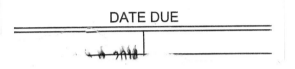

PUSHING THE LIMITS

PUSHING THE LIMITS

Katie McGarry

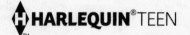

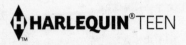

HARLEQUIN®TEEN

ISBN-13: 978-0-373-21049-7

PUSHING THE LIMITS

This edition published by arrangement with Harlequin Books S.A.

For questions and comments about the quality of this book please contact us at Customer_eCare@Harlequin.ca.

® and TM are trademarks of the publisher. Trademarks indicated with ® are registered in the United States Patent and Trademark Office, the Canadian Trade Marks Office and in other countries.

www.HarlequinTEEN.com

Printed in U.S.A.

Recycling programs
for this product may
not exist in your area.

PUSHING
THE LIMITS

Echo

"My father is a control freak, I hate my stepmother, my brother is dead and my mother has…well…issues. How do you think I'm doing?"

That's how I would have loved to respond to Mrs. Collins's question, but my father placed too much importance on appearance for me to answer honestly. Instead, I blinked three times and said, "Fine."

Mrs. Collins, Eastwick High's new clinical social worker, acted as if I hadn't spoken. She shoved a stack of files to the side of her already cluttered desk and flipped through various papers. My new therapist hummed when she found my three-inch-thick file and rewarded herself with a sip of coffee, leaving bright red lipstick on the curve of the mug. The stench of cheap coffee and freshly sharpened pencils hung in the air.

My father checked his watch from the chair to my right and, on my left, the Wicked Witch of the West shifted impatiently. I was missing first period calculus, my father was missing some very important meeting, and my stepmother from Oz? I'm sure she was missing her brain.

"Don't you just love January?" Mrs. Collins asked as she opened my file. "New year, new month, new slate to start over on." Not even waiting for a reply, she continued, "Do you like the curtains? I made them myself."

In one synchronized movement, my father, my stepmother and I turned our attention to the pink polka-dotted curtains hanging on the windows overlooking the student parking lot. The curtains were too *Little House on the Prairie* with the color scheme of a bad rave for my taste. Not a single one of us answered and our silence created a heavy awkwardness.

My father's BlackBerry vibrated. With exaggerated effort, he pulled it out of his pocket and scrolled down the screen. Ashley drummed her fingers over her bloated belly and I read the various handpainted plaques hanging on the wall so I could focus on anything that wasn't her.

Failure is your only enemy. The only way up is to never look down. We succeed because we believe. How much wood would a woodchuck chuck if a woodchuck could chuck wood?

Okay—so that last one didn't make the wall of sayings, but I would have found it amusing.

Mrs. Collins reminded me of an overgrown Labrador retriever with her blond hair and much too friendly attitude. "Echo's ACT and SAT scores are fabulous. You should be very proud of your daughter." She gave me a sincere smile, exposing all of her teeth.

Start the timer. My therapy session had officially begun. Close to two years ago, after the incident, Child Protective Services had "strongly encouraged" therapy—and Dad quickly learned that it was better to say yes to anything "strongly encouraged."

I used to go to therapy like normal people, at an office separate from school. Thanks to an influx in funding from the state of Kentucky and an overenthusiastic social worker, I'd become part of this pilot program. Mrs. Collins's sole job was to deal with a few kids from my high school. Lucky me.

My father sat up taller in his seat. "Her math scores were low. I want her to retake the tests."

"Is there a bathroom nearby?" Ashley interrupted. "The baby loves to sit on my bladder."

More like Ashley loved to make everything about her. Mrs. Collins gave her a strained smile and pointed to the door. "Go out to the main hallway and take a right."

The way she maneuvered out of her chair, Ashley acted as if she carried a thousand-pound ball of lead instead of a tiny baby. I shook my head in disgust, which only drew my father's ice-cold stare.

"Mr. Emerson," Mrs. Collins continued once Ashley left the room, "Echo's scores are well above the national average and, according to her file, she's already applied to the colleges of her choice."

"There are some business schools with extended deadlines I'd like her to apply to. Besides, this family does not accept 'above average.' My daughter will excel." My father spoke with the air of a deity. He might as well have added the phrase *so let it be written, so let it be done.* I propped my elbow on the armrest and hid my face in my hands.

"I can see that this really bothers you, Mr. Emerson," Mrs. Collins said in an annoyingly even tone. "But Echo's English scores are close to perfect…."

And this was where I tuned them out. My father and the previous guidance counselor had this fight my sophomore year when I took the PSAT. Then again last year when I took the SAT and ACT for the first time. Eventually, the guidance counselor learned my father always won and started giving up after one round.

My test scores were the least of my concerns. Finding the money to fix Aires' car was the worry that plagued my brain. Since Aires' death, my father had remained stubborn on the subject, insisting we should sell it.

"Echo, are you happy with your scores?" asked Mrs. Collins.

I peeked at her through the red, curly hair hanging over my face. The last therapist understood the hierarchy of our family and talked to my father, not me. "Excuse me?"

"Are you happy with your ACT and SAT scores? Do you want to retake the tests?" She folded her hands and placed them on top of my file. "Do you want to apply to more schools?"

I met my father's tired gray eyes. Let's see. Retaking the tests would mean my father hounding me every second to study, which in turn would mean me getting up early on a Saturday, blowing the whole morning frying my brain and then worrying for weeks over the results. As for applying to more schools? I'd rather retake the tests. "Not really."

The worry lines forever etched around his eyes and mouth deepened with disapproval. I changed my tune. "My dad is right. I should retake the tests."

Mrs. Collins scratched away in my file with a pen. My last therapist had been highly aware of my authority issues. No need to rewrite what was already there.

Ashley waddled back into the room and dropped into the seat next to me. "What did I miss?" I'd honestly forgotten she existed. Oh, if only Dad would, too.

"Nothing," my father replied.

Mrs. Collins finally lifted her pen from the page. "Ask Mrs. Marcos for the next testing dates before you go to class. And while I'm playing the role of guidance counselor, I'd like to discuss your schedule for the winter term. You've filled your free periods with multiple business classes. I was wondering why."

The real answer, because my father told me to, would probably irritate multiple people in the room so I ad-libbed, "They'll help prepare me for college." Wow. I'd said that with all the enthusiasm of a six-year-old waiting for a flu shot. Bad choice on my part. My father shifted in his seat again and sighed. I considered giving a different answer, but figured that reply would also come off flat.

Mrs. Collins perused my file. "You've shown an incredible talent in the arts, specifically painting. I'm not suggesting you drop all of your business courses, but you could drop one and take an art class instead."

"No," my father barked. He leaned forward in his seat, steepling his fingers. "Echo won't be taking any art classes, is that clear?" My father was a strange combination of drill instructor and Alice's white rabbit: he always had someplace important to go and enjoyed bossing everyone else around.

I had to give Mrs. Collins credit; she never once flinched before she caved. "Crystal."

"Well, now that we've settled that…" Ashley and her baby bump perched on the edge of the chair, preparing to stand. "I accidentally overbooked today and I have an OB appointment. We may find out the baby's gender."

"Mrs. Emerson, Echo's academics aren't the reason for this meeting, but I understand if you need to leave." She withdrew an official letter from her top drawer as a red-faced Ashley sat back in her seat. I'd seen that letterhead several times over the past two years. Child Protective Services enjoyed killing rain-forests.

Mrs. Collins read the letter to herself while I secretly wished I would spontaneously combust. Both my father and I slouched in our seats. Oh, the freaking joy of group therapy.

While waiting for her to finish reading, I noticed a stuffed green frog by her computer, a picture of her and some guy—possibly her husband—and then on the corner of her desk a big blue ribbon. The fancy kind people received when they won a competition. Something strange stirred inside me. Huh—weird.

Mrs. Collins hole-punched the letter and then placed it in my already overwhelmed file. "There. I'm officially your therapist."

When she said nothing else, I drew my gaze away from the ribbon to her. She was watching me. "It's a nice ribbon, isn't it, Echo?"

My father cleared his throat and sent Mrs. Collins a death glare. Okay, that was an odd reaction, but then again, he was irritated just to be here. My eyes flickered to the ribbon again. Why did it feel familiar? "I guess."

Her eyes drifted to the dog tags I absently fingered around my neck. "I'm very sorry for your family's loss. What branch of the armed forces?"

Great. My father was going to have a stinking coronary. He'd only made it clear seventy-five times that Aires' dog tags were to stay in the box under my bed, but I needed them today—new therapist, the two-year anniversary of Aires' death still fresh, and the first day of my last semester of high school. Nausea skipped and played in my intestines. Avoiding my father's disappointed frown, I took great pains to search my hair for split ends.

"Marine," my father answered curtly. "Look, I've got a meeting this morning with prospective clients, I promised Ashley I'd go to her doctor's appointment and Echo's missing class. When are we going to wrap this up?"

"When I say so. If you're going to make these sessions difficult, Mr. Emerson, I will be more than happy to call Echo's social worker."

I fought the smile tugging at my lips. Mrs. Collins played a well-choreographed hand. My father backed down, but my stepmother on the other hand…

"I don't understand. Echo turns eighteen soon. Why does the state still have authority over her?"

"Because it's what the state, her social worker and myself think is in her best interest." Mrs. Collins closed my file. "Echo will continue therapy with me until she graduates this spring. At that point, the state of Kentucky will release her—and you."

She waited until Ashley nodded her silent acceptance of the situation before continuing. "How are you doing, Echo?"

Splendid. Fantastic. Never worse. "Fine."

"Really?" She tapped a finger against her chin. "Because I would have thought that the anniversary of your brother's death might trigger painful emotions."

Mrs. Collins eyed me while I stared blankly in return. My father and Ashley watched the uncomfortable showdown. Guilt nagged at me. She didn't technically ask me a question, so in theory, I didn't owe her a response, but the need to please her swept over me like a tidal wave. But why? She was another therapist in the revolving door. They all asked the same questions and promised help, but each of them left me in the same condition as they found me—broken.

"She cries." Ashley's high-pitched voice cut through the silence as if she were dispensing juicy country-club gossip. "All the time. She really misses Aires."

Both my father and I turned our heads to look at the blond bimbo. I willed her to continue while my father, I'm sure, willed her to shut up. God listened to me for once. Ashley went on, "We all miss him. It's so sad that the baby will never know him."

And once again, welcome to the Ashley show, sponsored by Ashley and my father's money. Mrs. Collins wrote briskly, no doubt etching each of Ashley's unguarded words into my file while my father groaned.

"Echo, would you like to talk about Aires during today's session?" Mrs. Collins asked.

"No." That was possibly the most honest answer I'd given all morning.

"That's fine," she said. "We'll save him for a later date. What about your mother? Have you had any contact with her?"

Ashley and my father answered simultaneously, "No," while I blurted, "Kind of."

I felt like the middle of a ham sandwich the way the two of them leaned toward me. I wasn't sure what prompted me to tell the truth. "I tried calling her over break." When she didn't answer, I'd sat next to the phone for days, hoping and praying my mother would care that two years before, my brother, her son, had died.

My father ran a hand over his face. "You know you're not allowed to have contact with your mother." The anger in his voice hinted that he couldn't believe I'd told the therapist this tantalizing tidbit. I imagined visions of social workers dancing in his head. "There *is* a restraining order. Tell me, Echo, landline or cell phone?"

"Landline," I choked out. "But we never talked. I swear."

He swiped at his BlackBerry and his lawyer's number appeared on the screen. I clutched the dog tags, Aires' name and serial number embedding in my palm. "Please, Daddy, don't," I whispered.

He hesitated and my heart pressed against my rib cage. Then, by the grace of God, he dropped the phone to his lap. "We're going to have to change the number now."

I nodded. It stunk that my mom would never be able to call my home, but I'd take the hit…for her. Of all the things my mother needed, prison wasn't one of them.

"Have you had contact with your mother since then?" Mrs. Collins lost her friendliness.

"No." I closed my eyes and took a deep breath. Everything inside of me ached. I couldn't keep up the "I'm fine" facade much longer. This line of questioning ripped at my soul's freshly scabbed wounds.

"To confirm we're on the same page, you understand that contact between you and your mother while there is a restraining order, even if you initiate it, is forbidden."

"Yes." I took another gulp of air. The lump in my throat denied the entry of the precious oxygen. I missed Aires and, God, my mom, and Ashley was having a baby, and my dad was on me all the time, and…I needed something, anything.

Against my better judgment, I let the words tumble out of my mouth. "I want to fix Aires' car." Maybe, just maybe, restoring something of his would make the pain go away.

"Oh, not this again," my father muttered.

"Wait. Not what again? Echo, what are you talking about?" asked Mrs. Collins.

I stared at the gloves on my hands. "Aires found a 1965 Corvette in a scrap yard. He spent all of his free time fixing it up and he was almost done before he went to Afghanistan. I want to restore it. For Aires." For me. He didn't leave anything behind when he left, except the car.

"That sounds like a healthy way to grieve. What are your thoughts on this, Mr. Emerson?" Mrs. Collins gave great puppy dog eyes—a trait I had yet to master.

My father scrolled again through his BlackBerry, his body present but his mind already at work. "It costs money and I don't see the point in fixing up a broken-down car when she has a car that works."

"Then let me get a job," I snapped. "And we can sell my car once I get Aires' working."

All eyes were on him and now his were on me. Without meaning to, I'd backed him into a corner. He wanted to say no, but that would bring down the wrath of the new therapist. After all, we had to be perfect in therapy. God forbid we take advantage of it and hash out some issues.

"Fine, but she has to pay for the car herself, and Echo knows my rules regarding employment. She has to find a flexible job that will not interfere with her schoolwork, the clubs we agreed upon or her grades. Now, are we done here?"

Mrs. Collins glanced at the clock. "Not quite. Echo, your social worker extended your therapy until graduation because of your teacher evaluations. Since the beginning of your junior year, each of your teachers has noted a distinct withdrawal from your participation in class and in your social interactions with your peers." Her kind eyes bored into mine. "Everyone wants you to be happy, Echo, and I'd like you to give me the opportunity to help."

I cocked an eyebrow. Like I had a choice about therapy, and as for my happiness—good freaking luck. "Sure."

Ashley's perky voice startled me. "She has a date for the Valentine's Dance."

Now my father and I took our turn speaking simultaneously. "I do?"—"She does?"

Ashley's eyes darted nervously between me and my father. "Yes, remember, Echo? Last night we discussed the new guy you're into and I told you that you shouldn't dump your friends at school while you obsessed over some guy."

I deliberated over which part disturbed me more: the imaginary boyfriend or that she claimed we'd had an actual conversation. While I was deciding, my father stood and put on his coat. "See, Mrs. Collins, Echo is fine. Just a little lovestruck. As much as I enjoy these sessions, Ashley's appointment is in twenty minutes and I don't want Echo to miss any more class."

"Echo, are you really interested in making money to fix your brother's car?" Mrs. Collins asked as she stood to escort my father and stepmother out.

I pulled at the gloves I wore to cover my skin. "More than you could possibly imagine."

She smiled at me before walking out the door. "Then I've got a job for you. Wait here and we'll discuss the details."

The three of them huddled together on the far side of the main office, whispering to one another. My father wrapped his arm around Ashley's waist and she leaned into him as they nodded at Mrs. Collins's hushed words. The familiar pang of jealousy and anger ate at the lining of my gut. How could he love her when she'd destroyed so much?

NOAH

Fresh paint and the scent of drywall dust made me think of my father, not school. Yet that smell slapped me in the face when I walked into the newly remodeled front office. With books in hand, I sauntered toward the counter. "'Sup, Mrs. Marcos."

"Noah, why you late again, muchacho?" she said while stapling papers together.

The clock on the wall flipped to nine in the morning. "Hell, this is early."

Mrs. Marcos stepped around her new cherry desk to meet me at the counter. She gave me crap when I came in late, but I still liked her. With her long brown hair, she reminded me of a Hispanic version of my mother.

"You missed your appointment with Mrs. Collins this morning. Not a good way to start the second term," she whispered as she wrote my tardy slip. She tilted her head toward the three adults huddled together in the far corner of the room. I assumed the middle-aged blond woman whispering to the rich couple was the new guidance counselor.

I shrugged and let the right side of my mouth twitch up. "Oops."

Mrs. Marcos slid the tardy slip to me and gave me her patented stern glare. She was the one person at this school who didn't believe that me and my future were completely fucked.

The middle-aged blonde called out, "Mr. Hutchins, I'm thrilled you remembered our appointment, even if you are late. I'm sure you wouldn't mind taking a seat while I finish a few things." She smiled at me like we were old friends and spoke so sweetly that for a moment, I almost smiled back. Instead, I nodded and took a seat on the line of chairs pushed against the office wall.

Mrs. Marcos laughed.

"What?"

"She's not going to put up with your attitude. Maybe she'll convince you to take school seriously."

I rested my head against the painted cinder-block wall and shut my eyes, in need of a few more hours' sleep. Short one person for closing, the restaurant hadn't let me go until after midnight, and then Beth and Isaiah kept me up.

"Mrs. Marcos?" asked an angelic voice. "Can you please tell me the upcoming dates for the ACT and SAT?"

The phone rang. "Wait one sec," said Mrs. Marcos. Then the ringing ceased.

A chair down the row from mine shifted and my mouth watered from the aroma of hot cinnamon rolls. I snuck a peek and noticed red, silky, curly hair. I knew her. Echo Emerson.

Not a cinnamon roll in sight, but damn if she didn't smell like one. We had several of our main courses together and last semester one of our free periods. I didn't know much about her other than she kept to herself, she was smart, a redhead and she had big tits. She wore large, long-sleeved shirts that hung off her shoulders and tank tops underneath that revealed just enough to get the fantasies flowing.

Like always, she stared straight ahead as if I didn't exist. Hell, I probably didn't exist in her mind. People like Echo Emerson irritated the crap out of me.

"You've got a fucked-up name," I mumbled. I didn't know why I wanted to rattle her, I just did.

"Shouldn't you be getting high in the bathroom?"

So she did know me. "They installed security cameras. We do it in the parking lot now."

"My bad." Her foot rocked frantically back and forth.

Good, I'd succeeded in getting under that perfect facade. "Echo…echo…echo…"

Her foot stopped rocking and red curls bounced furiously as she turned to face me. "How original. I've never heard that before." She swept up her backpack and left the office. Her tight ass swayed side to side as she marched down the hallway. That wasn't nearly as fun as I'd thought it would be. In fact, I kind of felt like a dick.

"Noah?" Mrs. Collins called me into her office.

The last guidance counselor had major OCD issues. Everything in the office perfectly placed. I used to move his plaques just to mess with him. There'd be no such entertainment with Mrs. Collins. Her desk was a mess. I could bury a body in here and no one would ever find it.

Taking the seat across from her, I waited for my ass-chewing.

"How was your Christmas break?" She had that kind look again, sort of like a puppy.

"Good." That is if you considered your foster mom and dad

getting into a screaming match and throwing everyone's gifts into the fireplace a good Christmas. I'd always dreamed of spending my Christmas in a hellhole basement watching my two best friends get stoned.

"Wonderful. So things are working out with your new foster family." She said it as a statement, but meant it as a question.

"Yeah." Compared to the last three families I had, they were the fucking Brady Bunch. This time around, the system had placed me with another kid. Either the people in charge were short on homes or they were finally starting to believe I wasn't the menace they'd pegged me to be. People with my labels weren't allowed to live with other minors. "Look, I already have a social worker and she's enough of a pain in my ass. Tell your bosses you don't need to waste your time on me."

"I'm not a social worker," she said. "I'm a *clinical* social worker."

"Same thing."

"Actually, it's not. I went to school for a lot longer."

"Good for you."

"And it means I can provide a different level of help for you."

"Do you get paid by the state?" I asked.

"Yes."

"Then I don't want your help."

Her lips flinched into an almost smile and I almost had an ounce of respect for her. "How about we shoot this straight?" she said. "According to your file you have a history of violence."

I stared at her. She stared at me. That file was full of shit, but I learned years ago the word of a teenager meant nothing against the word of an adult.

"This file, Noah." She tapped it three times with her finger. "I don't think it tells the whole story. I talked to your teachers at

Highland High. The picture they painted doesn't represent the young man I see in front of me."

I clutched the spiral metal binding of my calculus notebook until it stabbed the palm of my hand. Who the hell did this lady think she was digging into my past?

She flipped through my file. "You've been bounced around to several foster homes in the past two and a half years. This is your fourth high school since your parents' death. What I find interesting is that until a year and a half ago, you still made the honor roll and you still competed in sports. Those are qualities that don't usually match a disciplinary case."

"Maybe you need to dig a little further." I wanted this lady out of my life and the best way to do that was to scare her. "If you did, you'd find out I beat up my first foster father." Actually, I had punched him in the face when I caught him hitting his biological son. Funny how no one in that family took my side when the cops arrived. Not even the kid I defended.

Mrs. Collins paused as if she was waiting for me to give her my side of the story, but she was sadly mistaken. Since my parents' death, I'd learned that no one in the system gave a crap. Once you entered, you were damned.

"Your old guidance counselor at Highland spoke highly of you. Made the varsity basketball team your freshman year, honor roll, involved in several student activities, popular amongst your peers." She surveyed me. "I think I would have liked that kid."

So did I—but life sucked. "Little late for me to join the basketball team—halfway through the season and all. Think coach will be fine with my tattoos?"

"I have no interest in you re-creating your old life, but together I think we can build something new. A better future than the one you will have if you continue down your current path."

She sounded so damn sincere. I wanted to believe her, but I'd learned the hard way to never trust anyone. Keeping my face devoid of emotion, I let the silence build.

She broke eye contact first and shook her head. "You've been dealt a rough hand, but you're full of possibilities. Your scores on the aptitude tests are phenomenal and your teachers see your potential. Your grade point average needs a boost, as does your attendance. I believe those are related.

"Now, I have a plan. Along with seeing me once a week, you will attend tutoring sessions until your G.P.A. matches your test scores."

I stood. I'd already missed first period. This fun little meeting got me out of second. But since I'd actually gotten my ass out of bed, I intended to go to class sometime today. "I don't have time for this."

A slight edge crept into her tone, so subtle I almost missed it. "Do I need to contact your social worker?"

I headed for the door. "Go ahead. What is she going to do? Rip my family apart? Put me in the foster care system? Continue to dig and you'll see you're too late."

"When was the last time you saw your brothers, Noah?"

My hand froze on the doorknob.

"What if I could offer you increased supervised visitation?"

I let go of the doorknob and sat back down.

If only I could wear gloves every moment of the day, I'd feel more secure, but the stupid dress code wouldn't let me. Because of this, my wardrobe consisted of anything with long sleeves—the longer the better.

I clutched the ends of my sleeves and pulled them over my fingers, causing my blue cotton shirt to hang off my right shoulder. My freshman year, I would have freaked if people stared at my white skin and the occasional orange freckle. Now, I preferred for people to look at my bare shoulder instead of trying to catch a glimpse of the scars on my arms.

"Did she say who it was? I bet you it's Jackson Coleman. I heard he's failing math and if he doesn't get his grades up he'll lose his scholarship to college. God, I hope it is. He is so hot." My best friend, Lila McCormick, took her first breath since I'd given her the rundown on my counseling session and the tutoring job Mrs. Collins spontaneously created. With her nonstop mouth and tight clothes, Lila was Eastwick High's own version of Glinda the Good Witch. She floated in her own beautiful bubble spreading happiness and cheer.

As Lila moved her tray down the lunch line, the smell of pizza and French fries made my mouth water, but the nausea roiling in my stomach kept me from buying food. My heart thundered and I hugged my sketch pad closer to my chest. I couldn't believe I was actually in the lunchroom. Lila and I had been best friends since preschool and the one thing she'd asked of me for Christmas was that I ditch the library and reclaim my old spot at our lunch table.

It may have sounded like an easy request, but it wasn't. The last time I'd eaten lunch in the cafeteria was at the beginning of May during my sophomore year: the day before my entire world fell apart. Back then, no one stared at me or whispered.

"Who's hot?" Natalie cut the line by sliding her tray between me and Lila. A group of guys behind us groaned at her boldness. As usual, she ignored them. Natalie was the second of two people who refused to treat me like a social pariah because of the gossip flying about me at school.

Lila pulled her sleek golden hair into a ponytail before paying the cashier. "Jackson Coleman. Echo is going to tutor some lucky guy and I'm guessing it might be him. Who would you like to add to our list of hot yet stupid boys?"

I followed them to the lunch table as Natalie's eyes roamed the cafeteria, searching for the right combination. "Nicholas Green. He's dumber than dirt, but I could eat him for dessert. If you're tutoring him, Echo, think you could introduce me?"

"Introduce who to who?" asked Grace. Natalie and Lila took their seats and I hesitated.

Grace's smile fell when she spotted me. She was the main reason why I didn't want to return to the lunchroom. We were total best friends before the incident and, I guess, even after. She visited me every day in the hospital and at home during the summer, but when our junior year began and my social status took a nosedive, so did our friendship…in public that is. In private she claimed to love me like a sister. Everyone else at school treated me like I didn't exist.

"Natalie to Nicholas Green." Lila patted the seat between her and Natalie. Attempting to hide, I dropped into the chair, slouched and propped my sketch pad against the edge of the table.

The other girls whispered to each other as they glimpsed me. One giggled. From the time I'd come back to school, I never had a social shot. The rumors about why I was absent for the last month of my sophomore year ranged from pregnancy to rehab to attempted suicide. My gloves became the kindling and my memory loss the match. When I returned that fall, the rumors exploded into a firestorm.

Lila continued her explanation. "Echo's going to be tutoring some dumb hottie. We're trying to guess who it will be."

"Well, don't hold out on us, Lila. Who is Echo tutoring?" Grace's eyes flickered from Lila to the girls on her squad sitting at the table. When we'd returned for junior year, Grace had found out she had a shot at making head cheerleader—a difficult feat since she'd always hovered in the periphery of popular in that crowd. I'd assumed things between us would go back to normal once she was voted in. I'd been mistaken.

"Ask Echo." Lila's teeth crunched into the apple, her hardened gaze locked on Grace. Our table became eerily silent as the most beautiful girl at school openly defied the most popular girl at school. A lull fell over the cafeteria as the student body prepared to watch the showdown in progress. I would have sworn a tumbleweed blew past the table and that weird Western whistle song played on the loudspeaker.

I gave Lila's foot a nudge, begging her in my mind to answer for me, instead of forcing Grace to acknowledge me in front of other people. Seconds ticked by as neither flinched in the stare-down.

I couldn't take it. "I don't know. I meet him this afternoon." Mrs. Collins didn't want to say who I'd be tutoring. She'd mumbled something about smoothing over a few details with him before we met.

Movement and chatter resumed in the cafeteria. The muscles in Grace's face relaxed and she took a relieved breath before taking stock of the reaction of her public friends. "I'll play guess the stupid hunk." She sent me a private wink. For the billionth time, I wished my life could go back to normal.

When Grace threw out a name the rest of the group also decided to play. I sketched Grace as they talked. Her new short blond haircut framed her face perfectly. I listened to their name-dropping and the new school gossip that accompanied their guesses.

"Maybe Echo's tutoring Luke Manning," Lila said with a not-so-gentle nudge of my arm. "He fits hunk and less-than-bright."

I rolled my eyes and did my best to fix the dark line her nudge had created on my drawing. Lila held on to the false hope that Luke, my boyfriend from my life before, still harbored feelings for me. She substantiated her claim with made-up stories of how he watched me when I wasn't paying attention.

"Luke and Deanna broke up over the winter break," said Grace. "Deanna says she broke up with him. Luke says he broke up with her. Who knows if we'll ever find out the truth?"

"Who would you believe, Echo?" Natalie asked. Gotta give

her credit. She wanted me to participate in the conversation, regardless of whether I wanted to be included.

I focused on shading the shadow Grace's hair created against her ear. After meeting Luke in freshman English, I'd dated him for a year and a half. This made me the table's Luke expert. Since our breakup, every table with a female contained a Luke expert. "Hard to say. I broke up with Luke and he didn't claim any differently, but he's changed a lot since then."

"Noah Hutchins," Natalie said.

I stopped sketching, confused about what Noah had to do with Luke. "What?"

"Guess the hunk, remember? Noah Hutchins is definitely hot. I'd tutor him." Lila stared over at the stoner table, practically drooling. How could she swoon over the guy who'd made fun of me?

Grace's mouth gaped. "And take the social hit? No way."

"I said I'd tutor him, not take him to prom. Besides, from what I've heard, quite a few girls have ridden that train and loved every second of it."

Grace glanced at Noah, eyes wandering up, then down. "You're right. He's hot, and rumor has it he's only into one-nighters. Though Bella Monahan tried to force a relationship. She followed him around like a pathetic puppy dog. He wanted nothing to do with her if it didn't involve the backseat of his car."

Lila loved dirt. "She lost her boyfriend, her virginity, her reputation and her self-respect in less than a month. That's why she transferred to another school."

Guys like Noah Hutchins ticked me off. He used girls, used drugs and had made me feel like crap this morning. Not that I should be surprised. I'd had a couple of classes with him last semester. He'd stride into the room like he owned the earth and smirk when girls fell all over themselves in his presence. "What a jerk."

As if he heard me from across the room, his dark eyes met mine. His shaggy brown hair fell over them, but I could tell he was looking at me. The stubble on his face moved as he smiled. Noah had muscles, looks and trouble stalking him. Somehow, he made jeans and a T-shirt look dangerous. Not that I was into girl-using stoners. Yet, I took another peek at him while sipping my drink.

"Harsh words, Echo. You're not talking about me, are you?" A chair scraped the floor. Luke flipped it around so he could straddle it between Natalie and Grace. Come freaking on. Luke and I had barely spoken a word to each other since we broke up sophomore year. Why was everyone pushing me into social mode today?

"No," said Lila. "We talked about you earlier. Echo was calling Noah Hutchins a jerk." I kicked her under the table. She sent me a glare in return.

"Hutchins?" Luke Manning: six foot two, built like a freight train with black hair, blue eyes, captain of the basketball team, hot and full of himself. To my horror, he sized Noah up. "What's stoner boy done to deserve your wrath?"

"Nothing." I returned to my sketch pad. My cheeks burned when one of Grace's public friends mumbled something about my weirdness. Why couldn't Lila, Natalie and Luke just leave me alone? The gossip only became worse when I crept out of my shell.

Unfortunately, Lila chose to ignore my red cheeks and my warning kick. "He made fun of Echo this morning, but don't worry, she told him off."

The pencil in my hand bowed from my tighter grip as I fought the urge to yank Lila's gorgeous hair out of her head. My teachers and Mrs. Collins were so wrong. Interacting with my peers stunk.

Luke's eyes narrowed. "What did he say to you?"

I stomped on Lila's toes and stared straight at her. "Nothing."

"He told her that she had an effed-up name and then did the stupid 'echo' thing people did in elementary school," said Lila. Oh, God, I wanted to murder my best friend.

"You want me to talk to him?" Luke stared at me with a familiar hint of possessiveness. Both Grace and Natalie smiled like Cheshire cats. I refused to look at Lila, who bounced in her seat. Now I would never hear the end of her fantasies about Luke and me getting back together.

"No. He's a stupid guy who said a stupid thing. He probably doesn't even remember saying it."

Luke chuckled. "True. That whole table's screwed up. Did you know that Hutchins is a foster kid?"

The girls at my table gasped at the new gossip. I checked out Noah again. He appeared deep in conversation with some girl with long black hair.

"Yep," Luke continued. "Heard Mrs. Rogers and Mr. Norris discussing it in the hallway." The bell rang, ending Luke's spotlight on the forbidden information on Noah Hutchins.

While I threw away the remains of my lunch, Grace sidled up beside me and whispered, "This was huge, Echo. If Luke's into you again, life will change. Who he talks to and dates changes everyone's opinion. Maybe things will finally get back to normal."

One of Grace's public friends called out to her and she left my side without a second glance. I sighed as I pulled my sleeves over my fingers. What I wouldn't give for normal.

NOAH

I'd told Mrs. Collins the truth. I didn't have time for tutoring or counseling. In June, I would turn eighteen and graduate from foster care. That meant I'd need a place of my own, and rent meant a job. But Mrs. Collins had played me like a street hustler. An occasional supervised visit with my brothers wasn't enough. She dangled them in front of me like a damn needle to a heroin addict.

My shift at the Malt and Burger started at five. I glanced at the clock hanging over the reference librarian's desk. What part of "meet the guy you're tutoring directly after school at the public library" did my know-it-all misunderstand? Mrs. Collins might have mentioned who would be tutoring me, but I'd stopped listening after a few minutes. The lady talked too much.

I focused on the double doors. Five more minutes and I could happily call this session a failure, a fact I would be thrilled to throw in Mrs. Collins's face.

One door opened and cold air swept in, causing goose bumps

to rise on my arms. *Ah, hell.* I leaned back in my chair and folded my arms across my chest. Echo Emerson glided into the library.

Her eyes swept the room while her gloved hands rubbed her arms. Like the cold could penetrate that fancy-ass brown leather coat. A light, sunshine smile rested on her face. It appeared Mrs. Collins had kept us both in the dark. The moment she saw me, her smile faded and her green eyes erupted with thunderclouds. *Join the fucking club.*

From under the table, I kicked out the chair opposite me. "You're late."

She set her book bag on the table and scooted the chair in as she sat. "I had to go to the office and find out testing dates. I could have gotten the information this morning, but some jerk got in my way."

Advantage Echo, but I smiled at her like I had the upper hand. "You could have stayed. I never asked you to leave."

"And let you harass me some more? No, thanks." She shrugged off her jacket, but kept on her knitted gloves. She smelled of cold and leather. Her blue cotton shirt dipped below her beige tank, exposing the top of her cleavage. Girls like her enjoyed teasing guys. Little did she know, I didn't mind looking.

Catching me staring, she readjusted her shirt and her cleavage disappeared from view. *Well, that was fun.* She glared at me, possibly waiting for an apology. She'd be waiting a long time.

"What subject are you failing? All of them?" Those green eyes danced. It appeared Echo also enjoyed dishing out shit.

All right, I'd screwed with her this morning for no reason. She deserved to get a couple blows in. "None. Mrs. Collins is calling the shots on this."

Echo opened her backpack and withdrew a notebook. A

shadow crossed her face when she slid off the gloves and immediately pulled her long sleeves over her hands. "What subject do you want to start with? We have calculus and physics together, so we could start there. You've got to be a complete moron if you need help with business technology." She paused. "And weren't you in my Spanish class last term?"

I lowered my head so my hair fell into my eyes. For a girl who didn't know I existed, she sure knew a lot about me. "Yeah." And this term, too. She barely beat the bell walking into class and took the first seat available without giving anyone a second look.

"*Qué tan bien hablas español?*" she asked.

How well could I speak Spanish? Pretty damn decent. I shoved away from the table. "I gotta go."

"What?" Her forehead crinkled in disbelief.

"Unlike you, I don't have parents to pay for everything. I've got a job, Princess, and if I don't leave now, I'll be late. See you around."

Grabbing my books and jacket, I left the table and immediately exited the library. The cold January air smacked me in the face. Ice covered several spots on the pavement.

"Hey!"

I glanced over my shoulder. Echo bounded after me, leather jacket on one arm and pack slung over her back.

"Get your damn jacket on. It's cold outside." I didn't stop for her, but I slowed my pace, curious as to why she followed me out.

She caught up quickly and kept step beside me. "Where do you think you're going?"

"I told you, to work. I thought you were smart." I'd never met anyone so fun to mess with.

"Fine. Then when are we going to make this session up?"

I slammed my books on the piece of crap I called a car, causing rust to scatter to the ground. "We're not. I'll make you a deal. You tell Mrs. Collins that we're meeting as many days after school as you want, collect whatever volunteer hours you need for whatever little club you belong to, and I'll back you up. I won't have to see you and you won't have to look at me. I get to continue with my screwed up life and you get to go home and play dress-up with your friends. Deal?"

Echo winced and backed away as if I'd slapped her. She lost her footing when she hit a patch of ice. My right hand swept out and snatched her wrist before her body could smack the ground.

I kept hold of her while she steadied herself using the trunk of my car. Embarrassment or cold flushed her white cheeks. Either way, I found it funny. But before I had a chance to make fun of her, her eyes widened and she stared down at the wrist I held.

Her long blue sleeve was hiked past her elbow and I followed her gaze to the exposed skin. She attempted to yank her hand away, but I tightened my grip and swallowed my disgust. In all the horror-show homes I'd lived in, I never once saw mutilation like that. White and pale red, raised scars zigzagged up her arm. "What the fuck is that?"

I tore my eyes away from the scars and searched her face for answers. She sucked in several shallow gasps before yanking a second time and successfully jerking out of my grasp. "Nothing."

"That ain't nothing." And that *something* had to hurt like hell when it happened.

Echo stretched her sleeve past her wrist to her fingertips. She resembled a corpse. The blood rushed out of her cheeks and her body quaked with silent tremors. "Leave me alone."

She turned away and stumbled back to the library.

Echo

"Nothing," said Lila. "Not a word, not a peep, not a sound. Natalie, Grace and I even put a few feelers out to the juniors, but there is absolutely no gossip flying about you. Well, at least nothing involving Noah Hutchins."

Lila sat in the passenger seat and I sat in the driver's side of Aires' 1965 Corvette. She'd come home with me to act as my barrier for Family Friday—or as I liked to refer to it, Dinner for the Damned.

In the garage, the radio played from my 1998 forest-green Dodge Neon. Aires' Corvette still had its original radio. Translation: a piece of crap, but the rest of the car was totally beast. Flashy bloodred with black pinstriping running horizontally—Aires typically lost me at this point, but he would still continue talking even though my eyes glazed over—three functional, vertical front, slanting louvers on the sides of the front fenders; a blacked-out, horizontal-bars grille and different rocker panel moldings.

I had no idea what that meant, but Aires said it enough that I had the description memorized. The car looked awesome, but it didn't run. Thanks to Noah Hutchins, my chances of it ever running lessened each day. I tightened my hands on the steering wheel and remembered Aires' promise to me. Days before he left, he had hovered over the open hood as I sat on the workbench.

"It's going to be okay, Echo." Aires' eyes had flicked to my rocking foot. "It's only a six-month deployment."

"I'm fine," I'd said as I blinked three times. I didn't want him to leave. Aires was the only person in the world who understood the craziness of our family, plus he was the only one capable of keeping the peace between me, Ashley and our father. He wasn't Ashley's biggest fan, but regardless of his feelings, he always encouraged me to give her a break.

He chuckled. "Next time at least try to stop your telltale sign of lying. One of these days Dad will pick up on it."

"Will you write?" I asked, changing the subject. He'd talked a lot about our father before he left.

"And email and Skype." He wiped his hands on an already greasy rag and stretched to his full six feet. "I'll tell you what. When I get home and finish the car, you can be first to drive it. After me, of course."

My foot stopped rocking and I was flooded with the first real feeling of hope since Aires told me of his deployment. Aires would return home as long as his car waited for him. He'd given me a dream and I held on to it after he left. My dreams died with him on a desolate road in Afghanistan.

"Whatcha thinking about?" asked Lila now.

"Noah Hutchins," I lied. "He's had all week to tell the whole school about my scars. What do you think he's waiting for?"

"Maybe Noah doesn't have anyone to tell. He's a stoner foster kid who needs tutoring."

"Yeah, maybe," I answered. Or maybe he was waiting for the perfect moment to make my life a living hell.

Lila played with the rings on her fingers, signaling nerves.

"What?" I asked.

I had to strain to hear her mumbled answer. "We told Luke."

Every single muscle in my neck tightened and I released my grip on the steering wheel, terrified I'd rip the plastic to shreds. "You what?"

Lila turned in her seat, wringing her hands in her lap. "He's in our English class. Instead of proofreading each others' papers, Natalie, Grace and I were discussing the Noah situation and your scars and…Luke overheard a few things."

My heart pounded in my ears. For almost two years, I'd kept this horrible secret and in one week two people had forced their way into my personal nightmare.

When I didn't say anything she continued, "Those scars are not your fault. You have absolutely nothing to be ashamed of. Your mom definitely does and possibly your dad, but you? Nothing. Luke already knew your mom was freaking psychotic and he never told anyone. He's a moron, but even he could figure out your mom hurt you."

Should I be mad? Relieved? I settled for numb. "She's not psychotic," I murmured, knowing that anything I said regarding my mother fell on deaf ears. "She has issues."

In a slow, deliberate movement, Lila placed her hand over mine, giving my fingers a reassuring squeeze. A reminder she'd love me regardless. "We think you should tell people. You know, take the offensive instead of the defensive. That way if Noah tells everybody, people will already know the real story and think he's a jerk for making fun of you."

I stared at Aires' workbench. My father never tinkered with tools. If something broke, he called someone to fix it. Aires had loved to tinker. He spent every moment here in this garage. God, I needed him. I needed him to tell me what to do.

"Please say something, Echo." The heartbreak in Lila's voice broke mine.

"Whose idea was it?" I asked, even though I knew the answer. "Grace?" She'd wanted me to tell the whole school what'd happened immediately.

"That's not fair." Lila exhaled. "Not that Grace has been fair to you either. She swore this whole public versus private thing would end after the head cheerleader vote, but here's the thing, Echo. She wants what we all want—everything back to normal. As long as everyone thinks you're a cutter or tried to commit suicide you'll always be on the outs. Maybe this whole Noah thing is a blessing in disguise."

I looked at Lila for the first time since she'd broken the news. "My mom is off-limits."

"We'll back you." Lila rushed out the words. "Luke said he'd tell his friends about the crazy mom episodes he witnessed when the two of you were dating. You know, to add legitimacy to your story. And when Grace heard that, she agreed to tell everyone what she, Natalie and I saw in the hospital. We saw the cops. We heard your father yelling at your mother. Grace wants this so badly—we all do."

"Because having a crazy mom and no memory of the night she tried to kill me is so much better than people guessing I'm a cutter or tried to commit suicide."

Lila spoke softly. "People will feel bad for you. Being a victim...it makes it different. That's what Grace has been trying to tell you all along."

Anger snapped my frail patience. "I don't want their sympathy and I don't want the worst night of my life up for discussion for the whole school. If I ever tell anyone what happened, I want to be able to tell them the truth, not that I'm some pathetic moron who remembers nothing." I rapped the back of my head against the seat and stared at the ceiling of the car. *Deep breaths, Echo. Deep breaths.*

I remembered absolutely nothing about that night. My father, Ashley and my mom knew the truth. But I was forbidden to speak to my mom, and Dad and Ashley believed what the therapists said. That when my mind could handle the truth, I'd remember.

Whatever. They weren't the ones who lay in bed at night trying to figure out what happened. They weren't the ones who woke up screaming. They weren't the ones wondering if they were losing their minds.

They weren't the ones who felt hopeless.

"Echo..." Lila faltered, took a deep breath, and stared out the windshield. This had to be bad. Lila always could make eye contact. "Have you ever thought that maybe you've brought some of this on yourself?"

I flinched and fought to control the anger shaking my insides. "Excuse me?"

"I know it was rough coming back after what happened between you and your mom, but have you ever wondered if maybe you'd come back in September and continued life as normal, people would have eventually moved on? I mean, you sort of became a recluse."

The anger gave way to a hurt that shoved my heart into my

throat. Was this how my best friend saw me? As a coward? A failure? "Yeah, I did think of that." And I waited before speaking again to keep my voice from cracking. "But the more I put myself out there, the more people talked. Remember last year's dance team tryouts? People tend to gossip about what they see."

Her head lowered. "I remember."

"Why?" I asked her. "Why bring this all up now?"

"Because you're trying, Echo. You actually came to lunch. You're talking to people. It's the first time since our sophomore year that I've seen you try and I'm terrified you're going to go back into your shell." She turned to face me with a strange spring in her movements. "Don't let what Noah saw scare you off. Come to Michael Blair's party with me tomorrow night."

Had she lost her mind? "No way."

"Come on," she pleaded. "It's your birthday tomorrow. We have to go out for your birthday."

"No." I wanted to forget that the day even existed. Mom and Aires used to make a holiday out of my birthday. Without them....

She clasped her hands together and placed them under her chin. "Please? Pretty please? Pretty please with hot fudge? Try it my way and if it doesn't work I swear I'll never bring it up again. And did I mention I overheard Ashley tell your dad that she wanted to take you out to dinner? At a restaurant. A fancy one. With five courses. One little yes to me and I can get you out of it."

Dinner for the Damned on Fridays was bad enough. Dinner for the Damned in public would be inhumane. I took another deep breath. Lila had stuck with me through it all: my mother's insanity, my parents' divorce, Aires' death and now this. She may not know it yet, but Lila was about to receive *her* birthday present. "Fine."

She squealed and clapped her hands together. In one long, continuous sentence, she described her plans for the next night. Maybe Lila and Grace were right. Maybe life could go back to normal. I could hide my scars and go to parties and just lie low. Noah hadn't told anybody and maybe he wouldn't.

Besides, only four more months till graduation and after that I could wear gloves every day for the rest of my life.

NOAH

Twenty-eight anxious days had passed since I'd visited this bleakly decorated room in the social services building. The clowns and elephants painted on the wall were meant to invite happiness, yet the longer I looked, the more sinister they became. Nervous as hell and holding two wrapped gifts, I sat on a cold folding chair. I didn't need this reminder of how screwed up my family had become. My little brothers used to shadow my every footstep, worshipping the ground I walked on. Now, I wasn't sure if Tyler remembered our last name.

I waited like a caged jack-in-the-box ready to spring. The social worker needed to bring my brothers in before my nerves exploded. For some reason, Echo and her rocking foot came to mind. She must be wound twice as tight as me.

My mother's voice chimed in my head. "You must always look presentable. It's important to put your best foot forward."

I'd shaved, which I normally didn't bother doing every day. My mom and dad would have hated my hairstyle and any sign of stubble on my face. With my mother in mind, I didn't let my hair grow past my ears on the sides, but, out of self-preservation, I'd let the top grow a little long, denying people access to my eyes.

The door opened and I automatically stood with the gifts still in my hands. Jacob flew through the door and rammed his body into mine. His head reached my stomach now. I tossed the presents on the table, lowered myself to Jacob's level and wrapped my arms around him. My heart dropped. Man, he'd grown.

My social worker, a heavyset black lady in her fifties, paused in the door frame. "Remember, no askin' personal questions about their foster parents. I'll be on the other side of that mirror."

I glared at Keesha. She glared back at me before she left. At least the hate was mutual. After I hit my first foster father, the system had labeled me emotionally unstable and I'd lost the right to see my brothers. Since I'd had no outbursts with any of my other foster families and showed "improvement," I'd recently regained once-a-month supervised visitation.

Jacob mumbled into my shoulder, "I missed you, Noah."

I pulled away and looked at my eight-year-old brother. He had Dad's blond hair, blue eyes and nose. "I missed you, too. Where's Tyler?"

Jacob diverted his gaze to the floor. "He's coming. Mom...I mean..." he stuttered. "Carrie is talking to him in the hallway. He's a little nervous." His eyes met mine again, full of worry.

I faked a smile and messed up his hair. "No worries, bro. He'll come when he's ready. You want to open your present?"

He flashed a smile that reminded me of Mom and nodded. I handed him his gift and watched him open the box that contained twenty new packs of Pokémon cards. He sat on the floor and lost interest in me as he tore open each pack, occasionally telling me random facts about a particular card he liked.

I glanced at the clock and then at the door. I only had so much time with my brothers and some bitch had Tyler. Even though I'd told Jacob it was okay, it wasn't. Tyler was only two when our parents died. I needed every minute I could get to help him remember them. Hell, who was I kidding? I needed every minute to help him remember me.

"How are things with Carrie and Joe?" I tried to sound nonchalant, but this question made me nervous. I had firsthand experience with shitty foster parents and I'd kill anybody who tried to treat my brothers like those people had treated me.

Jacob organized the cards into different categories. "Fine. They told us on Christmas that we could start calling them Mom and Dad if we wanted to."

Son of a bitch. My fist clenched and I bit the inside of my mouth, drawing blood.

Jacob looked away from his cards for the first time. "Where you going, Noah?"

"To get Tyler." I only had forty-five minutes left. If they wanted to play dirty, so could I.

The minute I entered the hallway, Keesha stepped out of the observation room connected to mine, shutting the door behind her. "Get back in there and visit with your brother. You already complain that you don't see them enough."

I pointed my finger at her. "I earned at least two hours a month with my brothers. At *least*—not limited to. If they don't get Tyler in that room in thirty seconds, I'm going to call a lawyer and tell him you're knowingly keeping me from my brothers."

Keesha stared at me for a second then started to laugh. "You're a smart boy, Noah. Learnin' the system and usin' it to your advantage. Get back in there. He's on his way." I turned, but Keesha called out, "And Noah, if you ever point your finger at me again, I'll break it off and hand it to you."

Jacob gave me Mom's smile again when I reentered. I focused on shoving the anger out of my system. Jacob was easy. Jacob remembered. Tyler—Tyler was a whole other animal.

Carrie, the perfect adult with perfect brunette hair, entered the room with Tyler wrapped around her like a baby monkey to his mother. I held out my hands. "Give him to me."

I towered over her. Easy to do since she only came to my shoulder. Instead of handing him over, she slipped another arm around him. "He's scared."

Correction. She was scared. "I'm his brother and you're not related to him. He'll be fine."

When she made no move to release him, I continued, "I have the right to this visit."

She licked her lips. "Tyler, baby, it's time to see Noah and play with Jacob. It looks like Noah got you a present."

At those words, Tyler lifted his head and stared at me. The face of my youngest brother almost brought me to my knees. It wasn't because he looked like me and Mom, but because the entire right side of his face was bruised. My heart beat faster when I saw the patch of shaved brown hair and at least five staples in his skull.

My head snapped to the transparent mirror, a clear indication that if Keesha didn't get her social worker ass in here, I was going to kill this woman.

I sucked in a calming breath. Tyler was only four and my anger would frighten him. I reached out and took him from her. She held her arms out as if I'd stolen her puppy. "It was an accident," she whispered.

"Hey, lil' bro. Would you like to open your present?" I asked Tyler.

Tyler nodded. I placed him next to Jacob and handed him his gift. Keesha walked in as Carrie scurried out. Keesha held her hands up. "It was an accident. I should have told you before Tyler came in, but it slipped my mind."

My eyes narrowed as I looked straight at her. "We'll discuss this later." I returned to my brothers and prayed that Tyler would speak at least one word to me before the session ended.

Once again, I sat on the folding chair, but I wasn't nervous this time. I was fucking pissed.

Keesha took the seat opposite me. "Carrie and Joe got Tyler a bike for Christmas and they let him ride it a couple of days ago without a helmet. When he fell, they took him immediately to the hospital and notified me. They feel horrible."

"They should," I barked. "How do you know they didn't hit him?"

Keesha picked up the blue ribbon from Tyler's package. "They're good people. I don't believe they would intentionally hurt your brothers."

Yeah. Genuine saints. "If they're so great, then they should stop stonewalling me and let me see my brothers."

"They took on the boys after the incident with your first foster family, Noah. They'd heard that you were emotionally unstable. That alone proves how much they care for those boys. Carrie and Joe don't want to see them get hurt."

My fist closed and I kept my hand under the table to prevent myself from pounding the wall like I wanted. Keesha would love more leverage to prove my instability. "I would never hurt them."

"I know that," said Keesha with a hint of defeat. "Why do you think I suggested that Mrs. Collins take you on?"

I should have known. "So she's your fault."

She leaned forward, placing her arms on the table. "You're a great kid, Noah. You've got a lot of potential in front of you if you'd just lose the attitude."

I shook my head. "I thought I proved myself already. Christ, you've placed me in a home with another teenager."

"I told you. This can be a slow process. Just come to the visitations, behave and work with Mrs. Collins. By the time you graduate, I'm sure we can move on to unsupervised visitation."

Unsupervised visitation? A muscle in my jaw jumped. Bullshit. "I'll be eighteen by the time I graduate. I'll have custody by then."

Keesha's face twitched with amusement, but then became solemn. "You think you could raise your brothers while workin' at a fast-food joint? You think a judge would choose you over Carrie and Joe?"

Choose me over Carrie and Joe? The realization that the judge might have this choice created a disturbing nausea in my gut. Jacob had said they wanted him to call them Mom and Dad. "Carrie and Joe are filing for adoption, aren't they?"

The moment she looked away I knew the answer. There was no way in hell anyone but me would raise my brothers. "You're right, Keesha. I've learned a lot in the past two and a half years. I've learned that this state takes blood into consideration and that the excuse of me being emotionally unstable must not be sticking if I've been placed in a home with another foster kid. I may not be able to take care of my brothers now, but in four months I will."

Ready to leave, I pushed away from the table and stood. Keesha's eyes crunched together in anger. "Don't mess those boys' lives up over an accident."

I spun around and pulled up my sleeve, pointing at the round scar on my bicep. "Gerald called that an accident. The best way to describe Don is as an accident. What type of accident would you call Faith and Charles Meeks? I've got words for them, but you forbade that type of language. My brothers will never be accidents of this system."

With that, I stalked out, slamming the door behind me.

Echo

Watching beer pong typically bored me, but not when Lila continued to kick everyone's butt. The girl was on fire. Plus anytime the opposing team hit her cup, she asked some random guy to drink it. Guys always lined up to do her bidding.

"Are you going to play?" Luke asked.

Caught up in my own thoughts, I'd missed his approach. "Nope. This is all Lila." Plus I didn't do anything that drew attention to me.

"Tonight should be all about you. It is your birthday." He paused. "Happy birthday, Echo."

"Thanks."

"So you gonna watch her all night?" Luke appraised the game with his thumbs hitched in his pockets. If I didn't know better, I'd say he was up to something.

"Buddy system. I've got Lila and Lila's got me. Natalie and Grace are around here somewhere." I surveyed the kitchen, half expecting them to spontaneously appear.

"Smart, yet annoying." Luke placed his palm on the wall next to my head, but kept his body a safe distance from mine. When he used to do that, he would crowd me with his body, causing butterflies to pole-vault in my stomach. Then he would lean in closer and kiss me. Those days were long gone—the crowding, the butterflies, the pole-vaulting and especially the kissing. "I was going to ask you to dance."

I made a show of looking around. "Who you trying to make jealous, Luke?"

He withdrew his hand and laughed—really laughed. Not the fake one he used in the cafeteria with his girl of the week. "Come find me when Lila's done playing games."

Lila threw her hands in the air and yelled as she demolished, once again, another team. At this point, I was sure they were letting her win just so she'd continue to play. Luke disappeared.

She grabbed one of the remaining cups of beer and walked away from the table, to the dismay of the guys who hung on her every movement. She drank half then handed the rest to me. "Here. Nat's still DD, right?"

"Yep." I took the cup from her and finished it off. I didn't particularly care for the taste, but when at a kegger...

I enjoyed the warm fuzzy feeling the beer eventually brought on. The edges of my life didn't seem so bad then. Week number two of the second term had brought on my first one-on-one therapy session with Mrs. Collins, no job, and the fear that Noah Hutchins would change his mind and tell everyone about my scars. The two of us had gone back to ignoring each other. "Mrs. Collins asked me this week if I drank. I'm really tired of lying to her."

Michael Blair, host of the party, walked by with a tray full of beers for another round of beer pong. Lila stole two and passed one to me. "Adults want us to lie. They expect us to lie. They want to live in their perfect little worlds and pretend we do nothing more than eat cookie dough and watch reality TV."

I sipped the beer. "But we do eat cookie dough and watch reality TV."

Lila stumbled before narrowing her eyes at me. "Exactly. We do that to take them off guard."

The warm fuzzy feeling that helped take the edge off also slowed the thought process. I ran through what she said twice. "That doesn't make any sense."

She waved her hand around like she was going to explain. Her hand kept moving, but her mouth stayed shut. Finally she dropped her hand and took another drink. "I've got no clue. Let's dance, birthday girl."

We threw our empty cups in the garbage and wove through the crowd to the source of the pumping music. Music...dancing...Luke had said I needed to find him. I opened my mouth to tell Lila when she abruptly stopped. "I've gotta pee." She took a sharp left and closed the bathroom door behind her.

I leaned my right shoulder against it and listened for dry heaves. Nope, she was definitely peeing.

Pain shot down my left arm when someone ran into me and kept walking. I glanced over my shoulder. "Watch it!"

A girl with long black hair, dressed in black from head to toe and sporting a nose ring, stepped toward me. She stood close enough that I could count her eyelashes over her bloodshot eyes.

"Get out of my way and there wouldn't be a problem."

Okay. I was a complete wuss. I'd never gotten into a fistfight in my life. Did anything to avoid people yelling at me. Worried at night that I may have offended someone. So when this biker-looking chick stood there with her arms stretched out wide, waiting for my witty comeback or me to throw a punch, I considered puking.

"Back off, Beth," a deep, husky voice called out behind me. Crap. I knew that voice.

Biker Beth's gaze settled right behind my shoulder. "She yelled at me."

"You ran into her first." Noah Hutchins stood beside me. His biceps touched my shoulder.

The corners of her mouth stretched up. "You didn't tell me you were fucking Echo Emerson."

"Oh, God," I moaned. She knew me—and she thought I was doing "it" with him. The room tilted and the warm fuzzy feeling I loved faded. *Happy birthday to me.*

"She's my tutor."

I leaned against the wall and wished everything would stop moving.

"Whatever. I'll see you outside when you're done studying." Biker chick Beth waggled her eyebrows and walked away.

Fantastic. Another rumor to worry about. I needed to get away from him. Noah Hutchins meant nothing but bad news. First he made fun of me. Then he saw my scars. Then he destroyed my hopes of fixing Aires' car. Then he made people think we were doing "it."

I tried the doorknob to the bathroom, hoping to join Lila in there, but it didn't budge. Locked doors were in direct violation of the buddy system. Screw it. I pushed off the wall and stumbled to the back door. Air. I needed lots of air.

I inhaled deeply the moment I stepped out onto the patio. The cold air burned my lungs and immediately nipped at the exposed skin on my neck and face. I heard laughter and voices in the darkness beyond the patio line. Probably the stoners smoking their crap.

"Do you have some sort of issue with jackets?"

Come freaking on. Why couldn't I get rid of him? I spun around and nearly ran into Noah. Depth perception and beer obviously weren't related. "Are you determined to ruin my life?" *Shut up, Echo.* "I mean, do you have nothing else to do but destroy me?" *That's enough. You can stop anytime now.* "Did you come to this party to tell everyone about my scars?" And I officially became the after-school special on why teenagers shouldn't drink.

I stared into his eyes and waited for his response. Neither one of us moved. Dear God, Lila and Natalie were right. He was hot. How could I have missed a body built like this? His unzipped jacket exposed his T-shirt, so tight I could see the curve of his muscles. And those dark brown eyes...

Noah straightened his head and coolly responded, "No."

A cold wind swept across the patio, causing me to shiver. Noah shrugged off his black leather jacket and tossed it around my shoulders. "How are you going to tutor me if you get fucking pneumonia?"

I cocked an eyebrow. What an odd combination of romantic gesture and horribly crude wording. I clutched his jacket, resisting the urge to close my eyes when a sweet, musky scent surrounded me. My slow mind turned one wheel. "That's twice you brought up tutoring."

He shoved his hands in his pockets. His hair fell into his eyes, blocking my new favorite view. "Nice to know that your mind still works when you're fucked up."

"You use that word a lot." I swayed. Maybe I didn't need space. I needed a wall. I stumbled and leaned my back against the cold brick. A small mutinous part of my brain chanted "buddy system" over and over again. *Yeah, I'll get on it—in a few.*

Noah followed and stopped less than an inch in front of me. So close, the heat from his body enveloped every inch of mine.

"What word?"

"The *f* one." Wow. He stood closer to me than Luke had earlier. Close enough that, if he wanted to, he could kiss me.

His dark eyes searched mine and then moved down to inspect the rest of my body. I should tell him to stop or make a sarcastic comment or at least feel degraded, but none of that happened. Not until his lips turned up.

"Meet your approval?" I asked sarcastically.

He laughed. "Yes." I liked his deep laugh. It tickled my insides.

"You're high." Because no one in their right mind would find me attractive. Especially when that person had seen the infamous scars.

"Not yet, but I'm planning on it. Want to come?"

I didn't need full use of my brain for this answer. "No. I like my brain cells. I find they come in handy when I…oh, I don't know…think."

His wicked grin made me smile. Not my fake smile—my real one.

"Funny." In a lightning-fast move, he placed both of his hands on the brick wall, caging me with his body. He leaned toward me and my heart shifted into a gear I didn't know existed. His warm breath caressed my neck, melting my frozen skin. I tilted my head, waiting for the solid warmth of his body on mine. I could see his eyes again and those dark orbs screamed hunger. "I heard a rumor."

"What's that?" I struggled to get out.

"It's your birthday."

Terrified speaking would break the spell, I licked my suddenly dry lips and nodded.

"Happy birthday." Noah drew his lips closer to mine; that sweet musky smell overwhelmed my senses. I could almost taste his lips when he unexpectedly took a step back, inhaling deeply. The cold air slapped me into the land of the sober.

He ran a hand over his face before heading toward the tree line. "See you soon, Echo Emerson."

"Wait." I began to pull off his jacket. "You forgot this."

"Keep it," he said without looking back. "I'll get it from you on Monday. When we discuss tutoring."

And Noah Hutchins—girl-using stoner boy and jacket-loaning savior—faded into the shadows.

NOAH

"What I don't get is why you gave her your jacket." Beth's head and hair dangled off the mattress. She took a hit off the joint and passed it to Isaiah.

"Because she was cold." I slouched so far back into the couch that if I relaxed any further it might open up and consume me. I chuckled. This was good shit.

After my run-in with Echo, I bought some pot, gathered Beth and Isaiah from the woods behind Michael Blair's house and herded us back to Shirley and Dale's. I couldn't depend upon either one of them to stay sober enough to drive me home, and I intended to get fucked up beyond belief.

According to my social worker's file, Isaiah, another foster kid, and I slept in bedrooms upstairs. In reality, this frozen hellhole, more cement block than basement, was where the three of us lived. We took turns sleeping on the old king-size mattress and couch we'd found at Goodwill. We let Beth have the bed upstairs, but when her aunt Shirley and uncle Dale fought, which was most of the time, she shared the mattress with Isaiah while I slept on the couch.

Besides my brothers, Isaiah and Beth were the only people I considered family. I'd met them when Keesha placed me at Shirley and Dale's the day after my junior year ended. Child Protective Services had placed Isaiah here his freshman year. It was more like a boardinghouse than a home.

Shirley and Dale became foster parents for the money. They ignored us. We ignored them. Beth's aunt and uncle were okay people, though they had some anger issues. At least they saved their anger for each other. Beth's mother and boyfriend of the week, on the other hand, liked to take their anger out on Beth, so she stayed here. Keesha remained unaware of this arrangement.

Beth flipped so she could see me straight. "For real. Are you doing her?"

"No." But after standing so damn close to her, I couldn't stop thinking about the possibility of her warm body under mine. I wished I could blame it on the pot, but I couldn't. I had been as sober as the day of a court-ordered drug test standing next to her on that patio. Her silky red hair had glimmered in the moonlight, those green eyes looked up at me like I was some sort of answer, and, damn, she smelled like cinnamon and sugar fresh out of the oven. I rubbed my head and sighed. What was wrong with me?

Ever since that day at the library, I couldn't get Echo Emerson out of my head. Even when I visited my brothers, I thought of her and that rocking foot.

She plagued me for several reasons. First, as much as I hated to admit it, I needed the tutoring. If I intended to get my brothers back, I needed to graduate high school, on time, with a job a hell of a lot better than cooking burgers. I'd missed enough class that I was behind and someone who attended class daily could help me catch up.

"Here. There ain't much left, but give it a try." Isaiah sat on the floor between the bed and the couch. He passed me the joint.

I took the last hit and held the smoke until my nostrils and lungs burned. And then there were the reasons that confused me. I exhaled. "Tell me about her."

"Who?" Beth stared at the floor.

"Echo." What crackhead names their kid Echo? I knew her, yet I didn't. I only pursued girls who showed an easy interest in me.

Isaiah closed his eyes and rested his head against the couch. He kept his hair buzzed close to his scalp. His ears were pierced multiple times and tattoos ran the length of his arms. "She's out of your league."

Beth giggled. "That's because she turned you down flat freshman year. Isaiah thought he could date up and asked a sophomore out. Little did he know Ms. Perfect had been dating King Luke for a year."

Isaiah's lips twitched. "I seem to remember Luke switching lab partners behind your back so he could sit next to her."

Beth's eyes narrowed. "Dick."

"Focus for me. Echo? Not your pathetic lives." Like an old married couple, the two of them enjoyed bickering. Isaiah and Beth were a year behind me, but the age difference never bothered us.

Beth sat up on the mattress. She loved to dish dirt. "So Echo's sophomore year, she's the star of the school, right? She's on the dance team, advanced classes, honor roll, art guru, Miss Popularity, and she's got Luke Manning feeling her up between classes.

One month before school lets out—she disappears." Beth's eyes widened and she spread her fingers out like a magician doing a trick.

This was not where I thought this story would go. Isaiah watched my reaction and nodded. "Poof."

"Gone," added Beth.

"Vanished," said Isaiah.

"Lost."

"Evaporated."

"Gone," repeated Beth. Her eyes glazed over and she stared down at her toes.

"Beth," I prodded.

She blinked. "What?"

"The story." This was the problem with hanging out with stoners. "Echo. Continue."

"Oh, yeah, so she disappeared," said Beth.

"Poof," added Isaiah.

Not this again. "I got it. Moving along."

"She comes back junior year a completely different person— like Body Snatcher different. It's still Echo, right? She's got red curly hair and a rockin' body," said Beth.

Isaiah laughed. "You just called her body rocking."

Beth threw a pillow at him before continuing, "But she's not Miss Social anymore. Luke and her are history. He moved on to some other girl. Though the rumor is she broke up with him before her disappearance. She quits the dance team, stops entering art contests and barely talks to anyone. Not that I would have talked to anyone either, the way rumors flew around about her."

"The gossip was brutal, man," said Isaiah. Beth, Isaiah and I understood gossip. Foster kids and those from bad homes lay low for a reason.

"What did they say?" I had a sinking feeling where this conversation was headed and it didn't sit well with me.

Beth wrapped her arms around her knees. "On the first day of our junior year she came back wearing a long-sleeve shirt and the same thing the day after that and on and on. It was ninety degrees for the first three weeks of school. What do you think people said?"

Isaiah made a circling motion with his finger. "Her little friends circled the wagons and kept her out of sight."

"And she started meeting with the school counselor." Beth paused. "You gotta feel bad for her."

My eyes had been drifting closed, but Beth's statement shocked them open. "What?" Beth lacked the sympathy gene.

She lay down on the bed, her eyes fluttering. "Obviously something fucked-up happened to her. Plus, her brother died a couple of months before she disappeared. They were super close. He was only three years older than her and took her to parties and stuff when he was in town. I used to hate her for having an older brother who cared." Now Beth's eyes shut completely.

Isaiah stood. "Roll over."

Beth rolled against the wall. Isaiah grabbed a blanket off the floor and draped it over her. Our storyteller passed out.

Isaiah joined me on the couch. "Most people call Echo a cutter. Some said she tried to commit suicide." He shook his head. "It's all messed up, man."

I was tempted to say I agreed and tell him what happened at the library, but I didn't. "What happened to her brother?"

"Aires? He was a good guy. Cool to everyone. Joined the Marines out of high school and got himself blown to hell over in Afghanistan."

Aires and Echo Emerson. Their mother must have hated them to give them names like that. Now I needed to find a way to make nice with the girl. She was my ticket to getting my brothers back.

Echo

I held Noah's black leather jacket over my arm and headed toward my locker. The temptation to wear it overwhelmed me. I loved the way it smelled, how warm it made me feel and how it reminded me of our moment together outside Michael Blair's house.

Get a grip, Echo. You're not an idiot. I knew the gossip regarding Noah. He only attended parties to get high and browse the drunken female crowd for a one-night stand. If I'd gone off to get high with him, I would have been it. I wasn't interested in a one-night stand, but it was nice to be considered. After all, since my sophomore year, no other guy at this school had showed an ounce of interest in me.

"What's your problem? You look like a four-year-old who lost her balloon." Lila joined me as I walked down the hall.

"I'm destined to die a virgin." My own admission shocked me. Had those words left my mouth? I rubbed the smooth material of Noah's jacket. Maybe I should have gone off with him. Not to get high, but to…well…not die a virgin.

Lila laughed so loudly several people gawked as we walked past. I lowered my head, let my curls hide my face and willed everyone to look away. We reached our lockers and I opened mine with the hopes of crawling inside.

"Hardly likely. But I thought you weren't into hookups." Lila rifled through her own locker, which was next to mine.

"I'm not. I held out with Luke because I wasn't ready. I never imagined there would come a day when nobody would want me."

I stared down at my gloved hands, causing seasickness to hit me on dry land. When the bell rang, I'd have to take them off. This wasn't about sex. "No guy's going to get close enough to ever love me."

Lila closed her locker and bit her lip. "Your mom sucks."

I inhaled deeply to keep from falling apart. "Yeah. I know."

Her eyes narrowed on the jacket I still clutched. "What's that?"

"Noah Hutchins's jacket," Natalie said, appearing out of nowhere and snatching it out of my hand. Her brown hair swung from side to side. "Follow me! Now!"

Lila's eyes widened to the size of cantaloupes as we trailed Natalie into the restroom. "Why do you have Noah Hutchins's jacket?"

I opened my mouth to answer, but Grace slammed the door to the bathroom shut. "We don't have time for small talk. He's coming."

Natalie used one finger to push each stall door open to confirm we were alone. The place smelled of disinfectant and a sink dripped every couple of seconds.

"Stop it," said Grace. "I already checked."

Lila grabbed Grace's hand. "Whoa. I need answers. Who's coming? Why does Echo have Noah's jacket and where did you get that sweater?"

"Luke. For Echo. You were so drunk at the party that you messed with the buddy system and now Echo has Noah's jacket. She can't be seen with it." Grace jerked it out of Natalie's hand. "We are getting Echo's life back."

I pried the jacket from Grace's fingers. My friends had officially lost their minds. "It's a jacket, not crack. He's in my first period class. I'll give it to him then. And who cares that Luke is looking for me?"

Grace pointed a red fingernail at me. "You held out. Luke asked you to dance at the party and instead of dancing with him we had to take Lila home. Now he's looking for you to find out why you stood him up. This is the answer to all of our prayers."

I clutched the jacket closer. "What? I mean, so? Luke and I are friends." I guessed. He'd wished me a happy birthday. Friends do that.

Lila started her annoying bouncing dance. "So? Dancing with you at a party is way past friendship. It means he's into you again."

"Exactly," said Grace. "If Luke's into you then everyone else will be into you, too."

Lila waved her hands in the air. "More importantly, you are not going to die a virgin." She sucked in a dramatic breath. "Luke cannot see you with another guy's jacket. Grace, take the jacket to your locker and we'll figure out a plan later."

Grace raised an eyebrow. "No way. I'm sure that thing reeks of drugs. What if they bring drug-sniffing dogs to school?"

"Oh, my God, you are worthless," Lila said.

Tossing some of my curls over my shoulder, Grace straightened my shirt. "Go on, get out there before he misses you and heads to class."

Lila and Natalie pulled me out the door and I clutched Noah's jacket closer to me. "You guys are way overanalyzing this," I said as Lila speed dialed the combination to my locker.

"He's coming," Natalie sang.

Lila plucked the jacket from my hands, threw it in my locker, pushed me out of the way and slammed it shut. She and Natalie leaned against my locker, adding a second layer of security.

"Hey, Echo."

I turned and faced Luke. "Hey." So much had happened in the past three minutes, my mind became a tilt-a-whirl.

Luke's eyes flickered over Natalie and Lila. His eyebrows inched closer together. I remembered that look: he had something he wanted to say without an audience. But if Luke remembered nothing else about me, he'd recall I was a package deal.

"I waited for you," he said.

"It's my fault," Lila blurted. "She didn't have time to dance with you because I wanted to go home. I drank too much."

Both Luke and I stared at her and then at each other. One Mississippi of awkward silence. Two Mississippi of awkward silence. Three Mississippi of awkward silence.

"Can I walk you to class, Echo?" he finally asked.

"Sure." I glanced at Lila and Natalie over my shoulder as I accompanied Luke down the hallway. Both flashed quick thumbs-ups. I sucked in a deep breath and smiled when I noticed Luke grinning at me. Wow—normal. Maybe it really was possible.

That is, if normal meant hiding Noah Hutchins's jacket in my locker...and pretending that I wasn't thinking about how close he'd come to kissing me.

NOAH

"Hold this." Mrs. Collins shoved a steaming to-go cup at me and went back to war with the school's locked doors. We could barely see in the pale morning light, making it hard for her to find the right key on the overloaded chain. I considered giving her crap about her lack of organizational skills, but decided not to. It took some major balls to be alone with a punk like me.

The warmth of the coffee reminded me how cold it was outside. Goose bumps pricked my exposed arms. I owned one long-sleeved shirt and only wore that for my brothers. Being jacket-less sucked.

Her eyes settled on the tattoo on my biceps and her forever smile fell a centimeter. "Where's your jacket, Noah? It's cold."

"I gave it to someone."

A relieved sigh escaped her mouth when the third key she tried unlocked the door. She waved for me to go in. Instead, I held the door and nodded for her to go first. It would be my luck that a security guard would see me, shoot, then ask questions.

Our footsteps echoed down the empty hallway. Thanks to our school's new green policy, the lights flashed on as we approached. It put me on edge. On top of the system that stalked my every movement, now the building did, too.

"Who did you give your jacket to?" Mrs. Collins entered the main office and unlocked her office door on the first try.

"A girl." A girl who'd ignored me all day Monday and had yet to return said jacket.

"A girlfriend or a friend that's a girl?"

"Neither."

Mrs. Collins gave me the pity look then busied herself with her purse. "Do you need a coat?"

I hated the pity look. After my parents died, everyone I knew wore that look. Eyes slightly rounded. The ends of their mouths curved up slightly while their lips pulled down. The entire time they fought to look normal, but they only came across as uncomfortable.

"No. I'm getting it back today."

"Good." She flipped open my file. "How are your tutoring sessions with Echo?"

"We're starting today." Only Echo didn't know that yet.

"Glorious." She opened her mouth to ask another asinine question, but I had my own.

"What do you know about my brothers?"

She picked up a pen and tapped it against the desk, keeping time with the second hand on the clock. "Keesha and I had a chat regarding your visit this weekend. What happened to Tyler was an accident."

What the hell? "You're a school counselor. What are you doing talking to my social worker? And what are you doing talking to her about Tyler?"

"I already told you. I'm a clinical social worker, and I'm the guinea pig for the pilot program. My job isn't to handle a part of you, but to handle all of you. That means I have access to your brothers. I'll be communicating with their foster parents and sometimes I'll be talking to Jacob and Tyler as well.

"As for where I fit in here at Eastwick, Mrs. Branch handles the typical guidance counselor issues and I handle…" She bobbed her head. "The more enlightening students. School fills your mind with knowledge, but we tend to ignore the emotional. I'm here to see what happens if we pay attention to both."

Yay for me. Having Keesha up my ass was bad enough. Now I had Sally Sunshine in my business, too. I ran my hand over my face and shifted in my chair.

Mrs. Collins continued, "Keesha also told me that you're threatening to petition for custody of your brothers after you graduate. If that's true, Noah, you've got some major changes you need to make in your life. Are you willing to make them?"

"Excuse me?" Did she just challenge me to get my shit together so I could get my family back?

She put the pen down and leaned forward. "Are you willing to make the changes necessary to possibly care for your brothers after graduation?"

Fuck, yeah. Hell, yes. "Yes, ma'am."

Mrs. Collins picked her pen back up and wrote in my file. "Then you're going to have to prove it to me. I know you have no reason to trust me, but this process will go faster and smoother if you can find a way to do it. You need to focus on yourself right now and trust Keesha and me to see to the welfare of your brothers.

"The reality of the situation is this. If you continue to harass Keesha about visitation and if you continue to pump Jacob for information on his foster parents, specifically their last name, then you are making it appear as if you aren't willing to play by the rules. The visitation you have now is a privilege, Noah. A privilege I want to see you keep. Do we have an understanding?"

The chair jerked beneath me as I pointed at her. "Those are my brothers."

The lack of information about who had my brothers—their foster parents' last name, their address, their phone number… the fact that I couldn't see Jacob and Tyler whenever I wanted… I lost all of those "privileges" the day I hit my first foster father. My throat swelled and my eyes stung. The realization that I was on the verge of tears pissed me off. I stood, unsure what to do… or who to blame. "You have no right. They're my responsibility."

Mrs. Collins stared at me straight-faced. "They're safe. You need to believe me on this. You're putting your experiences on your brothers. I understand your need to protect them, but right now it isn't necessary. If you want to see them on a regular basis then you need to learn to work with me, and I've explained how you can do that."

"Go to hell." I grabbed my books and left her office.

Echo

Mrs. Collins's plaques had moved by a fraction of an inch, revealing black marks on the wall. For once, I found myself wishing for Ashley's attendance. The imperfection would have driven her insane.

Just like last week, the blue ribbon sat on Mrs. Collins's desk and just like last week, the placement of the ribbon changed—each time closer to my seat. It was as if the ribbon contained a force field that enveloped me—a pull I couldn't explain.

"How are things with your boyfriend?" asked Mrs. Collins. Another Tuesday afternoon, another therapy session.

I drew my eyes away from the ribbon. Thank God Luke had asked me out on a group date for Saturday night. One less lie for me to tell. "Ashley misunderstood. I don't have a boyfriend, but I am dating somebody." Kind of. Sort of. If one date was considered dating.

Her eyes brightened. "Wonderful. Is it that basketball player I've seen hanging around with you in the hall?"

"Yes." Great, a stalking therapist. Was that even legal?

"Tell me about him."

Um…no. "I don't want to talk about Luke."

"All right," she said, totally unruffled. "Let's talk about Noah. He told me today is your first tutoring session."

I blinked several times in succession. Crap. Was it? Maybe I should have discussed Luke. I still had Noah's jacket in my locker since I'd let Lila and Grace convince me I couldn't simply hand it to him during school. They were still devising a plan to get it back to him. "Yes. Yes, it is."

"Would you like some unsolicited advice?"

I shrugged and yawned simultaneously, preparing for the just-say-no-to-drugs-sex-and-alcohol lecture. After all, in theory, I was tutoring Noah Hutchins. "Sure."

"Noah is more than capable of doing the work. He just needs a small push. Don't let him fool you into thinking otherwise. And you, Echo, are the one person at this school I believe can challenge him academically."

Allllrighty. That was a totally strange pep talk. "Okay." I covered my mouth as I yawned again.

"You look tired. How are you sleeping?"

Awesome. I slept a whole two hours last night. My foot began to rock.

"Echo, are you okay? You look pale."

"I'm fine." If I kept saying it then maybe it would come true. And maybe, someday, I could sleep a full night without horrible dreams—strange dreams, scary dreams, full of constellations, darkness, broken glass and, sometimes, blood.

"Your father mentioned that you don't take your prescribed sleeping pills even though you still have night terrors."

Nightly. Scary enough I didn't want to fall asleep. Frightening enough that if I lost the battle and did sleep, I woke up screaming. My father and Ashley kept the pills in a locked cabinet in their bathroom and only gave them to me if I asked. I'd rather have poked my eye out with a bleach-laced needle than ask Ashley for anything. "I said I'm fine."

With the word *fine,* my eyes shot back to the ribbon. What was it about that thing that attracted me to it? I felt like a moth flying toward an electric bug zapper.

"You appear very interested in the ribbon, Echo," said Mrs. Collins. "You're more than welcome to hold it if you'd like."

"No, I'm good," I replied. But I wasn't good. My fingers twitched in my lap. For some insane reason, I wanted to hold it. Mrs. Collins said nothing and the silence sort of creeped me out.

My heart stuttered as I finally shifted forward and took the ribbon in my hand.

This wasn't one of those cheesy blue ribbons. This was the real deal—large and made of silk. I rubbed the fabric between my thumb and forefinger. First in Show: Painting—Kentucky Governor's Cup.

Someone at my school won the Governor's Cup. How freaking cool was that? Every high school artist dreamed of winning that competition.

Maybe some lowerclassman had remarkable art talent. Screw my dad—the moment Mrs. Collins released me, I planned on checking out the art room and seeing this talent for myself. To win first place in the Governor's Cup, you had to be a stinking genius.

As I ran my fingers over the ribbon again, applause echoed in my head. A still frame image of my outstretched arm accepting the ribbon sprang into my mind.

My eyes snapped to Mrs. Collins as my heart thundered in my chest. "This is mine."

The thundering moved to my head and my chest constricted as another image squeezed out. In my mind's eye I was accepting not only the ribbon, but a certificate. I didn't see the name printed there, but I saw the date. It was *the* date.

Jolts of electricity shot up my arms and straight to my heart. Horrified, I threw the ribbon across the room and bolted from my chair. My knee slammed against the desk, causing needle-sharp pains to shoot behind my kneecap. I fell to the floor and scrambled backward, away from the ribbon, until my back smacked the door.

Mrs. Collins pushed slowly away from her desk, crossed the room to retrieve the ribbon, and held it in her hand. "Yes, it's yours, Echo." She spoke like we were sharing a pizza instead of me having a panic attack.

"It's… It…can't be. I…never won the Governor's Cup." Fog filled a portion of my mind, followed by a bright flash of red. A moment of clarity revealed a younger me filling out a form. "But I entered…my sophomore year. I won the county, then regionals, and moved on to state. And then…then…" Nothing. The black hole swallowed the red and the gray. Only darkness remained.

Mrs. Collins smoothed her black skirt as she sat down in front of me. Maybe no one told her, but sitting on the floor during a therapy session was abnormal. She reined in her Labrador enthusiasm and spoke in a calm, reassuring tone. "You're in a safe place, Echo, and it is safe to remember." She stroked the ribbon. "You had a very happy morning that day."

I cocked my head to the side and squinted at the ribbon. "I… won?"

She nodded. "I'm a huge art fan. I prefer statues over paintings, but I still love paintings. I'd rather go to a gallery than a movie any day of the week."

This lady was a feather-filled quack. No question about it. Yet in the middle of those annoyingly cheerful plaques hung honest-to-God legitimate degrees. The University of Louisville was a real school and so was Harvard, where she'd apparently continued her studies. I focused on breathing. "I don't remember winning."

Mrs. Collins placed the ribbon on the edge of her desk. "That's because you repressed the entire day, not just the night."

I stared at the file on her desk. "Will you tell me what happened to me?"

She shook her head. "I'm afraid that would be cheating. If you want to remember, then you need to start applying yourself during these sessions. That means you answer my questions honestly. No more lying. No more half lies. Even if your parents are here. In fact, especially if your parents are here."

I reached up to where Aires' dog tags would have rested around my neck if I had worn them. My eyes never left my file. "Did you bother reading that thing?"

One finger methodically rubbed her jaw. "Of course."

I bit the inside of my mouth. "Then you know. I tried to remember once and you know it isn't possible." Not without my mind fracturing in two. The summer after the incident, one psychologist tried to open the steel door in my brain and demons raced out from the crack. I lost myself for two days and woke in the hospital. My nightmares escalated into night terrors.

"You want the truth?" I asked. "You're right. I want so badly to know what happened. To prove I'm not...to know...because sometimes I wonder...if I'm crazy like her."

I could hear my father yelling at me to shut up in the dark recess of my mind, but the dam had burst open on my fears. "Because I'm like her, you know? We look the same, we're both artists, and people always say that I have her spirit. I'm proud to be like her. Because she's my mom, but I don't want..." To be crazy.

Mrs. Collins placed a hand over her heart. "Echo, no, you're not bipolar."

But why tempt fate? I'd tried once. Wasn't that enough? Mrs. Collins didn't understand. How could she? "If you tell me, I'll know. I think my mind cracked because that therapist tried to make me relive it. Maybe the memories are too horrible. Maybe if you tell me, you know, just the facts, then the black hole in my brain will be filled, the nightmares will go away and I won't lose my mind in the process." I stared straight into her kind eyes. "Please."

Her lips turned down. "I could read you the account from the police, your father, your stepmother and even your mother, but it won't take the nightmares away. You're the only person who can do that, but that means you need to stop running from the problem and face it head-on. Talk to me about your family, Aires, school, and yes, your mother."

My mouth hung open to speak, but then I snapped it shut, only to attempt to speak again. "I don't want to lose my mind."

"You won't, Echo. We'll take it slow. You run the race and I'll set the speed. I can help you, but you'll have to trust me and you'll have to work hard."

Trust. Why not ask me to do something easier, like prove the existence of God? Even God had given up on me. "I've already lost a piece of my mind. I can't trust you with what's left."

NOAH

After school, I spotted Echo weaving through the crowded hallway. She swung into the main office seconds before I caught up to her. Tuesday was my only night off and I'd planned on shooting hoops with Isaiah. I slammed my fist into the locker beside me. Now I had to wait for some stuck-up head case to be done with her therapy appointment.

I wandered the halls before settling across from Echo's locker. She hadn't had her backpack or coat with her, so I figured she'd have to come get them before she left for the day. Forty mind-numbing minutes later, I was questioning my decision. Echo had coat issues. Waiting by her car would have been smarter.

Heels clicking against the linoleum floor signaled her approach. Echo's red spiral curls bounced with each step. Clutching her books tight to her chest, she kept her head down. Every muscle in my body clenched when she walked past. I'd tolerated her ignoring me during school, but to flat-out diss me in an empty hallway was beyond cold. With her back to me, she tried the combination on her lock. The metal locker lurched open.

"You are the rudest damn person I have ever met." I shoved off the ground. Screw her, Mrs. Collins and tutoring. I'd find a way to bring myself to speed. "Give me my damn jacket."

Echo spun around. For a second, pure pain slashed her face, but then another storm brewed in her eyes. A storm that required hurricane warnings and evacuations. "No wonder you need tutoring. You have the worst vocabulary of anyone I know. Have you ever even bothered learning anything beyond four-letter words?"

"I've got another four-letter word for you. Fuck you. You got back with your boyfriend and couldn't stomach giving me my stuff in front of other people."

"You don't know anything."

"I know crazy when I see it." The moment the words flew out of my mouth I regretted them. Sometimes when you see the line, you think it's a good idea to cross it—until you do.

For the second time since meeting her, Echo looked as if I'd slapped her. Water pooled at the bottom edges of her eyes, her cheeks flushed red and she blinked rapidly. She'd succeeded in making me feel like a dick...again.

She reached into her locker and flung my jacket at me. "You are such a jerk!" She slammed shut her locker and stalked off.

Dammit. Just dammit. "Echo!" I ran after her. "Echo, wait."

But she didn't. I caught up to her, grabbed her arm and turned her toward me. Dammit all to hell, tears poured down her face. What was I supposed to do now?

She sniffed. "I didn't know you were waiting for me. I didn't see you." She wiped the tears with the back of her hand. "I should have given you your jacket back yesterday, but..." Her slender white neck moved as she swallowed. "But I wanted normal and for a few minutes that's what I was. Like two years ago…like before…" And she trailed off.

If I'd had the thinnest chance at normal again, I would have burned the damn jacket. I was sure she wanted her brother back as much as I wanted mine. To have a home again, and parents, and dammit. Normal.

I took a deep, pride-eating breath. In the wise words of Isaiah—poof. My muscles relaxed and my anger disappeared. Lowering her head, Echo withdrew into her hair. I would never understand why this girl made me grow a conscience. "I'm sorry. I shouldn't have yelled at you."

She revealed her pale face and sniffed again. One red curl clung to her tearstained cheek. My hand reached out to release it, but I hesitated a mere heartbeat away from her skin. I swear to God she quit breathing and even blinking, and for a second so did I. In a deliberate movement, I freed the curl.

She exhaled a shaky breath and licked her lips when I lowered my hand. "Thanks."

For the apology or the curl, I had no idea and wasn't going to ask. My heart pounded in tune with thrash metal. We'd read about sirens in English this fall; Greek mythology bullshit about women so beautiful, their voices so enchanting, that men did anything for them. Turned out that mythology crap was real because every time I saw her, I lost my mind.

Normal. She wanted normal and so did I. "You know what's normal?"

"What?" She wiped away her remaining tears.

"Calculus."

No doubt, Echo Emerson equaled siren. She gave me the same smile I'd seen on Saturday night. That type of smile caused men to write those pussy-ass songs that Isaiah and I made fun of. I'd sit in Mrs. Collins's office for hours and wake my ass up early to go to calculus in order to see that smile again. This was fucked up.

"All right," she said. "Let's do normal."

And we did. For an hour, we sat against the lockers and she caught me up on a few lessons. She used her hands to describe things, which was pretty damn hilarious since we were discussing math. Her green eyes shone when I asked questions and she gave me that siren smile each time I clued in. That smile only made me want to learn more.

She took a deep breath after finishing her explanation of a derivative. I'd understood a derivative five minutes ago, but I loved the sound of her sweet voice. Part angel, part music.

"You know a lot about math," I said. You know a lot about math? What type of statement was that? Right along of the lines of "Hey, you have hair and it's red and curly." Real smooth.

"My brother, Aires, was the math genius of our family. The only reason I can keep up is because he tutored me. He never turned in his calculus book, knowing I'd need all the help I could get." Handling it with the same reverence my mother had carried the family Bible, Echo pulled out an old, tattered math book from her backpack and began turning pages. The book contained copious notes written in blue or black ink in the margins. "Guess that makes me a cheater, huh?"

"No, it means you have a brother who cared." Was my brothers' foster mom helping them with their homework, or was she like Gerald's wife? Locking herself in the bedroom, she'd pretended none of her foster kids existed and that he didn't beat us.

She stroked the handwritten words on the page. "I miss him.

He died two years ago in Afghanistan." Echo clutched the book like it was a life raft. "IED."

"I'm sorry." I'd said that phrase more to her today than I had said it over the past two and a half years. "About your brother."

"Thanks," she said in a lifeless voice.

"It doesn't get better," I said. "The pain. The wounds scab over and you don't always feel like a knife is slashing through you. But when you least expect it, the pain flashes to remind you you'll never be the same."

Why I was telling her this, I didn't know. Maybe because she was the first person I'd met since my parents died who could understand. I stared at the pulsating fluorescent light hanging from the ceiling. On. Off. On. Off. I wished I could find my pain's off switch.

A warm, tickling touch crashed me back to earth. Maybe it sent me straight to heaven. Either way, it dragged me out of hell. Echo's pink fingernails caressed the back of my hand. "Who did you lose?"

"My parents." No pathetic sympathy crossed her face, only plain understanding. "Think Mrs. Collins put the two most depressed people together on purpose?" I flashed a smile to keep the honesty of the statement from corroding the remainder of my heart.

Her hand retreated. "Wow. I thought I was the only person at this school faking every moment."

Craving more of her touch, I shifted on the floor so my arm touched her shoulder. Echo's lips never moved, but my siren sang nonetheless. Her song seared my skin and my nose burned from her sugar and cinnamon scent.

Her back pocket vibrated, flinging me back to hell...sorry—

high school. I needed one of Beth's cigarettes and I didn't even smoke.

She skimmed a text message on her iPhone. Probably that lucky son-of-a-bitch ape boyfriend. Any trace of the siren smile I worked so hard to put on her face faded. That in itself was a fucking tragedy.

"You okay?" I asked.

"Yeah. My stepmom stalking my every move," she said with forced lightness.

I took a relieved breath. Better her stepmom than the ape. "At least you've got someone who cares." I doubted Shirley or Dale knew I owned a cell phone. "I am sorry for making you cry earlier. I promise I'll play nice in the future."

"Does this mean that I'm actually tutoring you now?"

"Yeah, I guess it does."

Echo pulled her sleeves over her hands. "You didn't make me cry. You didn't help, but you didn't make me cry."

She had exposed her hands while she tutored me—when she touched me. Shit. I'd forgotten about her scars. Hell, *she'd* forgotten about her scars—until now. I wanted that moment back, and to see her smile again. "Then who did? It's been a while since I've been in a fight. My rep will be ruined if I'm good for too long."

She fought it, but I won. The smile returned for a brief dazzling moment. "You'd be expelled if you got into a fight with Mrs. Collins. So thanks, but no, thanks."

I hit the back of my head against the locker. "She fucked with me today, too. Must be a third date thing." I chuckled when Echo looked at me like I'd tattooed my forehead.

"Third date thing meaning what?"

Did she live in a box? "After the third date, people generally have sex. Today was my third session and Mrs. Collins royally screwed me over. And by the looks of it, she did a number on you, too."

Her perfectly shaped eyebrows furrowed as she ran through what I said. I loved how her lips twitched in humor and a blush touched her cheeks.

"You know what sucks?" she asked.

"Mrs. Collins?"

"Yes, but that's not what I meant. Everything I need to know is in that freaking file she keeps on me. It's like the key to the magic door that opens the magic kingdom." She kicked her backpack across the hall. "I could finally find some real peace if I could get my hands on that stupid, stupid folder."

As she spoke, my mind whirled like a tornado. Mrs. Collins was in touch with Tyler and Jacob's foster parents, which meant she had their information: their last names, their phone number, their address. Echo was right. Those files were a gold mine. If I got my hands on my folder, I could check on my brothers. I could prove they were in an abusive home and gain custody. "You, Echo, are a genius."

Echo

Stage one of Operation Read My File consisted of my father, Ashley and me waiting for Mrs. Collins to call us in for our meeting. My father stood in the corner, speaking harshly to someone on the other end of his BlackBerry while Ashley and I sat next to each other on the row of chairs.

Ashley flung her hand over her stomach. "Oh. Oh, Echo, the baby kicked."

"You can come in now," called Mrs. Collins.

I flew out of my seat. "Thank God." For months, Ashley had bored everyone with endless baby chatter. Okay, maybe not everyone. My father hung on her every word like she was Paul preaching the gospel. He'd never paid this much attention to my mother. If he had, I wouldn't be the school freak.

Three weeks ago, Mrs. Collins had begun the term wearing business suits and then jeans and a nice shirt on casual Fridays. Each week casual Friday moved up a day. Today, Tuesday was the new Friday. From behind her desk, she flashed her never-ending smile. "Mr. and Mrs. Emerson, how wonderful to see you, but our group session is next week."

With eyebrows raised, my father sent a questioning glance to Ashley, who sat stunned with her mouth open. "No. The family calendar clearly stated..."

I cut her off. "I told them to come this week."

Mrs. Collins did that weird thing where she shifted her entire mouth to the right. "I know we had a rough session last week, but did you really think you needed to bring bodyguards?"

"Echo?" My father asked. "What happened last week?"

My heart squeezed and dropped. His concern sounded real. I'd give anything if it was. I stood and walked to the window. Students mingled in the parking lot before heading home. This session had the possibility of stinking as much as last week's. "Something good."

"That's fantastic. This family needs good news." Ashley's perky voice grated like sandpaper against my skin. "I read in a magazine that babies can sense negativity."

A car pulled out of its spot, revealing Noah sitting on the hood of his rusting car next to some guy with lots of earrings and tattoos and biker chick Beth. His two friends stared at me when he gave me his mischievous grin. His friends gave me the creeps. Noah's smile gave me flutters.

Not that I should have flutters for Noah Hutchins. I was dating Luke, not him—that is if you called Luke's one-sided nighttime phone conversations and a single awkward group outing to the local pizza place dating.

I sighed and shook Luke out of my head. Noah and I had made a deal and I intended to uphold my end of the bargain. The plan was simple: I needed to push back my appointment so he could move his session from the morning to my current afternoon slot. With our appointment times near each other, one of us would distract Mrs. Collins while the other snuck a peek at the files.

"Echo?" my father prodded, the hint of concern still present. "What's good?"

Inhaling deeply to calm the nerves squeezing my stomach, I turned to face him. I loathed confrontation and I hated confrontation with my father more. "Why didn't you tell me I won the Governor's Cup?"

"Excuse me?" No concern left in my father's tone now.

A twinge of hurt joined the nerves. Why, on top of everything else, did he take art away from me, too? "I wanted to win so badly. You could have at least told me that much."

Mrs. Collins eyed me warily and kept her hands folded on her lap. I expected her to jump in and defend herself, but she remained annoyingly cool. Ashley placed her hand over my father's. "Owen?" Was that guilt flickering in her blue eyes?

Scaring the crap out of me, he turned an unusual color of gray. "You remember?" His eyes grew round, making him look lost and terribly sad.

I thought he wanted me to remember. My forehead wrinkled in confusion. Wasn't that the point of all this therapy?

Gray turned to red as he faced Mrs. Collins. "This is unacceptable. We saw two psychiatrists and had three separate psychological evaluations. Each of them had a different opinion of how to proceed, but after her breakdown, every single one of them told us to leave that day alone. I knew when you asked for that ribbon to put in this room we should have opted out of your program. How could you force her to remember?"

"I didn't force anything, Mr. Emerson. I simply placed the ribbon on the desk during her sessions. It's called desensitizing. Her mind decided it was safe to remember, so she did."

Springing from his chair, my father ran a hand through his hair. "My God, Echo. Why didn't you tell me earlier? You have to understand..."

"Mr. Emerson, stop!" Mrs. Collins tried to keep her voice level, but I felt the slight urgency in her tone. "She only remembered receiving the ribbon. That's all."

My father's chest rose and fell rapidly. He reminded me of one of those paper bags people blow into during a panic attack. Then, as if to prove the impossible possible, he pulled me into him and hugged me. One of his arms wound around my back. His other hand cradled my head against him. I stood stiff.

Yet I felt warm. Secure. Safe. Like when I was a child and my mother spiraled into an episode and I was scared. Memories of my mother wide-eyed, yelling incoherently, her wild, red hair falling from a ponytail filled my mind. I used to run to my father and he would hold me—just like this. He protected me and kept me safe. I listened to his heart beating and I almost allowed myself to hug him back. Stilettos clicked against the floor when Ashley fidgeted.

Unbelievable pain stung my heart and I pushed him away. "You chose her."

My father held a hand out to me, his mouth hanging open. "What?"

"You chose Ashley. She weaseled her way into our home and she tore our family apart. You chose her over us."

"Echo, no. It wasn't like that." Ashley's plea was pathetic and fake. "I loved you and then I fell in love with your dad. Your parents' marriage was over way before the divorce."

My foot tapped the floor. Liar. She was a liar. "Yes, because of you."

"We're going home. This is a family matter." My father reached for his jacket and Ashley stood. "Mrs. Collins, I appreciate the state's willingness to place Echo in your program, but I believe it's best if my family seeks private counseling someplace else."

I panicked. In the parking lot, Noah was waiting for his turn to set our plan into motion. So far, I'd failed miserably. My father needed to stay until I accomplished my goal. In theory, I had one ally in this room. "Mrs. Collins?"

She gave me a nod. "Mr. and Mrs. Emerson, with all due respect this is exactly the kind of matter that should be discussed here."

My father held out Ashley's coat for her. "I'm capable of deciding what's appropriate for my family. My divorce from my ex-wife and my marriage to Ashley have nothing to do with Echo's memory loss."

"I beg to differ. They're issues Echo needs to deal with."

Oh, God. They were going to leave and I'd never learn what happened to me. I had to say something to keep them in the room. "I like her."

All three adults froze. "That's why I brought you here." I focused on the words I'd practiced since Noah and I had come up with the plan. "I wanted to tell you that I like the job Mrs. Collins found for me and that I'm done lying to her. I'm not fine and I'm not happy at home. I like her and I want to keep seeing her."

And oddly enough, I didn't blink.

Mrs. Collins's lips turned up, the exact reaction I hoped for. In order for Noah's plan to work, she needed to think I trusted her. Now, if I could build a time machine, go back to twenty minutes ago, and stop myself from telling my father how I really felt, my plan would be back on track. Telling Ashley off felt good, but that only disappointed my father. I sighed. In an effort to make this up to him, I'd be the only college freshman still attempting a perfect ACT score.

"I'm sorry, Daddy. I was out of line." Ugh. I'd rather eat cockroaches than say this. "And you, too, Ashley. My comments to you were rude." But true.

My father nodded and finished helping Ashley into her coat. "I don't blame you, Echo." He stared at Mrs. Collins, making it perfectly clear who he blamed for my outburst. "If you want to keep seeing Mrs. Collins then I'll let you. On a trial basis only. That means these next few sessions will be scrutinized."

Ashley rubbed her baby bump. "I'm glad you're making progress, Echo. It was a wonderful day when you got that ribbon. It was the first time I ever felt like the three of us were a real family."

"Why wasn't my mom there?" Silence. Ashley's hand froze mid-rub and my father stood motionless. I continued, "You said three. Mom would have never let you squeeze her out of that moment. She loved my paintings. She encouraged me more than the two of you combined."

The black hole pulsed in my head and a faint memory squeezed out. "I invited her to the ceremony and she accepted."

My mother's overly excited voice filled my head. "I wouldn't miss it, my little goddess."

"You're asking good questions, Echo, and I'm thrilled that you want to keep working with me. But I think we've had enough for today," Mrs. Collins said, bringing me back to the present. "We can pick this up in another session."

Speaking of another session…I was veering off course again. I had to set up Noah. "Daddy, there's one more thing."

He pinched the bridge of his nose, no doubt praying for the day I would be off to college and out of his house. Then he could focus all of his attention on his new family—the replacement family. "Yes?"

"If it's okay with Mrs. Collins, I want to move my counseling sessions back an hour. I'm thinking of rejoining the dance team or at least helping them with their routines."

Ashley beamed and I considered taking the statement back if only to annoy her. The worry lines around my father's eyes lessened and his mouth actually hinted at a smile. "Of course. Do you need money for a new outfit or costume?" He pulled his wallet out and held toward me green dollars with zeros.

I shook my head and smiled a little. I'd made my father happy. Part of me flew high in the sky. "No. No, thanks. I have plenty of stuff to practice in and I'm not sure about the costume thing yet. I may not even compete."

"Take it anyhow—in case you need it." He bounced his hand insistently. I took the cash, feeling a little ashamed and guilty. I'd never intended to rejoin the dance team—it was an excuse for Noah to rearrange his appointment time to my slot. Now, I had to accept Natalie's offer. If rejoining the dance team made my father smile at me and not at Ashley for a few minutes, I'd do it.

"Echo, would you mind leaving me and Ashley alone with Mrs. Collins? There are some things I'd like to discuss."

Uh—no. I hoped Mrs. Collins would tell my father whatever he had to say to her could be said in front of me, but no such luck. "Why don't you wait in the main office? I'd like to schedule our next appointment before you leave."

I shut the door behind me. With the staff gone for the day, the main office sat eerily quiet.

"Is it working?"

Startled, I knocked over a cup of pens on the counter. Noah leaned against the door frame, laughing.

I busied myself with picking them up. "I think so. My dad and Ashley are on board with me moving my time back, but Mrs. Collins hasn't committed yet. Though I think I just rejoined the dance team. What are you doing here?"

"It's cold outside and warm in here."

Having nothing left to fidget with, I rested against the counter and tried not to stare at Noah. But I wanted to. He had his jacket off and his black T-shirt fit him perfectly. Today, during lunch, Grace had turned her nose up when she spotted the bottom of his tattoo on his right bicep. I'd silently agreed with Lila's comment—*yum*.

My insides had melted when Noah produced his wicked grin and gazed at me like I was naked. Luke used to give me butterflies. Noah spawned mutant pterodactyls.

A cabinet door clicked closed in Mrs. Collins's office and jolted me back to reality. "But what if Mrs. Collins sees you? We shouldn't be seen together."

He chuckled. "You're my tutor, remember? She expects to see us together. Besides, I didn't show for my session this morning and she sent me a note informing me that I was to come as soon as possible." He held out his hands. "So here I am."

"When did you get the note?"

"First period."

I sucked in air. "And you're just now showing up?" I couldn't imagine missing a session, much less disregarding a request from an adult.

"It's all part of the plan, Echo. Chill."

Tapping my foot against the floor, I regarded the closed door. "You think she knows we're up to something?"

Noah crossed the room. The back of my neck exploded in heat when his body brushed mine. In a movement so nonchalant, it signaled he was impervious to temperatures only known in the Sahara Desert, he leaned his hip against the counter. He rubbed one of my curls between his thumb and forefinger. "You are paranoid. I'm glad you didn't get high with me. You'd be a major downer." He let the curl drop.

I folded my hands across my chest, attempted to ignore the warmth filling my cheeks, and said as dryly as I could, "Thanks." Nothing increased your confidence level like being insulted by a stoner.

Keeping time with my foot, my fingers drummed against my sleeve.

"What are you worked up about?"

"My dad and Ashley are in there with Mrs. Collins discussing me."

Noah picked up a phone from behind the counter. "Wanna hear what they're saying? I've watched Mrs. Marcos do this plenty of times. Mrs. Collins's phone is screwed up and it doesn't make the beeping noise anymore, so Mrs. Marcos has to introduce herself quickly."

I opened my mouth to protest, but Noah gently placed two warm fingers against my lips. He raised an eyebrow and flashed a pirate smile. "Shh."

He removed his fingers, leaving my lips cold, and pushed buttons on the speakerphone. Adrenaline pumped in my blood and my head felt featherlight. I'd never done anything so wrong in my life. In order to hear better, I leaned in closer.

My father was speaking. "...don't understand. If Echo wants to discuss her feelings regarding the divorce with you, that's one thing. I'll support any efforts to help her repair her relationship with Ashley. But you need to leave the rest alone. She's obviously back on track. She makes straight A's. She's active in several clubs and rejoining the dance team."

"Owen's right," Ashley said. "Socially, Echo is doing beautifully. She's going out with her friends, talking on the phone and texting. She and Luke are dating again. It's like she's finally fitting back into her old skin."

"What Ashley and I are trying to get at," my father added, "is that Echo is becoming Echo again. Child Protective Services was right to get involved after what happened, but now, it's overkill. Her mother is no longer an issue. Echo has this new job and, I'll admit, you were right. Working toward repairing the car has given her a healthy way to grieve Aires. Therapy was needed when she couldn't cope, but Echo is no longer simply coping. She's living."

"And her memory loss?" asked Mrs. Collins. "The nightmares? Her insomnia? The fact that Echo refuses to expose her arms to anyone?"

My stomach churned. I craved my father's answer, but to my utter mortification, Noah Hutchins had already heard too much. I reached out to disconnect the line, but Noah shook his head and placed a steady hand on my back.

Dizzy from nerves, I swayed to the right. Noah took a small step toward me while guiding me into him using gentle pressure on my back. I shouldn't be touching him, but I wanted to hear the answer and I needed someone to lean on. Just one time—this one moment only—would I rely on him. I allowed my muscles to relax when he combed his fingers through the curls hanging near my shoulder blades.

"Do you want my honest opinion, Mrs. Collins?" my father asked.

"Yes."

"You're right. She's not one hundred percent, but she is doing better than she was a year ago. Leave the past alone. Let her try to move on with her life."

"Without ever remembering?" Mrs. Collins pressed. "Without ever dealing with the emotions buried inside of her?"

"I think it would be best if Echo never remembered. I have a hard time understanding how her mother could hurt her. How can a child grasp the extent of the madness?" My father paused. "The nightmares are bad. Echo still has issues, but I'm concerned the truth will only hurt her, not help. Echo's mind cracked when the first psychologist pressured her to remember. What if you pressure her and she cracks again? Are you willing to risk my child's sanity?"

I clamped my hand over my mouth, to keep both words and vomit from coming out. Noah ended the call and placed the phone back on the other side of the counter. The room tilted and sweat formed between my breasts. Even my dad believed that if I tried to remember, I'd lose my mind...again.

"Echo?" Noah's deep, raspy voice hummed inside of me, but I couldn't look at him.

Pressing my lips together, I shook my head and withdrew into my hair.

"I won't tell anyone. I promise."

Noah brushed my hair behind my shoulder and tucked a straggling curl behind my ear. It had been so long since someone touched me like he did. Why did it have to be Noah Hutchins, and why did it have to be now?

"Look at me."

I met his dark brown eyes. His fingers skimmed the back of my hand. The sensation tickled like a spring breeze yet hit me like a wave rushing from the ocean. His gaze shifted to my covered arms. "You didn't do that, did you? It was done to you?"

No one ever asked that question. They stared. They whispered. They laughed. But they never asked. My entire world collapsed around me as I answered, "Yes."

NOAH

I leaned against my locker, scanning the students heading to lunch. Isaiah and Beth stood across from me near the side doors, waiting for the hallway to clear. If Echo stopped by her locker before lunch, she had to walk this desolate area to reach the cafeteria. I needed to know if she'd pushed back her appointment. That's what I told myself. Our plan wouldn't work if she failed.

Honestly, she put me on edge. She'd refused to make eye contact with me during calculus and fled the room the minute the bell rang. After her admission yesterday, she left the office. One moment, she'd relaxed her warm body next to mine, taking my comfort and strength. Seconds later—gone.

"Are you even listening to me, man?" Isaiah asked. Two blondes walked past us, huddled together. One sneered as she stared at the sleeve of tattoos on Isaiah's arms. He smirked while appraising their chests.

"Yeah." No. Something about cars and his jacked-up job at the local auto shop.

"No, you're not," said Beth. "You're looking for Echo Emerson." She waggled her eyebrows. Part of me regretted asking her for Echo's background. "Screwed her yet?"

"No." The look I gave her made football players shit their pants. Beth simply shrugged and rolled her eyes.

She flicked the unlit cigarette she held in her hand, anxiously waiting for the teachers to go into the lunchroom so she could sneak open the side door. "What's your obsession with her anyhow? Every time that girl comes around you stare at her like you're the Coyote and she's the Road Runner. Either fuck her or move on. You and the ex-popular chick will never be homecoming court material."

We could have been. If life was different, if my parents had never died, if I'd never gotten screwed by the system, if… I shut down the *ifs*. "She's my tutor, and she's helping me out with some stuff. Leave it—and her—alone."

"Don't say you haven't thought about it, man. She's… How did Beth put it? Oh, she has a rocking body," Isaiah said.

Beth slid her left hand underneath Isaiah's elbow and flicked the lighter. Isaiah jumped out of the way, smacking the flames lapping his shirt. "You're crazy."

"Damn straight," she replied.

The hallway finally emptied of students and teachers. Beth opened the side door, poked her head out and lit the cigarette. She took a long draw and blew the smoke out the door. "Maybe you've been alone for too long. Whatever happened to that Bella chick?"

"We ain't living through Bella again. Remember how clingy she got?" said Isaiah.

She flicked the ashes. "Yeah, I forgot. Bella's off the list. What about Roseanna? She basically ran out the door anytime Isaiah and I came downstairs."

"I screwed Roseanna, not Noah. He had Rose."

Our stroll down memory lane reeked like a garbage dump. "I'm not lonely and I don't need a girl. Drop it, Beth."

"I don't mind if you hook up with Echo. Have at it. In fact, I'll stay the night at my mom's house and let Isaiah have the bedroom if you need an all-nighter with privacy. But here's the truth, Noah. Echo might be on the outs since she became a cutter and all, but she's still a popular chick. She'll bail on you and treat you like shit in the end." She took another draw. "There's only so many times people like us can have our hearts ripped out. She's a ripper."

The muscles in the back of my neck knotted. "For the last time, I'm not screwing her or anyone else. But call her a cutter again and I'll set fire to every single pack of cigarettes you buy."

Beth laughed. "Jesus, Noah. You've got it bad. Don't say I didn't warn you."

"If you two are done, I'd like to get some lunch. Only thing left in the fridge this morning was a slice of bologna and mustard," Isaiah said.

Beth flicked her cigarette out the door and shut it. "Mustard. I ate the bologna for breakfast."

SHE NEVER CAME TO LUNCH. Her entire table full of porcelain doll rejects did, but not Echo. I didn't sweat it, at first. I waited patiently for her to show in physics and then business technology. No show in either class. Echo's favorite gal pals went out of their way to snub me, though. Each stuck their little china noses in the air while staring in my direction. I simply smiled, aggravating the shit out of them.

"'Sup, man," said Rico Vega, joining me in the back of Spanish class.

"'Sup," I answered. "How can they let you take Spanish when that's what you speak half the damn time?"

"Why they let a bunch of *gueros* take English? You gringos gotta be stupid if you ain't got it down in eighteen years."

Before I could hand crap back to Rico, Echo entered the room. She had that bunny-locked-in-a-pet-store-cage look, but at least she made eye contact this time. Until her stuck-up friend breezed in and redirected Echo to a seat in front.

"Why Lila glaring at you, *hombre?*" asked Rico. "Though I wouldn't mind a hot piece of *culo* like that acknowledging my existence." Rico puckered his lips, sending a mock kiss in Lila's direction. I laughed when she flipped her golden hair over her shoulder and stared at the dry-erase board.

Mrs. Bates, a real-life condom ad, waddled through the doorway. She was knocked up with triplets. "*Hola*. Today we are going to work on our conversational Spanish."

Excitement rippled through the room. Conversational Spanish meant picking a partner and doing nothing for the rest of the period. Rico and I bumped fists. I needed some sleep.

"Yeah, yeah. Don't get too excited. I've already picked your partners. I expect to hear Spanish flowing in my room."

She eased back into her chair and it squeaked when her ass hit the seat. "Lila McCormick—you're partnered with Rico Vega."

Lila groaned, "No," while Rico pumped his fist twice to his heart and then raised a finger to the sky. "*Gracias a dios.*"

Lila approached the desk. "Please, Mrs. Bates. I'll do anything. Let me and Echo partner."

Mrs. Bates winced and rubbed a hand over her stomach. "Miss

McCormick, do I look sympathetic to your plight? Go find a seat next to Rico. Noah Hutchins, you're paired with Echo Emerson."

Lila clutched her hair as her voice dropped. "No."

Mrs. Bates continued with her list of assigned partners while Lila knelt next to her, begging for a change of heart.

Rico chuckled. "I'm off to peel my partner off the floor." He yelled to Lila as he walked toward her, *"Casate conmigo, diosa."*

Echo gathered her books and made the long trip down the aisle to me. The universe had a strange sense of humor. Last semester, Echo and I barely made eye contact. Now, we were thrown together at every turn. Not that I minded. She sat in Rico's seat and stared at the fake wood desktop.

"First trip to the back?" I asked. Everyone partnered out, most moving their desks together so others couldn't hear their screwed up Spanish. When she didn't say anything back, I continued, "I'm impressed. The rule-follower skipped a few classes today."

"No, not skipped. Mrs. Collins excused me so I could prep for the ACT this weekend." She inhaled deeply, causing her cleavage to expand. Lines worried her forehead. "Noah, about yesterday…"

Echo had permitted me a peek into her world yesterday. The least I could do was let her into mine. Even if the thought made me nervous as hell. *"Mi primer padre adoptivo me pegaba."* My first foster father hit me.

Her wide eyes met my gaze. *"Lo siento."* I'm sorry.

I tapped my pencil against the desk and continued to speak in Spanish. "We're even now. You've got dirt on me and I know something about you. No need to avoid me anymore."

She bit her lip, translating in her head, before she replied, *"Tú hablas bien el español."* You speak Spanish well. Echo sent me a soft, shy smile that told me we were beyond good.

"*Mi madre era una profesora de español.*" *My mother was a Spanish professor.* I'd never told anyone that before. Images of my mother laughing and speaking to me in Spanish filled my head.

"*Mi madre era una artista. Muy brillante.*" *My mother was an artist. Very brilliant.* Echo's foot began to bounce under the desk.

We sat in silence. Murmurs of broken Spanish and English hummed in the room. Soon the pen she held in her hand drummed in time with her foot. I understood her rhythm. That feeling of everything inside twisting to the point that if you didn't find a release you'd explode. I craved to grant her peace.

I placed my hand over hers. My own heart rested when I rubbed my thumb over her smooth skin. She dropped the pen and grasped her sleeve in her palm, her constant defense mechanism. No. If she grasped anything, it would be me. My thumb worked its way between her fingers and her sleeve and released her death grip on the material. I wrapped my fingers around her fragile hand. Touching Echo felt like home.

Her ring finger slid against mine, causing electricity to move through my bloodstream. She moved it again. Only this time the movement was slow, deliberate and the most seductive touch in the whole world. Everything inside of me ached to touch her more.

Beth had been both wrong and right. Echo couldn't hurt anyone, especially when she seemed so breakable herself. But the need I felt to be the one to keep the world from shattering her only confirmed Beth's theory. I was falling for her and I was fucked.

The PA system in the classroom beeped. Echo pulled her hand

away from mine, ending perhaps the most erotic moment of my life. I shifted in my seat, trying to find my damn mind.

"Mrs. Bates?" called Mrs. Marcos through the loudspeaker. "I need Noah Hutchins to report to Mrs. Collins's office."

"You heard her, Mr. Hutchins. Get going."

I had no doubt the head shrinker was ticked at me. I hadn't waited around long enough yesterday to find out why I'd been summoned. When Echo left the office, I'd followed. Partly to make sure she made it to her car okay and partly because I was shaken from what I'd overheard. Dealing with Mrs. Collins required me to be one hundred percent and after learning about Echo, I hadn't even been close to fifty.

I stood to leave, half relieved, half disappointed. I'd connected with the girl, but not in the way I intended. Echo placed her sleeve-covered fingers on my wrist. Her neck and cheeks flushed red. "I moved the appointment time. I meet with her at three forty-five on Tuesday afternoons instead of at two-thirty."

Searching for a brief reminder of the moment we had lost, I brushed my thumb across her sleeved hand. "I knew you wouldn't let me down."

WHEN I WALKED INTO THE MAIN office, Mrs. Collins stepped out of hers with her coat and purse in hand. "Great timing. I'm glad to see you have your coat—you're going to need it."

"What?"

She locked her office door. "We're taking a field trip. Let's go."

Mrs. Collins brushed past me. My mind remained blank as I watched her walk down the hallway. For the first time, I missed the brain cells I'd fried.

"Come on, Noah."

I caught up to her right as she walked out to the teacher parking lot. "Where are we going?"

"You didn't show for your appointment yesterday morning, nor did you come when I requested." She held out a remote and pushed a button. Lights flashed on a black Mercedes. Figured. "Irresponsible. Get in."

I opened the door and was greeted by the smell of leather. My gut twisted. I've been down this road before. "I've got four months to graduation, they can't move me again." The mistake of becoming attached to Beth and Isaiah roared to life. Anger and hurt pricked my chest with needles. And Echo...

Mrs. Collins shut her door and leaned over the middle console. "Unless your current foster home has become a dangerous situation, you're not being moved. Get in or you'll miss the fun."

Fun? I slid into the seat. The engine purred to life. She floored the accelerator and the car jerked forward. She took a hard right and the tires screeched when she pulled out onto the main road. I gripped the armrest. "Who the fuck gave you your license?"

"Watch your language, Noah, and the state of Kentucky. Why did you miss your appointment?"

I loved fast driving. Isaiah and I had drag raced all last summer. What I didn't love was a middle-aged nut job who couldn't steer straight. "You want to pull over and let me drive?"

Mrs. Collins laughed and cut off a tractor trailer merging onto the freeway. "You're a riot. Focus, Noah. The appointment."

Oh—yeah. Echo had gone through hell to move her appointment. I could, at least, change mine before I became part of a fireball when we hit that tanker. "I work most evenings and close the place. It's hard to get up in the mornings. I was wondering if we could move our session to right after school."

She cut over three lanes and took the next exit ramp. "It's

your lucky day. I happen to have an opening at two-thirty on Tuesday. But I expect you to make it to your first period class on time. I won't accept that excuse for anything else."

"Yellow light. Yellow light!" And she ran right through the red. "Jesus Christ, you can't drive."

"I'm afraid we're going to be late." She pulled into a crammed parking lot and found the first spot available. "We've got to book it."

She sprang out of her car and ran toward the town's convention center. Unable to imagine one thing Mrs. Collins could offer me worth running for, I lazily followed. I breezed into the building a few seconds behind her and saw her enter an auditorium.

I grabbed the door before it closed and blinked when the crowd applauded around me. Row upon row of chairs faced a large, wooden stage. The room was crushed with people. Mrs. Collins waved me over to the side and the two of us leaned against the wall. She whispered, "Good, we're just in time."

A stout man in a shirt and tie propped his arms on the podium. "I have the privilege of introducing the Young Authors first-place winner in the second grade division, Jacob Hutchins."

My heart slammed past my rib cage as I searched wildly for my brother. There he was, speed-walking down the middle aisle from the back of the room to the stage. I took a step to follow him, but Mrs. Collins placed a hand on my arm and shook her head. "This is his moment."

I peeled my eyes off him to browse where he'd been sitting. Carrie and Joe sat next to his empty seat. Sitting on Carrie's lap, Tyler rested his head on her shoulder and glanced around. Everything inside me twisted in pain and relief. My brothers. I was in the same room as my brothers.

My eyes met Tyler's and a smile tugged at his lips. I sucked in a breath in order to pull back the millions of emotions eating at me. Tyler remembered me. "Thank you," I breathed, not sure who I was thanking or why—Mrs. Collins for bringing me here, Tyler for remembering me, or God for both of those.

Mrs. Collins watched my reaction, but I didn't care. I waved at Tyler and, to continue the miracle, he waved back.

Joe caught the movement, glanced behind him and spotted me. His face paled and he shook his head at Tyler in reprimand while pointing at the stage. Tyler turned away.

"He remembered you," said Mrs. Collins.

"If that dickhead had his way, he'd forget me." I wanted to rip Tyler from their evil paws.

Mrs. Collins sighed. "Language, Noah."

Jacob smiled from ear to ear when he shook the man's hand on stage. The man then handed him a trophy. "Tell the audience about your book."

My little brother confidently walked up to a microphone his height and beamed to the crowd. "I wrote about the person I love the most, my older brother, Noah. We don't live together so I wrote what I imagine he does when we're not together."

"And what is that?" prodded the stout man.

"He's a superhero who saves people in danger, because he saved me and my brother from dying in a fire a couple of years ago. Noah is better than Batman." The crowd chuckled.

"I love you, too, lil' bro." I couldn't help it. To see him standing there, still worshipping me like he did when he was five… it was too much.

Jacob's smile reached a whole new level of excitement. "Noah!" He pointed right to me. "That's Noah. That's my brother, Noah!"

Ignoring his foster parents, Jacob flew off the stage and ran down the middle aisle.

Joe lowered his head and Carrie rubbed her eyes. Jacob raced into my arms and the crowd erupted into applause.

"I've missed you, Noah." Jacob's voice broke, bringing tears to my eyes. I couldn't cry. Not in front of Jacob and not in front of Mrs. Collins. I needed to be a man and stay strong.

"I've missed you, too, bro. I'm so proud of you."

I continued to hug Jacob as I searched for Tyler. He clung to Carrie and the sight dampened what should have been a joyous moment. Jacob was mine and the faster I could get Tyler away and help him remember his real family, the better.

Echo

I stood outside of the girls' locker room, palms sweating and my foot tapping uncontrollably on the floor. Why had I told Dad I'd rejoined the dance team?

My file. I wanted, no, *needed,* no, was totally obsessed with seeing my file. Today, Noah had passed me in the hallway, given me his wicked grin and mumbled, "Done deal." He'd successfully changed his appointment time to the slot before mine. Now, we needed to hatch our half-baked plan. He somehow believed that combined, we could distract Mrs. Collins. Noah exuded confidence. Me? Not so much, but it was definitely worth a try.

The door to the locker room opened and Natalie came out with two other senior girls. The two girls stopped laughing when they spotted me and forced smiles back on their faces. Natalie, on the other hand, shined at me like I'd hung the sun. "Get your butt in there and dress out, girl. Warm-up in five."

"I was just walking in." Into a Stephen King novel. Young girl, tragically scarred, attempts to return to her normal life, only to find out her normal life doesn't want her back. I entered the locker room, where all the lowerclassmen on the team gossiped and laughed.

"Hi," came a faint voice from the back of the room. Every single girl in the room froze and stared at me as if laser beams were going to shoot out of my eyes or even worse—I'd roll up my sleeves and show them my demon scars.

"Hey," I replied.

I'd rather have watched reruns of bad seventies sitcoms than weave through this room to dress out, but standing there like an idiot didn't seem like a great option either. Why couldn't I have Noah's confidence? He didn't care what anybody thought.

I lacked confidence, but I could pretend. I chanted in my mind, *Pretend you're Noah. Even better, biker chick Beth*, held my head high and crossed the crowded locker room toward the bathroom where I intended to change in a private stall. Biker chick Beth confidence or not, there was no way I could change in front of them.

Shaking off the tension that runway walk created, I shut the stall door and changed. If entering a locker room resembled the opening of a Stephen King novel, dance practice ought to be like starring in a horror movie.

Thankfully, the locker room had emptied by the time I hurried to join warm-ups. In the hallway, two juniors giggled by the water fountain. "Can you believe that Echo Emerson is rejoining the dance team? What a nightmare."

"Like, because Luke is all over her it gives her an excuse to pretend she's not a freak."

I ducked back into the bathroom. My heart in my gut, my stomach in my throat, my pretend confidence in tatters.

WITH MY JEANS, BROWN COTTON shirt and tank top back on, I roamed the hallways. I had an hour to kill for five days a week until graduation. Maybe only four. I could move Noah's tutoring session back to right after school on Mondays.

I turned a corner and a part of my soul took a deep breath when I noticed the artwork littering the walls. I followed the trail of paintings and drawings to what used to be my favorite room—art. Several canvases rested on easels, waiting for their masters to return. A bowl of plastic fruit sat on a table in the middle of the easel circle.

I assessed each painting in turn. I admired the way the first one used shadowing. The second one paid nice attention to detail. The third one?

"Good to see you, Echo." My old art teacher, Nancy, exited the connecting darkroom and weaved through the easels and tables toward me. She insisted that her students call her by her first name. She despised rules and formalities. Her hair, bleached blond with black streaks, was a testament to her attitude.

I gestured to the third painting. "Abstract expressionist?"

Her boisterous laughter vibrated in the room. She adjusted her black horn-rimmed glasses. "Lazy student who thought art would be an easy A. She claims to be an impressionist."

"What an insult."

"I know. I asked if she knew what an impressionist was and when she shook her head, I showed her your paintings." Nancy stared at the mess in front of her as if trying to find something redeemable in it. "I've missed you."

Familiar guilt tiptoed through my insides. "I'm sorry."

"Don't be, kid. It's not your fault. Your father informed me you were no longer allowed to take an art class. I took that to mean I'd never see you."

I walked to the fourth picture. "Nice lines."

"Are you still painting?"

Hoping to make it look like I was extremely interested in the color chosen for the banana, I tilted my head, but I wasn't. The black hole in my mind widened, interrupting any thought of painting. "No, but I still sketch. Mostly in pencil. Some with charcoal at home."

"I'd love to see them."

Nancy snatched the sketchbook I pulled from my backpack. She sat on the table with the fruit and flipped it open. "Oh, Echo. Simply amazing."

I shrugged, but she missed it, too infatuated with my sketchbook. "We won."

She tore her eyes away from the sketches and stared at me in silence. I continued to busy myself with the other artists' work. After a few seconds, she returned to studying my drawing of Grace. "No, you won. I was merely along for the ride." She paused. "You remember?"

"No." Surely Nancy would take pity on me and fill in some of the gaps. "Were you there?"

"Mmm, girlfriend. You're itching to get me in trouble with your father and Mrs. Collins. Your father I could take, but Mrs. Collins?" She shuddered. "Between you and me, she scares me. It's the friendly ones that'll get you in the end."

I snickered, missing Nancy's honesty. "I wish I could remember." The fifth canvas was completely blank. The oil paints and brushes sat unused. "Do you mind?"

In her classic deep-in-thought stance, Nancy rubbed the bottom of her chin. "He only said you couldn't take an art class, not that you couldn't paint."

I picked up a flat brush, dipped it into the black paint and made circles on the canvas. "It's like I have this large black hole in my brain and it's sucking the life out of me. The answers are in there so I sit for hours and stare. No matter how hard and long I look, I only see darkness."

I chose a fan brush and mixed black and white paint together to create different shades of gray. "There are edges around the black and every now and then a flash of color streaks out of the gray. But I can never really grasp any of the slivers of memories that emerge."

Clutching the paintbrush, I stared at the canvas that now represented my brain. "I wish someone would just tell me the truth and end the madness."

A warm hand pressed hard against my shoulder, causing me to blink out of my zone. Wow, five o'clock. Dad would kill me if I didn't get home soon. Nancy kept her hand on my shoulder and her eyes locked on the canvas. "If this is madness, then madness is brilliant. Are you going to finish this?"

For the first time in two years I felt like I could breathe. "You mind me hanging out after school?"

IN THE FIGURE BELOW, RAY *AB was constructed starting from rays AC and AD. By using a compass, C and D were marked equidistant from A on rays AC and AD. The compass was then used to locate a Point Q, distinct from A, so that Q is equidistant from C and D. For all constructions defined by the above steps, find the measures of BAC and BAD.*

If Aires was here, he would know what to do.

I mean, come freaking on—was there even a question in there? If so, simple English required a question mark. Was the triangle-looking drawing below supposed to help? Did I need a compass? And why did the answers below have numbers? There weren't any freaking numbers in the story problem.

"Breathe, Echo," Aires would tell me. "You're psyching yourself out. Take a break and come back to it later."

And he was right. Aires was always right. God, I missed him.

I tossed the ACT study book to the floor and rested my head on the back of the couch. I hated this room. Tacky pink flowered wallpaper hung on the walls to match the tedious curtains and upholstery. The moment she kicked my mother out the door, Ashley traumatized all interior designers of the world with her redecorating. She may have glued paper on the wall to wipe out my mother's influence, but I knew what remained underneath—the mural of Greece my mother had painted.

I typically studied in Aires' car, but Ashley had nagged at me until I lugged my books back into the house. I must have killed a lot of cows in a past life for Karma to hate me this much. Maybe I'd died two years ago and unknowingly entered hell. Doomed to spend the rest of eternity living with my father and stepmother and retaking the ACT over and over again.

"How was dance team practice today?" Ashley asked. The Wicked Witch and my father walked into the living room hand in hand. Good God, I must have died, because I'd hate to see the real thing if this wasn't hell.

"Good." I blinked several times. Crap—I always blinked when I lied. Worried they'd catch on, I lowered my head. Wait. Dad had attention issues and Ms. Scarecrow Brain wouldn't notice a flying monkey if it smacked her in the face.

My father eased into his recliner and Ashley sat on his lap. *Dear God, I am so sorry for whatever I did, but honestly, was my sin that bad?* Dad kissed her hand. Swallowing bile, I turned my attention to the fireplace.

"Are you ready to take the ACT on Saturday?" my father asked.

Did chickens enjoy being put on trucks labeled KFC? "Sure."

"You studied word lists earlier. Focus purely on math. That's where you have problems."

Problems? My math scores were way above average, but of course that wasn't good enough.

Dad continued, "Did Mrs. Collins excuse you from some of your classes so you could prepare?"

"Yes."

"I noticed fliers for the Valentine's Day Dance in the office. Are you and Luke going?" When Ashley fished for information her irritating voice entered a higher pitch of annoying. Dogs in Oklahoma winced.

"Luke asked me today. Don't worry. Our family's precious reputation will stay intact. Mrs. Collins will never know that you lied to make yourself look better."

"Echo!"

Crap. I cringed at the disappointment in my father's voice. The automatic apology fell out of my mouth. "Sorry, Ashley." Though it was true.

"It's okay. When do you want to go dress shopping?"

Do what? I tore my eyes away from the fire and stared at her. My father rubbed her baby belly while she caressed his cheek. Gross. "I don't need a new dress."

"Yes, you do. Everything you own is either strapless or spaghetti-strapped. You can't go to a dance with those scars showing."

"Ashley," my father whispered. His hand froze on her belly.

My throat swelled as if someone had rammed it with a two-by-four and my stomach cramped as if someone had whacked it. I sat up and my head swayed with the room. Disorientation in full force, I pulled down my sleeves. "I'm going…to go…up-stairs."

Ashley slid off my father. "Echo, wait. I didn't mean it like that. I just want you to have a good night. A night you can look back at pictures of and remember how much fun you had."

I brushed past her to the stairs. I needed my room. The one place Ashley's bad decorating hadn't completely ruined. The place where my mother's colorful paintings hung, where pictures of me and Aires cluttered my desk, the only place I felt comfortable.

My heart ached. I wanted more than my room, but that was all I had. I wanted my mom. She may have been nuts, but she never put me down. I wanted Aires. I wanted the one person who'd loved me.

Ashley called to me from the bottom of the stairs. "Please, let me explain."

I paused in my door frame. If she had never entered our lives, my mother and Aires would still be here, I wouldn't be a scarred monster, and I would know love, not the hate currently boiling in my veins. "I liked you better when you were my babysitter. I hope when I graduate from high school I don't turn into a royal witch like you." I slammed the door behind me.

AFTER THAT LOVELY EXCHANGE with Ashley, I spent the rest of the night in my room hiding. I lay in bed and stared at the one part of my room Ashley had gotten to—my ceiling. She'd painted over my mother's hand-painted constellations. The witch had done it while I recovered in the hospital. My mother used to lie in bed with me for hours staring at the ceiling, telling me Greek myths. Having few good memories of my mother, I despised Ashley more for stealing the one I had.

The knock on my door at 11:30 surprised me. The rule of thumb in the house required me to apologize first. Ashley probably wanted to show me in person why my current dresses wouldn't work. No need to prolong the inevitable. "Come in."

I bolted upright the moment my father walked in. He never came to my room. The first two buttons of his dress shirt were unbuttoned and his tie hung loose. Worry lines were carved around his tired eyes. He looked old. Too old to be married to a twenty-some-odd bimbo and too old to be having another baby. "She's sorry, Echo."

Of course he'd come on Ashley's behalf. God forbid anything in this house not revolve around Ashley. "Okay. My apology will have to wait until morning. I'm a little beat." We both knew what a cop-out that was. I'd be lucky if I slept for an hour.

Surprising me even more, my dad did something he hadn't done since I came home from the hospital—he sat on my bed. "I'm going to contact your social worker. I don't think this new therapist is working out."

"No." I said it too quickly and my dad caught on. "I already told you, I like her. She's easy to talk to. Plus you said that you'd give her another try."

"I know things between you and Ashley have been tough since you found out about our relationship, but you've been lashing out at her more than normal. She's pregnant. I don't want her under stress."

My big toe began to rock. Would it kill him to love me? "I'll try harder. Just let me keep seeing Mrs. Collins." I needed to give him a reason to back off. "She's the one that convinced me to focus on my friends and to date." Lie.

Some of the worry lines disappeared. "I don't think that's her.

That's you. I'll leave it alone if you try harder with Ashley. She loves you. And you used to adore her."

Yeah, when on her eighteenth birthday, she let me stay up late and eat popcorn at the age of six or when she let me wear makeup on my first day of fourth grade. Crazy thing happened—she slept with my father and then left my family drowning in a wake of destruction.

"If you really want to show me you're trying, let her take you dress shopping. She had a whole day planned and is devastated that she upset you. Let her have fun and I'll drop the SAT retake."

I raised an eyebrow. My father never negotiated. "Really?"

"The next SAT date is too late for your application deadlines anyway. We'll have to work with what you got. Your scores should be good enough to get you into some of the best business colleges in the state."

He typically said accounting, but he must have caught me wincing whenever he said the word. "I'm happy you're back with Luke and even happier you're going to the Valentine's Dance. You loved getting dressed up and going to dances. I thought maybe that part of you died." He stared down at my sleeve-covered arms. "I have to say, you've really made me proud."

No freaking kidding. I made straight A's, did whatever he said, and he's proud of me for going to a dance. Let's see, if he came to my room over a Valentine's Dance, maybe he'd do something crazy for prom, like tell me he loved me. My father patted my knee and rose from the bed.

"Daddy?"

"Yeah."

"Do you ever check on Mom?"

The worry lines returned. "She's not my responsibility any-more."

"Then is she mine? I am her only living relative."

A muscle in his jaw jerked. "Your social worker would never allow that and neither would I." His eyes softened, his jaw un-clenched. "Are you scared she's going to hurt you? She will never hurt you or anyone else again. Don't worry about her."

But I did. My mother might be crazy and she'd tried to kill me, but she was still my mom. Someone should take care of her, right?

NOAH

I'd seen my brothers. Who knew a miracle could occur? And I'd get to see them again on the second Saturday of February. This called for a celebration. I hoped Isaiah got some weed because I planned on rolling the biggest damn J any of us ever saw.

Last to return for the night, I parked my piece of crap on the street. Dale worked swing shift at the local truck plant. We didn't know from one day to the next what hours he'd work. I'd made the mistake of parking in the driveway once. Instead of moving my car, Dale took out my driver's-side mirror.

Lights blared from every window in the house—not a good sign. I stepped into the tiny living room and noticed towels covered in blood. "What the fuck?"

Isaiah appeared instantly by my side. "The bastard beat the shit out of her."

"I'm fine." Beth's voice trembled. She sat in the kitchen with her arm extended on the table. Her aunt Shirley cleaned several cuts and cigarette burns.

Beth's entire body shook like a seizure. The right side of her face was bruised, scraped and puffy, and her right eye swollen shut. Blood soaked her favorite T-shirt. She raised the cigarette to her mouth and sucked in a long draw. "Mom's new fuck wears a class ring. He must have stolen it from someone."

"Son of a bitch. Why the hell did you go home, Beth? You knew this asshole was bad news." Three steps and I knelt beside her in the kitchen.

She took another draw as a tear fell from her left eye. "It was Mom's birthday and the stupid bastard didn't want to share her, so…" She shrugged.

Pure anger raged through my body, every muscle tightening, preparing to fight. "When are the police getting here?"

"They're not," said Shirley. She placed gauze over a burn and taped around it.

I fought for control. "And why not?"

"She's sixteen and her mom was there. They'll lock my sister up along with that no-good boyfriend. I don't agree with how she lives her life, but I won't send my sister to jail and Beth isn't interested in it either."

I waited for Beth to confirm the theory. She put out her cigarette in the ashtray, placed another in her mouth and fumbled with the lighter. It clicked several times as she unsuccessfully struck the wheel against the flint. I took it from her and, in one smooth motion, lit the cigarette.

"Thanks," she said weakly.

The phone rang once, twice, a third time. It stopped ringing and Beth's cell began to play The Cure's "Lovesong"—her mom's ring tone. Her hand shook as she flicked ashes into the ashtray. "She keeps calling. She wants me to come back home."

"Why?" I snarled.

"He got tired of beating me and fell asleep, passed out, whatever. Probably woke up and missed his piñata."

I tried to rub the anger out of my neck. "Call the police, Beth."

"And what do you think's going to happen to you and Isaiah if she does?" Dale wandered into the kitchen, his dark hair slicked back from a recent shower. "Your social worker has been a little nosy recently, Noah. We put a phone call in to the police, they'll figure out Beth's been living here. We can kiss you and Isaiah goodbye."

Beth's voice broke. "I can't lose you guys." And there it was. She sat here bleeding because she loved me and Isaiah. For the millionth time, I wished the system was a person. One person I could name, know and hold responsible for screwing every single one of us. Right now, Beth's mom's new boyfriend would have to do.

I stood up and kissed the top of Beth's head. "You ready, bro?"

"I've been waiting for you to catch up, man." Isaiah opened the front door, his eyes cold and deadly.

Beth's one good eye widened. "No," she whispered.

"I ain't bailing you boys out," said Dale.

"Never asked you to," I said and walked for the door.

A car swerved coming up the street and flew into the grass of the front yard. The passenger door opened before the car stopped, and Beth's mother hopped out. Her blond hair fell from a ponytail, eyes bloodshot, a bruise forming under her right eye. "I want my baby. I need to tell her I'm sorry."

"Go to hell," said Isaiah. "She ain't your doll to play dress-up with."

The Beamer's headlights stayed on. A large man staggered from the driver's side. "Shut your trap. Sky wants her slut daughter. Tell her to come out or I'm going in to get her."

Isaiah and I stood side by side, a silent agreement that we'd kill him before he got to the front door. My brothers flashed through my mind. As much as I wanted to protect Beth, I also needed to protect them. "Leave now before I call the police."

God damn, this guy had to be at least six and a half feet tall and he looked familiar. He stood toe to toe with Isaiah and me. The stench of alcohol rolled off of him. His eyes shifted nervously and his body flinched.

"He's tweaking, man," Isaiah said to me.

Fabulous. This night had shifted from the best to bad to *Saw* in record time. The man turned the ring on his finger. That was no regular ring—that was a damn Super Bowl ring. "Go ahead, call the police. Everybody loves me. I ain't going to jail."

"Aren't you that asshole that got kicked off that loser team a couple hours from here?" I said, trying to keep his eyes off the house.

He blinked a couple of times, like his fucked-up mind understood for three seconds that a two-hundred-and-fifty-pound linebacker shouldn't be picking fights with a sixteen-year-old girl and her two stoner friends.

"I'm tired of this bullshit, man," Isaiah whispered to me seconds before he hauled back and hit the bastard in the jaw. The impact would have sent me to the ground, but this guy only turned his head. Dammit all to hell…everything about this was going to suck.

The bastard raised his fist to retaliate, but found himself on the ground when I tackled him right at his knees. I had the fleeting thought that I should thank my gym teacher, Mr. Graves, for the three weeks of football instruction.

I rolled away from him before he could throw a punch. Isaiah came too close and the asshole swept Isaiah's legs out from underneath him and pounded him in the gut as he fell to the ground. The sound of Beth's mom screaming irritated the shit out of me.

The bastard rose, as did I, and I punched him in the kidney before he had a chance to kick Isaiah, who lay on the ground with the wind knocked out of him. Tweaker turned and swung for my head, but I ducked and landed a punch on his stomach. He grunted and swayed, but stayed upright.

I needed to get this loser back on the ground. I attempted to tackle him again, but aimed too high. My sides stung when he threw two good punches into my rib cage. The two of us crashed into his car as Isaiah stood up and cracked the guy in the back with his fist.

A gunshot screamed into the night. Both Isaiah and I froze. I prayed to God that nothing warm or wet left my body, and I wasn't referring to piss.

"Sky, you and this trash get off my property," Dale said in a surprisingly calm voice. He stood on the front stoop, hunting rifle cradled in his hands. "You boys okay?"

"Super," said Isaiah through clenched teeth.

"Never better." Dammit, my knuckles throbbed.

"Get in the house before Beth goes into hysterics," said Dale.

I pushed off the Beamer and did my best to not stumble to the house. Isaiah came up beside me. "Think she could have told us we were going to fight the NFL."

"Would that have stopped you?"

"No."

"Me neither." The laughter between the two of us echoed into the night.

BETH CRIED HERSELF TO SLEEP—in Isaiah's arms.

I lay on the couch, watching some eighties movie on television. The sound was so low, I had no idea what anyone said for an hour. My ribs ached, my knuckles throbbed, but damn, I felt good. Dale and Shirley had told Sky never to come back and that Shirley was heading to Sky's tomorrow to collect Beth's stuff. Dale and Shirley had issues, but they were good people at heart.

Beth whimpered when she shifted in her sleep. Isaiah soothed her with hushed words and ran his hand through her hair. She wrapped her arms tighter around his chest and placed herself practically on top of him. Isaiah continued to rub her back.

"How long have you been into her, bro?" I asked Isaiah.

Isaiah let his head fall back onto the wall. "A while. Terrified to tell her, but now…I can't keep letting her be with guys that use her or just watch as she goes to her mom when she needs to feel loved. What am I going to do, man?"

"You're asking the wrong guy." What did I know about love? All I knew was that I couldn't get Echo Emerson out of my mind. No doubt, I wanted her. I couldn't rid my mind of images of her body writhing in pleasure against mine. That siren voice whispering my name. But she appealed to me in more than a physical way. I loved her smile, the light in her eyes when she laughed, and damn if she couldn't keep up with me. "If you figure it out, let me know."

Echo

"I'm sorry," I said for the third time. "I didn't know you were in such a hurry."

Luke kept my hand and dragged me through the crowded mall toward the movie theater. When the crowd gave way, he pulled me next to him. "I'm with your dad on this one. It's a car. I mean, that car's a beast and all, but still a car. You'd be better off selling it and making some major cash than wasting any more money or time on it."

The movie started at eight instead of the eight-forty-five he originally told me. I'd made an appointment at six with a mechanic willing to come to the house to look at Aires' car. I'd taken the ACT again this morning, come home, accidentally fallen asleep (had a day terror—if that's what you call a night terror that occurs during the day), and then woken up less than twenty minutes before the mechanic arrived. Luke had waited a whole patient ten minutes before he told the mechanic to leave because we had plans. The mechanic had gone, telling me he'd email the estimate.

"It's all I have left of Aires." We entered the carpeted area of the movie theater. I yanked my hand away. "I thought you would understand."

Going out with Luke was exactly like I remembered—at least the last two months of our relationship, minus the pawing. On our group date last weekend, I asked him if we could take things slow and he agreed—for the first few dates. I had a feeling tonight was going to be the end of Luke's hands-off promise. So far, dating him the second time around stunk.

Luke placed his hands on his hips. "It's a good thing Stephen and Lila got here on time to get tickets. It's sold out."

Self-absorbed, egotistical jerk… "This isn't going to work," I said.

He balled his fist and then forced himself to relax his hands. "Look, I want this to work. You're just mad because I'm siding with your dad on this stupid car thing. Lila's dating Stephen. Grace is with Chad. You and I make perfect sense." He caressed my cheek. That touch used to melt me into a puddle. All I felt now were calluses, a wart and dry skin. "I know it's rough trying to figure us out again. I think our problem is that we're taking it too slow. I deserve an award for keeping my hands off of you."

Luke took a step toward me, slipped a hand around my back, and pressed me into him. Every muscle I had tensed. This didn't feel natural at all.

"Let's go see the movie and afterward we can go back to my place. I think you'll feel a lot better once I help you remember what we're so good at doing." His breath fanned over my face and I swear a few spit particles did, too. Why was I doing this again?

"Echo! There you guys are. The movie theater is already packed." Lila bounced beside me. Relieved for the interruption, I stepped away from Luke.

Stephen and Luke exchanged some sort of weird male handshake. Stephen pointed at theater three. "Come on. It's starting. We couldn't get six seats together, but we saved two for you in the back." Stephen gave Luke a high five. Boy, Luke would be disappointed when he figured out nothing was going to happen in the back.

The guys walked ahead while Lila and I fell behind. Lila asked, "You okay?"

"I don't think Luke and I are going to work. He hasn't changed a bit." Why, like everything else, did this have to be complicated? Why couldn't anything be simple, the way it had been freshman year?

Lila took a deep breath and pressed her lips together. "We'll talk later. Let's enjoy the movie, okay?"

She caught up with Stephen and Luke grabbed my hand. "You just need to focus on being like you used to be. You know—normal," he said.

Lila sent me a pleading glance. I sank in the seat next to Luke and let him put his arm around me. All of us prayed for normal. But so far, normal only meant more misery.

In the first five minutes of the movie we met a teenager who graduated from high school and joined the Marines. Ten minutes in, we watched him graduate from boot camp. Twenty minutes into the movie, I dry heaved.

Nausea swelled my throat, my tongue felt ten sizes too big

and I couldn't breathe. No matter how much air I tried to suck in, none of it went into my lungs. I sprang from my seat and tripped down the dark stairs of the theater to the sounds of men screaming in agony to God and their mothers.

I raced for the women's bathroom, busted past the door and clung to the cold sink. The mirror revealed a nightmare. Red curls clung to the sweat on my forehead. My entire body shook like an earthquake.

The image of the man's friend stepping on an IED flashed in my mind. The bile inched up my throat. Oh, God—Aires. Was that what happened to him? Did he scream in agony? Did he know he was dying? The face of the blood-drenched actor merged with Aires' face. My body wrenched forward, my stomach cramped and I coughed with the dry heave.

He was dead and he'd died in misery, terrified.

A stall door opened. A little old lady stared at me with pitying old eyes. "Boy troubles?"

I snatched a paper towel to wipe my eyes and hide my face. Gasping for air, I reminded myself that I'd come here to be normal, not a spectacle. "Yes."

The old lady smiled at me in the mirror while washing her hands. "A pretty girl like you will find someone new quickly. By the way, I love your gloves. It's not very often that you see a young person wearing them." She left.

My cell phone vibrated in my back pocket. Luke texted me: Whr r u?

In the girl's bathroom losing my mind. There was no way I could go back: 2 violent 4 me. shpg. Meet u aftr movie.

I waited a few seconds and my phone vibrated again: cool cu then.

Eight-thirty. I had two and a half hours to blow until the end of the movie. Seemed to be a recurring theme in my life.

The food court sat right next to the movie theater. I needed something to drink. But like an idiot, I'd brought no money, not even my purse. Luke insisted that I leave it at home. Blah, blah, blah…our first night to the movies together…blah, blah, blah…he would pay for everything…blah, blah, blah…he took me to see the worst movie ever…

The employees of the food court were cleaning and preparing to close. But some places stayed open to feed the night owls. I headed to one, the burger joint that had stools next to the counter.

I sat on a stool and watched some tall guy flip burgers. Lila would so love that cute butt. "Excuse me?"

The cook turned and I slid off my seat. "Noah?"

He flashed his wicked grin. "'Sup, Echo. Miss me?"

I sat again. "No." Kind of.

Noah scooped the burgers off the grill, placed them on some buns and called out a number. A lady came and carried the burgers away. He sauntered to the counter. "What can I do for you?"

The red bandana he wore held back the hair that typically covered his eyes. I loved his eyes. Chocolate-brown, full of mischief and a spark ready to light the world on fire. "Can I have a glass of water, please?" And please let it be free.

"Is that it?"

My stomach growled, loud enough for Noah to hear. "Yep, that's it."

He fixed me a glass and handed it to me. "Are you sure you wouldn't like a burger? A nice thick burger on a toasted bun with salty fries on the side?"

I sucked on my straw, gulping the ice water down. Funny, water didn't give me that warm, fuzzy, full feeling like a burger and fries would. "I'm fine, thank you."

"Suit yourself. You see that nice-looking piece of meat right there?" He motioned to the patty frying. The aroma made my mouth water. "That's mine. When it's done, my shift for the day is over."

He returned to the grill and lifted the fabulous patty onto a toasted bun, topping it with various vegetables. He then tossed an ample amount of French fries on the plate. "Hey, Frank. I'm outta here."

Somebody called from the back, "Thanks, Noah."

Noah slid his bandana and apron off and threw them into a container. He left his plate next to me on the counter, made himself a Coke and then walked around to take the seat beside me. "Shouldn't you be on a date with your ape boyfriend?"

He bit into his burger. I watched every delicious movement. "I was. I mean, I am. Luke's still in the movie theater. But he's not my boyfriend. Not now. He was—a long time ago, but he's not now. We're just, you know, dating. Or something." Right? And why was I rambling?

Noah chewed his food while he narrowed his eyes. "If you're on a date, why aren't you in there with him?"

I stared down at the fries. They looked so golden and crispy.

"Do you have any money?" he asked.

"What?"

He rubbed his fingers together. "Dinero? Cash? Do you have any on you?"

Unsure where this was headed, I shook my head. He reached over the counter and grabbed a knife. He cut the burger in half and slid the plate between us. "Here. Don't bogart the fries."

"Are you serious?"

Noah took another bite of his half. "Yeah. Don't want my tutor to starve to death."

I smacked my lips like a cartoon character and bit into the succulent burger. When the juicy meat touched my tongue, I closed my eyes and moaned.

"I thought girls only looked like that when they orgasmed."

The burger caught in my throat and I choked. Noah stifled a laugh while sliding my water toward me. If only drinking it would erase the annoying blush on my cheeks.

"I think I missed your answer to my previous question. If you're on a date, why are you out here sharing dinner with me while Luke's in there fondling himself?"

I cleared my throat. "Do you always have to be so crude?"

"No. I'll rein it in if you answer the question."

"We were running late and I didn't know what movie he'd chosen until it started. *Enemies at War* is a little too violent for me." I stirred my water with my straw, focusing on sounding nonchalant while the images of war tortured my mind.

Noah balled up his napkin in his hand, his playful demeanor gone. "So why isn't he out here with you?"

Good question. "I told him to stay and watch the movie. He's been looking forward to it."

"You deserve better." He pushed the plate in front of me, his part of the hamburger gone, but all the fries still on the plate.

Like a guy who would share his dinner with me and give me all the fries? A guy who broke rules so I could listen to my father talk to my therapist? A guy who gave me his jacket when I was cold? A guy who set me on fire with a simple touch? But Noah couldn't possibly want a girl like me.

I finished my hamburger and pushed the plate back to him. "Thanks. I guess I should let you go home."

"What are you going to do?"

A few teenagers gathered around a table in the middle of the empty food court. A janitor set up a sign indicating a wet floor. A homeless guy clutched his shopping cart and stared at me and Noah from across the room. *Oh, I don't know. Wander around by myself, probably end up dead, stuffed in the bottom of that guy's shopping cart.* "Maybe head to the arcade and hope someone left some quarters on the table so I can play pool."

Noah raised an eyebrow. "You play pool?"

"Aires taught me." The sound of Aires' laughter as we played replaced the screaming in my head.

Noah hopped off the stool and enveloped my hand in his. The gesture took me by surprise and caused my heart to stutter. He pulled me off the seat. "Come on, let's go see if Aires taught you pool like he did math."

We walked toward the arcade and Noah shifted his hand to allow his fingers to rest beside mine. My heart galloped like a horse. This was Noah Hutchins. The Noah Hutchins that refused steady relationships or even dating. The Noah Hutchins that only wanted one-night stands. A stoner. My opposite. And right now, everything I wanted.

NOAH

Echo withdrew into her hair the moment she entwined her fingers with mine. I hadn't touched weed in over a week yet somehow I floated above the ground, my blood ran warm in my veins and I felt high—no, not high...invincible.

"Can I ask you a question? I won't mean to offend you by it," I said.

Her hand went limp, but I clung to it, not allowing her escape. "I guess."

"Is there a meaning behind your name?"

We reached the arcade. A few middle-schoolers hovered around a game with a mock machine gun. The sound of bullets flying amid screams blared from the game. A college student flipped through a comic book behind the glass counter full of cheap prizes from ski ball tickets. I squeezed Echo's hand tighter and led her past the game to the empty pool tables in the back.

Reluctantly, I let go of her hand and pushed a couple dollars into the coin machine.

"My mom was obsessed with Greek myths. I'm named after the mountain nymph, Echo."

Aires' name suddenly made sense, too. I plunked two quarters into the table and the balls rumbled out of the slot. Echo immediately tossed them onto the table. "Eight or nine ball?"

"Eight." Nine was more complicated. I already planned on playing at sixty percent capacity, hoping she'd have a good time. "What's the myth?"

She set the balls into the rack and flipped the triangle away. "There are several, actually. You break."

I'd met several girls like her; terrified to break because they couldn't hit more than a few balls off the group. Better she break and get one in than nothing at all. "Ladies first." I couldn't wait for this game to be over so I could teach her how to break properly. Images of her body pressed against mine, bending over the table, caused my jeans to get tighter.

"Your funeral," she sang and my lips turned up at her flash of confidence. Echo twirled her pool cue like a warrior going into battle, never once taking her eyes off the cue ball. She leaned over the table. I focused on her tight ass. My siren ate me alive with every movement. As she took aim, she no longer resembled the fragile girl at school, but a sniper.

The quick and thunderous cracking of balls caught me off guard. The balls fell into the pockets in such rapid succession, I lost count. Echo rounded the table, once again twirling the cue, studying the remaining balls like a four-star general would a map.

Damn—the girl knew how to play.

"Stripes," she called. Echo bent over the table to make her second shot. Her beautiful breasts were right there for me to see, but I wanted to do more than observe, I wanted to…

"You should put your tongue back in your mouth. You'll get all cotton-mouthed if it dries out." She sank two stripes with one shot.

"I can't help it you're hot." I loved it when she dished it out. "The myth?"

After sinking two more shots she finally missed. Now it was my turn. Sixty percent capacity wouldn't cut it with her. Hell, one hundred percent may not even be enough.

I worked the table while Echo settled onto a stool. "Zeus enjoyed affairs with nymphs on earth and his wife, Hera, didn't quite approve of his extracurricular activities. So he sent Echo, a beautiful wood nymph, to distract and entertain Hera while he did a little entertaining of his own. Hera finally figured it out and punished Echo by taking her voice, cursing her to only repeat what others said.

"After this happened, Echo fell in love with a jerk who didn't love her back. Echo wandered the woods, heartbroken, crying until there was nothing left to her but her voice, which still haunts the earth."

Some of us were named after Bible personalities, others from a dart thrown at a baby book. Echo was named after a psychotic Greek myth. I sank two balls into the right pocket. "She didn't like the names from normal fairy tales?"

Echo laughed. "Those were my fairy tales. I grew up understanding the story behind every constellation. What Greek god was mad at whom. Love, lust, anger, revenge. I slept with the light on for a long time."

I missed my shot and swallowed the curse. Echo pranced to the table with a wicked grin on her lips. I craved nothing more than to kiss that pretty little smirk off her face. Instead, I yanked one of her silky red curls. Her laughter tickled my skin.

"Your turn to answer a question," she said.

"Shoot."

"Why do you want to see your file?" She aimed for the eight ball and sank the shot.

No one, except Keesha or Mrs. Collins, had asked me a question that personal in years. I placed two more quarters into the table. "Are you going to tell me why you want to see yours?"

Echo arranged the balls again. "You already know most of it. You break this time."

Feeling off balance, I leaned on the pool stick. "I have two younger brothers. Jacob's eight and Tyler's four. We were separated after my parents died. They're in a shitty home. I want to prove it and hopefully win custody of them after I graduate. That file lists where they live. If I can catch these bastards hurting my brothers, then I can get them out, and make us a family again."

I broke the balls with more strength than I'd intended. I couldn't get the picture of Tyler's bruised face out of my head. My brothers wouldn't become victims like Beth or turn into hard-asses like me. The cue ball bounced several times after hitting the group of balls. "Solids. Your turn to answer."

"My mom hurt me and I don't remember it."

She sounded detached, but I knew she wanted in her file as much as I wanted in mine. I'd told her my story, I wanted hers. "Tell me what you do know."

Echo rolled the pool cue in her hand. "I don't know you well enough."

How the hell would I get her to trust me? On some level, she did. But not like I wanted her to. My reputation with girls at school preceded me like cheerleaders in front of a marching band. Shit, what if she did trust me? What would I do with it?

I rested my hip against the pool table. "What if we only have one shot at those files? I'm not telling you my personal shit because I'm into group therapy, I'm telling you because if you have the opportunity to get into the files, I need you to find my brothers' foster parents' information. Last name, address and phone number. If I get a crack at yours, what am I looking for?"

Damn if she didn't turn into a vampire. Absolutely no blood remained in her gorgeous face. "Swear you won't tell anyone."

What could be worse than being called a cutter? "Whatever it is..."

"Swear it," she hissed. The tilt of her head, the way her eyes flashed a deep green and narrowed like a savage animal's warned me that a joke may not be the smartest move.

"I swear."

Echo left her pool stick against the wall and walked to the table. It appeared all games were over for the night. She picked up the cue ball. "My mom is bipolar. You know, manic depressive. There are two types of bipolar and my mom is number one. Not like one is the bottom, one as in Category 5 hurricane, 10.0 earthquake. She was misdiagnosed for years and then when I was six..."

Echo rolled the cue ball onto the table, hitting multiple balls. "She had a major breakdown and got help. My mother was great when she stayed on her meds."

She wrapped her arms around herself and stared down at the table. Her foot tapped against the floor. "I only know what little my dad and my friends told me. She came off her meds, went into a manic episode, I went to her apartment and she tried to kill me."

I was terrified to move, breathe, exist in this moment. On TV, teenagers were portrayed as happy, carefree. Echo and I would never know such a life. My parents died. I got screwed by a system supposedly in place to protect me. Echo...Echo was betrayed by the person who should have laid down her life to protect her.

She raised her hand like a claw to her forehead. "Do you know what it's like to not remember something? My mother loved me. She wouldn't hurt me. Do you know what it's like to have horrifying nightmares night after night? I go to bed one night, my life perfect, and then wake up in agony two days later in a hospital and my whole world is torn apart. I need to know. If I know, maybe I'll feel whole again. Maybe..."

Echo reminded me of the statue of a saint my mother had once placed in her flower garden. Arms outstretched, seeking an answer from a God that hated us both. "Maybe I'll find normal again."

"Tell me about Aires." I grasped for any straw to help.

By pure miracle, my statement snapped her out of misery. She blinked, coming back to the beeping and ringing of the video arcade. "Aires loved cars. He salvaged this 1965 Corvette and spent years working on it. That's why I'm tutoring you. I need to make money to finish fixing it up."

So she wasn't some nerd looking for extra credit or service hours. She wanted to honor her brother—her family. Echo and I were more alike than I'd thought. "What's wrong with it?"

She picked up her pool cue and placed it back on the rack. "I have no idea. For all I know, it needs twenty dollars in gas and new spark plugs. Or it could need something huge and expensive. I got a mechanic to come and look at it today, but I have a feeling he's going to take me to the cleaners."

"I know a guy who's a genius with cars. He'd love to be in the same zip code as a '65 Vette. Would you mind letting him have a crack at it?"

Her siren smile appeared and her eyes lit up the room. "Yes. Totally. Yes."

She'd probably lose some of that excitement once she met Isaiah. "Isaiah's a little rough around the edges, but a good guy. I don't want you to be shocked when someone like me shows up."

Her laughter sounded like music. "What, you don't hang out with missionaries in your downtime? When the rest of us go home and slip into sweatpants and T-shirts, you kick back in a polo shirt and khakis."

No one but Isaiah and Beth teased me. People ran from me. Yet this little nymph thoroughly enjoyed this game. "Keep it up, Echo. I'm all about foreplay."

She laughed so loudly, she slapped a hand over her mouth, yet the giggles escaped. "You are so full of yourself. You think because girls swoon over you and let you into their pants on the first try that I'll follow suit. Think again. Besides, I have your number now. Every time you try to look all dark and danger-ous, I'll picture you wearing a pink striped polo, collar up, and a pair of pleated chinos."

No way. I stalked over to Echo, feeling like a tiger after its prey. She backed up against the wall, but I kept up my approach. I pressed against her, feeling each sensual curve. I wanted to touch every inch of her body. Her sweet smell intoxicated me.

Her eyes kept their laughter, but her smile faded as she bit her lower lip. Damn, did she have any idea what she was doing? For a girl hell-bent on keeping me away, she sure did everything to turn me on.

"You were saying?" I lowered my head and inhaled the warm

cinnamon scent at the nape of her neck, allowing my nose to skim along her inviting skin.

Her chest rose and fell at a faster pace. My hand melted on the curve of her stomach, centimeters from her hip. I reeled with the decision of moving up or down, both areas I'd dreamed of touching.

"Noah," she breathed out, unknowingly fulfilling one of my many fantasies involving Echo. If I played my cards right, maybe she'd fulfill a couple more. I barely brushed my lips down her cheek as I moved toward her mouth. Her nails tickled my chest, driving me insane. Kissing her became my single reason for breathing.

Her hands applied pressure to my chest and her lips moved against mine. "I can't."

She pushed me away. "I...I...can't." Any traces of humor were gone, her eyes wide. "I'm on a date with Luke and this—" she motioned with her hand between us "—cannot happen. You're Noah Hutchins and I'm not the girl that does 'it' with ...with..."

I closed my eyes to regain some control over my body. I finished for her. "Me."

"Yes...no...I don't know. I want normal, Noah. Can you give me normal?" Funny, she talked about normal as she tugged at the gloves on her hands.

"When are you going to figure out that doesn't exist for people like us?" I wasn't sure who I wanted to hurt more, myself or her. She could pretend, but she'd never return to the girl without scars. Hell, maybe I said it to remind me that a guy like me could never have Echo.

She whipped around, the same anger spewing from her that I'd seen that first day in Mrs. Collins's office. "What should I do, Noah? Give up like you? Get stoned, skip school? Say fuck it to everything?"

"It's a hell of a lot better than pretending to be someone I'm not. Why's it so important to be with some guy who'd dump you to see a damn movie?"

Echo rubbed her face with both of her hands, her anger dying out. "Are you going to take me to the Valentine's Dance? Am I going to be more than another girl in the backseat of your car or will I be a joke between you and your friends?"

I don't know. The truth stuck in my throat. I wanted to tell her that she'd be more, but I couldn't. I didn't do attachments and here was this amazing creature, asking me for one.

She ran a hand through her hair. "It's fine. Don't blow a blood vessel over it. I'm your tutor and you...you need help. We'll work together to get into our files and you'll live your life and I'll live mine. I've gotta go. Thanks for the meal and the game."

Echo brushed past me, bringing me to life. "Wait."

She glanced over her shoulder. Dark circles hung under her eyes and her shoulders slumped forward. How come I'd never seen the exhaustion before? She talked about nightmares. When was the last time she'd slept? Not my concern—my silence confirmed that. When I said nothing, the best thing that happened to me in three years left. Damn, I was an idiot.

Echo

Two thousand dollars. That's how much the mechanic wanted to get Aires' car running. So, I made ten dollars an hour and, if I was lucky, I tutored Noah two hours a week. If I took out federal, state and local taxes and social security I'd get Aires' car fixed in...never.

Sunlight streamed in through the cracks of the venetian blinds. The light perfectly hit the picture on my dresser of me, Aires and my mother.

"Hey, beautiful." Luke entered my room, shutting the door behind him.

In rabbit-swift movements, I bolted upright in bed, grabbed a sweatshirt and pulled it over my head, more importantly over my arms. "What are you doing here?"

"I told you I might stop by." He strolled across the room and plopped himself, belly-first, on my purple comforter.

"No. What are you doing here, in my room?" On my bed?

"Your dad and Ashley said I could come up."

I raised an eyebrow. "My dad? Said you…could come…up?"

"Yeah. I think you're misjudging him. He's cool now. Nothing like he was when we were going out before."

"Before. We were a steady thing before. Now—we're dating." *Going out* implied serious feelings and the only thing I felt seriously about right now was I didn't want him in my room, specifically on my bed. With me. "What happened to Sunday morning basketball with Stephen and the guys?" Luke had had the same Sunday morning ritual since he was eight.

"I'm meeting them in a half hour. I know you're going dress shopping today and I wanted to talk to you before you went." He placed his hand over mine and rubbed his thumb over my skin. "Look, I'm going to say it again since when I said it last night you didn't say anything back. I'm sorry. Really, Echo, I am. I didn't make the Aires connection until after the movie, I swear."

"It's fine." *Really—we're even. You took me to a crappy movie. I left and almost kissed a really hot guy. A guy who made my toes curl and shared his food. A guy I should really stop obsessing over because God knows he's not thinking about me.*

Luke diverted his eyes to the mural of the sea on my wall. "I can't believe you keep that shit. After what your mom did to you."

I placed a hand over my stomach as it twisted. "She's still my mom."

My heart sank when his eyes widened to the are-you-nuts look. People had given my mother that look plenty of times. Being the recipient of it for the first time stunk. "Is that all?"

"No. You know I think you're smokin'-hot." Luke looked hungry and I didn't think he wanted the rest of the bagel sitting on my bedside table. "And those dresses you used to wear to dances were rebellious." He closed his eyes and licked his lips. I'd lay odds he was remembering football homecoming sophomore year. Blue satin dress, short skirt and the backseat of his father's Lincoln. Even I had fond memories of that night.

He opened his eyes and the hunger faded. "But I was wondering what type of dress you were going to get. You know, so you won't be embarrassed."

Wow. Maybe he should go to the dance with Ashley. "Are you asking if I'm going to expose my scars?"

"Yes. No. Yes." Shifting closer to me, Luke massaged my outer thigh. I fought the urge to pull away. "I want you, Echo. You know that. You're the one putting the brakes on the physical—not me. And to be honest, I'm getting pretty damn tired of it. I've got plenty of girls who'd sleep with me."

Luke loved a good monologue, but I didn't. I cut him off. "Then by all means, go sleep with them. You're not going to guilt me into sex."

Thank God, he withdrew his hand from my leg. "This isn't going like I planned."

"Then tell me exactly how you thought this would go. Did you think you could tell me that you're mortified I'd expose my scars and then I'd fall into your arms and we'd make out?"

He tilted his head. Oh, crap. He really had thought that. "Get out."

"Come on, Echo." I'd forgotten how fast he could move. He slid up the bed and placed a heavy arm over my waist to keep me from escaping. "I still love you."

Funny how the word *love* directed at me could melt my fury. The muscles in my stomach relaxed, as did the rest of my body. Sensing my give, he slipped both his arms around me and pulled me into his chest.

I used to love lying with Luke, especially when he told me that he loved me. Once upon a time, my world had revolved around him. I missed those days. I missed knowing that someone loved me and lying here, I realized I missed loving someone in return.

"I never stopped loving you. It hurt when you broke up with me." He rubbed his hand up and down my back. The touch felt familiar and right now, familiar felt right.

"Then why did you push so hard for sex? Why couldn't you wait until I was ready?" My heart had also broken when I left him, but I'd been sick of the constant fighting. He'd pushed at me every second—asking, wanting more.

"I don't know. I wanted to know what it was like to have sex. I thought if I gave you time we'd get back together after a couple of weeks, but then..." Thanks to my friends, he knew what happened next. "Can I ask you a question?"

Not really sure I was up for any more of Luke's "questions," my body rose and fell with an exaggerated sigh. "Sure." Why not?

"Do you still love me?"

I leaned up on my elbow and forced myself to look at Luke. Really look at him: his blue eyes, black hair and that face I used to love to kiss and caress. "I'll always love you, but I'm not 'in'—not yet. Never in my wildest dreams did I imagine you'd want me back after I became the freak."

His finger skimmed my cheek. "You were never the freak, Echo. Not to me. I spent the past year and a half waiting for you to work out whatever you needed to work out. My entire world fell into place the day you came back to the cafeteria."

My eyes widened. Wow. Simply wow.

"I want you 'in' again and I think the best way for you to fall is to jump. I think we should pick up where we left off. I think we should have sex."

My intake of air made a loud gasping sound. "What?"

"Not now, but soon. I bet if we do, you'll be 'in' again."

I knew I must resemble a goldfish in a small bowl, with my mouth opening and closing over and over again. Odd, I'd gotten my wish—I could have sex with someone who loved me—but I'd forgotten to add that I wanted to love him back. "I don't know."

He simply smiled. "Sleep on it."

Sleep. Oh, how funny.

"HOLY CROW, ECHO. YOU hibernate for a year and a half and wake up with a bang." Lila finished changing out of her church clothes and into a tight pink sweater and blue jeans. "Luke tells you he still loves you—and by the way, told you so. And Noah stinking Hutchins tries to kiss you. And you complained you were going to die a virgin."

I continued to sketch while lying on the bed Luke had abandoned moments before Lila walked in. "Don't count that out yet."

"Ha." She pulled her golden hair up into a slicked-back ponytail. "Luke's begging for it, and Noah, well, from what I hear, sex is what Noah does best."

"Hear from who?" I asked, way too quickly and with too much enthusiasm. I kept my eyes on the sketch pad and forced my hand to keep working. Maybe Lila had missed my sudden and very loud outburst.

Lila bounced over to the bed. "Ooh, my little Echo is crushin' on a boy toy. I'd love to see him with his shirt off. I bet his abs are to die for. Emma from the dance team had Noah as a snack between guys last summer. Rather, he had her for a snack. She said he blew her mind."

The tip of my pencil broke. *Jerk, jerk, jerk, jerk. Incredibly hot, extremely sweet jerk.*

"Soooo, which will it be? The boy that loves you or the boy you're lusting after?"

How could such a question come out of the mouth of someone who looked so ethereal? Glinda the Good Witch had a dirty mind. No use hiding behind my sketch pad anymore. I tossed it and my broken pencil onto my nightstand. "Luke may love me, but he's not exactly thoughtful."

Lila lay down beside me and took my hand. "True. He's self-absorbed and has a one-track mind—anything that pleases him. But you have feelings for him."

"But I'm not 'in' with him." Not like I was "in" with Noah either. I internally sighed. God forbid I go three seconds without brooding over Noah.

"Noah's hot," said Lila, "but you know that's not going anywhere. You just got your life back. Dating him would be a social nightmare. Besides, you don't have feelings for him."

He'd shared his hamburger with me and made me laugh. Not polite laugh. Not fake laugh. Like laugh so loud people stare at you. Spit-out-your-milk-through-your-nose laugh. And I'd told him about my mom and he'd found a way to make me feel better.

"Echo," said Lila sternly. "Please tell me you don't have feelings for this guy."

"It doesn't matter," I mumbled. "He isn't going to the Valentine's Dance."

"Yeah. That was a totally weird answer, but I'll take it. So, topic switch. You need to be on birth control."

Twice in one day I found myself sympathizing with a goldfish. "No. I don't."

"Yes. You do. I'll bet my Big Buddha bag that you'll join the rest of the lunch table and have done the deed by graduation. With who, I don't know." She immediately whispered, "Luke," before returning to her normal tone. "But you definitely need to be on birth control."

Birth control? Birth control meant talking about sex, and I counted myself lucky as I'd avoided the sex talk with any parental figure. "My dad is gonna freak."

Lila rolled off the bed, grabbed my hand and dragged me up. "Oh, no, sista, we're not hitting up Daddy. Let's go dress shopping!"

FIVE TORTUROUS HOURS LATER, Ashley and Lila finally agreed on my homecoming dress. Unless I planned on appearing like the mother of the bride, I couldn't find a dress with long sleeves. We settled on a black satin strapless dress, midthigh skirt, with matching black satin gloves that reached to my biceps.

Lila and I sipped our lattes at a table in the food court while Ashley finished paying the barista.

"Now," whispered Lila.

"Now what?" My feet and head hurt.

"Stepmom is all giddy from girl day. Keep to the script and you'll be fine."

My eyes widened. *Oh, crap.* Now as in this was the moment we were going to con stepmom into putting me on birth control.

Ashley sat at our table. "I've had so much fun with you girls. Remember when we used to go shopping every weekend?"

Yeah. Before you stabbed my mom in the back by sleeping with my father. Lila kicked me under the chair. "I have painful periods."

My leg throbbed as Lila took another whack. Ashley blinked, obviously startled. "Excuse me?"

Lila cleared her throat. "What I think Echo meant to say was that we're thrilled to be spending time with you because there's an issue she needs to discuss. A girlie thing. You know, like a men-don't-understand type of thing. See, over the past year her periods have become very heavy and the cramping has gotten worse. Right, Echo?"

"Ow," I said plainly while trying hard not to blink my eyeballs out. I really stunk at this. She kicked me again. "I mean, yes. Lots of blood and cramps. Wow. Really bad cramps. Like cramps from Hades. Yeah, I really hate cramps. Cramps, cramps, cramps."

This time, Lila stomped on my foot. "As Echo's best friend, I told her that she should talk to you. My mom put me on the pill when my periods became heavy."

Ashley's face fell for a moment while she glanced back and forth between me and Lila. Which one would win out? The wife who knew my father would crush his BlackBerry in his hand if he found out his only daughter was on birth control, or the woman desperate to make herself feel better for ruining my life?

"Yes. Yes, Lila. You were right to tell Echo to talk to me." A small smile touched her lips, but her eyes still darted in worry. "How long has this been going on?"

Never. "Over a year."

"Why didn't you come to me sooner, sweetheart?"

I shrugged.

Ashley took a long drink from her latte. "How are things going between you and Luke?"

Crap. "Ashley, can we focus on my period issues?"

Ashley's eyes brightened. Guilt had won. "I have an appointment with my OB Monday. Why don't you tag along and we'll have her take a look at you and give you a prescription. I have an ultrasound scheduled. Your dad can't make it and I was so bummed when we didn't find out the sex last time. How exciting will it be for you to see your younger brother or sister?"

For a moment, I thought Ashley was going to break out into song. This time, instead of a kick, Lila reached under the table and took my hand. I squeezed her hand as I answered, "Yeah. That'll be great."

NOAH

"Stop sulking already. If you would have screwed her when you first met her, like I told you to, you wouldn't be twisted like a damn pretzel." Beth slammed her tray on the lunch table.

I pushed my pizza away and leaned back in the chair. So far, Echo had done little more than make fleeting eye contact with me today. Just like she'd said, she'd gone back to her life and, in theory, I'd gone back to mine. Problem? I didn't like mine, not without her.

Isaiah placed his tray on the other side of me. "Let him be, Beth. Sometimes you can't help who you fall for." Words of wisdom from the guy who ignored his feelings for Beth.

Beth scowled as she stabbed a fork into her chicken patty. She kept her hair in her face to hide the bruises the makeup couldn't cover. "What's eating you, Isaiah? You've been brooding almost as bad as Noah. Please don't tell me you've fallen for some unreachable, stupid girl, too."

Isaiah changed the subject. "So, Beth, I heard Mrs. Collins called you into her office."

"What for?" I asked. Mrs. Collins messing with one of us was enough.

"I'm assuming one of my teachers turned me in when they noticed the bruises. I told her I fell down the steps at my dad's house." She winked at Isaiah and the two laughed at their shared joke. Neither of them had any clue who their fathers were.

My heart quickened when I caught a flash of red entering the lunchroom. At the corner door farthest from me, Echo paused and performed a quick scan. She held her books tight to her chest, sleeves clutched in her hands. Our eyes met. Her green eyes melted and she gave me that beautiful siren smile. My lips quirked and I motioned for her to come over to the table. What the hell was I doing?

Beth had evidently become a mind reader. "What the hell are you doing?"

While watching Echo's eyes widen, I quickly turned to Isaiah. "Would you like to work on a 1965 Corvette?"

"Do I want a million bucks? Hell, yeah."

"Got plans after school?" I asked. Echo glanced over to her lunch table and then back to me. *Come on, my little siren. Come to me.*

"We haven't skipped in a while," said Isaiah.

"I'm game," said Beth. "And I don't need the excuse of a car to skip."

"No skipping." I kept my eyes locked on Echo's. She shifted from one foot to another. She needed a reason to come. I picked up my calculus book and showed her the cover. She exhaled enough that a couple of curls moved with her breath. Finally, my nymph approached.

"Hey." She spoke so softly I had to strain to hear her. Her eyes flickered from me to Beth to Isaiah, then back to me.

"Want to sit?" I asked, knowing the answer. By standing next to my table, she was breaking a hundred of her stuck-up little friends' social rules.

"No, my *friends* are expecting me." She emphasized the word before purposely glancing over to the table of girls who stared at our interaction. *Score one, Echo.* I'd messed Saturday night up so badly she didn't even consider us friends. Beth smiled and tauntingly waved at Echo's table of gal pals. Echo cringed externally while I inwardly flinched.

"What do you need, Noah?" She stared at Beth while she asked and then let her eyes narrow on me.

"This is Isaiah."

She raised both eyebrows. "Okay."

"He's going to look at Aires' car after school. We can study at your house while he assesses what needs to be done."

Her face brightened. "For real?"

"What's for real?" asked a familiar voice. Dammit—the overgrown ape. Just when I'd started to manipulate Echo back into my corner, her loser boyfriend swooped in and draped an arm around her shoulder.

Echo continued to beam. "Isaiah's going to look at Aires' car for me."

The corners of my mouth turned up as Luke's turned down. "When?" he asked.

"Today. After school," answered Isaiah. He shifted in his chair to let Luke have a good look at him, earrings, tattoos and all his punked-out glory.

"Echo!" called one of her friends.

She glanced behind her, then rifled through her backpack.

"I'll be leaving after lunch for an appointment and won't be back, but after school will totally work."

Echo bent over and scribbled her phone number on a napkin. Her shirt dipped, exposing a hint of her cleavage. The glare I gave Isaiah warned him off from looking and the smile I sent Echo's ape boyfriend when she slid the napkin to me made the ape's fist curl.

"My phone will be off," said Echo. "But text me your number so I can give you directions. See you guys after school." She took a step, but Luke didn't follow. "You coming?"

"I'm going to grab something to eat first."

Echo bit her bottom lip and stole a look at me before walking away. So I hadn't screwed everything completely up. I had at least one more shot at Echo.

A chair scraped against the floor and Luke took a seat at our table.

"What is the deal with you popular people? Can't you leave the losers alone?" mumbled Beth.

Luke ignored her. "We played basketball against each other freshman year."

Both Beth's and Isaiah's heads snapped toward me. I never discussed my pre–foster care life. I folded my arms across my chest. "Yeah. We did."

"I defended you and you kicked my ass. Your team won."

He brought up that game like it was yesterday. For me, it was eons ago. Those memories belonged to a boy who died alongside his parents in a house fire.

When I didn't respond he continued, "You won that day, but you ain't winning now. She's mine. Not yours. Are we clear, amigo?"

I chuckled. "Way I hear it, Echo's fair game. If you're not man enough to keep her satisfied, well…" I held my hands out to let my reputation speak for itself.

Luke sprang from his seat, face flushed red. "You go near her and I'll beat the shit out of you."

Homecoming king probably never fought a day in his life. His body shook. I stayed seated, knowing my calmness would scare him more. "Bring it. I'll kick your ass like I did in basketball. Only this time, no referee is going to save you."

Luke slammed his chair into our table and stalked away. Beth and Isaiah broke out into laughter. I joined them until I noticed the horror on Echo's face. Before I could move, she sprinted from the lunchroom. Dammit.

ECHO LIVED IN ONE OF THOSE nice neighborhoods. Not the rich fancy kind, but the ones with large trees in the front yard, amateur but nice landscaping, two-story brick fronts and porches with swings. I used to live in a place like this—before. I bet it looked real pretty in the spring. Probably smelled like daffodils and roses—like my house used to. Now, all I could smell was dirt and cold. February sucked.

The two-car garage door opened when we shut our car doors. Echo had parked her Dodge Neon on a narrow strip of concrete next to the house, leaving the red Corvette as the only car in the garage. From the driver's side, one of Echo's jean-clad legs dangled.

"I've got a hard-on just looking at her, man," said Isaiah as we strolled up the drive.

"You're ate up," I replied, hoping he meant the car, not Echo. I'd hate to throw down with someone I considered family.

Beth squeezed between me and Isaiah. "Sick in the head, more like it."

"Both. Jesus, are those the original fenders?" Isaiah slid his hand over the body of the car.

I walked into the garage and into a bubble of warmth. A heater hung from the rafters, along with several shop lights. The moment the three of us entered, the garage door closed behind us. Wooden tool benches lined the left and back walls. Tools hung on pegboards. Pictures of cars and people littered the cabinents.

"Maybe you'd keep a girl if you touched her like that." Beth leaned against a bench.

Isaiah smirked while inspecting the pinstriping. "I meet a girl that could purr like this kitten, I'd caress her all night."

"Are you guys high?" Echo's voice drifted from the car. The hoarse catch in her tone swiped a claw at my heart.

Beth scowled in my direction. "Unfortunately, no. Your goody-two-shoes attitude is rubbing off on my boy." I'd hear Beth complain for days over this. But she, Isaiah and I were more than loser stoners and I wanted to prove that to Echo.

She stayed in the driver's seat and had yet to show her face. I kept my focus on the car, pretending I had the slightest clue what the hell Isaiah mumbled about. One shot. That's what I'd bought myself. If I screwed today up, I'd be watching ape boy living life with Echo. Everything inside me wound tight. Shit. I was nervous over a girl.

Isaiah continued to slide his hand up the car toward the hood, mumbling incoherent nonsense. He threw out words like fenders, chrome, body and slants. "Can I take her to second base?" Isaiah's eyes flickered into the car and then immediately to me. He tilted his head toward Echo before running his hand under the hood, waiting for her to pop it open.

Hell. Isaiah had never won awards for being observant. My stunt with Luke must have pissed her off. I wandered up to the driver's side to translate for my dumb-ass best friend. "He wants you to pop the hood."

Echo held a photo album in her lap, with her fingers touching an image. She had that lost look again. The same one she'd worn last semester when she walked into class seconds before the bell rang, pretending no one else existed. Only now I realized that she wasn't pretending. In this moment, Echo lived in her own little world.

She'd said she had an appointment, but mentioned nothing else. Did something go wrong? I crouched next to her, lowering my voice so only she could hear my concern. "Echo."

Awakening from her dreamworld, she took a deep breath. "Yeah. The hood."

She slid her hand under the console and pulled the lever. Isaiah's eyes sparkled when the latch released with a pop and the door to his magical world opened. "Beth, you've got to see this."

"Your car obsession is unnatural." She acted like she didn't care, but Beth pushed off the bench toward Isaiah. "How on earth do you get girls to screw you?"

"Come on, you know the words *big block V-8* make your panties wet."

"Oh, baby," Beth said dryly. "Take me now."

Echo checked out my eyes. "Are you sure you guys aren't high?"

Several sarcastic comments entered my mind, but I reminded myself—one shot. "This is your house and I wouldn't disrespect you like that."

The right side of her mouth turned up. "Thanks." She closed the album. "You ready to delve into the world of physics?"

I glanced around the garage. "Where?"

"I typically study in here."

"You're kidding." The serious look in her green eyes told me she wasn't, as did her backpack sitting on the passenger side. "You know, most people use tables and chairs."

Echo shrugged, taking her physics book out of her pack and then placing the pack on the floor next to me. She lowered her voice. "Most people don't have scars running up their arms or go to 'strongly encouraged by Child Protective Services' therapy once a week either. Are we studying or not?"

I opened the door to the passenger side and took a seat. Taped to the dashboard was a picture of Echo with her arms wrapped around a taller guy with brown hair. Appeared Beth had left out a boyfriend in her history of Echo lesson. Imagine that—a stoner who forgot something. "Who's that?"

A soft smile touched her lips, but not her eyes. Those eyes held so much pain that I felt a knife slash through my gut. "That's my brother, Aires. It's our last picture together." Her hand absently stroked the album in her lap.

Isaiah and Beth were bantering back and forth, giving our conversation some privacy. "You're lucky. Everything that meant a thing to me burnt up in the fire. Everything but my brothers. I don't have a single picture of my parents. Sometimes I'm terrified I'm going to forget what they looked like." And the sound of their voices. My father's deep laughter and my mom's hearty giggles. The fragrance of my mom's perfume when she got ready for work. The smell of my dad's aftershave. The sound of them cheering from the stands when I made a shot. God, I missed them.

I had no idea I'd traveled into my own universe until Echo's cold fingers squeezed mine. "Want to do normal?"

And my heart clenched in pain and joy at the same time. I

missed my parents beyond words and this beautiful nymph understood. "I'm all over normal." I opened my physics book.

THE SLAMMING OF THE HOOD startled me and Echo. We'd spent two hours reviewing for our physics test. If I didn't pass the son of a bitch tomorrow, I'd never pass a test.

If I didn't know better, I'd say Isaiah was on the best trip of his life with that crazy smile on his face. "I know how to get her going."

Echo brightened to the level of supernova. "Really?" She dropped her physics book and hopped out of the car.

I fought the urge to stand behind Echo and wrap my arms around her as she bounced in front of Isaiah in delight. For a second, it appeared Isaiah would join in the happy dance. "Just a few parts, minor really. I'll find them at the junkyard. It'll take me some time and probably cost up to two hundred."

Echo's eyes widened and my heart sank. She didn't have the money. How much could she make tutoring a loser like me? I had the money. I saved every dime to move into my own place after graduation and rescue my brothers. I could loan it to her and we could increase our tutoring sessions until she made enough to pay me back. "Echo…"

She threw herself at Isaiah, tackling him in a hug. "Thank you. Thank you. Thank you. Do you need the money now or later? I've got cash, if that's okay."

Isaiah paled and stared at me with his arms held out to his sides. "I swear to God, I'm not touching her, man."

"Yeah, but she's touching you." The dark shadows in Beth's eyes prompted me to take action.

Oblivious to the black-haired threat behind her, Echo released Isaiah, glowing as if Jesus had appeared and turned water into wine. A pang of jealousy nagged at my gut. To keep Beth from tearing Echo to pieces, I stepped between the two. "Told you I could help." Shitty of me to attempt to take the credit, but I couldn't help it. I wanted to be her champion.

Her cheeks filled with color and her eyes lit like sparklers. "Noah." She gasped, out of breath. "We did it. We're going to fix his car. Oh, God, Noah..." She threw her arms around my neck and pressed her head into my shoulder.

Everything within me stilled. I wrapped my arms around her warmth and softness, closing my eyes to savor the peace Echo's presence brought to me. Life would almost be enjoyable if I could feel this way all the time. I nuzzled the top of her hair with my chin, sending Isaiah a glance of gratitude. He nodded once and shifted his footing as he caught a glimpse of Beth.

She had a hand on her throat, disbelief draining her face of color. "Isaiah, I..." She took two steps backward before turning and bolting.

"Beth!" Isaiah raced after her. The door to the garage slammed shut behind him.

Using my arms as chains, I kept Echo locked against me when she pulled her head off my shoulder. "What's wrong?" she asked.

My messed-up friends are ruining my moment. "Isaiah's into Beth and doesn't want to admit it and Beth doesn't want to be into anyone. At least not the guy she considers her best friend. But your hugging him got her riled up."

"Oh." She unlocked her hands from my neck and pushed her body against my arms, but I wasn't ready to let her go—not yet. "Noah?"

"Yeah?"

"I'm kind of done hugging you."

Reluctantly, I let go. One shot. One fucking shot. *What the hell do I do now? What the hell do I want?* Echo. To feel her body wrapped around mine, to smell her enticing scent, to let her deliver me to that place where I would forget everything but her.

She packed her books in her bag, speaking the words on my mind. "What's going on between us?"

I don't know. I rubbed my hand over my face before glancing at Echo. A hint of her cleavage peeked from her shirt. Damn, she was sexy as hell. I wanted her, badly. Would one night be enough, even if she gave it to me? Echo already felt like a heavy drug. The kind I avoided on purpose—crack, heroin, meth. The ones that screwed with your mind, crept into your blood and left you powerless, helpless. If she gave her body to me, would I be able to let go or would I be sucked into that black veil, hooks embedded into my skin, sentenced to death by the emotion I reserved for my brothers—love? "I want you."

Echo zipped up her pack and threw it at the door to the house. It smacked the wood with a bang and slid to the floor. "Do you? Really? Because these scars are sexy."

How did she see herself? "I don't give a fuck about your scars."

She stalked toward me, hips swaying side to side, eyes hardened with anger. Echo pushed her body against mine, parts of her fitting perfectly into parts of me. I swore under my breath, fighting for control over my body.

"How are you going to react when we're this close and you take off my shirt? Are you still going to want me when you see red and white lines? Are you going to flinch each time you accidentally touch my arms and feel the raised skin? How about when I touch you?"

She pulled away from me, leaving my body cold after experiencing her warmth. "Or will you forbid that? Will you tell me how to dress or what I'm allowed to take off?"

Her anger only fed mine. "For the last time, I don't give a *fuck* about your scars."

"Liar," she spat. "Because the only way anyone will ever be okay with me is if they love me. Really love me enough to not care that I'm damaged. You don't love people. You have sex with them. So how could you want to be with me?"

She'd summed me up perfectly. I didn't love people—only my brothers. Echo deserved more. Better than me. *One shot. Take it or go home.* Kiss her and risk an attachment or leave her and watch some other guy enjoy what could have been mine.

Echo

When I graduated from high school I planned on painting a plaque for Mrs. Collins: *Therapy Stinks*. Pink and white with polka dots to match the curtains on the windows.

"Sorry I had to reschedule your session and take you out of business technology. The conference in Cincinnati was fabulous! Are you ready for the Valentine's Dance tomorrow? When I was a teenager, we had dances on Fridays instead of a Saturday like you." Mrs. Collins hunted through the growing stacks of papers and folders on her desk for my file. How could she misplace the thing? Thanks to her copious note taking, my three-inch file had grown to four.

She placed a folder off to the side and the name caught my eye—Noah Hutchins. We hadn't talked in a week and a half. Okay—not totally true. Last week, he'd taken thirty seconds before calculus to download his latest plan of attack. He planned on disrupting my therapy session to ask Mrs. Collins for some type of form. He hoped she'd leave the office and I could gain access to our files. It didn't happen. Noah stormed out of her office ten minutes before the end of his session and never returned.

I wanted to talk to him on Monday when he, Beth and Isaiah came over for the next tutoring/car repair session, but he kept our conversation exclusively on calculus. When we finished studying, he cut up with Beth and Isaiah, purposely keeping me out of their loop.

Not that I blamed Noah for avoiding me. I'd said some pretty horrible things to him in my garage. Things I had no idea how to take back. Besides, how would I even begin to explain why I'd been in such a foul mood?

Earlier that day, I'd learned that Ashley carried a boy in her precious little baby bump. Ashley had lain on the table, staring at the black-and-white swishing screen, and said, "Oh, Echo. You'll have a brother again." Again. Like I lost a puppy and she cooked me up another. I wasn't interested in a replacement.

Noah had come over to my house that afternoon and rocked my world with Isaiah's car knowledge. He didn't have to bring Isaiah, or share memories of his family. Once again, he showed me what an incredibly awesome guy he really was and what did I do? I threw it in his face that he slept with every girl who offered herself up to him. I told him he didn't know how to love because he couldn't tell me what I wanted so badly to hear from him. That he wanted more than my body—that he wanted me.

"Yes. I'm ready for the dance," I told Mrs. Collins, returning to reality.

"Fantastic. Ah, there it is." She flipped open my file and rewarded herself with a sip of her new addiction, Diet Coke. "I'd like to discuss your mother today."

"What?" No one discussed my mother.

"Your mom. I'd like to discuss your mom. Actually, there's an exercise I'd like to try with you. Can you describe her in five words or less?"

Bipolar. Beautiful. Erratic. Talented. Unreliable. I chose the safe answer. "She loved Greek mythology."

Mrs. Collins sat back in her seat, revealing jeans and a blue button-down shirt. "I think of chocolate chip cookies when I think of my mom."

"I'm pretty sure you know my mom isn't the cookie-baking type." Or the mom type.

She chuckled. I didn't mean it to be funny. "Did she teach you the myths?"

"Yes, but she focused on the constellations."

"You're smiling. I don't see you do that in my office very often."

My mom. My crazy, crazy mother. "When she was on, my mother was on. You know?"

"No. Explain."

My foot began to rock. "She...um... I don't know."

"What do you mean by your mom being on?"

My mouth dried out as if I hadn't drunk in days. I really hated talking about her. "I realize now that my favorite moments with my mom were her manic episodes. It kind of stinks because now the only good memories I have are tainted. The way she smiled at me made me feel so important. She painted the constellations on my ceiling with glow-in-the-dark paint. We'd lie in bed and she'd tell me the stories over and over again. Some nights she'd shake me to keep me awake."

Mrs. Collins tapped her pen against her chin. "Constellations, huh? Think you could still pick them out?"

I shrugged, shifting in my seat. My foot clicked repeatedly

against the floor. What temperature did she have the room set at? Ninety? "I guess. I haven't looked at the stars in a while."

"Why not?" Mrs. Collins's demeanor changed from friendly Labrador to pure business.

Sweat crept along the back of my neck. I twisted my hair in a bun and held it up. "Um...I don't know. Cloudy? I don't go out at night very often?"

"Really?" she asked dryly.

Anger flashed in my bloodstream. I wished lasers would shoot out of my eyes. "I lost interest, I guess."

"I want to show you some pictures that may trigger a memory. As long as that's okay with you, Echo?"

Um...not really, but how could I say no? I nodded.

"Your art teacher gave me these smaller paintings you did your sophomore year. I could be wrong, but I believe they're constellations."

Mrs. Collins held up the first one. A first-grader could name it. "The little dipper, but in Greek mythology it would be Ursa Minor."

The next painting was familiar to me, but maybe not to others. "Aquarius."

The third one stumped me for one second. My mind wavered in that gray hazy area I detested. I snatched out the answer before the black hole could swallow it. Dizziness disoriented me, allowing me only to whisper, "Andromeda."

My heart pounded and I let go of my hair to wipe the perspiration forming on my forehead. Nausea rolled in my stomach and up my throat. Good God, I was going to puke.

"Echo, breathe through your nose and try to lower your head."

I barely heard Mrs. Collins over the ringing in my ears. The black hole grew, threatening to swallow me. I couldn't let it. "No."

It couldn't grow. The black hole was already too large and this had happened once before. That time I almost lost my mind.

"No to what, Echo?" Why did she sound so far away?

I squeezed my hands against my head, as if the motion could physically stop me from falling into that dark chasm. A bright light ripped through the blackness and for a brief few seconds I saw my mother. She lay next to me on the floor of her living room. Red curly hair falling from a gold clip. Her eyes wide—too wide. My heart raced faster. She reached toward me, whispering the words, "And Perseus saved Andromeda from her death. Aires was our Perseus. We'll be with him soon."

Raw fear—nerve-breaking, horror movie, chain-saw-carrying fear—pushed adrenaline through my body. "No!" I yelled, shoving my hands out to stop her from touching me.

"Echo! Open your eyes!" Mrs. Collins shouted, her warm breath hitting my face.

Every inch of me trembled and I reached out to steady myself, only to be caught by Mrs. Collins. I blinked rapidly and shook my head. This couldn't be happening again. I had no memory of standing. Several of the stacks of files perched on the edge of her desk now cluttered the floor. I swallowed quickly to ease my dry mouth and calm my nerves. "I'm sorry."

Mrs. Collins swept my hair away from my face, her expression a mixture of delighted and compassionate. If she had a tail, she would have wagged it. "Don't be. You experienced a memory, didn't you?"

I don't know. Did I? I clutched Mrs. Collins's arms. "She was telling me the story of Andromeda and Perseus."

She took a deep breath, nodded and helped lower me to the floor, next to all the overturned files. "Yes. She did."

The heat that had overwhelmed me earlier retreated, only to

be replaced with cold and clammy goose bumps and uncontrollable shivering. Mrs. Collins handed me an unopened Diet Coke before returning to her desk. "Drink. The caffeine will help. I think we've done enough for today. In fact, I think you should probably go home. Your choice, of course."

I stared at the bottle, unsure I had enough strength to open the cap. "Why was she telling me stories? And why did she say we'd be with Aires soon? Did she forget he was dead?"

Mrs. Collins crouched in front of me. "Stop. You've had a huge breakthrough and you need to let your mind and your emotions rest. Echo?"

She waited until she had my full attention. "You didn't lose your mind."

I sucked in a breath. I hadn't. I'd remembered something and I hadn't lost my mind. Hope swelled within me. Maybe it was possible. Maybe I could remember and stay in one piece.

"Now, tell me, home or school?"

The Diet Coke shook in my hand. "I'm not sure I can do school."

She gave me a soft smile. "All right. Is it okay if I step out and call your father and Ashley to tell them what happened and that you're coming home?"

"Sure."

"By the way," she said, "I'm proud of you."

Mrs. Collins shut the door behind her. Thank God. The last thing I needed was anyone in the office seeing me shaking like a leaf on her floor surrounded by a mess of files. Files. Files!

I scanned the floor and within seconds spotted Noah's, but mine sat there on her desk—open. It was there—every moment, every secret, every answer. Noah's first. But my eyes drifted back to mine. The need to fill the black hole pressed upon me. But

Noah needed small things—fast things—last name, address, phone numbers, and…I'd yelled at him. His first, then mine.

Crawling on my hands and knees, I snatched his file and quickly scanned the pages, searching for any trace of the names Jacob and Tyler. The first page—nothing. Second page—nothing. Third, fourth, fifth. I stared at my file. God, I was running out of time. Sixth page, seventh, eight. Ninth—Tyler and Jacob Hutchins. Placed in foster care by the state of Kentucky after the death of their parents. Currently placed with Carrie and Joe…

The door clicked open and I threw the file to the floor. "Echo, are you okay?"

I sat back on my knees. "I tried to get up, but got a little dizzy." I blinked three times in a row.

She rushed over to me, concern ravaging her tone. "I am so sorry. Am I the worst therapist on the planet or what? Leaving you in here as weak as a kitten. Your father would have my license for sure." Mrs. Collins helped me to my feet. "Let's get you to the nurse's office and let you lie down for a while. The bed in there should be more comfortable than the floor."

"NOAH!" HE IGNORED ME THE first time I yelled his name. The nurse had finally released me with only ten minutes left of lunch. When I entered the cafeteria, he, Isaiah and Beth pitched their trash and left.

He may not have heard me call to him in the cafeteria, but I knew for sure he heard me in the hallway. I barely had the energy to run after him as the three of them headed to the lockers on the lower level. Clutching the railing for support, I dragged myself down the stairs. "Noah, please."

They kept walking, but he glanced quickly over his shoulder then stopped dead in his tracks. He dropped his books and doubled back toward me, catching me as I stumbled down the last step. "What happened? You look like hell."

Weak kitten? Try comatose jellyfish. My legs gave and Noah helped me sink to the floor. He sat beside me, one strong hand stroking my face. "You're scaring the shit out of me."

"Peterson. Tyler and Jacob's foster parents are Carrie and Joe Peterson. I'm sorry. Mrs. Collins walked back in before I could get any more information." I rested my hot face against the cool cinder-block wall. Oh—that felt so good.

"No apologies. I could kiss you right now." Judging by the look in his chocolate-brown eyes, he meant it.

"Don't. I think I'm gonna puke." I loved the way his lips turned up—part mischievous smile, part man of mystery.

"Noah," Isaiah called out. He and Beth waited at the other end of the hall.

His hand fell from my face and I inhaled air. We weren't friends anymore. Why did that hurt my heart? "Go ahead. I'm fine."

"I'll be there in a few." His eyes never strayed from me. "You got into your file then?"

"Never got a crack at it. I went for yours first."

Noah ran a hand over his face. "Why? Why did you read mine first?"

"It was closer." Because I needed to do this—for him. "Besides, I had a flash from that night. Not much, but it was enough to scare the crap out of me." And add fuel to my nightmares for weeks. Who needed more than three hours of sleep a night? Not me.

The bell rang, dismissing lunch. Noah stood and helped me to my feet. "Come on, I'll get you to class."

I held on to his warm hand simply because I wanted to. "I'm

going home. My mind's a little fried. Mrs. Collins called Ashley to tell her that I'm on my way and she'll probably go postal if I don't show soon. I didn't know I'd have to chase you the length of a football field."

He squeezed my hand. "Yeah. Sorry. I was…being a dick."

At least he admitted it. I let go of him and pushed open the side door. "It's okay. Tell me on Monday what I missed in class."

NOAH

"Make sure you talk about me. I want your brothers to know who I am when they come and live with you." Beth became lost in a cloud as steam hissed and rose from the iron. She methodically slid the iron over the arms of my white button-down shirt.

"Will do." I continued to scrub polish on the pair of black boots I'd found at the Goodwill. They fit, but were scratched to hell.

Isaiah flew down the stairs to the basement, swiped one of the boots and a rag, and joined me on the couch. "Why do you do this, man? They're your brothers. They don't give a shit if you show up in a pair of ripped jeans and an old T-shirt."

"It's not for them. It's for my social worker and that stuck-up couple. Everything I do and say is judged. I need them to see me as an upstanding citizen." To trust me to take care of the two most important people in my life.

"So..." Isaiah exchanged a glance with Beth. "What's going on with you and Echo?"

The iron gurgled when Beth set it on the ironing board. She inspected the shirt for missed wrinkles before handing it to me. "What happened to business only? You know, hands and emotions off of Echo."

I shrugged on the shirt. The warmth from the ironing eased some of the tension in my neck. "Still the plan."

Beth plopped next to Isaiah, resting her head against him. "Then what the hell was yesterday?"

I had a hard time accepting a rubbing from the king and queen of denial. Isaiah and Beth lived in a strange world where emotions were left unsaid, yet the two gravitated together like a couple. My gut told me that one of these days I'd find them naked in bed. "Echo snuck a peek at my file and found my brothers' foster parents' last name. I may not be able to give her a relationship, but I can't turn away friendship. Only a real friend would stick themselves out like that."

"Or a girl who's into you," mumbled Beth.

I shoved the boots onto my feet and laced them up. Did I have more than one shot? My past told me no, but miracles had occurred since Echo had entered my life. "What would you guys do if I did bring Echo around?"

Beth grunted in disgust. "Buy some glue for when she shatters you. Look at everything you've done for the girl and where is she going to be tonight? At the dance with King Luke, not you."

The image of that ape with his arm draped over her caused my blood to spew lava. I shoved the emotion down. My only concern was my brothers and if I didn't get my ass moving, I'd be late. "See you tonight."

Beth yelled after me, "Tell them that their aunt Beth loves them."

I walked past Dale and Shirley eating lunch without either of them acknowledging my existence. When Tyler and Jacob moved in with me, life would never be like that. We'd talk all the damn time. I'd know everything going on in their lives. Outside, the February air nipped at my freshly shaved face.

"Hey," Isaiah called from the house, following after me. He pulled at his earring before he spoke. "Look, man, I get it. We don't do attachments. We depend on something or someone and the system rips it away from us. But Echo's not the system, man. She's a girl who looked like shit yesterday and chased you down when we all decided you should play the dick instead of being her friend."

I ran my hand through my hair and then shook it back over my eyes. "Beth's right."

"Beth can't see this one clearly. You ever tell Beth I told you this and I'll kick your ass. Luke screwed her over the summer before her sophomore year. She honestly believed that asshole loved her. She was a virgin, man. He never called, texted, nothing. Me and you, we're bad shit, too, but at least we're up front. No girl expects a cuddle or a call from us."

If I never had a reason to kick Luke's ass before, which I did, I had one now. Beth was my sister, regardless of blood. "What's this got to do with Echo?"

"Those popular pricks—they're Beth's equivalent of the system. We've got social workers and judges making our life hell. Luke and Grace—that's her hell. Echo and Luke were legend when Beth and I were freshmen. Beth honestly believes Echo is just like Luke."

"But she isn't," I said, climbing into my car. The need to defend Echo against any attack rocked my system.

The defeated set of Isaiah's jaw told me he'd already walked that road with Beth. He headed toward the house. "You know, you look like you're going to a dance, man."

I flipped him off and backed out of the drive.

To my surprise, Mrs. Collins was sitting at the table in the visiting room wearing a knee-length black sequined dress. I hated being on the same continent as this woman, but today? Didn't care. In five minutes I'd see my brothers. "'Sup, Mrs. Collins."

She gave a hearty laugh. "I feel honored. I never thought you'd grant me the privilege of your patented 'sup greeting."

"Maybe you've never been to one of these things, but they aren't that formal. Check this out." I opened my bag and pulled out a box. "I loved this game as a kid. Me and my dad used to play it over and over again." I'd always chosen black and he'd let me drop my round piece into the slot first. Whoever got four in a row won. I won more often than my dad.

"Thanks for the tip. I'm heading to the dance after this. Will you be escorting some lucky young lady?" Mrs. Collins did that thing where she appeared as harmless as a puppy while she asked a question that could bite me in the ass if I answered wrong.

"Sorry. No dance for me."

"Hmm, pity." She drummed her fingers against the table. "What happened to that girl you loaned your jacket to last month?"

Damn, I'd backed myself into that one. I stared at the door, praying my brothers would come barreling in to save me. "She's got a date."

"She's missing out."

I clasped my hands between my knees. The uncomfortable silence building between Mrs. Collins and me took hell to a whole new level. Echo's foot would have dug a hole to China by now. Echo, the girl embedded in my brain.

The second hand on the clock over the door ticked loudly. Where were my brothers? "Why are you here?"

Her eyebrows lifted as she smiled. "We talked about this, Noah. As your clinical social worker, I'm involved in every aspect of your life. That includes your brothers."

"Noah!" Jacob's scream from the hallway pierced my heart. I jumped up to find him, but Mrs. Collins blocked my path.

"No." She pressed her manicured hand against my chest. "Trust me, he's fine."

A good foot taller than her, I purposely towered over her. "In case you haven't caught on, I don't trust you. Now get out of my way, before I remove you."

Shocking me, she kept her hand on my chest. "He had a basketball tournament this morning and fell asleep on the way here. Joe put him on a couch in another room to let him sleep. Jacob doesn't sleep well and Carrie and Joe didn't have the heart to wake him. I promise you will have your two hours."

I glanced at the door and back to Mrs. Collins. "You've got thirty seconds to explain before I bust past you and the door." She took a deep breath, wasting my time. "One…"

"How well do you think a child would sleep if he suffered something traumatic?"

Her words stopped me short and Echo's issues pushed forward in my mind. "Are you saying he has night terrors?"

"I'm not saying that, but I know a child who does, and I'll tell you that in three years that child has never slept through the night."

I closed my eyes. So many things were wrong with this picture. "Why was I never told?"

"Because it's private information. Besides, Jacob wants you to view him the way he sees you—as strong, as a hero."

The last part of her statement blew my mind, but I couldn't focus on that, not when Jacob needed me. "Private?" I opened my eyes and the only color in the room was red. "I'm his brother."

Her gaze bored into mine. "That's right. You're Jacob's older brother, not his guardian. You know you're not allowed private information." I wasn't. I lost all rights to my brothers the moment my fist connected with my first foster father's jaw.

"Noah!" His bloodcurdling scream echoed into the room. Fuck it.

"Please, let Carrie and Joe handle this," pleaded Mrs. Collins, but I hustled around her and exited the room. Keesha stood in the hallway holding Tyler. What was their excuse for keeping Tyler away? I'd deal with that later.

"Get your butt back in that room, boy. Carrie and Joe have this covered," Keesha said.

I ignored her completely as I walked past, placing a hand on Tyler's head for a brief moment. Muffled cries carried out of the room next to mine. I shoved the door open to find Carrie and Joe sitting on the carpet beside Jacob, who thrashed uncontrollably.

Joe's eyes widened when I entered the room. "What are you doing here?"

Tears soaked Jacob's cheeks and basketball jersey. His face flushed red, hands clutched tight to his chest, mumbling incoherently. I knelt beside Carrie, inches from my brother. She grabbed hold of my wrist as I went to touch him. "Touching him makes it worse."

I flicked my arm from her hold and placed my hand on Jacob's head, mimicking the way Mom used to stroke mine. "J-bird, it's me. Noah. Can you wake up for me, buddy?"

His body shook and he moaned, "Noah."

"You don't understand, he's not awake. He doesn't know you're really here." The woman wiped her eyes. "We know what to do. We're the ones who take care of him. Not you."

"Looks like you're doing a fantastic job. Killed any goldfish lately?" I scooped my brother up and sat on the couch with him cradled in my arms. I sang Mom's favorite song in his ear.

I continued to whisper the song until Jacob's tears and convulsions faded. Finally, he opened his eyes, awareness more pronounced than confusion. "Noah?"

"Hey, bro."

TYLER DREW ME PICTURES DURING our visit. Lots and lots of pictures. He smiled and hugged me before he left, but still never said a word. Jacob sat in my lap while we played the game at least a hundred times. When Keesha told us our time was up, it felt like someone had ripped out my heart, cut it into pieces and poured alcohol all over it. Jacob locked his arms around my neck so tightly, he constricted my air passage.

"I'm scared, Noah," he whispered to me.

"Jacob, it's time…" started Carrie.

Mrs. Collins shushed her while motioning with her hand for me to continue. My eyes widened and I held him tighter. Dammit. What type of questions did Mrs. Collins ask me? "What are you scared about?"

"What if there's another fire? You're not going to be there to save me."

"I'll always save you." Because I would. I'd move heaven and earth. I'd willingly walk into hell and stay there. I'd give up anything and everything for him.

He sniffed and his body began to shake. I absently rubbed his back. "It's okay, bro."

"But if there is another fire…"

Mrs. Collins pointed to Jacob and then to Carrie and her pathetic husband, her meaning clear. I'd rather go back to some of my earlier foster homes than tell him to trust those idiots. "There won't be another fire."

Mrs. Collins raised her hands in exasperation, shaking her head. He whispered in my ear, "How do you know?"

I kissed his cheek and whispered back, "I know."

His voice barely audible, Jacob said, "Please don't tell anyone."

"Never."

"DON'T TELL ANYONE WHAT, NOAH?" Mrs. Collins stared into the two-way mirror, fixing her hair.

"What?" I put on my jacket and grabbed Tyler's drawings.

"Jacob whispered to you not to tell anyone and you agreed." She turned and smiled. "I read lips."

Of course she did. What the fuck didn't she do? Oh, drive. "You must have misunderstood."

"No. I didn't." She straightened her dress. "What do you think of the dress, too much? I've never chaperoned a dance. Not that it matters, I won't have time to change. Keeping secrets isn't helping your brother."

What the hell? Was the lady incapable of a coherent line of thought? Dresses, chaperoning dances, my brothers? Screw good impressions. She treaded on territory I wanted her far away from. "You don't know anything about me and my brothers, so I suggest you butt out."

"This is a hard way to live. Not trusting anyone," she said in that annoying I'm-older-and-wiser-than-you voice. "It's not you and your brothers against the world. Aren't you tired of being miserable? Don't you want to know what it feels like to be happy again?"

Yes, but the world didn't work that way—not for me.

She picked up a drawing Tyler had done for her. "You're not going to find happiness until you learn to trust. If you're going to start somewhere, why not with me?"

I had a million reasons why not—with her.

Echo

I tugged at my gloves for possibly the millionth time this evening. When Luke brought up the idea of joining Lila, Grace, Natalie, a few other girls and all their dates for a limo ride, I'd jumped at the opportunity. I made the mistake of thinking that would keep Luke's wandering hands from touching my body. Guess not.

The limo pulled in front of the school's gym. Luke's hand brushed the side of my breast and he whispered in my ear, "You're so hot, Echo."

I shifted away from him and his beer breath and peeked to see if anyone had noticed the inappropriate way he touched me. I whispered back, "Stop it. People are watching."

He downed the rest of the beer, shoving his body against mine again. "Tell me it'll be tonight. My parents will be gone until tomorrow afternoon and your dad told me you didn't have a curfew. We'll have all night." His hand dropped to my butt.

Great—obviously Daddy wanted me to get laid. I smacked Luke's hand away. "You told me you'd give me time to think."

"You've had plenty of time to think. Come on, you look ssso beautiful." How wonderful, he was slurring and we hadn't even had our first dance yet.

The limo came to a stop and Stephen opened the door. "Ladies first." He motioned for Lila to get out, but I bolted from the limo like my clothes were on fire.

Lila followed. Her breath also hinted of beer. "You okay?"

"I'm fine," I lied. Luke had marked his territory over the past few weeks by performing the high school equivalent of a dog peeing on a fire hydrant (holding my hand, wrapping his arm around me, sitting with me at lunch) and made me, once again, acceptable. For Lila, Grace and Natalie life was finally back to normal.

For me, "normal" felt worse. Sure, people talked to me now, but dating Luke and having Grace back as a public friend didn't stop the stares or the whispers. That big gaping wound inside of me hadn't filled like I had expected. In fact, the hole grew wider and deeper.

"You're not fine." Lila stopped talking when Grace wrapped her arms around both of us.

"I love it!" Grace kissed my cheek, then Lila's. "We are back."

Luke offered me his hand. I took it and let him escort me into the dance. The decorating committee had attempted to transform the gym into an island paradise. Three glittering palm trees and an ocean backdrop for the photographer didn't hide the basketball goals or bleachers, or mask the stench of smelly socks from the boys' locker room.

Luke only slow danced, leaving me to dance to the faster songs with Lila, Grace and Natalie. As we did, Luke wandered in and out of the boys' locker room with his friends. Unfortunately, he came back to the dance a little more sloshed each time.

"I hear everyone is heading back to Luke's when the dance is over," Grace said as the two of us took a breather at our table. She leaned her head on my shoulder, and a portion of my heart lightened. I loved having Grace back as a public friend.

"He mentioned it." Along with the idea I should sneak into the boys' locker room with him and take a drink to loosen up. I watched Lila and Stephen grind, excuse me, dance, on the hardwood floor. School dances were the loophole to PDA rules.

"Are you ready?" Grace asked.

"Let's wait for one more song and then I'll be ready to dance again. These heels are pinching my toes." Circulation returned to my aching feet the moment I kicked them off. I scanned the dark room and caught sight of Luke laughing with some guys from the basketball team. "I should probably dance with Luke."

Grace laughed. "No, silly. For tonight. I overheard Luke asking you to do it."

My blood and energy levels dropped to my feet, out my body and onto the floor. The dark shadows under my eyes, which I'd painstakingly hidden with makeup, dragged heavier. I rubbed my eyes, hoping to reenergize myself. No. I wasn't ready.

"Hey, beautiful."

Luke gave me that loopy one-sided grin he only wore when he was drunk. Grace patted my knee and slunk away, leaving me alone with Luke. Not only was I not ready, but I had to inform him. Tonight stunk. I forced a smile on my face and stood. "Can we talk?"

His hand, sweaty from God knew what, touched my cheek. "Sure. In a sec. I'm going to get another drink." His eyes brightened like he'd found the cure for cancer. "You want to come? We smuggled Lila and Natalie in earlier."

"No." The third slow song for the night began to play. Grace waved at me, her eyes full of desperation. A reminder not to screw this up. "Dance with me, Luke. Then we'll take a walk together and talk, okay?" A good talk. One of those where you tell each other how you really feel. One of those mind-blowing talks where you learn something so raw and real about the other person that you can't help but fall in love.

I could tell him I wasn't ready for sex and Luke would tell me that he was okay with that. He'd tell me that he loved me so much that he'd wait forever and then tell me something he'd never told anyone else. I could tell him how scared I was that I'd never know what happened to me and even more frightened to know the truth. He'd tell me that he didn't care about my scars and that I could show them to the whole world and he'd still stand by me. And me? I would fall in love with him and, all of a sudden, I would be okay with doing "it."

Like with Noah. I slammed that door shut.

Touching his face, I let my gloved fingers trace his jaw, a move he loved. His lips twitched up. "See, beautiful, I told you we'd figure each other out again."

And we could—maybe. "Yeah."

He took my hand and began to pull me toward the dance floor. This was it. Normal. A boyfriend who loved and accepted me. Surely this would fill the gaping hole. I glanced over to my friends and flashed my real smile to Grace, Natalie and Lila. My heart sang when the three of them lit up like firecrackers, knowing, for the first time in ages, they were seeing me happy.

Happiness—it was so close I could taste it. Then I stopped. My feet, my heart, my happiness, all of me, stopped. We'd bypassed the dance floor and entered the hallway leading to the bathrooms. "Where are you going?"

"I told you, the locker room," Luke answered.

I yanked my hand away. "What happened to dancing and then talking?"

"Yeah, sure, whatever. Later. We're getting to the bottom of the barrel with our supplies. If I don't go in now, I'll miss my chance."

In more ways than he could ever imagine. "Yes, you will."

His deranged male mind misunderstood and he kissed my cheek. "I knew you'd understand." And Luke walked away.

I leaned against the door frame. Half of me in the shadowed gymnasium. The other half of me in the lighted hallway.

Idiot. I was an idiot. I blinked several times to keep any tears at bay and hugged myself. My heart should hurt, but it didn't. Because I'd never invested my heart into this second chance with Luke. I'd poured in an ample amount of hope, but I'd never put my heart on the line. My soul ached from disappointment. I'd tried normal and I'd failed. Me...a failure.

Unlike the ACT, I couldn't retake this part of my life and erase an unpleasant score. There was no blank canvas to start a new painting or sketch pad for a fresh drawing. My mother had failed me and my arms guaranteed I would always fail.

"I told you that you deserved better."

My heart lifted at the sound of that deep, mischievous voice. "Noah?"

Like a thief, he drifted from the shadows in a white button-down shirt, black tie loosened to the third button, blue jeans and black army boots. His dark brown hair fell casually over his eyes. "Echo, you look..." He let his eyes wander down my body and then slowly back up. A wicked grin spread across his face. "Appetizing."

I laughed out loud, causing several lowerclassmen passing by to gawk. For the first time in a long time, I didn't care. "Like chicken wing appetizing or succulent hamburger appetizing?"

His chuckle tickled my insides. Noah stepped closer, definitely invading my personal space. "Appetizing as in your boyfriend's a moron to leave you alone."

"He's not my boyfriend." And never would be.

"Good. Because I was going to ask you to dance."

As if on cue, another slow song started. Noah didn't offer me his hand to take me to the dance floor. Instead, right there between the entrance of the gym and the locker room, he wrapped both of his arms around my waist and pulled me close. God, he felt good—warm, solid. I slid my arms to his neck, letting my gloved fingers skim his skin.

"I thought you didn't do dances."

Noah held me close enough to see those chocolate-brown eyes. "I don't. And, this afternoon, I had no intention of coming here." He swallowed. "This dance seemed so damn important to you. And you…you're important to me." He stopped swaying from side to side and looked away from me. My heart beat so loudly he had to hear it, if not feel it through my chest.

"Echo, I can't tell you what's going to happen because I don't know. I don't hold hands in the hallway or sit at anyone else's lunch table. But I swear…on my brothers that you'll never be a joke to me and you'll be much more than a girl in the backseat of my car."

The proximity of his body to mine made voicing the thousands of emotions raging inside of me impossible. My fingers drifted from his neck to his head. I clutched his hair and guided his head to mine. I couldn't tell him, but I could show him.

"Get away from my girl, Hutchins."

In lion-fast movements, Noah maneuvered us into the hallway and placed me behind him. He stood between me and Luke. "She's not yours."

Luke's face reddened and he fisted his hands. Stephen, Chad and a few other guys stumbled out of the locker room. Their laughter faded the moment they noticed Luke, Noah and then me. Crap.

My now-ex stared straight at me. "Come here, Echo."

"We should talk. In the gym. " And get the heck out of here. Back where lots and lots of teachers hovered to prevent scenes like this. I inched toward the gym, but neither Noah nor Luke moved.

Stephen stepped beside Luke. "It's not cool to be up on another man's girl."

Hello? Did anyone hear me? Recap—I needed to talk to Luke and we were all going to go into the gym so we could be monitored by adults. I wrapped my fingers around Noah's hand and tugged gently. "Noah."

He squeezed back before pulling away. "Why don't you go on in? I'll be there in a few."

"Um, no. Not without everyone else."

Luke took a drunken step toward Noah. "Yeah, go, Echo."

This was not happening. Luke didn't stop his advance. In fact, he picked up speed and slammed into Noah. The two of them crashed into the wall. "No!"

Luke punched Noah in the jaw. Blood trickled from Noah's lip as he drove his fist into Luke's stomach and pushed him away.

"Come on, man," Noah said, wiping the blood from his lip. "You don't want to do this."

"I warned you to stay away from her," Luke yelled as he rammed into Noah again.

Prepared this time, Noah punched Luke in the gut and pushed him to the ground.

"Stay down, Manning," he hissed.

Luke staggered up, staring at Noah. I raced toward them. This had to stop. Only I was a little too late. Luke launched himself at Noah at the same exact moment I stepped between them. Cement hit my stomach. I lost the ability to breathe, followed by massive amounts of pain.

"Echo!" multiple voices yelled from various parts of the hallway.

My stomach hurt way too much to move, open my eyes or speak. Oh, God. Absolutely no air entered my body. I forced my mouth open and fought to suck in oxygen. Nope, nothing. One more time...*yes*. Not much, just a little, but it was air...regardless of how much it hurt. The cold floor touched one of my cheeks and my hair touched the other. Crap. It had taken me an hour to get all of my hair in that clip. Dear Lord, I think I broke something, like my liver.

"Jesus...Jesus, I hurt her," Luke mumbled from close by.

"Get away from her, asshole," Noah barked. Warm fingers touched my face, brushing back my hair. He lowered his voice. "Echo? Are you okay?"

Those warm fingers left my face and then covered my hand. I focused all of my energy on exerting pressure onto Noah's. He applied pressure back. "I've got you. I promise."

"What's going on out here?"

I moaned, not from the pain, but due to the person who entered the hallway—Mrs. Collins. "Echo? Echo!" Heels clicked rapidly toward me. Another hand, colder and delicate, touched my face. I forced my eyes open and blinked the double vision away.

"Are you okay?"

No. "Yes." Against the scream of every muscle in my body, I picked my head off the floor. Noah placed his hands on my back and helped me sit up, hovering centimeters behind me.

Mrs. Collins's kind eyes softened. "What happened?" She checked out the hallway, taking stock of the situation. Funny thing, Luke's friends had disappeared. "Noah, you're bleeding."

Noah wiped his mouth. "Yes, ma'am."

"You're Luke, correct?"

Luke sat at my feet, eyes wide. "Yes."

Mrs. Collins sighed heavily, shaking her head. "I'm not going to like this at all, am I?"

"Nope," answered Noah.

"I tripped," I said.

Mrs. Collins's lips tightened into a thin line. "And Noah's mouth?"

"Me, too."

She stared at Luke. "And the nice bruise forming on your jaw is from?"

Luke absently rubbed his jaw, but he kept his eyes locked on me. "I got into a fight earlier tonight."

"But not here, right?"

"No, not here."

Mrs. Collins closed her eyes and sighed again. The three of us held our breath, waiting on her verdict. Finally, she reopened them. "Luke, why don't you return to the dance? I'd like to speak with Echo and Noah."

Luke continued to stare, as if he physically couldn't take his eyes off of me. My dazed mind began to function. He wasn't staring at my face, but my arms. The glove on my right arm no longer protected my scars from the outside world. It hung limply around my fingertips. Before my eyes, though, it suddenly slipped back up my arm. Noah mumbled several words directed at Luke as he placed an arm over the glove he straightened.

"Echo," Luke said. I forced myself to look at him. "I'll be waiting." His eyes flicked back to my arms, the disgust clear. Somehow, he walked into the gym without stumbling.

Mrs. Collins sat on the floor beside me, kicking off her heels. "Guess I'll need to dry clean this dress. I hoped to avoid it. I have a habit of forgetting my clothes there and they end up chucking them." She produced a tissue from the small purse hanging on her wrist. "Here, Noah. No need to bleed all over the place."

Noah settled against the wall, pulling me into his chest between his legs. He took the tissue from Mrs. Collins while keeping a protective arm on me. Too tired to care what Mrs. Collins thought, I rested my head against him.

"So, Noah, Echo's the coat girl." I had a nickname?

Noah chuckled. "Yeah."

"Echo, is your father aware of this relationship?"

"Would you believe me if I told you I didn't know about it?"

Her eyes laughed. "Yes." She stared at us like we were rats in a maze. "I should have seen this coming, but I didn't. So much for my intuitive powers. Anyhow, let's get the two of you to the nurse's office. She's here tonight in case of sudden illness or accidents."

Noah startled me by saying "No" at the exact same time as I did.

"I'm fine," he said.

"Me, too," I added. "Fine, I mean."

"If you're sure." Mrs. Collins collected her shoes and lifted herself off the floor. "I expect the two of you to remain professional in your tutoring sessions. I've been extremely pleased with your attendance and progress reports from your teachers, Noah. I see a negative change and I'll be in the middle before the two of you can say group therapy. Am I making myself clear?"

We both mumbled something and watched her fade into the dark gym.

Noah nuzzled my hair. His warm breath sent shivers down my spine. "Truth, Echo. Are you okay?"

"Yeah, I'm fine," I whispered, enjoying the sensation of his lips skimming the back of my neck. "Noah?"

"Yes?" The husky sound of his voice set me on fire.

I hated to end this moment, but… "I need to talk to Luke."

He tensed then dragged me with him from the floor. "One-time offer, Echo. You and me, but you've gotta dump the ape. I'll wait outside. You've got twenty minutes."

Noah left me. I stood with my hair half fallen from my mother's clip, feeling suddenly alone. I unlatched the hook, letting the rest of my hair fall to my shoulders.

As I walked into the gym, I could barely see several feet in front of me. The glittering disco ball created the only light available. Fortunately, my friends found me.

"Oh, my God, Echo. Stephen told me what happened. Are you okay?" Lila grabbed hold of me. My heels dangled in her hand. Natalie and Grace flanked her on either side.

A lump grew in my throat. Would she stand by me? My best friend since kindergarten? She'd stood by me through so much already. If I chose the wrong guy in her eyes, would I destroy the one relationship I absolutely needed?

Grace pushed a few curls out of my face. I'd lose Grace. Definitely Grace, but had we really been friends to begin with?

"Echo?" prodded Natalie. She'd follow Lila. She always followed Lila.

"I need to talk to Lila," I said. When I saw the hurt in Grace's and Natalie's eyes I quickly made something up. "Mom issues."

Grace and Natalie both gave me encouraging smiles as they turned away. They left any conversation regarding my mother to Lila.

Lila placed her hands on her hips. "I'm not buying the mother card. You're breaking up with Luke and you want my permission."

"I'm not 'in' with him and I'm not going to be. I can handle losing Luke. I can handle becoming a social reject again, but I can't handle losing you."

"Are you falling for Noah Hutchins?" Glinda the Good Witch looked suddenly...serious.

Terror and joy fluttered inside of me. If I chose Noah, I might push Lila too far and destroy the only real friendship I ever had. But the mere thought of Noah's name made my heart skip beats. It brought a smile to my face. It made my skin tingle for his touch. "Yes."

She hugged me. "I expect a report on his abs. Real details, not romance novel nonsense."

"What about Grace and Natalie?"

She sighed heavily, pulling away. "You know Nat will be fine. I'll take care of Grace, but I'll expect a picture of his abs for that one. Anyway, only three more months to graduation."

"Echo?" said Luke from behind me.

Lila kissed my cheek, stuffed my shoes into my hand and left to join Natalie and Grace.

"Luke." I tugged at my gloves.

He had his dress jacket off with his sleeves rolled up past his elbows. "I'm sorry for running into you. I saw you, but I couldn't stop."

"It's okay." I shifted from one uncomfortable foot to another, sensing the sand running into the bottom of the hourglass. "Luke…"

"He touched you—Noah. He saw your scars, didn't flinch, and then he touched them." Luke rubbed the back of his head. "I'm going to sound like a real dick, but I wouldn't have been able to do that. Touch them or pretend they weren't there. I thought I could, but…"

I rubbed my arms. Regardless of the words I'd planned on saying to him, the truth still stung. "Luke, it's okay, because here's the truth…" This sucked. "I'm not 'in' with you and I'm not going to be. Part of me really wanted us to work, but that's what we became—work. We didn't have to work the first time around."

Luke nodded his head and then lowered it. His shoulders drooped forward and he stared at the floor for a second before wiping his nose. Then he raised his head and straightened to his full height. He forced a grin, but there wasn't a light in his blue eyes. "Deanna came stag and she was hoping to get a ride in the limo to my house…"

"She can have my spot." I didn't need to rub it in that I planned on leaving with Noah.

He took a step toward me and whispered into my ear, "I really did love you." Leaving out the unsaid word, *once*.

"Me, too." Once.

NOAH

I should have thrown her over my shoulder and dragged her from the gym. Instead, like an idiot, I'd given her the choice. The choice to rip my heart out and hand it back to me. Why didn't I listen to Beth? Why did I listen to Isaiah? Beth had experience down this road and Isaiah gave me advice he refused to take himself. I needed my damn head examined.

Fifteen minutes. Fuck it. She wasn't coming and I wasn't going to continue to stand here in the freezing cold like a moron. I had a party to go to. A party where there would be plenty of girls willing to give themselves to me and plenty of shit to smoke and enough alcohol to help me forget.

I pushed off the brick wall of the gym, shoving my hands in my jeans pocket for my keys. The door flew open, almost smacking me in the face. I opened my mouth to yell at the asshole busting out the door, but stopped the moment I came face-to-face with my own personal siren, my nymph—Echo. This time, she wouldn't walk away.

Wrapping my arms around her, I walked her backward into the brick. "Tell me you chose me, Echo."

She licked her lips. Those green eyes smoldered, calling me to her. "I chose you."

For the first time in three years, the coil forever tightened in my gut relaxed. "You will never regret it. I promise." Letting my hands skim the curve of her waist, I leaned into her soft body.

I wanted her. All of her, but Echo deserved more than a quick thrill and better than a guy like me. Everything needed to be slow and deliberate. I wanted to blow her mind with every touch and every kiss so her every thought always came back to me. I would never touch anyone else again without thinking about her.

I'd promised she would be more and I needed to keep that promise. Tearing myself away, I took her delicate hand in mine and headed toward my car. "Come on."

"Where are we going?"

I opened the passenger door and turned to face her. Echo's innocent eyes were wide with confusion. She shouldn't be with me. We'd both been through hell, but Echo deserved better. Still, I wasn't all bad. I used to be good, like her. She needed to know that. "Someplace special."

"I'M BUYING YOU A COAT." And I meant it. I opened the car door and slung my leather jacket around her shoulders. "It's February. Why don't you ever have a damn jacket on?"

Echo slid her arms through my coat, closing her eyes as she inhaled. When she finally opened them, she fluttered her eyelashes, giving me a look of pure seduction. "Maybe I like wearing yours instead."

I swallowed. I had plans, and those plans did not involve

kissing her against my car. Dammit, she was going to kill me. "Congratulations, it's yours."

Her laughter warmed me in ways a jacket couldn't. "Are you going to be a big pushover now?"

Appeared so. I entwined my fingers with Echo's and walked her across the empty street, toward the fountain. Red and pink lights lit up the water trickling from the three flowered tiers.

"It's beautiful." Echo stared at the fountain, her eyes darting to the different flowers etched in the metal. No, she was beautiful.

"I helped build this."

"What?"

I motioned toward the houses that encircled the fountain. "The houses. I helped build these houses. My mom and dad were involved with Habitat for Humanity. It's how they met. Instead of partying in Cancun for spring break, they went to eastern Kentucky and built houses. They got married and kept doing it."

Echo let go of my hand and stared at the small vinyl houses with porches and swings. My dad had made sure every house had a swing. As she turned completely around, she caught sight of the plaque on the side of the fountain: *In memory of David and Sarah Hutchins*.

"Your parents?"

My throat tightened, leaving me unable to answer. I nodded.

"Every time I think I've got you figured out, Noah, you surprise me."

Which was why I brought her here. "We didn't finish that dance."

Her anxious gaze went to the windows of the small neighborhood. All the shades were drawn. Some had lights on, some didn't, but no one watched. "Here?"

"Why not?"

Echo's high heel tapped against the sidewalk, the telltale sign of nerves. I took a deliberate step forward and caught her waist before she could back away from me. My siren had sung to me for way too long, capturing my heart, tempting me with her body, driving me slowly insane. Now, I expected her to pay up.

"Do you hear that?" I asked.

Echo raised an eyebrow when she heard nothing but the sound of water trickling in the fountain. "Hear what?"

I slid my right hand down her arm, cradled her hand against my chest and swayed us from side to side. "The music."

Her eyes danced. "Maybe you could tell me what I'm supposed to be hearing."

"Slow drum beat." With one finger I tapped the beat into the small of her back. "Acoustic guitar." I leaned down and hummed my favorite song in her ear. Her sweet cinnamon smell intoxicated me.

She relaxed, fitting perfectly into my body. In the crisp, cold February air, we swayed together, moving to our own personal beat. For one moment, we escaped hell. No teachers, no therapist, no well-meaning friends, no nightmares—just the two of us, dancing.

My song ended, my finger stopped tapping the beat, and we ceased swaying from side to side. She held perfectly still, keeping her hand in mine, her head resting on my shoulder. I nuzzled into the warmth of her silky curls, tightening my hold on her. Echo was becoming essential, like air.

I eased my hand to her chin, lifting her face toward me. My thumb caressed her warm, smooth cheek. My heart beat faster.

A ghost of that siren smile graced her lips as she tilted her head closer to mine, creating the undeniable pull of the sailor lost at sea to the beautiful goddess calling him home.

I kissed her lips. Soft, full, warm—everything I'd fantasized it would be and more, so much more. Echo hesitantly pressed back, a curious question for which I had a response. I parted my lips and teased her bottom one, begging, praying, for permission. Her smooth hands inched up my neck and pulled at my hair, bringing me closer.

She opened her mouth, her tongue seductively touching mine, almost bringing me to my knees. Flames licked through me as our kiss deepened. Her hands massaged my scalp and neck, only stoking the heat of the fire.

Forgetting every rule I'd created for this moment, my hands wandered up her back, twining in her hair, bringing her closer to me. I wanted Echo. I needed Echo.

A car door slammed shut, startling her. She swiftly pulled away and turned her head toward the sound of the engine. We watched as the red taillights glowed toward us, then away when the car accelerated down the street.

Her eyes met mine again. "So what does this mean for us?"

I lowered my forehead to hers. "It means you're mine."

Echo

Monday morning ushered in a new phase of my life—dating Noah Hutchins in public.

The moment Noah came up behind me and kissed the side of my neck, I was torn between leaning into him and skirting away. Every muscle in my body screamed to fall into him. My brain told me to run. With a sigh, I followed my head. "You are breaking so many of the school's public display of affection rules."

Noah chuckled while I closed my locker. "So?"

So? "I don't want detention."

"You are way too uptight. I think I know what will help you chill."

The way his eyes devoured me hinted I shouldn't take the bait, but I did anyhow. "And what would that be?"

Noah pressed his body into mine, pushing me against the lockers. "Kissing."

I held my books close to my chest and fought the urge to drop them and pull him close. But that would only encourage his behavior, and good God, bring on his fantastic kissing. Fantastic or not, kissing in public would definitely mean detention and a tardy slip.

I ducked underneath his arm and breathed in fresh air, welcoming any scent that didn't remind me of him. Noah caught up to me, slowing his pace to mine.

"You know, you may have never noticed, but we have calculus together," he said. "You could have waited for me."

"And give you the chance to drag me into the janitor's closet? No, thanks."

Noah held his books at his side, his other hand shoved into his jeans pocket. As promised, he didn't hold my hand or drape an arm around my shoulder, but he did pay more attention to me than the hallway in front of him or the other students roaming the halls.

We entered calculus and I swear, every person in the room froze and watched as Noah paused by my desk. "Isaiah, Beth and I will be by later."

"All right." Tutoring, car repair, hopefully a little kissing.

He flashed his wicked grin and lowered his voice. "Mrs. Frost always runs late. I could kiss you now and give the crowd what they're looking for."

That would be an awesome way to start class. I licked my lips and whispered, "You are going to get me in so much trouble."

"Damn straight." Noah caressed my cheek before heading to his seat in the back.

I settled in my seat and spent the entire hour trying to keep my mind focused on calculus and not on kissing Noah Hutchins.

LILA PUSHED OFF THE WALL AND joined me as I walked toward the cafeteria. "Took you long enough. Where were you anyway?"

"I had to go to my locker before lunch." Actually, I didn't, but I'd used the excuse so I could walk past Noah's locker and steal a few seconds—okay, a few kisses—from him. I finally understood why he and his friends preferred that desolate hallway to the cafeteria.

"Uh-huh. So tall, dark and mysterious isn't going to sit with us at lunch?"

"Nope." I shoved the optimism in my voice, forcing myself to be okay with it. After all, I really didn't have a choice. I guessed I could sit with Noah, if I really wanted. I'd stalled long enough. "So, what's the verdict on my social status?"

"It's all down to lunch."

Lovely. She could have warned me before we glided into the cafeteria. Why oh why couldn't Glinda the Good Witch wave her magic wand and make the people of munchkinland love me?

Reminiscent of the first day of junior year, people stared and whispered as I walked past. At least they weren't staring at my arms this time, but between me, Luke and Noah's empty lunch table.

"Grab a tray, we're getting food," Lila mumbled as we breezed past our table. Natalie sent me a weak smile, while Grace busied herself with a container of yogurt.

My heart sank. The opinions of the rest of the school honestly didn't matter to me. Their laughter and whispered comments stunk, but in the end, didn't matter. But Grace's rejection broke my heart. I slid my tray behind Lila's, not touching a single item of food.

Uncharacteristically, Lila grabbed a plate of fries and two fudge brownies. "The school's divided. Deanna told her friends that Luke only used you to make her jealous, which leads you back to the world of pathetic. Thanks to the fight at the dance and your and Noah's make-out session before first period, some people think you dumped Luke for Noah, officially putting you on the road to freakdom."

Awesome. Maybe I could be the queen of freakdom, the ruler of emotionally scarred people everywhere. Kind of like a stepsister to the Good Witch.

"And the rest of the school thinks that you and Luke used each other, that he belongs with Deanna and that you and Noah are hot." Lila gave me a sly smile and winked as she handed her money to the cashier.

I followed her and caught sight of Luke hovering over Deanna, grinning at her like a fool. I did dump Luke for Noah, but Luke dumped me, too. Truth be told, I'd used him for normalcy. Had he used me to win back Deanna?

Deanna caught me looking. Her eyes narrowed. Luke gave me a half smile while taking Deanna's hand. Maybe he'd used me, but I was okay with that. In this case, two wrongs made a major right. "Let me guess, you and Natalie make up that last group."

"We're the only part that matters, right?"

I joined Lila at the condiment station. "If the majority of the school has thrown me on the freak bus, why's lunch a big deal?"

Lila squeezed honey mustard all over her fries. "Grace." Sitting next to Natalie and another of her public friends, Grace stirred her yogurt over and over again.

"I'm surprised she hasn't already made the decision. Rep versus friendship. Rep always wins, right?"

"She's trying. Give the gossip some time to die down and she'll come around."

Yeah, maybe she would. I placed my empty tray on the condiment table. "Tell Natalie I said hi, okay?"

"Where are you going?"

"To paint."

NOAH

"'Sup, Mrs. Collins." I strolled straight into her office and plopped down in the chair across from her. I had an hour to kill before I started my Friday night shift. Steam and the stench of nickel coffee rose from the untouched mug on the corner of her desk.

She glanced up from a file and gave me a weak smile. "I'm impressed. You responded to a summons on the same day. I didn't think I'd hear from you until next week."

"You wrote the magic words: Jacob and Tyler."

"Hmm." Mrs. Collins's eyes drifted back to the file. Lines strained the skin around her eyes and she lacked her ever-present puppy enthusiasm.

"Are my brothers okay?"

She rubbed her forehead, looking suddenly exhausted. I sat on the edge of my seat. If those bastards hurt my brothers... "Mrs. Collins, are they okay?"

"Yes. Yes, your brothers are fine. Sorry." She waved her hand over the file before closing it. "I'm a little distracted and tired. TGIF, right? Or do you kids not say that anymore?"

Mrs. Collins forced a kind smile onto her worn face, placing her hand over the four-inch thick file. That was when I caught sight of the label. It was Echo's file. My gut twisted. Something was wrong.

"As you know, Tyler's fifth birthday is rapidly approaching and I talked Carrie and Joe into letting you have an additional day of visitation."

"No shit."

A little tension eased off her face as she chuckled. "No shit, but I'd prefer you not say that around me again, or around your brothers." She picked up a small white envelope on the edge of her desk and handed it to me. "Party invitation. The boys are making a big deal out of it. It's an exclusive party at the visitation center with you as the only guest. Oh, and me. Maybe you could pick up some balloons for the visitation room. I'll bring streamers. Be there or be square."

Jacob had chicken scratched my name on the envelope. I never thought I'd see the day where I could celebrate any important event with my brothers. "How did you pull that off?"

"I told you if you concentrated on working on you, I'd take care of the situation with your brothers. When I give my word to someone, I plan on keeping it." She rested her open palm over Echo's file and stared down at it again. Was that the problem? Had she made a promise to Echo that she couldn't keep?

I tried fishing. "Echo wants to remember what happened to her. Do you think you'll be able to help?"

"I can't discuss Echo with you, just like I won't discuss you with her."

Fair enough. Attempt number two. "She told me what happened with her mom. Actually, she told me what people told *her* what happened with her mom, which isn't jack. To be honest, nutcase or not, I can't imagine any decent mom hurting her kid."

Mrs. Collins relaxed in her chair, still looking exhausted, though a spark lit her eyes. "Of course you wouldn't. You had a very close relationship with your mother."

Suddenly filled with the urge to beat my head against the wall, I slumped in the chair. I'd walked myself into this one. "Yeah, I did." How the hell could I turn this back around to Echo?

Her puppy enthusiasm returned. "Jacob loves to write, but you know that already. Anyhow, Carrie and Joe let me read this endearing story about how your mom declared the first Friday of every month as family campout night. It sounded absolutely delightful. Was it fact or fiction?"

Mrs. Collins craved trust. I'd give the dog a bone. "Fact. My mom and dad started the tradition when I missed my first Tiger Scout campout because I got sick. That was Mom's way of making me feel better." She'd always found a way to make everything better.

"The rest of the story is also fact? The ghost stories, s'more making, everyone sleeping in the tent in the living room?" Mrs. Collins laughed. "You must have been a cool big brother."

My grip on the invitation tightened. "Still am, but I can't take credit. The campouts were all about my parents."

"Then why were they upstairs instead of in the tent with your brothers the night of the fire?" Her eyes pierced through me. "I think you know why Jacob is having night terrors."

I stood up. "I've got to get to work."

"Noah, tell me about that night. Give me the opportunity to help your brother."

"Like you're helping Echo?"

Mrs. Collins blinked. Good—for the first time, I'd screwed with her. "That's what I thought."

WATER RUNNING INTO A STEEL sink mingled with the sound of banging as I walked into the classroom. The art teacher busied herself cleaning bowls while Echo sat on a stool with a wet paintbrush in hand. Several bright blue spots dotted her cheek and she created new ones when she absently tapped her index finger to her chin, causing the brush in her hand to mark her face in the same rhythm.

"May I help you?" The water turned off.

"I'm here for Echo." Work would have to wait. If Echo had problems, I wanted to know.

Echo continued to tap her finger to her chin and created more dots on her face while she stared at the canvas. The intensity of her stare shocked me.

The art teacher stacked the bowls and walked toward the door. "She's in the zone. Good luck getting her attention. Do me a favor. If she ends up painting her whole face, grab my camera from my desk and take a picture. I'll add it to my collection." She gazed at Echo and smiled. "I'll title that one *Smurf*. Nice tats, by the way."

"I'm focused, not deaf," mumbled Echo after the teacher left. She put down the paintbrush and attempted to wipe her face with a rag.

The blue only highlighted the red in her hair. "You're smearing it."

"It's a bad habit of mine." Echo gave up, leaving the blue paint on her cheek. She hopped off the stool and stretched. "What are you doing here?"

The night sky stretched across Echo's canvas. The curvature of the earth was lit on fire with bright yellows, reds and oranges. Bright blues quickly faded into darkness with stars glittering in the sky. Everyone said she was an artist, but I'd had no idea. "Echo, this is…"

"Crap." She wrinkled her nose.

"No, really…"

"Whatever," she said, rolling her eyes. "What do you need?"

"You."

I loved how her face glowed. She stood up on her tiptoes and gave me a quick peck on the lips. "If I do any more I'll get paint on you."

Everything Echo did or said became sexual in my mind, and I fought hard to expel the images of her naked and covered in paint. "Mrs. Collins snagged me an invitation to Tyler's birthday party."

"Really? That's fabulous!"

"Yeah." But not why I'm here. "She was browsing through your file and she looked kind of…worried." Echo's smile fell. Throughout the week, her spirits had lowered with each passing day, but I let it slide when she'd come to life for me. No more sliding. I wanted answers. "You haven't been at lunch this week. What's going on, baby?"

She shrugged. "Nothing."

I snagged one of her belt loops and brought her body against mine.

"Noah, the paint."

"Fuck it. I can change clothes." I tugged on her chin to force her to face me. "I don't know much about this boyfriend stuff, but I'm not only interested in kissing you."

"I know, and that means a lot to me. It's just…I'm buying Grace time." She tried a half smile, but failed.

When she'd told me earlier in the week about her shitty little friend, my response made her cry. Luckily, I'm a quick learner, so I kept my mouth shut—at least when it came to Grace. "What's got Mrs. Collins so down?"

"I don't know."

I took a deep breath to keep the anger under control. "Echo, if you can't trust me…"

She raised her voice. "I don't know! Mrs. Collins has gotten very serious, asking me more questions about Mom and what I think about restraining orders, and Dad and Ashley have taken annoying to a whole other level. They took my car away from me this morning and announced that they will be driving me to and from school. They made up some lame excuse and said they wanted to detail it. Who details a Dodge Neon? I'll tell you—nobody. Ashley may be brainless, but even she knows that!

"Ashley answers every call at home and my cell phone has lost its service. Dad tells me he's working on it, but I don't believe him."

Mrs. Collins talking to her about restraining orders? Her father taking away her ride and her means of communication? Red flags shot to the sky. Echo's mother meant danger. "Has your mom contacted you?"

Her head fell back. "Not you, too."

Well aware that wasn't an answer, I felt a menacing coil churn inside of me. No one messed with my girl. "Echo?"

"No." With a defeated sigh, she relaxed into me. "I know it sounds crazy, but sometimes I miss her."

It did sound crazy, yet at the same time it sounded sane. I kissed the top of her head and rubbed her back. Echo either didn't see the signs or refused to acknowledge them: her family and Mrs. Collins were worried about her mother making a reappearance in her life. A tug of war raged in my brain between telling Echo my theory and keeping her happily in the dark.

But then again, they could be upset for other reasons. "Is it me? Are they giving you a hard time because you're with me?"

Echo pressed against my arms for release and I let her go. I rubbed my neck to ease the tension. "It's okay to tell me."

"Ashley and my father don't even know about you. I was going to introduce you this weekend when we went out, but now I'm not so sure."

That entire statement was loaded. "I'm going to meet your parents this weekend and we've got plans?"

Her face reddened. "Sorry. I, um, assumed that, you know, that since you said I was yours, that we would kind of, I guess…" Damn, she was cute when she stammered.

"I planned on taking you to a party tomorrow night, but if you've made other plans, I'm flexible. I'm okay with meeting your dad. I can't promise he's going to be okay meeting me."

The blush remained on her cheeks, but I got a smile out of her. "No, the party is fine." Her forehead wrinkled. "Though I don't know of anyone throwing one. My dad will be okay. Just don't curse. You are capable of not cursing, right?"

"I was a Boy Scout."

She giggled, then returned to the painting of the night sky, all traces of humor disappearing.

"It really is a beautiful painting," I said.

"Mom constantly painted the constellations. Now, I'm stuck doing the same thing." She paused. "On the rare occasion my mom decided to be a mom, she would tell me the story of Andromeda and Perseus before I fell asleep. Why was she telling it to me the day I got hurt? I'm so close to the truth."

My heart hurt to see her in pain and, for one second, I shut down all emotion. One day, she'd figure out she was too good for a loser like me and when she left, I didn't know how I'd deal with the pain. Echo tapped the paintbrush against her face. Hell, she was worth it. I enfolded her into my body once more, kissing the side of her neck. "Then let's get serious. Tuesday, we're getting into your file."

Echo

"They're brooding." I snuck a peek out my bedroom window, searching for any sign of Noah while holding the cordless phone tight to my ear. No cell phone service for twenty-four hours. Living prior to the nineties must have stunk.

"Because Noah is every father's dream come true," Lila said, her disdain clear. "And I've asked around. There's no party. I'll bet you his party consists of drugs, a parked car and him showing you the backseat."

"You said you were going to support me."

"I said that you will always be my best friend. Anyhow, I kind of thought you'd make out with the guy and move on. Not get all serious about him." Lila sighed. "Come with me and Stephen to the movies. Bring Noah if you must."

Images of Noah standing stoic next to a ticked-off Stephen filled my mind. Noah had agreed to be with me, not become BFFs with the popular crowd. "Maybe next weekend." Or never.

A rumbling engine grew louder as it approached the house. "Gotta go. Noah's here."

I bounded down the stairs, hoping to answer the door before Ashley or my father.

"Echo." Too late. Brainless swept into the foyer. "You know your father's rules. He answers the door while you wait in the living room. It's only proper that we meet your date."

"We," meaning Ashley, created this rule when she found out I dumped Luke.

My father's recliner snapped shut in the family room and he entered the foyer. His typical worry lines were carved deeper than normal and dark circles of exhaustion hung under his eyes. The annoyed set of his jaw said he was just as excited as me about "his" rule.

Ashley primped in the hall mirror. I probably should keep an eye out since she did have a thing for other women's men. So far, I'd been able to keep her away from Noah since we studied during the time she watched her favorite talk show.

My father leaned against the corner of the wall, waiting for the doorbell to ring. He closed his eyes and let his head fall back. My father always wore worry and stress like a St. Bernard carried medicine, but today he appeared worse than normal. It reminded me of the days before he and mom divorced or when I'd returned to school after the incident. "You okay, Daddy?"

His eyes popped open. "Yes. Work has been demanding."

We stared at each other for a second, both searching for a topic of conversation or, heck, a coherent sentence. What was Noah doing out there? Did the engine rust and fall out so he had to push his car up the drive?

My father cleared his throat. "Some odd things happened with your cell phone account and you'll be getting a new number on Monday. Do me a favor and try to hand it out only to people who really need it." Because my popularity equated to large phone bills.

"And my car?" It should look like a Porsche after all that detailing.

The doorbell rang, saving my father from answering. He placed his hand on the doorknob and sent me his you-can-change-your-mind look. "I really liked Luke. You should give him another chance."

I shoved my hands in my pockets, making a mental note to grab my gloves before I left. "I like Noah, Daddy. So can you try not to be—" overbearing, controlling, mean "—you."

My father actually smiled and it touched his eyes. As quickly as it appeared, it disappeared and he opened the door. My father and Noah exchanged a muffled greeting. Seconds later, Noah stinking Hutchins stood in my foyer looking hot as ever and unrepentant for being so sexy. When my father turned his back to close the door, Noah flashed a pirate grin and winked.

His face fell solemn as my father entered the living room, beckoning both of us to accompany him. Noah walked beside me and whispered, "He's kidding."

"Wish he was." In eighteen years, I'd only had two boyfriends, Luke and now Noah. Although the term *boyfriend* didn't seem to fit Noah. I liked to consider us...together. When I was a freshman, my first date had consisted of Luke's mom driving him to my house so we could watch a DVD. My father had no such silly dating rules then. Luke's driver's license opened up a whole new world for the two of us, but my father had had close to a year to warm up to him by then. Noah came out of nowhere.

I sat on the couch and squeaked in shock when Noah took a

seat right beside me, resting his hand on my knee—a motion noticed by my father's overly observant eyes.

My obviously pregnant stepmother eased into the new three-hundred-dollar glider she'd bought for the baby and my father sat in his recliner. "So, Noah, how did you meet Echo?"

Wow, had it gotten really hot in here? My eyes shifted to Noah, expecting to see panic. Instead, a relaxed smile settled on his face. "Echo and I have class together."

Ashley brightened and pressed a hand to her belly. "Really? Which one?"

"Calculus."

"Physics," I added. "And business technology."

"Español." Had he purposely made his voice all deep and sexy? His hand moved up a fraction of an inch and squeezed my leg, exerting delicious pressure on my inner thigh. I twisted my hair away from my neck to release some of the heat. Noah either choked on his own spit or stifled a laugh.

Thankfully, my father missed the show. "What do your parents do?"

Uh-oh. I should have prepped Ashley and my father for Noah's home situation. Okay, I'd considered it, but then I hoped the subject would never come up. I opened my mouth, but he answered, "Shirley stays at home and Dale works at the truck factory."

My father and Ashley exchanged a long, concerned look. Ashley shifted in her chair and cupped both hands over the balloon meant to replace my brother. "You call your parents by their first names?"

"They're my foster parents."

I swear to God, I heard myself blink. I possibly could have heard Ashley and my father blink, but neither of them had done that yet. Noah withdrew his hand and rubbed the back of his neck. "At the end of my freshman year, my parents died in a house fire."

My father clasped his hands and leaned forward in his seat, staring a burning laser hole through Noah. Ashley placed a hand over her mouth. "Oh, my, I'm so sorry."

I inched toward the edge of the couch, wanting to get out of here before they asked him anything else. "We should probably get going." Not that I had any idea where we were getting to.

"Where are you taking my daughter?" My father spoke to Noah with the malice I thought he reserved only for my mother. He'd clearly stopped listening after the words *foster parents*.

The temperature jumped another ninety degrees. Why couldn't anyone in my life see how awesome Noah was? I shoved up my sleeves, welcoming the cold air on my skin.

"Echo, stop!" Ashley propelled herself out of the glider.

I froze and then remembered Ashley was damaged. I was going on a date, not to Vegas with Noah to elope.

Noah's strong hand slipped over my wrist before he entwined his fingers with mine. The sensation of warm flesh against an area I allowed no one to see, much less touch, caused me to shiver. My eyes widened, realizing my mistake. This was what had freaked Ashley out. What had come over me? I never pulled up my sleeves. I spent all my time pulling them down. When had I become…comfortable?

He rubbed his thumb over my hand. "I planned on taking her to my house to meet some of my friends."

Noah could have told them he was taking me to the ghetto and buying us crack and they wouldn't have heard him. Ashley stood in place, staring at my exposed scars while my father stared at our combined hands. I reached over to pull down my sleeve, but Noah casually placed his hand over my forearm, preventing me from doing it. My lungs squeezed out all the oxygen in my body. Noah Hutchins, in fact, a human being, was overtly, on purpose, touching my scars.

I'd stopped breathing moments ago, as had Ashley. Noah continued as if nothing earth-shattering had happened. "What time does Echo need to be home?"

Blinking myself back to life, I answered for them, "My curfew is eleven."

"Midnight." My father stood and extended his hand. "I didn't have a chance to properly introduce myself earlier. I'm Owen Emerson."

NOAH

Echo kept silent on the way to Shirley and Dale's. Stretching the material each time, she repeatedly tugged her gloves up while she yanked her sleeves down. She clearly needed some time to deflate after that interesting meeting. My favorite punk band played on the radio and I drummed my fingers with the bass on the steering wheel. I still had a hard time registering it. Echo Emerson sat in my car, intentionally hanging out with me. Mom would have loved her.

Several shitty cars lined the streets. I'd worked the evening shift at the Malt and Burger for so long, I forgot what hanging out with friends felt like. Sure, they were still around when I got home, but they were too stoned by that time to be any fun.

I parked on the street behind Rico's gangster piece of crap. Echo stared out the window at the small boxed house. "Where are we?"

"My foster parents' house. Dale and Shirley are at their trailer down at the lake."

Her foot tapped against the floorboard as she assessed the house. The vinyl either needed to be replaced or repainted. Isaiah and I had cleaned a strip in the back once and discovered that the vinyl used to be yellow instead of gray from the grime currently coating it. The house matched the other crappy ones stacked together in the neighborhood—bare with no shrubs or landscaping. On the stoop, three large shadows smoked cigarettes and bellowed deep, rough laughs.

I got out of the car and quickly moved around to open her door. She stepped out, never once peeling her eyes off the house. "How many people are in there?"

"Ten or so."

The end of February brought warmer air during the days, so the nights weren't so crisp. Still, Echo shoved her hands in her jacket like she was freezing to death. At least she was wearing a jacket for once. I wanted her to be comfortable, yet I also wanted to hang out with friends and spend time with my girl. Using my body, I backed her against my car. "Isaiah and Beth will be in there."

Her eyebrows rose. "Beth hates me."

I chuckled, loving Echo for calling it straight. I framed her face with my hands, letting my fingers enjoy the feel of her satin skin. "You're my world, so I'd say that evens things out."

Echo's eyes widened and she paled. Why was she upset? My mind replayed every moment carefully and then froze, rewound, replayed and froze again on the words I'd said.

It had been so long since I'd let myself fall for anybody. I gazed into her beautiful green eyes and her fear melted. A shy smile tugged at her lips and at my heart. Fuck me and the rest of the world, I was in love.

Echo's gloved hands reached up and guided my head to hers.

I let myself bask in her warmth and deepened our kiss, enjoying the teasing taste of her tongue and the way her soft lips moved against mine. Very easily, I could lose myself in her…forever.

"Didn't one of your fucked-up foster moms teach you manners? At least bring the girl in and give her a beer before you feel her up," Rico called from the stoop.

I kissed Echo's lips lightly, my fingers burning from the heat blazing from her cheeks. Her arms fell to her sides while I contemplated the best way to pay Rico back for embarrassing her. "Vega, you got some major balls harassing my girl."

The porch light flashed on and Rico swore under his breath when Echo and I stepped into the glow. "Sorry, *vato*, I didn't know you brought Echo."

"How many girls do you kiss against cars?" asked Echo in a clipped manner.

My mouth gaped, but no sound came out. Rico and his two cousins cackled at my expression. I snapped it shut when Echo winked. Damn, I loved it when she dished it back.

"Echo Emerson, please don't tell me you're really with this loser." Rico's cousin, Antonio, stepped off the stoop, smiling from one ear to another.

I reached out to pull her close to me, but Echo unexpectedly leapt forward, throwing her arms around him. "Oh. My. God. I can't believe you're here."

Jealousy lurched in my stomach when Antonio lifted Echo off the ground, swinging her by her feet. "You're gorgeous as ever."

I would never figure this girl out. Antonio was one initiation rite away from a gang. Echo didn't look at me the entire first term, yet she throws herself at this asshole.

He finally lowered her to the ground. Echo bounced in excitement. "So, how is it?"

Antonio rubbed his jaw and his smiled waned. "Unbelievable. The teachers, the students, the classrooms, it's…" He glanced away from her. "It's shitty you're not there."

Echo's excitement faded and she forced the smile in place. "At least one of us got to go to Hoffman. They could have deleted the spot when my father turned it down."

My brain clicked so loudly, I was surprised no one else heard it. Antonio attended Hoffman, the only creative and performing arts school in the county, which admitted only juniors and seniors. Spots were granted based on talent and the competition to get in was furious. Jealousy still rolled through my body. I needed to confirm my theory before I ruined a friendship. "You went to Eastwick?"

"Echo and I had every art class together our freshman and sophomore year. Hoffman offered me her spot when she was no longer able to take it." Antonio held his hand out to me. "Beth's pestering Maria. Think you could tell your sister to give her a break?"

I clasped his hand, happy Antonio had brought a girl of his own. "Beth doesn't like anybody, and me telling her to give your girl a break is only going to make things worse."

"Yeah, you're right. So, how did you convince a classy girl like Echo to hang out with a bastard like you?" Antonio applied pressure to my hand before releasing it. He may not be interested in her, but he cared about her enough to not like the idea of me being with her. Which spoke volumes about his friendship with Echo. Until now, Antonio never cared what or how many girls I brought home to sleep with.

Not sure how I felt about Antonio and Echo, I linked my fingers with hers. Antonio cocked a surprised eyebrow. *Damn straight, bro. I did just mark my territory.* Rico punched his cousin in the shoulder. "Noah's gone all serious. Even went to a dance."

Antonio relaxed his position. "No shit. Gonna do prom next? I'd pay money to see you dressed up like a monkey."

"Very funny." I pushed past Rico and his hyena cousins and led Echo inside.

The already small living room seemed to have shrunk a few sizes thanks to several teenagers strewn across the furniture and floor. Beth sat on the kitchen table, beer in one hand and cigarette dangling from the other. Isaiah stood beside her, making ridiculous faces, enjoying every time Beth howled in laughter. Looked like the two of them had made a head start on the dime bag we bought this morning.

The sound of a car screeching came from the television. Several people called out a greeting and told me to move out of the way so they could see the TV.

"'Sup, man." Isaiah pulled me into a half hug and smiled like an idiot. "Echo."

Echo pressed closer to me and I took advantage of the situation by wrapping my hand around the curve of her waist. My mouth watered from her sweet scent. Man, she smelled good.

"Hi, Isaiah. How are you doing, Beth?" Echo asked.

Beth took a long draw off her cigarette, glaring at Echo. Standing her ground, Echo stared back, pretending Beth's fury didn't matter to her. Pride flooded my body. Beth broke first, blowing smoke to the side. "I went to the store today, Noah, and bought glue. The crazy kind."

Echo's entire body flinched and I wasn't the only one who noticed. Isaiah hissed something into Beth's ear as she took a long drink from her beer. Her bloodshot eyes sparked with happy condemnation.

"Come on, let me show you the house." Like a house tour could help salvage this situation. I applied pressure with my hand on Echo's back, pushing her toward the hallway.

"Enjoy the grand tour, Princess!" yelled Beth.

When Echo stepped away, I hissed to Beth, "Knock it off."

She shrugged and took another sip of beer.

Unfortunately, we didn't have far to go. Four steps later we stood in the middle of the hallway, next to the pink-and-green-tiled bathroom. Echo stared at the cracked white paint on the ceiling, probably wondering how to escape.

"The room behind us is Beth's and the other one is Shirley and Dale's," I said.

Echo tugged at the gloves on her arms. She had to know that this one time, Beth meant to tear me down. "Echo, what Beth said...that was a shot at me, not you. She thinks she's going to have to put me back together after you rip my heart out and shatter me."

Laughter erupted from the living room and Rico cursed. Twice in one night I'd declared my emotions to her and she had yet to say a thing back. The silence between us dragged. She finally asked, "Are you any good at Xbox?"

It couldn't be that easy. Anytime Beth tore down a girl I brought here, I spent more time convincing them to let it go than I did trying to get into their pants. I wanted to play, but I also wanted Echo to enjoy herself. "Yeah."

"Then why don't you prove it?" She yanked on my hand and led me to the living room. Was this some sort of test? Should I be protesting, telling her we should leave because Beth made her uncomfortable? That's what the other girls had wanted.

But she seemed persistent as we entered the living room and motioned for me to join in the game. I'd find out soon enough if this was a test. I snagged the open spot on the couch and pulled Echo down on my lap. "Hey, Rico, hand me a controller."

"Yeah, Rico, give it to someone who can actually play," said Isaiah. More laughter and insults followed.

"You'd play better without me on your lap," she whispered.

I added myself to the game and prepared to kick some ass. As everyone else selected their player, my lips grazed Echo's earlobe. I loved how she closed her eyes and leaned into me. "But then I couldn't do this."

After a half hour, Antonio lured her away by throwing around words like *technique* and *shading*. I planned on joining her in the kitchen when the game ended, but decided against it when she grabbed a pencil and spoke rapidly as she sketched. I'd wanted her to be comfortable and I'd wanted to hang with my friends. Somehow, I got both my wishes.

An hour and a half later, Antonio sat in the kitchen chair opposite from Echo, making out with his girl. He occasionally mumbled something to Echo while she sketched and nursed a beer.

Beth emerged from the basement, bag of pot and rolling papers in hand. I tossed the controller onto the couch. "I'm out."

Several of the guys groaned when Rico snagged my controller. Isaiah threw an empty beer can at me. "Come on, man, Rico sucks. I can't believe you're leaving me hanging."

I ignored the comments they made regarding my manhood in their attempt to draw me back into the game. Echo's hand flew rapidly over the paper, her eyes darting after it. I ran my fingers through her curls, gently pulling them straight, just for them to bounce back.

She was a genius. She drew Antonio and Maria, locked in an embrace. The picture on the paper looked like it could come to life. How could she accomplish something like that in such a short period of time?

Beth sat at the table and began to roll a joint. I wanted Echo out of here, immediately. "I haven't shown you where Isaiah and I live yet."

"Hold on a sec. I want to get this shading right." Echo was lost in her world and oblivious to me. Hell, Beth had never rolled a J that fast before. She placed it in her mouth and lit it. The familiar smell drifted into the room, catching everyone's attention, including Echo's.

Echo watched as Beth inhaled and held her breath. Since living here, I'd never refused a hit, but there was no way I was going to do this in front of Echo. Beth released the smoke. Her lips twisted up as she held the joint out to Echo. "Want some?"

Everyone in the room watched and waited patiently for their turn, thus putting Echo on the spot. Her foot tapped against the floor and she laid the sketch pad on the table, shoving it toward Antonio. "No, thanks." Her eyes shot sharply to me. "Don't let me stop you."

Nice, exactly what I hoped to avoid. I held my hand out to her. "Come on."

Echo

I claimed Noah's hand, giving Beth a wink as I let him lead me away. Being nice to Beth had gotten me nowhere and for once, it felt good to be nasty. The scowl on her face was worth whatever cosmic payback I'd get later.

Noah opened the basement door and motioned for me to head down first. The temperature dropped at least twenty degrees the moment my feet hit the concrete floor. A box spring and mattress lay against the corner of the wall. An old plaid couch faced the bed and a television sat on the wall between them. Jeans and T-shirts were folded in two laundry baskets.

The door shut behind us and the wooden steps groaned with Noah's heavy footfalls. I shoved my hands in my pockets and surveyed the ceiling. My neck twinged with the image of the hundreds of tiny spiders waiting to assault me.

"What do you think?" he asked.

"It's…ah…cozy." I'm sure the spiders loved it. Along with those strange bugs that curled into a ball when you touched them.

Noah swept my hair behind my shoulder and placed a delicious kiss on the nape of my neck. "Liar," he whispered in my ear.

Ugh—moral choice: couch or bed, couch or bed? The decision was taken out of my hands as Noah hooked a finger on my back belt loop and tugged me, backward, toward the bed. His arms snaked around my waist and pulled me down alongside him.

Noah propped himself up on his elbow, his wicked grin in place. "Do you have any idea how long I've wanted to see you on this bed?"

"Nope." The hem of my sweater rode up from our fall, exposing my belly button. Noah traced circles onto the skin of my stomach, down to the material of my low-rise jeans. His touch sent a combination of tickles and chills through my body. My heart sped up and I struggled to keep my breathing normal.

Every Noah rumor had been right. His kisses curled my toes and now his simple touch rocked my body. Fear mingled with the pleasure in my bloodstream. "Noah?"

"Yes?" His dark eyes followed his fingers as they teased my belly button.

"When did you start smoking pot?"

He laid his palm flat against my tummy. "You're going to make me work for this."

I nodded, afraid I'd squeak instead of answering. Things were moving fast, way too fast for a slow girl like me.

Noah kicked off his shoes and inched up the bed to the pillows. "Come on." My hand shook when I unzipped my black boots and lined them neatly on the floor next to his tossed-upside-down shoes. Why was I so nervous? This was Noah—study with, talk to, laugh and plot with Noah.

As I crawled up the bed to sit beside him, my pterodactyl butterflies somersaulted in my stomach. Good God, he was gorgeous and I was in bed with him. I leaned my back against the wall, pulling my knees to my chest. He lay. I sat. No, this wasn't awkward.

Noah's smile faltered. "Don't do that, Echo."

I raked a shivering hand through my hair and fought to control my voice. "Do what?"

He clutched my hand and gently rubbed his fingers over it. "Be scared of me."

Noah sat up a little and I sank low enough to rest my head on his shoulder. I could compromise. "I'm not scared of you." *What you do to my body, maybe, but not you.*

"What are you afraid of?"

"You answer my question first."

He stretched his arm around my shoulder and settled his head against mine, enveloping me in a warm little bubble. "I was a lot like Luke my freshman year—the basketball star, the guy who dated all the right girls and had all the right friends...I tried to remain that person my sophomore year, but no matter how hard I tried, I kept failing. I couldn't stay on a sports team because I couldn't afford the equipment or my foster parents would make it impossible for me to make practices or games. Finally, I got tired of working so hard to fail, so I quit. One day a guy asked me if I wanted a hit, so..." He trailed off.

So, Noah smoked pot. I drank beer. We made a beautiful couple. "I'll never smoke pot or do drugs. I don't want to do anything that messes with the mind. It's a delicate thing."

Because I was terrified to do anything that would flip the switch that would make me like my mother. Studies suggested there was anywhere between a four and twenty-four percent chance I'd inherit her manic little genes. "If you're going to try to get custody of your brothers, aren't you scared they're going to do a drug test at some point? I mean, if I was the judge, I would."

He had been feathering kisses into my hair, causing goose bumps on the back of my neck, when he abruptly stopped. "I guess you're right."

I pulled away and stared into his eyes. "I don't care that you smoke pot. I mean, I'm not going to join you and I'd prefer to hang out with you when you're sober, but I'm not looking to change you."

Noah shifted so that his hair fell into his eyes and kept his face expressionless, not even a smile. He scratched at the stubble on his face. "Why didn't you go to Hoffman?"

"Because my father thinks art is as evil as the devil himself." And that if I continued to indulge my talents, I'd turn exactly into my mother.

"That makes no sense."

No, it didn't, but what could I do? "My mom was an artist. He associates her talent with her behavior."

Noah tugged on a curl. "You're not crazy."

I tried to force a reassuring smile onto my face, but came up short. "My mom came off her meds because they inhibited her creativity. For every painting my mom accomplished, I could tell you the time frame of her manic episode. Like when I turned nine and instead of taking the time to sing happy birthday, she painted the Parthenon on our living room wall. You can't blame my dad for wanting to protect me from becoming someone who could do this." I held out my sleeved arms as proof.

Noah reached for my arms, but I snapped them away. He pressed his lips together and then unexpectedly yanked off his shirt, revealing all of his six-pack glory. He thrust his bicep in my face.

I sucked in air. "Oh, God, Noah." A circle of red skin protruded from his arm, the same exact size as—my stomach dropped—a cigar. I reached out to touch it then withdrew my hand.

"It's okay. You can touch it. It stopped hurting a few days after it happened. It won't bite your fingers off. It's a scar. Nothing more. Nothing less."

I placed my fingers over my mouth, swallowing bile. "What happened?"

"Foster parent number one. My fault. I decided to go hero and keep him from beating his biological kid." He said it so plainly, so matter-of-factly, as if branding happened to everyone. "And this—" Noah touched the top tip of his tattoo on his other arm "—is from where I used my body to protect Tyler and Jacob from debris falling in the fire."

The one-inch wide scar ran down the middle of his cross tattoo and stopped at the bottom edge. The top of the scar continued onto his back. I tore my eyes away from it to study the design of his tattoo. A single rose weaved through the black Celtic cross. Each tip of the cross bore the name of his mother, father or brothers. The heaviness in my chest squeezed my lungs. I traced the line of the cross, not the scar.

"It's a beautiful tribute to them." I couldn't imagine losing everything. At least I still had my father. I might have to jump through hoops for the rest of my life to please him, but at least for the moment, I still had...I think...his love.

Noah took the hand tracing his tattoo and kissed my fingers. "Yes, it is. My parents would be proud of each scar."

My eyes snapped to his. "I didn't mean... I meant the...tattoo."

He licked his lips before flashing a mischievous smile. "I know. I showed you mine, now it's time you showed me yours."

I shook my head back and forth before he even finished his statement. "It's not the same. You're strong. You helped people. I...I trusted the wrong person and then I go all pathetic and don't remember a thing. Anyhow, you're a guy. Scars on guys are, like, sexy. Scars on girls...that's just...ugly." And there, I said it—out loud.

His hold on my hand tightened and his eyes darkened into thunderclouds. "Fuck that. There is no shame in trusting your mother. She fucked up. Not you. And as for that pathetic bullshit—fuck that, too. You are not pathetic. You had the guts to return to school and continue to live your life like nothing happened. Me? I lost it all and flushed anything left of me down the damn toilet. Now that's pathetic."

Noah released my hand and advanced on me like an angry lion. In lightning-fast movements he wrapped his arms around my waist and laid me flat on the bed. My heart pounded as he hovered over me. "Baby, no one would ever make the mistake of using the word *ugly* with you. Especially with me around." He pushed the curls off my face, his fingers leaving a burning trail. "Everything about you is beautiful and sexy as hell."

I turned my head to the side, unable to hold his gaze. "There's more." Because there's always more. My mother guaranteed that. I grabbed the hem of my sweater and before I lost my nerve, tugged the material over my head and twisted slightly, revealing not only my black lace bra and arms, but the one scar no one but my mother and father knew existed.

Noah's fingers lightly touched the long thick ridge below my left shoulder blade. His voice pitched low. "I'm sorry, baby."

"No one else knows, Noah. Not even Lila."

He kissed my back as he slid his hand over the scars on my arm. "You're beautiful," he whispered against my skin. Noah lifted my arm and kept eye contact as his mouth trailed kisses along the scars. Pure hunger darkened those chocolate-brown eyes. "Kiss me."

Raw emotions and the need to hold him close overwhelmed me. Every part of me ached for him—my mind, my soul and my body. Without hesitation, I closed the gap between us and pressed my lips eagerly to his.

Noah's hands were everywhere, my hair, my face, my back, and for the love of all things holy, my breasts. My hands roamed his glorious body just as greedily. After drugging me with delicious kisses for not nearly long enough, his warm lips skimmed my throat and kissed down the center of my breasts, causing me to arch my back and lose my ever loving mind.

Without meaning to, I moaned and whispered his name when his hands wandered to my thighs and set my world and blood on fire. Noah eased me back into the bed and my hair sprawled all around me.

"I love how you smell," he whispered as he suckled my earlobe. "I love how beautiful you are."

I reclaimed his lips and hooked a leg around his as we moved in rhythm with each other. In between frantic kisses, I whispered the words, "I love you." Because I did. Noah listened to me. He made me laugh and he made me feel special. He was strong and warm and caring and…everything. I loved him. I loved him more than I'd ever loved another person in my life.

· Every muscle in my body froze when Noah stopped kissing and stared down at me with wide eyes. He caressed my cheek twice over and tilted his head. "Make love to me, Echo. I've never made love."

No way. Noah's experienced reputation walked down the hallway before he did. "But…"

Noah cut me off with a kiss. "Yes, but never love. Just girls who didn't mean anything. You…" His tongue teased my bottom lip, thawing my body. "Are everything. I got tested over winter break and I'm clean and I've got protection." He reached to the side of the bed and magically produced a small orange square.

I froze again. Sensing my hesitation, Noah kissed my lips slowly while stroking my cheek.

"And since break?" I asked.

"There's been no one," he whispered against my lips. "I met you soon after and I could never think of touching anyone else."

I loved him and we were together. I entwined my fingers in his hair and pulled his head back to mine, but the second his hand touched the waist of my jeans, my heart shook and my hands snapped out to stop him. "Please. Wait. Noah…" Oh, God, I was actually going to say it. "I'm a virgin."

Now Noah froze. "But you were with Luke."

A faint smile grew on my lips. I was typically the tongue-tied one and found it amusing to see him confused for once. "That's why we broke up. I wasn't ready."

He shifted his body off of mine and tucked me close against his warmth. I laid my head on his chest and listened to the comforting sound of his beating heart. Noah ran his hand through my hair. "I'm glad you told me. This needs to be right for you and I'll wait, for as long as you need."

NOAH

Almost all the cars were gone when I returned home. I'd dropped Echo off at midnight then driven around for a couple of hours, attempting to process everything that had happened between us. Seeing her expose herself to me, trust me when I deserved no one's trust, it was…life-altering.

Rico slept on the couch with his body tangled with some chick's. Odds were she'd regret that in the morning. In the basement, light flickered from the television with the sound muted. I grabbed the remote to turn it off when Isaiah stopped me. "I'm still watching it, man."

"My bad." I smiled, catching myself using one of Echo's phrases. The smile fell when I noticed the bare back of a girl passed out in Isaiah's arms. I immediately turned to head back up the stairs. "Sorry, bro. I didn't know you had company." Wouldn't be the first time he forgot to lock the basement door.

"Stay. It's Beth."

That answer only made me want to run. I'd gone this long

without seeing her naked and had no intention of starting now. "I'm good."

"Wait and we'll have a beer." Isaiah mumbled something to Beth and she gave a groggy reply.

In the kitchen, I opened the fridge and grabbed two beers. Isaiah emerged from the basement clad only in jeans. I handed him a beer and twisted off the cap of mine. "I told Echo she was mine."

"I made out with Beth."

The two of us leaned against the counter and drank our beers. "You and Beth a couple?"

"Hell if I know. You know how she is. I'll be lucky if she doesn't bolt to her mom's for a month when she wakes up and realizes what we did. Worst case, she makes out with the next loser guy to prove she doesn't need anyone. Fuck, Noah, I screwed this up."

I let him have the silence to collect himself. Finally, he pulled at his lower hoop earring and spoke. "It happened. I'll deal with it. Even if I have to ignore it happened. It's just...we were both wasted and she smelled so damn good." Isaiah didn't need to explain. I knew all about girls that smelled good. If I didn't know better, I would have thought Echo lived in a bakery.

"So you gotta girl then?" asked Isaiah.

"Yeah." I was officially attached. We stood in silence again, both of us taking the occasional drink from our beer.

"I meant to say something to you guys earlier. I'm having problems finding one of the parts I need to fix her car. I'm going to have to buy it from a parts store."

My knowledge of cars was limited, but even I knew this couldn't be good. "How much?"

"One hundred."

Dammit. Echo depended upon our tutoring sessions for money and so far she'd given Isaiah everything she had. I knew her father had the money, but he refused to help. "Don't tell her. Buy what you need and I'll cover the cost."

"You sure?"

"Yeah." Echo wanted that car running and I wanted to see that siren smile. Several large sheets of paper with Echo's name on the bottom caught my eye. How did she draw so fast? She'd drawn a picture of Isaiah and Beth laughing with one another. The last one stopped my heart. I saw my mother's eyes.

Isaiah came up behind me. "She's a fucking artist, man. That drawing is the spitting image of you."

"YOU DIDN'T HONESTLY THINK you could leave school without me knowing?" Mrs. Collins closed her office door and shrugged on her coat.

I had considered walking out the side door near my locker, but Echo's pot comment convinced me to think ahead—something that no longer came easily to me. If I wanted to make a good impression, I'd better start following some rules, or at least give the impression I did. "I have a note from Shirley and Dale to let me out of school. This is totally legit."

She rolled her eyes and dug her car keys out of her massive purse. "When are you going to accept that I'm on your side? I'll drive and have you back in time for last period."

I finished writing my name on the sign-out log and tossed the pencil on the counter. "More like put me in the hospital," I mumbled. Mrs. Collins breezed past me and I followed her out to her car.

"Mind telling me how you know about this?" I asked as I shut the passenger door and securely fastened my seat belt.

"My husband volunteers for the Legal Aid Society and gave me a heads-up that you made an appointment."

Great. Would I ever ditch this woman? I clutched the armrest when she gunned the engine on the freeway and cut off a minivan. "That big red shiny thing inches from you was another vehicle."

She slapped the steering wheel and laughed. "Every time I think we aren't connecting, you tease me. I love it." Red taillights glowed in front of us. She accelerated instead of braking.

"Construction zone," I said. Mrs. Collins swerved in front of a tractor trailer without even looking in her mirrors and barely made the exit off the freeway. The light at the bottom of the ramp turned red. She waited to hit the brakes until we were less than five feet away. I whiplashed forward then slammed back into the seat. "I could teach you to drive if you're ready to admit you don't know how."

Mrs. Collins finally took a peek in her rearview mirror, but only to check her lipstick. "Would you like to tell me what you're going to discuss with a lawyer? I was under the impression you agreed to leave Jacob and Tyler's well-being to me."

"I guess it's a good thing I'm not discussing that." I kept my eyes peeled on the road before us. Mrs. Collins may act like an idiot and be the worst driver on the face of the planet, but she always knew more than she let on and I had a feeling this time was no exception.

THE LEGAL AID SOCIETY WEBSITE promised free legal help, which was good because I needed help and I needed it to be free. Located downtown, the Society was housed in one of those old historic homes my dad loved to drive past. I remembered him complaining to Mom about how difficult it was to keep the city from tearing down the old structures. He would have loved that the Society remodeled the old home into offices.

For a half hour, Mrs. Collins and I sat in wooden chairs across from the receptionist. Around me, other people waited patiently, some impatiently. Phones rang and murmured conversations drifted from offices. Like everything else in life, if it contained the word *free,* it implied slow. Mrs. Collins finished checking her email on her BlackBerry and turned to face me. I should have known my luck would eventually end.

"Why don't you go ahead and tell me why you're here?"

I leaned forward and rested my elbows on my knees. "You're smart, so I'm sure you figured it out."

"Yes, but I'd prefer to hear it from you."

Rubbing my hands together, I contemplated telling her the truth. If her husband worked here, she'd find out regardless, but somehow speaking the words to her invited her into my private world. The question was, did I trust her enough to let her in? "I want custody of my brothers when I graduate and turn eighteen. I need someone to tell me how to make that happen."

"Noah…" she began, then stopped. Her pause made the air between us heavy. "Do you have any idea how hard it is to raise an eight- and soon to be five-year-old?"

Couldn't be any worse than life now. "Do you have any idea what it's like to live without them?"

"Keesha and I are working on increased visitation."

A muscle in my jaw jumped and I had to focus to keep from yelling. "I don't want increased visitation. I want my family back together."

"Winning custody of Jacob and Tyler won't bring your parents back."

My heart slammed through my chest and I snapped my head

to look at her. "You don't think I know that? You don't think I've spent the past two and a half years knowing that my life will never be the same?"

"Exactly," she said. "It will never be the same. You won't be their brother. You'll be their father. There's a huge difference... have you honestly thought this through? What type of job do you think you can get fresh out of high school? How do you think you can afford to raise them and take care of yourself? There are programs out there to help *you,* Noah. You. Because you're a ward of the state, they'll pay for you to go to college. Think about the life you can create for yourself. Think about the future you can have."

A woman with slicked-back brown hair emerged from an office wearing a navy suit. She gave me the business smile. "Noah Hutchins?"

About damn time. I stood and stared down at Mrs. Collins. "My brothers are my future."

"Your brothers are fine." Her eyes pleaded with me. "I promise, they're safe."

I shook my head, trying to ignore the nagging voice that said that Mrs. Collins was the one adult who gave a shit and wouldn't lie. The image of Tyler's bruised face appeared in my mind. Trusting her would mean turning my back on my brothers and I would never do that.

I needed to stick to my plan: talk to Legal Aid about pursuing custody, clean up my act at school, find a decent-paying job before graduation and prove that Carrie and Joe were unfit parents. In order to do that last one, I needed to get my hands on my file.

Echo

"It'll work," Noah purred.

We'd finished studying an hour ago, thanks only to my utter persistence. I sat on his lap in the passenger side of Aires' car while Isaiah slaved over the open hood. Noah explained his new plan for getting into our files while driving my body to the brink of explosion with caresses and kisses. The asinine plot had plenty of holes, but his seduction fogged my mind and kept me from voicing my opinion, until now.

"You honestly believe that Mrs. Collins is going to fall for it?" I asked. "First off, she'll probably tell you to wait or she'll get it for you Wednesday or she'll see right through you and know we're up to something."

"She wants nothing more than for me to go to college and if I tell her I'm going to take the ACT she'll shit her pants. She's been dying for me to apply for late registration."

Noah trailed kisses down my neck, interfering with my decision-making skills. I opened the door and slid out of the car.

March had roared in like a lion, bringing severe but warm weather. I stood close enough to the edge of the open garage door that a few warm raindrops hit my shoes. Noah didn't crowd me with his body, like he normally would. Instead, he leaned against the garage door frame, away from me.

We'd failed at our latest attempt last week to get into our files. Our high failure rate only pushed us harder to succeed. Every now and then, I wondered if the only reason we were together was because of our joint goal of stealing those files. At times, it was the only thing we talked about, but then I'd see the warmth in his brown eyes and I'd know—he cared.

"If this works, which I'm not saying it will, I think you should go for your file first," I said. "I'm sorry the last name didn't help." He'd tried every avenue available—phone books, Google, Facebook—and had found nothing on Jacob and Tyler's foster parents.

"No. I saw your dad and Mrs. Collins speaking privately this morning. Something's going down and we need to figure out what." Noah stared out into the rain, looking more like a Calvin Klein underwear model than a down-and-out foster kid. "Besides, I think we'll have a good crack at both files since you'll be doing hypnosis on Thursday. When I lure Mrs. Collins out tomorrow, you take a crack at yours then I'll take a crack at mine on Thursday."

"It's not hypnosis. Its relaxation therapy and I haven't agreed to it yet."

"It's perfect. You and Mrs. Collins will be in the sickroom and the office staff will be gone for the day. Besides, you said last week that Mrs. Collins thinks you're on the verge of a huge breakthrough."

The rain pounded against the roof of the garage. I glanced

over to Isaiah and Beth. I hated seeing her perched on Aires' favorite tool bench, but I liked the spark she put in Isaiah's eye.

How odd would it be to finally put the pieces together? To understand why I kept painting the night sky over and over again. To understand why my mother had told me bedtime stories while I bled on her floor. Maybe the nightly terrors would finally end and I could sleep a full restful night for the first time in two years.

But what if it didn't work? Mrs. Collins had said she thought my mind was ready to remember a little more—with appropriate prompting. That tidbit of information sent Ashley into a newsmagazine conversation binge about how we should try hypnotherapy again. It turned out she had already done the research, found another hypnotherapist and checked his credentials. Mrs. Collins knew the therapist so she was okay with it, yet not thrilled. Wanting to make Ashley happy, my father reluctantly agreed, and like always, I agreed by not disagreeing.

Besides, we weren't going after the full memory. Instead, our goal was to see if I could remember some of the moments before my mom dragged me to hell.

Supposedly, this relaxation therapy would be different than the one that cracked my mind the summer after the incident. Mrs. Collins said that therapist was inexperienced and pressed too hard, too fast. Thursday, Ashley would bring in a reputable "professional." Mrs. Collins assured me over and over again that she would be there to watch the session and that I would be safe—that my mind wouldn't fracture again.

So far, she'd been right about most things, but... I whispered so no one else could hear, "What if my dad's right? What if my mind can't handle the truth?"

"Baby, you've got enough strength and tenacity to take down drug dealers. You'll be fine."

I wished I had Noah's confidence and faith in me. Nothing ever shook him and for some reason, he thought I could climb mountains then juggle them. Someday, he was going to be very disappointed when he saw me for who I really was—a weak, pathetic person.

"Where's your dad?" Noah asked. "He's usually home by now." Ever since my dad figured out that Noah and Isaiah spent every Monday afternoon in our garage, he made it a point to be home from work as soon as humanly possible. He may have accepted Noah as my boyfriend, but he didn't like said boyfriend being alone with me.

My foot tapped nervously. Dad's strange behavior had taken a turn onto Bizarre Boulevard. "The Neon didn't make it through detailing. He's picking up my new used car today."

I'd loved that car. Aires and I car shopped for weeks, trying to find the right combination of deal and longevity. When I finally bought it, we picked up Mom to celebrate with a trip to Dairy Queen for chocolate malts. Good thing Isaiah had promised to fix Aires' car. Otherwise, I would have curled into a ball and cried over another loss of Aires…and my mom.

I caught Beth sending me a death glare while listening to my and Noah's conversation. We talked openly in front of her and Isaiah, but we never flat-out mentioned my issues. Noah considered them family and trusted them. I trusted Noah and liked Isaiah. I tolerated Beth.

"Gym was interesting today." Beth lips turned up into the devil's grin. Very rarely did she speak directly to me. Noah's pterodactyls began feeding on my stomach lining.

"Really?" I asked, meaning, *please go back to ignoring me.*

"I got to listen to your little cheerleader friend, Grace, make fun of you. I have to say, it's the first time she ever said anything to make me laugh."

Beth's words confirmed what I already knew in my heart: that publicly dating Noah had pushed Grace over the edge and destroyed the fragile remains of our friendship. If Beth meant to gut me open like a fish, then she'd succeeded. My stomach hurt like the night Luke rammed into me.

Noah pushed off the frame and stalked toward Beth. "Son of a bitch, Beth. What the fuck is wrong with you?"

"With me? You're the one hanging with Ms. Crazy." Beth jumped off the tool bench, accidentally hitting a glass full of washers. It rolled toward the edge of the bench.

"Beth, grab it!" I yelled.

She reached out, but her fingers clutched air as it rolled off the edge and shattered on the floor. The sound of glass shattering vibrated in my head. Images flickered and the black hole in my brain grew and rotated. A fuzzy picture forced its way forward as hammers pounded sharp nails into my skull.

I lay on the beige carpet of my mother's living room floor. Colored glass surrounded me, and blood. Lots and lots of blood. Pain sliced and seared my arms. I flipped to escape it, only to scream in agony as something sharp slashed my back.

My eyes fixed on the front door. I had to get there. I had to make it outside. Ignore the pain. Fight through the fear. I rolled to my side, crying out as glass dug into my knees and arms. Glass crunched under my weight. Every large chunk embedded in my muscles sliced like hot coals and every tiny shard knifed its edges into my skin. I crawled my way forward. Exhaustion weighed every movement, my mind unclear and my stomach uneasy. Oh, God, where was he? He said he was coming. Oh, God, please, Daddy, please come.

"Echo!"

I blinked rapidly to find myself crouched on the floor of the garage with my hands grasping my head. My heart thundered and every part of my body shook.

Noah sank beside me, eyes wide, face full of shock. He tucked my hair behind my ear and spoke in a low, soothing tone. "Baby, what happened? Are you in pain? Are you dizzy?"

My eyes darted around, sensing danger. Isaiah and Beth gave me the crazy stare. Noah framed my face with his hands, returning my attention to him. "Please, baby."

I swallowed in an attempt to help my dry mouth. "Stained glass. That was my mom's newest project."

Understanding warmed his eyes. "You remembered something."

Lightning flashed and crackled in the sky. My muscles jumped past my skin. Noah drew me closer to him. "It's okay. I've got you."

The back of my neck burned and my teeth chattered with my shaking body. I sniffed to keep away the tears. If I felt like this when I remembered a flash, what would happen if I remembered the whole thing? Would I break?

Hot tears pooled at the edge of my eyes and I swiped at them with the back of my sleeve. "I'm tired of having nightmares." *I'm tired of wondering if I'm losing my mind.*

Noah stroked my hair and his hold on me tightened. "We'll figure this out, Echo. I swear we'll figure it out."

NOAH

"I wish I could sleep with you," Echo's sexy-as-hell drowsy voice mumbled through the phone.

"Say the word, baby, and I'll rock your world." I'd gotten in from work a little after midnight and decided to give Echo a call. I sat on the dryer, giving Beth and Isaiah the private time they both claimed they didn't need. Isaiah pretended their make-out session never happened and Beth did the same. The good news was, Beth didn't bolt to her mom's or let some other guy use her. The bad news was, Isaiah hurt like hell. For the moment, I tried to forget my best friends' problems and focused on remembering Echo's delicious Cinnabon smell instead of the basement's damp, musty stench.

My little nymph's laughter filled my soul. "You're so bad. I'm talking about sleep. Like real sleep. Not sex."

"We don't need to have sex. There are other things I can do to help you sleep."

"You're impossible," she said over the rustle of sheets. "You make me feel safe, Noah. Maybe if I felt safe I could sleep."

Was that why Jacob had night terrors? Did he not feel safe? "I'll sneak into your room one night and we'll give it a shot. Sleep only, I promise."

"My dad would kill you and then lock me up in a convent."

"I'll take my chances."

"So...." Echo said in an extremely light tone. "I told you the ACT story wouldn't work." She giggled, enjoying being right.

Ten minutes into Echo's therapy session, I'd walked into Mrs. Collins's office and announced my sudden interest in college. I was right about one thing. Mrs. Collins did shit her pants. Instead of jumping up to get the information, she spoke rapidly, telling me she needed time to gather crap. She then handed me an appointment card for Thursday, right after school and moments before Echo's hypnosis appointment. "And you love being right, don't you?"

"Shhh. I'm basking in my moment." Echo yawned loudly. Her nightmares had increased in frequency and terror thanks to her therapy sessions. My gut told me she slept only a handful of hours each night, forcing herself to stay awake to avoid the dreams.

My mind wandered to Jacob and his nightmares. "If you knew the cause of your nightmares, would you talk to Mrs. Collins about it?"

"Are you high?" She didn't even wait for my answer of no. "She knows the cause of my nightmares, but to answer your question, yes. The lady is crazy, but I think she knows what she's doing. Well...kind of...a lot more than the other idiots I've seen. I don't know. I guess I kind of like her." Her voice slurred toward the end.

"Go to sleep, baby. I'll see you at school tomorrow."

Echo yawned again. "I'll get off, but I think I'm going to read for a while. Love you." She hung up, knowing I wouldn't say it back. I wished I had her courage.

"Tell me you broke up with her," Beth called out.

I hopped off the dryer to find Beth and Isaiah curled up on the bed watching television. "Why would I do that?"

"Because she's crazy. And before you defend her, remember I saw her little breakdown."

I took off my shirt, tossed it in my laundry basket and settled down on the couch to sleep. First thing I planned on buying when I got my own place was a bed. A big king-size bed with fluffy pillows and sheets.

"Don't you dare ignore me! Isaiah, tell Noah he's breaking some sort of guy code. For instance, you don't date crazy chicks."

Too easy. I opened my mouth to shove it back at Beth, but Isaiah stopped me. "Don't, man. Just don't."

I picked up an old stained pillow and tucked it under my head. "Quit being a bitch."

"Thanks," Isaiah mumbled. Beth hated being called a bitch. But when the shoe fit...

"Whatever. Keep telling yourself you're not dating Sybil. Does she have different names for her personalities?"

"Tone it down, Beth," Isaiah said.

This needed to stop. The harder Beth pushed at me and the more I defended Echo, the greater the odds of Beth laying into her. She had enough shit going down without having to deal with my loudmouthed, non-blood-related sister. If she ever found out, Echo would be beyond pissed, but I had to do it—for everyone's sanity. I swung an arm over my face, hoping once I said it, I could finally go to sleep. "At the end of her sophomore year, she was attacked. Echo's mind repressed the memories and

Mrs. Collins is trying to help her remember. What you saw in
the garage was her remembering a sliver of that night. Give her
a break."

A laugh track played on the television, followed by a smart-
ass comment by an actor. I waited for Beth's shitty comeback. I
readjusted my arm and caught her horrified expression. Isaiah
smoothed hair away from her face and whispered something to
her. She blinked back to life. "I'm sorry, Noah," she whispered.
"I'm sorry."

"...AND I PUT SOME information in there regarding the University of Louisville and the University of Kentucky, though the
state will pick up the tab for any state school. They both have
admirable architecture programs." Mrs. Collins took her first
breath in five minutes. The afternoon sun made her office into
a prison hot box.

"Architecture?" I checked her eyes to see if she'd taken a recent hit.

"Architecture." She smiled brightly.

I halfheartedly flipped through the mountain of brochures
sitting on my lap. My father had been an architect. He designed
the Habitat houses we'd built, even let me help him with it. I
began to read the requirements for admission. What was I doing?
I shut the folder.

"Echo trusts you," I said. Not sure where that came from, but
I needed to redirect myself from paths I couldn't visit.

Her eyes softened, but she quickly put on her puppy game
face. "Now, now, I already told you we won't discuss Echo." She
swiveled back and forth in her chair. "I take that back. We can
discuss anything that involves your relationship with Echo. I'll
be honest. I'm dying to know the details."

I didn't gossip, especially with my therapist. But Echo had looked exhausted today and I thought she may have fallen asleep during calculus. If her nightmares were that bad, what was life like for Jacob? "I'm not sure if I trust you. I have a shitty track record with adults."

"Yes. You do. What's troubling you, Noah?"

I ran a hand over my face and swallowed. What if I was wrong about her? She could destroy Jacob and also my chances of getting my family back together.

Mrs. Collins leaned her arms on the desk. "I swear to you, whatever you say will stay between us unless you tell me differently."

"Do you believe in God?" I asked.

The question caught her off guard, but she answered, "I do."

"Swear it to your God."

"I swear to God that I'll keep whatever you say private unless you direct me to do otherwise."

Damn her to hell if she lied to me. "Jacob started the fire."

She sucked in a breath and quickly regained her composure. "That's not what the report from the fire marshal said. It was ruled an accident."

"It was an accident. He didn't mean to do it." I kept eye contact. She had to believe me. Jacob would never intentionally hurt anyone.

She rubbed her eyes and shook her head as if trying to dispel what I had said. "Are you sure? Maybe he misunderstood something and only thinks he started it."

"He started it. But it's my fault." The guilt of my decisions that night would hound me forever. "Instead of staying home to camp out with my brothers, I went to the county fair with some girl. At the time that date seemed so important, I…" The guilt

I tried so hard to bury underneath layers and layers of avoidance rose to the surface in the form of nausea. I fought to keep myself from dry heaving.

I shoved the emotion back down. This wasn't about me. "It doesn't matter." I wiped my nose as anger began to seep into my bloodstream. If I couldn't make it through this session without crying, I didn't deserve my brothers. I cleared my throat.

"Mom told Jacob we'd do the campout the next Friday instead, but Jacob was pissed. After Mom and Dad put them to bed, Jacob woke Tyler up to make s'mores. Mom had a candle in the hall bathroom. I guess she left the matches out. Jacob lit the candle, they roasted marshmallows and then they went downstairs to sleep in the living room. Dad had set up the tent there before he knew I was going out."

Mrs. Collins held her hands to her face as if she was praying. Her eyes glistened. "The fire started in the hall bathroom. They assumed one of your parents lit the candle and forgot to blow it out. They had no idea it was your brother."

She knew the rest. My parents died in their bedroom and I came home to a roaring fire. "Jacob told me in the hospital and I promised never to tell anyone." A promise I'd now failed to keep.

"Why?" Her exasperation was clear. "Why didn't you tell someone? A social worker could have helped him."

I welcomed the familiar edge of betrayal and anger. "They separated us. Who would you have trusted?" Now to complete my own betrayal. "Help my brother."

She wiped her eyes. "I will. I promise." She checked the clock, our therapy session over.

Having nothing left to say, I stood, shoved my arms in my

jacket and prepared myself to see Echo on the other side of that door.

"And Noah," Mrs. Collins said. "I plan on helping you, too."

I didn't want help. I didn't need help, but I wasn't going to argue with the woman who could save my brother. I opened the door to find Echo leaning against the counter and staring at the floor, her foot tapping uncontrollably.

Echo

Noah looked drained. His dark eyes were heavy and his shoulders slumped forward. He closed the door to Mrs. Collins's office behind him and I met him halfway. "Are you okay?"

He gave me a halfhearted smile and pulled me into his body. "I hope I'm doing the right thing." He clutched me tighter.

I rested my head on his shoulder and tried to reassure him by rubbing his back. "I'm sure you are." He worried about Jacob and the possibility of trusting Mrs. Collins. "You'd never do anything to harm your brothers."

"Thanks." He kissed my hair and came close to squeezing the breath out of me. "I needed to hear that."

We stood still for several seconds before he released his death grip. "I'm going to wander the hallway to give you time to set up in the sickroom, then I'll sneak into her office."

This sounded oddly like breaking and entering, moving our plans into the land of illegal. My stomach shifted uneasily. "I don't know. Maybe we shouldn't. I don't want you to get caught in her office." Or get in trouble or get thrown out of school or go to jail.

Noah shot me his mischievous grin. "Have I ever mentioned you're paranoid?"

I crossed my arms over my chest. "Several times."

He kissed me as Mrs. Collins opened her door. "I'm pretending that I'm not seeing this."

Noah winked at me before he left the office. Mrs. Collins grinned from ear to ear, wagging her imaginary tail. "You two are a very cute couple. Is he taking you to prom?"

What a very strange question. "I don't know. Prom's over a month away. Anyway, Noah doesn't give me the impression he does dances."

"He came to the Valentine's Dance." She walked past me and down the hallway of the main office to the sickroom, beckoning with her fingers for me to follow.

"I think that was a one-time deal." I followed, reluctantly. "You know, I never agreed to this."

She laughed—actually laughed at me. "Oh, Echo. You're going to, if only on the principle that I'm asking you to do it. Your authority issues sure come in handy at times."

I stood in the middle of the sickroom and shoved my hands into my pockets. "Doesn't that break some sort of therapist code? You know, using my issues against me."

"Possibly." She gave me another smile. "Echo, this is Dr. Reed."

A.K.A. the relaxation therapist Ashley had handpicked. The short man stood and shook my hand. "How are you doing today, Echo?"

Terrible. "Fine."

"You'll be more relaxed if you lie down," said Mrs. Collins.

It took every ounce of strength to not immediately hop onto

the bed. My fingers drummed nervously in my pockets and my heart thundered. I'd show her.

She tilted her head. "I think Noah's rubbing off on you. Now that you've proven to me you're overcoming being a pushover, which I'll take credit for, would you please lie down?"

Since she asked nicely and my heart surged like a heart attack... "Sure."

Mrs. Collins dimmed the lights while I lay down on the uncomfortable, plastic-covered bed. A nice thick comforter lay at the end and a fluffy pillow at the head. I cocked an eyebrow.

"I wanted you to be comfortable."

A couple of candles sat on the counter next to the sink. "Are you going to light candles?"

"I was." She sighed. "But I'm not feeling very candlish right now. Did you tell your father that we could be a while? I don't want him upset with me when you don't come home at your normal time."

Now I sighed. "Yes. Mr. Overbearing is fully aware and I'm under direct orders to call him the moment I'm done."

She chuckled. "Me, too. Mr. Overbearing, hmmm? It definitely has a ring." Mrs. Collins lost her playful tone as she spoke to Dr. Reed. "Whenever you're ready."

Grabbing the comforter and fluffing the pillow, I snuggled down like a bear preparing for hibernation. If I was really going to do this, I might as well be warm.

Dr. Reed started off with some breathing and meditative exercises. After a while, my mind began to wander and his voice became this soothing, magnetic sound. "Tell me when you last felt safe, Echo. Really, really safe."

"Noah makes me feel safe."

I followed the smooth and reassuring voice as I imagined

Noah's warm, strong body and sweet musky scent enveloping me in his safe protective bubble.

"Dig deep, Echo. Very, very deep." He continued to calmly speak. I burrowed deeper into the covers and listened to his voice prod my mind to discover that one time I felt safe. Memories flipped like a slide show until I found one that warmed my heart.

"Aires made me feel safe." He hid with me in the closet several times when my mother suffered from a particularly energized manic episode. By the time Aires found me, my father had taken care of my mother, but I refused to leave the closet. He'd stay with me and read stories by flashlight until I fell asleep.

"Ashley." Funny, my voice sounded like my own and the world seemed far away. As a child, the sight of Ashley meant games, warm baths and dinners, normal bedtime stories and nighttime songs.

"Daddy." My protector. My savior. He convinced my mother to take her medication and she did. For him. She loved him. He made us a family and during those dark moments when my mother's illness threatened to rip us apart, he held me. Like in the hospital, when I couldn't sleep, terrified of the first wave of nightmares, he lay with me in bed and held me, whispering over and over again how much he loved me.

The scene in my mind altered. I was safe. Somehow I knew that, but this…something was off…wrong…

Moonlight bathed my mother's living room, reflecting off thousands of pieces of glass scattering the floor.

Warm liquid trickled down my arms and I fought to breathe through the sobs of pain. Burning pain. Tearing pain. Throbbing pain. Every muscle screamed and my throat ran raw with each sensation. Struggling to keep upright on my hands and knees, I compelled myself forward. I couldn't let my eyes close. I couldn't.

But my eyelids were heavy and so were my muscles. I could rest. For a few seconds. Yes, I could rest.

I gave in to the weight of my body, collapsing onto the glass-filled serenity of the floor. If I didn't move, the glass could no longer shred me to pieces. I breathed with the slow steady rhythm of my heart and let my mind wander to other thoughts beyond pain and blood. Sleep. Yes. I needed sleep.

No! I forced my eyes open and blinked rapidly to focus. Edges of the clear glass now shone with red—blood. My blood.

"Daddy!" I whispered. Daddy should be here by now. I sent out a plea in my head, begging him to somehow hear me and know....

I focused on the door, but there was no way I could make it. Not now. My legs were dead to me—no control, no movement.

My arms. I could still move my arms, but the pain. "Oh, God!" The pain.

"I'm so sorry, Echo. I never should have let you stand up, but the pain will be over soon." Ignoring the glass, my mother lay down beside me, settling her head on the floor inches from mine. Her wide, glazed-over eyes held a hint of concern.

"Don't cry." Her callused fingers wiped the tears off my face. "We'll be with Aires soon and then there will be no more pain or sadness. Only joy and happiness and we'll be able to paint—you and I—and Aires will be able to tinker with as many cars as he wants."

I hardly recognized my own voice, hoarse and shaky. "I don't want to die, Momma. Please, don't let me die."

"Shhh," she cooed. "Don't think of it as dying." She yawned

and her eyelids fluttered. "We're going to sleep and when we wake, we'll be with your brother again."

She smiled and I sobbed, "Oh, God, Daddy."

My stomach sank. I'd never see my dad again. My father, who was supposed to pick me up, my father, who I prayed over and over again would walk through that door as promised. *Please, Daddy, please. I need you.*

"I'll tell you a story, just like I did when you were a baby. Cassandra had a beautiful daughter named Andromeda…."

I opened my eyes and blinked several times. Mrs. Collins stood in the door frame and Dr. Reed sat in the chair next to the sickbed. I kicked off the comforter. Sweat dripped down the side of my face. Blood hammered my head and my heart thrashed in the same rhythm. My skin stung as I peeled myself off the bed and my body felt light after experiencing the heaviness of the memory.

Cold air slapped me and disoriented my body and mind. I had fallen and shattered one of the stained glass windows my mother had propped in the living room, but why? Was it an accident? It couldn't have been, because she seemed so calm and peaceful…resolved. But she'd apologized.

"Daddy," I whispered. Tears stung my eyes and I immediately sought Mrs. Collins for an explanation. There had to be an explanation because he wouldn't have left me there—never. My throat closed and swallowing wouldn't open it up. "Where was he?"

Mrs. Collins said, "I think we've done enough for today."

I waved my hand in the air, refusing that answer. "No. No. I remembered something and now it's your turn."

"I understand your frustration, but your mind needs to handle this slowly."

A strange uneasiness clawed at my heart and everything within me twisted and dropped. A single word tore at my heart… *betrayal*. "Where was my father!"

From behind Mrs. Collins came my father's voice. "I forgot to pick you up."

NOAH

I wandered the hallways for twenty minutes. Echo had radiated nerves. I wanted to give her plenty of time to make it to the sickroom and be well underway before I attempted the office.

"Aires made me feel safe." Echo's voice carried to the front office. Dammit, Mrs. Collins had kept the door to the sickroom open. In theory, there would have been no need to close the door because the school should have been abandoned.

"Ashley." I froze. Echo sounded drowsy. Part of me wanted to stay there and listen, but then I wouldn't have a chance to find both of our answers.

My mother would sure be proud of me—breaking into my counselor's office, though I reminded myself that her door hung wide open. I tried to shove away the guilt eating at my gut, but it faded the moment I saw my name poking out from underneath two other files.

I grabbed the folder and immediately flipped it to the page with my brothers' information. On the back of one of the college brochures Mrs. Collins gave me, I copied their data, careful not to miss a single piece.

"Noah. What are you doing here?" Mr. Emerson scared the crap out of me, but I emptied all emotion from my face, discreetly closing my file before I spun around.

I held up my brochures. "College planning." Might as well rack up some brownie points.

"Good." He glanced back into the main office. "Good for you."

"I don't want to die, Momma. Please, don't let me die." Echo's distressed voice vibrated down the hallway. I could hear the underlying terror. Both Mr. Emerson and I took a step toward the sickroom. Our simultaneous movements caught each other's attention. She screamed, "Oh, God, Daddy!"

Mr. Emerson turned a weird shade of gray. "I think you should go."

My heart beat faster. Muscles tense, I glared at Mr. Emerson, waiting for him to give me some sort of explanation for why the girl I loved was screaming his name in panic and desperation.

He placed a hand on the wall and leaned into it. "Go on, Noah."

Should I go or should I stay? If I stayed, I'd have to explain my presence, risking being caught, and losing the information on my brothers. I also risked an argument with her father.

If I left, I was a dick. Not the champion Echo needed me to be. I'd make it up to her. I'd find a way. I left the office and dialed Echo's cell.

"It's me. You know what to do," said her sweet voice.

"Hey, baby. Call me when you can. I..." Love you. "I need to hear your voice."

Echo

"You forgot to pick me up?" Everything inside of me became as hard as a rock and just as numb. "Like you forgot to pick up eggs at the store or clothes at the dry cleaners? Like you forgot to pick up a piece of cereal that fell on the floor or a can that fell out of the grocery bag? You forgot to pick me up."

My father tugged his ear and kept his gaze on the floor. "I, uh…" He cleared his throat. "Ashley had her high school reunion that night and we were running late from the art show. I dropped you off at your mother's so you could tell her about winning the Governor's Cup and time got away from me."

My eyes flickered between my father and Mrs. Collins. Dr. Reed shifted, but I ignored him. Mrs. Collins stood uncharacteristically still, her eyes glued on me.

"Which was it?" I demanded. "Time got away or you forgot to pick me up?"

His Adam's apple bounced when he swallowed. The chaos in my head cleared for an instant as the lightbulb went on. "You were supposed to drop her off at the reunion, then come and get me. It was supposed to be a short visit, but Ashley convinced you to stay."

He barely nodded. "I'm sorry, Echo."

I pushed against the black hole in my mind. There had to be more. "Obviously Mom wasn't with it, so why did you leave me there?" Better question, why did I stay?

Mrs. Collins forced optimism into her tone and smiled. "Why don't we go into my office and talk this new progress through. We can get a drink. You like Diet Coke, right?"

Anger gave me a boldness I'd only dreamed of having. "I'm not going anywhere until he answers. Why did you leave me there?"

"Mr. Emerson, let's give Echo some time to collect herself while you and I have a chat."

"No way." I took a step toward my father. "He's answering me."

"Echo…" Mrs. Collins began to protest, but I put my hand up to stop her.

"You think he's controlling now? You should have seen him after the divorce. I didn't see my mom for two years. Do you know what middle school was like without a mom? Periods, training bras, boys. I had no one."

"You had Ashley," my father said. "I wasn't keeping your mother from you. She knew what she had to do to get visitation. She chose not to do it."

"No!" I bit. "You chose Ashley and ruined my mother. But Mom did get herself together, didn't she? She got help. She took her meds and you know what my father did, Mrs. Collins? He treated her like a serial killer. She had to jump through hoops of fire in order to see us. He never once allowed visitation unless he was a hundred percent sure she was stable. So tell me, *Dad,* why did you leave me there?"

"Because I was in a hurry and didn't check on her when I dropped you off." My father met my eyes for the first time and I saw the truth. "I was only supposed to be gone fifteen minutes. A half hour tops."

"Did I call?" Because I would have. Living through sixteen years of my mother's highs and lows had taught me that her on no meds equaled adult-supervised visitation.

He looked away again. "Yes."

The heaviness of his words crushed my heart. "Did you answer?"

My father shoved his hands into his pockets and closed his eyes.

Idiot. I was an idiot. No one loved me. Nothing I could do or say would ever change that fact. My father merely mentioned jumping and I asked if I needed to buy a trampoline. That wasn't love; that was control. Dad chose Ashley and Aires chose the Marines over me. Noah still hadn't told me that he loved me even though I'd said the words to him.

I used to believe my father cared. After all, he cared enough to try to control every aspect of my life and I let him. I let him because I loved him and I wanted so desperately for him to love me back. But I'd been wrong, so wrong. He didn't even care enough to answer the phone. I was unlovable before my mother ever touched me.

I brushed past him and grabbed my stuff out of Mrs. Collins's office.

"I'm sorry." My father blocked my path as I tried to leave. I ignored the hoarseness of his voice, stepped around him and bolted down the hallway. I was done being controlled.

NOAH

I should have stayed. If the roles had been reversed, she would have waited for me, but I needed to see my brothers. When she called me back, I'd run by and see her.

Newly built large, spacious houses formed a circle around a large park. The full deal—walking paths, trees, bushes, benches and the largest playground on the planet.

Two children flew out of a blue three-story house. My dad would have loved it—Second Empire architecture: mansard roof, dormer windows, square tower, decorative brackets and molded cornice. I remembered my dad laughing while showing me pictures. "Think *Lady and the Tramp,* Noah," he'd said.

As the children raced closer, I recognized Mom's smile. The two of them scrambled up the stairs of the play gym and flipped to the tallest slide. Jacob stopped repeatedly to help the struggling Tyler up several of the lifts.

I got out of the car and sat on a bench far from the playground and watched my brothers laugh and play. Everything inside me hurt. They were so close and all I wanted was to be with them. I pulled out my phone, reminding myself of my purpose—to prove that their foster parents were unfit.

Speaking of, where the hell was either Carrie or Joe? Jacob was only eight. Tyler wasn't even five yet. Shouldn't they be supervised? I raised my phone to take a picture of the situation when a voice caught me off guard. "A little to the right. She's sitting on the bench under the maple."

Mrs. Collins took a seat on the bench beside me. Sure enough, from a bench under the tree, Carrie watched my brothers' every movement. I shoved my phone back into my pocket.

"They like to slide—your brothers, that is. The two of them could spend hours flipping up and sliding down."

We sat next to each other in silence and listened to my brothers giggle from afar. I had no clue how to get out of this one. Silence: the defense of the guilty.

"So, were the two of you working together this entire time or did you jump at the opportunity when it presented itself?"

Might as well try denial. "I think you've lost your mind."

"I'm a slob, but I'm an organized slob. You put your file back in the wrong spot. Do you have any idea how much trouble you could be in for this?"

Dammit. "What do you want to know?" Maybe if I played, she'd cut me some slack.

"Were you and Echo working together?"

I would never sell Echo out. "Next."

Mrs. Collins sighed. "I promised Echo privacy and she trusted me. You shouldn't have been anywhere near that office today."

I swallowed down the guilt over leaving her. "Is she okay?"

Tyler squealed when Carrie pushed him on the swing. Mrs. Collins smoothed back her hair. "You should probably call her."

I clasped my hands loosely between my knees as I leaned forward. "What happened to never discussing Echo with me?"

"What can I say? It's been a bad day all around."

We sat in silence again. Joe pulled into the driveway and ran across the street to the park. Tyler leapt off the swing and jumped into his open arms. I felt like someone punched me in the gut.

"They're happy here, Noah. Are you that excited to rip them away from all of this?"

I had to admit, it was nice here. Guess financial gurus really did do well.

"What will you have to offer them? A two-bedroom apartment in a less-than-desirable end of town? I'm assuming you read the file. They go to the best private school in the county. In the state, actually. Both of your brothers have multiple extracurricular activities. How are you going to balance a full-time job and two little boys? How will you find the time to juggle their current schedule? Even better, how can you afford it?"

Joe covered his eyes with one hand and began to play hide-and-seek with my brothers. Jacob hid at the top of the slide while Tyler hid behind Carrie on the bench. When Joe stopped counting, he saw Tyler immediately but pretended he didn't, to Tyler's delight.

Mrs. Collins leaned into my line of sight. "There are other options. You can go to college. Continue your relationship with Echo. Become the man your parents intended you to be."

My muscles tightened. "What does Echo have to do with this?"

"Have you ever asked her what her plans for the future are? Do you think she's ready to date a single dad?"

I met Mrs. Collins's eyes for the first time. Sincerity screamed from them. I swore under my breath and returned to watching my brothers. Echo. In all of my imagined scenarios involving my brothers or Echo, I'd never once thought of them in the same future. Separate—yes. Together—no. How the hell did the two combine—or could they?

Carrie and Joe called out to the boys, informing them that it was time to go inside. Jacob and Tyler ran ahead. I watched as a black Suburban pulled out of a spot a few feet down from my brothers.

Everything in my world slowed. I jumped to my feet and began to run toward them as Jacob and Tyler bolted in front of the moving car. *No. Please, no. Not them, too.* Brakes squealed, a horn blared and Jacob wrapped himself around our younger brother.

My heart beat once when the car stopped inches from Jacob and Tyler. Carrie and Joe swooped them up and hurried into the house. My blood pulsed nervously through my entire body and I could only take shallow breaths.

Mrs. Collins placed a hand on my arm. "They are okay, Noah. They're safe."

Fuck that. "They'll be safer with me."

Echo

My father followed me home, running two red lights in order to keep up. His tires screamed when he flung his car into Park, door open before he turned off the engine. "Echo!"

Oh, there's the man I knew. Drill sergeant tone, fast as a rabbit. He could bark orders at me as much as he wanted. I'd discharged myself from his military. He grabbed my arm the moment he caught up with me in the kitchen.

He slammed the door behind him, causing Ashley to jump from the table. Her tabloid magazine fell to the floor. "What's happened?"

I jerked my arm away. "I'll tell you what happened. I was born. A couple of years later my genius parents figured out that my mother was bipolar. While she struggled to understand her condition you weaseled your way into our lives and tossed her out right when she finally accepted that she needed the meds."

Ashley blinked rapidly and looked to my father for reassurance. "Owen, what happened?"

She hurt me. Ashley may have not have dug the cuts into my arms, but she was every bit as responsible. My blood dripped from her manicured hands. "How many times did he start to answer his phone and you stopped him? Did you seduce him into staying later at your stupid reunion or did you remind him that I wasn't worth the effort?"

Her evil mouth fell into the shape of a round little O and her bloodred lipstick glowed against her now pale face. Disgust weaved through me. "Tell me, Ashley, when they brought my bloodless, lifeless body into the hospital, were you relieved when they told you that I may not make it? Did you celebrate that I was finally out of your life? After all, Aires was dead, my mom cast out for good. I was the only thing left standing in your way."

She shook her head repeatedly and a single fake tear ran down her cheek. "No. I have always loved you. You, Aires and your father. All I ever wanted to do is to be your mother."

The thin thread holding back any control snapped so loudly I blinked once. My eyes widened to the point of threatening to fall out of their sockets. "You are such a…"

"Stop it, Echo," my father bellowed while forcing himself between me and Ashley. "You're mad at me, not her. Leave Ashley out of this."

I screamed at him, "Leave her out of this? She's in this. She's all over this. Tell me she told you to accept the phone call. Tell me she explained that whatever pathetic thing you were doing wasn't more important than your own daughter!"

He said nothing, but a single muscle in his jaw jumped. I'd found it. The truth. The truth neither of them ever wanted me to know. My mother always told me that the truth shall set me free. I didn't feel free. Betrayal poisoned my bloodstream like a black sludge, taking over everything in its path. The two of them could no longer hide their sins. I'd remembered and I demanded penance.

My father stood stoically still. He'd killed my soul and I wanted his in return. "Mom fell apart after you left her for the nanny. And then you stole custody of us. You left her with nothing. You were her whole world. She had nothing left to live for, no reason to take the meds. You left her right when she was getting her act together!"

His eyes narrowed. "Are those words yours, Echo, or your mother's? You're right on one count. I did everything I could to make sure I got custody of you and your brother. I hired the best lawyers weeks before I served your mother to guarantee she'd never share custody with me. My only regret is that I allowed visitation, to give her time to spew those lies and to hurt you."

Mom had said Aires and I were a game to him. That he used us to hurt her. "You mean you regret having me. You regret that I found out that you will pick Ashley over everything and everyone else." I screamed so loudly my throat became raw. Every part of me shook and heat flushed my cheeks and the back of my neck. Had he ever loved me? Had he? "How could you abandon me?"

The anger drained out of my father's face, leaving him pale and old. "I'm sorry. You have no idea how sorry I am."

I sniffed and fought to keep the tears from falling. I would not cry in front of him. I wouldn't give him the satisfaction of knowing he'd ripped me into a thousand pieces. But I needed rest. I needed all the voices and nightmares to go away. I had no one now. No one. And damn them for making me beg for the one thing that could grant me a few hours' peace. "I want my sleeping pills. I'm tired and I need to sleep. For one night, I just need to sleep."

Ashley slid by my father's side, placing a hand on his shoulder. She never once looked at me. "I'll get them. The doctor said you can move up to ten mg."

"I'll be in my room." I left, not caring if I ever spoke to my father again.

NOAH

Last night, Echo called while I was at work. She left a message telling me that she was taking sleeping pills and wouldn't answer her phone until morning. She'd sounded...destroyed.

On edge, I waited by her locker before school, but she never showed, leaving me sitting there in business technology losing my damn mind. Three messages. I left the girl three messages. Hell, I didn't leave messages, yet I'd left this girl three. Where was she?

I stared at her empty seat in the front, willing her to magically appear. Mr. Foster droned on and on. Each second on the clock took three times longer than normal to tick away. My right pocket vibrated and I dropped my pencil in order to retrieve it. Both Isaiah and Rico shot me a glance the moment they heard the vibration.

When I checked the caller ID, my heart leapt. Echo.

"Mr. Hutchins?" asked Mr. Foster.

Damn. "Yes, sir." My phone stopped vibrating as Echo went to voice mail.

"Is that a cell phone I hear?"

"Yes," Isaiah piped up. "Sorry, sir. I forgot to turn mine off this morning."

Mr. Foster looked back and forth between me and Isaiah, obviously not buying it, but he held his hand out to Isaiah. "You know the rules. You can collect it at the end of the day."

Isaiah handed over his phone without another word, giving me a sly smile when he returned to his seat. I nodded my thanks. What did I do to deserve a brother like him?

He leaned over to me once Mr. Foster resumed his boring lecture. "Tell her I said hi."

I TORE OUT OF CLASS, HITTING the speed dial in record time. My heart stuttered with every ring. *Dammit. Pick up.* Her beautiful voice filled the line. "It's me. You know what to do."

"You're killing me, baby." I hung up.

I reached my locker, threw my books in and checked voice mail. Isaiah sauntered to the other side of the hallway and leaned against the wall. Beth joined him seconds later, unlit cigarette in hand. "What's going on?"

"Echo called last period and he missed it. Now he's pissed," Isaiah answered.

"No, I'm not," I snapped. Yes, I was.

Isaiah shrugged while suppressing a smile.

Echo had left a short, lifeless message, "Hey, I guess I'll try you later. Love you."

Dammit, Echo. You gotta give me more than that. Lunch and three more periods. I wasn't going to survive. "I'm going to grab some food. I'll see you guys in the cafeteria."

"Wait. We'll come," Beth called out. "I'll smoke later."

I took nothing with me to the cafeteria, so instead of heading to my table, I went straight for the line. Echo's little gal pals gathered at their table, oblivious to the fact that somewhere on the other side of the school walls, she was suffering. I did a double take when blue eyes met mine.

Lila typed furiously into her phone before calling out to me, "Noah!" Her entire table froze and stared at her.

"Lila?" Grace asked meekly.

Lila sent Grace a death glare and walked over to me. My opinion of her grew. "Have you talked to Echo?"

"Messages only. What's going on?"

Lila glanced over my shoulder. I followed her gaze to see Luke staring at us intently. She continued, "I don't know. She called me last night, but I was out with Stephen."

At that exact moment both of our phones chirped to notify us of a text message. We simultaneously pulled them out and I sucked in a breath as I read the message from Echo: I'm across the street.

Thank you, baby, for those four beautiful words. I turned on my heel and mumbled to Lila, "Let's go."

I hesitated when Lila continued to stare at her phone. "She needs me," she said and her phone chirped again. "But she says it's okay if I don't come." A war of emotions played over her face. "I have a test next period and…"

"You don't skip."

She smoothed her hair. "Look, she keeps telling me that you're this great guy. Do you think you could wow me and keep my best friend together until I can take over after school?"

I could do one better. I could take care of her now *and* after school. "Yeah."

"Tell her I love her, okay?" said Lila. "And I'll be right there as soon as I can."

"Yeah." This girl really did care about Echo. "I can do that."

WITH THE WINDOWS OPEN, ECHO sat in the driver's side of the gray Honda Civic her father had bought her to replace the Dodge Neon. I slid my car next to hers. As I was about to cut my engine, she turned hers on. She stared at me as I rolled down my window.

"I want to go someplace," she said, "but I don't want to go alone. I'm sorry I asked you to skip."

I wasn't sorry. "I'll drive you anywhere you want to go, baby."

I hoped for a smile, but instead she shook her head. Whatever happened yesterday had to be big. "Will you follow me? I kinda need a few more minutes to myself."

"Whatever you need." Even though I craved to be breathing the same air as her.

"Noah?" she said before I rolled my window up. "Thanks for skipping for me." And finally, she smiled. It wasn't huge or full of joy, but still it was there.

"Anything for you."

MOM LOVED DAYS LIKE THIS: spring warmth with those big fluffy white clouds against a royal-blue sky.

I hated this place, no matter the weather. Resthaven would always be that gray, rainy, muggy day in June, with my brothers and me standing under a half-assed thrown-together tent. Tyler strangled my neck, crying for Mom, and Jacob asked if Mom and Dad were going to get wet, explaining to me over and over again that Mom hated getting wet. She allowed no splashing in the bathtub. Dad was in a suit and Dad would be upset if it got wet.

For the first time in my life, I'd wanted to die. I wished I had been asleep in my bed and died right alongside my parents, but then if I'd been home, it never would have happened.

My guilt was a yoke around my neck. My burden to handle. And when I graduated, I'd make it right. I'd put my family back together again.

I parked behind Echo in the east garden, under the towering oak trees. Echo had caught the traffic light entering this place and I hadn't, giving her a head start. She sat cross-legged in the middle of the cemetery section, resting her head on her joined hands, staring at a white marble tombstone. Her red curls moved with the gentle breeze and the sun shined directly on her—an angel right in the middle of hell.

She never took her eyes off the tombstone. "Thanks for doing this, Noah. I know being here is hard for you, too."

Hard was an understatement, but it only showed how much I cared for her. "Do you think Mrs. Collins will blame me for your sudden urge to cut school?"

Echo opened her mouth to answer, but exhaled instead. I'd said it to lighten her mood, but she was too deep to see daylight.

I sat beside her. Unable to stop myself, I raked my hand through the curls flowing down her back. Touching her in this moment was a necessity. I liked the tombstone's simplicity: Aires Owen Emerson: son, brother, Marine.

"What did you remember?"

She rubbed her chin against her clasped hands. "He left me there. At my mother's. I called and he didn't answer. He…um… didn't." Echo lowered her head.

I continued to comb through her silky hair and listened to the birds calling out to one another. Her shoulders never shook. No tears streamed down her face. The worst type of crying wasn't the kind everyone could see—the wailing on street corners, the tearing at clothes. No, the worst kind happened when your soul wept and no matter what you did, there was no way to comfort it. A section withered and became a scar on the part of your soul that survived. For people like me and Echo, our souls contained more scar tissue than life.

She picked at the blades of grass. "I'm alone now. Aires is dead. Mom is God knows where. My friends...well...you know. Dad was a long shot, but I pretended I had him. I tried to become the daughter he wanted to love, but..." Echo shook her head. "It sucks to be alone."

"Come here, baby." And with my words, Echo leaned into me: soft, pliant, broken. "You're not alone," I whispered into her hair as I cradled her in my arms. "You're not alone, because you have me." *And I love you, more than you could ever know.*

Echo

Noah offered to call in to work so we could spend the evening together. A huge part of me hoped he would. I wanted to stay in his arms for the rest of my life. Because of that, it took every ounce of self-control to not jump on his offer. I knew he needed the money. Besides, Lila began texting me every two seconds the moment school let out.

"Your dad called my mom looking for you," Lila said from my right. "She told him you were here."

We sat on the massively wide stairs of her back deck, overlooking the field behind her house. Wind chimes tinkled with the gentle breeze and the sun kissed my bare arms. "Is he coming to get me?" He had to know I'd skipped school.

"No, but he did ask my mom to remind you that your curfew is midnight."

The urge to laugh shook my body and the harder I tried to keep it in, the more powerful it grew. Finally, I let it out. Lila smiled at first and then began to laugh with me. "What's so funny?"

I took a deep breath and wiped my eyes. "My father left me for dead and I've got a freaking curfew."

Lila giggled. "That is kind of funny." She sighed. "What are you going to do?"

"I don't know." And I didn't. The mere idea of going home grated on my nerves like sandpaper. "You know what I do know?"

"What?"

I extended my arms. "I miss the feel of the sun on my skin. Just curious, how would you react if I wore short sleeves to school?"

Lila's mouth twitched up. "No differently than if you wore long sleeves."

"Grace would have a coronary."

"Grace can go to hell." Lila's uncharacteristic outburst of anger surprised me. "We've got two months until graduation. You can live life to please everyone else or please yourself. Come next fall, I'll be living large at the University of Florida and forgetting that I ever made friends with people like Grace. I've made my decision. What's yours?"

NOAH

As soon as I finished my shower, I planned on calling Echo then heading to Antonio's for the rest of the party. At eleven, Echo would easily still be awake. Hopefully, Lila had helped lessen the blow of her new memory. I shouldn't have gone to work. I should have stayed with her. Man, I was a dick. I'd make it up to her tomorrow.

Three years ago, I'd imagined spending my senior year choosing where to play college ball, not negotiating my salary and benefits for becoming the day manager at the Malt and Burger. But how could I argue with a salary, insurance and steady hours? I wouldn't break the bank though I could afford something small and decent for me and my brothers. I had a long list of things I preferred to do over flipping burgers. Flipping burgers and teaching people to flip burgers: my fucking dream come true.

The hot water washed away the grease from my shift. Apartment hunting would be next: a two-bedroom, maybe one. I could sleep on the couch and give my brothers the bedroom.

Either way, my apartment required a good showerhead and lots of scalding water to erase the flipping-burger tedium.

After ten minutes, the hot water faded, leaving only steam. The fog crept into the bathroom and into my brain. What was I doing? My mother had taken me to her office on campus at least once a month. "College is a must, even if you're military bound. College first, then decide your future," her smooth voice preached.

I wiped the mirror and saw my mother's eyes staring back. "You didn't tell me what the fuck to do if you died."

Water droplets hung in the heavy damp air and on my body. The heater in the basement pounded several times before kicking on, sending cooler air through the vent on the floor. I stood there staring, waiting for her answer.

"Noah?"

A welcome voice—not my mother's, but welcome all the same: Echo. A smile spread across my face. This was too good. Me in a towel, alone in the house with my nymph. I left the bathroom. "'Sup, baby."

Echo peeked around the corner and red curls bounced when she rapidly turned her head in the opposite direction. "Oh, my God, I am so sorry. I'll wait outside or something until you... um...you know, get clothes on."

I padded into the living room behind her, running my hand down her back. "What are you doing here? You and Lila run out of girl gossip?"

"I, um, made a decision. Can you put some clothes on?"

"Cutting it close to curfew, aren't you?"

She shrugged and avoided looking in my direction.

"Come on." I grabbed her hand and led her toward the basement.

"No, really, Noah," she said. "I'll wait until you're dressed."

So I could miss that blush creeping across her face? No way. "Turn away if you want, but I don't mind you looking." I let go of her hand when we reached the bottom of the stairs and walked over to my basket of clothes, picking up a pair of jeans. "Turn away now. Or not." I glanced over my shoulder. Echo had her back to me and her eyes covered. I chuckled to myself. "What's going on, baby? You're not a rule-breaker."

"I don't feel like going home. At least not yet."

I zipped my jeans. "You can look now."

Echo turned and her smoldering emerald eyes drifted to my bare chest. She licked her lips and quickly focused on folding a blanket Beth had left on the couch. "You're still wet."

She wanted me—just not as badly as every throbbing muscle in my body wanted her. Behind the hunger in her eyes rested a quiet pain. Echo placed the expertly folded blanket back on the couch and smoothed it several times, insisting on finding perfection in a world where none existed.

"If you don't want to go home, what do you want to do?" I asked, sitting on the bed.

Echo plopped down on the couch, wrapping her arms around herself. "Lila told me I could stay the night with her, but Stephen ended up coming over…" Her tone indicated she'd rather embed nails in her forehead than return to that.

"Antonio's parents are out of town. Beth and Isaiah are already there and plan on spending the night." I didn't need to mention the amount of pot Beth had taken with her.

I barely heard her muffled comment of "Yay," but the sarcastic jazz hands were hard to miss.

"He specifically called and asked if I was bringing you." And that would be the reason I never brought up the party to Echo.

Homeboy or not, he was too friendly with my girl. But if hanging with another art guru made her smile, I'd take her.

"Can we…" Her knee bounced. "Can we stay here?"

"Yes."

She stretched her sleeves and stared at the ground. At least she didn't wear the gloves around me anymore. I could think of plenty of things to do with Echo in a house alone. Hell, I'd fantasized about moments like this, but damn if she didn't make me want to be a better man. "Want to do normal?"

A curious flicker crossed her face. "You want to study?"

"There are other normals." Discreetly readjusting my jeans, I picked up the remote, joined Echo on the couch and pulled her slender body next to mine. I relished the feel of her melting into me as I flipped to a promising channel. "I'll even make popcorn."

Throughout the movie, we moved to eat popcorn, shifted to get comfortable, only to end up uncomfortable; an awkward dance of keeping my hands and parts from familiar and unfamiliar areas of Echo's divine body. I was capable of being a gentleman for the length of one movie, at least. The credits rolled and my left hand, which I'd placed behind my head to avoid her tempting tummy, tingled with numbness.

My patience finally snapped. "This is ridiculous." I swept her up and swung her over my shoulder, her bare feet dangling in front of me.

Tinkling laughter filled the room. "What are you doing?" I tossed her onto the bed. Her fire-red hair sprawled over the pillow. My siren smiled up at me.

"Getting comfortable," I said.

Echo blinked and raw hunger replaced the laughter that danced in her eyes moments before. Her delicate fingers glided up my arm, exciting every cell. "You don't look very comfortable." The sultry tone caused something deep within me to stir.

I swallowed, attempting to push away the unexpected flutter of nerves in my stomach. "Echo…"

My heart swelled, causing my chest to ache and breathing to become nearly impossible. Paralyzed by her beauty, I hovered over her. She was no nymph, but a goddess.

Her hands continued their burning climb up my arm and onto my chest. Bold moves for her. Echo's breasts rose and fell at a faster rate. "I want to stay with you tonight."

I sucked in a breath as her fingers trailed down the indentations of my chest muscles and willed her to continue as they made their slow descent. Caressing the warm redness forming on her cheek, I sank onto the bed beside her. "Are you sure?"

"Yes."

"What about your dad?"

She whispered, "I'll handle my dad."

Tender hands wove into my hair, guiding my head to hers. I inhaled her delicious, warm scent: cinnamon rolls, straight out of the oven. The first taste of her lips didn't disappoint. Sweet sugar teased my tongue, heightening my awareness of the gift Echo offered to me.

This girl owned my soul and stole my heart. She'd opened herself to me, giving me love and never asked for anything in return. I deepened our kiss, the words *I love you* stuck in my mind.

Echo

Noah trailed a line of blazing kisses along the nape of my neck, confusing my brain. Part of me responded to him, clung to him, held him tighter to me. The other part froze in fear, absolutely terrified of the unknown, horrified of disappointing him. "Tell me what to do."

His warm breath tickled my ear. "Relax."

But against my will, my muscles did the exact opposite. Underneath Noah's typically inviting touch, I went rigid. "Please, Noah, I don't want to do this wrong. Tell me how to make you feel good."

He shifted so that his body rested beside mine, his leg and arm still draped over me. I felt small under his warmth and strength. His chocolate-brown eyes softened. "Being with you feels good. Touching you—" he tucked a curl behind my ear "—feels good. I have never wanted anyone like I want you. There's nothing you can do wrong when just breathing makes everything right."

I wanted to believe him, but Noah was experienced and I

…wasn't. He could be trying to make me feel better, yet bored with my lack of knowledge.

His hand framed my face and his tone was edged with husky authority. "I want you, but only if you want me."

"It hurts the first time. My friends, they all told me that." And the second and the third, and eventually, sometimes, it didn't hurt. "And I should tell you, I'm on birth control. So… you know…I'm protected from…" Babies. "Stuff. But you should use something too—because."

The wicked smile I loved spread across his face. His lips touched mine, tenderly drawing a response. "Relax and I'll take care of everything."

I kissed him back, allowing my arms to wrap around him. His fingers gently massaged my neck, releasing the tension, erasing my unease. The kiss became a drug and I craved more with every touch. Our bodies twined so tightly to one another, I had no idea where I began and he ended.

Noah felt strong and warm and muscular and safe and he smelled, oh, God, delicious. I couldn't stop kissing him if my life depended upon it: his lips, his neck, his chest, and Noah seemed as hungry as me. We rolled and we touched and we shed unwanted clothes. I moaned and he moaned and my mind and soul and body stood on the edge of pure ecstasy.

And I waited. I waited for that moment of pausing for protection and then the burning pain my friends described, but Noah never stopped and the pain never came, not even when I whispered his name and praised God several times in a row. Both of us gasped for air while kissing each other softly and I struggled to comprehend I was still a virgin.

He shifted off of me and tugged me close to him. My entire body became lazily warm, happy and sated. I listened to his heartbeat and closed my eyes, enjoying the relaxing pull of his hand through my hair. "Noah," I whispered. "I thought…" we were going to make love.

He tipped up my chin, forcing me to look at him. "We have forever to work up to that, Echo. Let's enjoy every step of the way."

My mind drifted this way and that. Mostly between focusing on his heart, his touch and the sweetest word I had ever heard: *forever.*

One clear thought forced my eyes open again. "You're putting me to sleep."

"So?" he asked a little too innocently.

I swallowed. "I'll have nightmares."

"Then we'll have an excuse to do this again."

NOAH

The familiar ring tone jerked me awake. My arms and legs were wrapped like tentacles around Echo, my nymph who lay sleeping with her back pressed against me. I released my grasp of her stomach to reach for the cell in my jeans, which had been tossed during our earlier activities.

"Hello?" I cleared my throat.

"Noah?"

"Yeah?" I didn't recognize the man on the other end. Echo remained blissfully asleep. I edged away from her, tucking the blanket tight around her slender form. Millions of thoughts raced in my exhausted mind. Had something happened to Isaiah or Beth? Were they hurt or in jail? Keesha or Mrs. Collins would have called if it were my brothers.

"It's Owen Emerson. Echo's dad." He paused.

Rubbing my head to wake my brain, I kept my mouth shut as I walked to the other side of the basement. It wouldn't be a good conversation starter to mention that his daughter lay in my bed, half naked.

"I'm sorry to wake you, but Echo left this morning rather upset with me and she hasn't come home." I craned my head to check out the clock radio on the floor next to the bed. Two in the morning. Her dad must be on the verge of a coronary. Oddly enough, he didn't sound like a rabid pit bull. "She turned her phone off and I've called her friends. Lila gave me your number and said she could be with you."

The blanket rose and fell with the steady rhythm of Echo's breathing. She'd come to me tonight, trusting me. If I told him, he'd come and take her away, breaking my heart and possibly her trust in me. "Mr. Emerson…"

"Please, Noah, she's my daughter. I need to know she's okay." I'd never heard a man sound so desperate in my life. Almost as desperate as my own need to know Jacob and Tyler were safe.

"She's here." My heart stopped beating, waiting for the patented father ass-chewing.

"Is she okay?" He sounded…relieved?

"Yeah. She's asleep. Has been for a while. I'd hate to wake her."

He paused again. "When did she fall asleep?"

Best guess? "Sometime near one."

"And she's slept through?"

Good thing I knew Echo's sleep patterns, or lack thereof. Otherwise, I would have thought this an odd line of questioning. "Yes, sir. Not a peep."

I waited in heavy silence as he debated his options: have me wake her to tell her to go home or let her sleep. "Do your foster parents mind her being there?"

"No." They were at the lake, but even if they were here and

paid enough attention to notice I'd brought a girl home, they'd only remind me that she couldn't live here once she got knocked up.

"Can I speak to them?"

No. "They're asleep."

"Of course, of course. Echo mentioned that you have a foster sister. I'm assuming she's sharing her living arrangements."

Technically—"Yes." When she was here, Beth did sleep on the bed.

"Have her call me the moment she wakes up in the morning."

"Yes, sir."

"And, Noah, thank you for telling me the truth."

"You're welcome." I hung up and crawled back in bed, burrowing into Echo.

I WOKE TO EMPTY ARMS. ECHO had kept her warm body close to mine all night. A vise gripped my chest. Where was she?

My eyes opened to find the sexiest sight in the world. In black bikini underwear and a tank top, Echo stretched out next to me. Her sketch pad lay on the bed, pencil moving rapidly in her hand. A photo of my brothers was propped up on the pillow.

"Hey, baby."

She gave me a quick glance and a shy smile. "Hey."

I glanced at the clock. Ten-thirty in the morning. Isaiah and Beth would probably roll in soon, but it would be a sin to see her put clothes on. "How did you sleep?"

The smile fell, but she kept drawing. "Better than usual."

My heart dropped. I wanted to be the answer to her problems. "You had nightmares?"

She nodded. "Not nearly as vivid, though. Plus I slept longer than I normally do."

"Why didn't you wake me?"

"Because you're cute when you sleep. See?" She turned the page and showed me the drawing of me sleeping.

"What are you working on now?" I snatched the pad and took her hand in mine when she tried to grab it back.

"Don't look. It's a work in progress. Just messing around really. Noah…"

I flipped the page to her work in progress and quit breathing.

"Please don't be mad. I wanted to give you something. Oh, God," she moaned. "This was a bad idea."

I tore my eyes away from the page, cupping her face with my hand. "No. It's the best present anyone has ever given me." I wanted to kiss her, but I couldn't. I had to look at the picture again. "How did you do it?" Somehow, she'd drawn my parents.

She scooted next to me, resting her head on my shoulder. "You talk about them a lot. Not like long monologues or anything, but enough that I've been able to create a picture in my head. You told me that Jacob looks like your dad and that you and Tyler resemble your mom. You said Mrs. Marcos reminds you of your mom. I saw this picture of your brothers and, I don't know…I put it all together."

I love you. Every part of me ached to say it. I gazed into those beautiful eyes and knew I loved her more than I loved myself. I'd known for weeks, but I couldn't say the words. Saying the words—it made Echo official. It made the attachment I already knew I had to her real.

But it was real and it was official. I was a pansy-ass for not saying the words. *Say them. Just say them.* I sucked in a breath, opened my mouth, then snapped it shut. No. Not here. I'd take her someplace nice. Someplace beautiful. Maybe back to my parents' fountain. "Your dad called last night looking for you. I told him you were here."

She drew away from me, wrapping her hands around her knees. "I guess I should probably head home." A bitter smile hung on her lips. "Think he'll forgive me for breaking the rules for one night?"

I didn't want her to go, ever. I wanted Echo in my bed every night with my arms and legs wrapped around her. But how? In two months she'd be a free woman. Free of high school and, if she chose, free of her father, but I wouldn't be free.

Taking care of my brothers wouldn't be like babysitting, it would be a job. A full-time job that required responsibility. How did I explain to young children the difference between a serious dating relationship and a committed, married relationship when they awoke to find Echo in my bed? Even better, would the judge allow me custody knowing half my heart belonged to someone else?

I wouldn't be their big brother. Fuck, Mrs. Collins was right—I'd be their dad and Echo…Echo would be the woman I was sleeping with. The words tumbled out of my mouth before I knew what I was saying. "Marry me."

Her eyes widened and her head tilted with a twitch. "What?"

I brushed my hair out of my face and sat up, putting the sketch pad down. "I know it's crazy, but after we graduate, marry me. We'll get custody of my brothers and you can get away from your dad and we'll be a family. I know you want a family as much as I do."

Her mouth gaped and her eyes flickered between the pillow and the sheets. "Noah…I…I don't know. I mean, how would we support ourselves? Where would we live?"

"Frank offered me the day shift manager position yesterday.

If you marry me, you'll get to be on my insurance. I know you'll nail one of those college scholarships you've applied for, so we don't have to worry about paying tuition. You can get a part-time job and help me take care of the boys. Maybe if things go well, I could take some night classes in a year."

Excitement rippled through me. Maybe I didn't have to negotiate. Maybe I could have it all, just at a slower rate than I would have liked. "It'll be perfect. You can go to classes and work while the boys are in school. I can get them ready and off to school before my shift and you'll be there to pick them up. There is absolutely no way the judge can tell me no."

"No." Echo's small voice caught me off guard. She grabbed her jeans and rolled off the bed. "No. Is this all I've ever been to you?" She shrugged them on and then threw on her shirt. "A pawn to get your brothers back?"

No. She was distorting my every word. I sprang off the bed. "No, baby. You have to know how much I care for you."

She shoved on her boots. "Really, Noah? You've never once told me that you love me, yet you're willing to marry me. I'm not sure if you were listening, but your proposal sounded something like this. 'Hey, baby, marry me and then you can take care of my brothers.'"

Everything inside of me twisted and began to shatter. I'd fucked this up. "You've got to know how I feel. Please, baby, I..."

She threw a hand up in the air. "Don't. Don't cheapen my feelings for you by lying to me. I'm the idiot in this situation. You told me I was yours, nothing more than a piece of property—a body to sleep with. You never promised me anything else. At least you kept your word and made me more than the whores in the backseat of your car. So thanks, Noah, thanks for not fucking me."

The basement door opened and Isaiah called out, "Coming down, cover up!"

Echo flew up the stairs as he came down. Isaiah stopped at the foot of the stairs watching her leave. "Where's the fire, Echo?"

"Echo, wait!" I yelled out to her. Isaiah blocked my path.

"What the hell, man?" he asked.

"Let me by," I growled and pushed past him. By the time I reached the front stoop, Echo had pulled off down the street. I slammed my fist against the house, but my throbbing hand couldn't match the pain tearing at my heart. I'd lost Echo.

Echo

Lying on my bed, I clutched my tank top to my chest and wished the knife would stop stabbing my heart. Noah's sweet musky scent lingered on my tank. It had hurt when I'd broken up with Luke, but nothing like this. I loved Noah. I really, really loved him.

His messages made sense. All of them. I stopped counting how many he left after five. He cared for me, wanted to be with me, and had spoken without thinking. Noah secretly had been wondering how to make it work between me and his brothers. If I only called him back, he promised to find a way. Sure, he'd like to marry me, but on my time frame, not his.

Yesterday morning, I'd been ticked, but as the day wore on I realized that the world didn't revolve around me. More than anything, I wanted to call Noah back, accept his apology and fall into his safe, strong arms, but he deserved better than selfish me.

Never thinking beyond my next tutoring session, I'd been

caught up in my own delusions of finding my lost memories. I hadn't thought about what would happen after graduation or what it would mean for him to gain custody of his brothers. I loved Noah more than I'd ever loved anybody else. I loved him enough to do the thing that hurt me.

I sniffed and wiped my face when someone knocked on my door. "Can I come in?" my father asked from the other side.

No, but my options were limited. I'd snuck past him and Ashley earlier to avoid a confrontation. Dad's rebuke had to happen at some point. I shoved my tank under my covers, sat up, and hugged a pillow to keep myself from falling apart. "Sure."

My father took a seat on my bed and stared at my mother's paintings. He looked as tired as I felt. "Promise me you won't break curfew again."

"All right." Giving in seemed easier at the moment.

He'd opened his mouth as I spoke, then shut it. Obviously, he'd thought we would fight. "Noah's called the landline twice. You guys have a fight?"

"We broke up."

He shifted on the bed. "Honey, he did the right thing by telling me you were there."

I wasn't having this or any other conversation with him. "Little late to play dad, isn't it?"

"I am your father and I have never considered you a game to be played."

Yeah, tell that to Mom. "Look, we've got a little over two months until I graduate. Let's just get through it, okay? As soon as I graduate, I'm leaving. I'll take early acceptance somewhere or I'll get a job and an apartment. I'll be done with you and you can be done with me. If we time it right, I can be out before the baby is born and you can have your fresh start."

Every worry line deepened. "Echo…"

I let the anger building inside burst free. "Go tell it to Ashley. She's the only one you've ever cared about."

"That's not…"

"You left me to die." I pointed at the door. "Get out of here and out of my life!"

My father lowered his head, nodded, and then left my room.

NOAH

Not bothering with my locker, I headed straight for the cafeteria. Echo had found a way to avoid me this morning, but I'd be damned if I let her slink away now.

"You could tell her I ordered the part for the car," Isaiah said when he sat next to me.

"I plan on it being my opening line." I stared at the doors, waiting for her to walk in. I'd give her five more minutes before I chased her around the building.

"You really fucked this up, Einstein." Beth tossed her tray full of food on the table.

"You hate her," I mumbled.

"She grew on me. Kind of like moss."

Where was she? The door opened to the cafeteria and her favorite gal pal glided in.

"Lila!" I pushed my chair back to go after her, but she changed direction and came to me.

She cocked an annoyed eyebrow. "Yes?"

I withered before very few people, but the look Lila gave me could scare the shit out of serial killers. "Do you know where Echo is?"

"Why? Need a babysitter?" she asked dryly.

Damn, Echo had to be pissed. Did she listen to any of my messages? "I fucked up and I want to talk to her."

"You can say that again."

"I bet you're enjoying this, prom queen," snarled Beth. "Were you scared that by hanging with real people like us, she'd figure out that you and the other little Barbie wannabes are full of shit?"

Lila's lip curled back. "Speaking of wannabes, do you have plans to go after Echo's leftovers again?"

Damn, not what I needed. Beth hurled herself at Lila, but Isaiah grabbed Beth by the waist and hissed at her to calm down. My chair flipped back when I stood. "Forget it. I'll find her myself."

ECHO SAT ON A STOOL STARING AT the canvas, but this time she didn't have a paintbrush in her hand. Her gloved hands were propped on her knees.

"You know it's rude not to call back." I held my breath, waiting for her wrath.

She gave a sad smile, hurting my heart. I would have preferred her anger over her pain anytime. "It's not the first time you thought I was rude." She glanced up at me. "Hey, Noah."

"Echo." I permitted myself to get closer, but not too close. "It's Monday, which means you should be tutoring me this afternoon."

"You never needed a tutor, just motivation."

Rubbing the tension out of the back of my neck, I continued,

"Look, I fucked up Saturday. I never should have brought up marriage. I was out of my mind. You drew that picture of my parents and then I thought about how much I love you and how I couldn't keep you and have my brothers. I added a fucked-up thought to another fucked-up thought and I created a pile of shit."

Echo's lips twitched up. "That's the worst apology I've ever heard, but I'll take it." She turned her gaze back to the blank canvas.

I'd uttered the words I never said to a girl—I loved her. Girls craved words like that, but the distance between us had widened. Maybe she didn't catch it. "I love you, Echo. You could never marry me and I'd still love you. We'll find a way to figure everything out. You are not responsible for my brothers."

"I know." She sighed and looked bone-weary. Her foot began to bounce on the leg of the stool. "I love you, too, and because of that, I think it's time we end this."

Pain seared through me, followed by a quick flash of anger. "But you said you forgave me."

She picked up a paintbrush, dipped it in black paint and smudged dots on the middle of the canvas. "I have up to a twenty percent chance of inheriting my mother's genes."

"What does that have to do with anything? You're not your mother. You are a far cry from that crazy bitch."

"She's ill, Noah, not crazy," she whispered.

This entire conversation was crazy. "She cut you to pieces. That's crazy."

She shut her eyes tight and flinched. "I fell."

I yanked the paintbrush out of her hand and threw it across the room. "Fuck that. If that was a damn accident, you'd remember." I ran a hand over my face, trying to wipe away the anger. "What the hell does this have to do with anything? With us?"

Echo opened her eyes and revealed a mind-numbing pain. "Everything."

The need to touch her overwhelmed me and I gave in. I stepped toward her, but Echo hopped off the stool and placed it between us. I shoved it out of the way and kept advancing. She pressed her hands against my chest and tried to push me away. "I can't think straight when you're this close."

I backed her up against the wall. "I don't like the thoughts running through your head. I plan on staying right here until you look me in the eye and tell me you're mine."

She lowered her head and hid in her hair. As she spoke, her tone reminded me of Jacob's when he finally understood Mom would never hold him again. "This isn't going to work. It never would have."

"Bullshit. We belong together." Echo sniffled and the sound tore at me. I softened my voice. "Look at me, baby. I know you love me. Three nights ago you were willing to offer everything to me. There is no way you can walk away from us."

"God, Noah…" Her voice broke. "I'm a mess."

A mess? "You're beautiful."

She finally raised her head. No tears, but the trails remained. "I'm a mental mess. In two months you're going to face some judge and convince him that you are the best person to raise your brothers. I'm a liability."

A nagging voice told me to shut up and listen. "Not true. My brothers will love you and you'll love them. You are not a liability."

"But how will the judge see me? Are you really willing to take that risk?" She swallowed. "Two months after the incident with my mom a therapist tried to reclaim the lost memories. Mrs. Collins said the person tried too hard. I cracked. I woke up in a hospital two days later with the memories still repressed. I've been lucky so far, but what happens to you if my luck runs out?

"Noah, look at it from an outsider's perspective. I'm scarred with no memory of what happened to me. I've already had one mental breakdown because I tried to remember. My mother is bipolar. Most people who are bipolar start to exhibit the symptoms in their late teens or early twenties. What happens if the judge finds out about me? What if he discovers what a mess you're dating?"

Breathing became a painful chore. Her lips turned down while her warm fingers caressed my cheek. That touch typically brought me to my knees, but now it cut me open.

"Did you know that when you stop being stubborn and accept I may be right on something, your eyes widen a little and you tilt your head to the side?" she asked.

I forced my head straight and narrowed my eyes. "I love you."

She flashed her glorious smile and then it became the saddest smile in the world. "You love your brothers more. I'm okay with that. In fact, it's one of the things I love about you. You were right the other day. I do want to be part of a family. But I'd never forgive myself if I was the reason you didn't get yours."

To my horror, tears pricked my eyes and my throat swelled shut. "No, you're not pulling this sacrificial bullshit on me. I love you and you love me and we're supposed to be together."

Echo pressed her body to mine and her fingers clung to my hair. Water glistened in her eyes. "I love you enough to never make you choose."

She pushed off her toes toward me, guiding my head down,

and gently kissed my lips. No. This wouldn't be goodbye. I'd fill her up and make her realize she'd always be empty without me.

I made Echo mine. My hands claimed her hair, her back. My lips claimed her mouth, her tongue. Her body shook against mine and I tasted salty wetness on her skin. She forced her lips away and I latched tighter to her. "No, baby, no," I whispered into her hair.

She pushed her palms against my chest, then became a blur as she ran past. "I'm sorry."

Echo

He loved me.

Noah Hutchins had told me he loved me, and that had made the past week at school absolute hell.

The bell rang. Everyone else snapped shut their books, zipped up their backpacks and left business technology for lunch. I stayed completely still.

My hand gripped my pencil as Noah walked past and left the room with his shoulders stiff and head high. He never acknowledged my presence. Isaiah, on the other hand, took his time and stared at me with sad eyes as he followed his best friend.

For seven days, this had been how Noah and I interacted. I waited for him to leave class. He bolted. I sucked in a breath, wishing the pain would stop as the room cleared out. Well, except for my best friend.

"Echo." Lila stood in front of my desk with her books clutched to her chest. "Are you okay?"

No. Nothing would be okay ever again. "I accidentally overheard in the bathroom this morning that Lauren Lewis is going to make a move on Noah." Tears threatened the edges of my eyes. "I shouldn't care. I mean, I broke up with him and he can…" *Sleep with whoever he wants…* But I couldn't say that because a lump formed in my throat.

"Lila," called Stephen from the hallway, "you coming to lunch or not?"

She started to shake her head no when I answered for her, "She's going."

"Echo," Lila said in reprimand.

"I'm fine." I faked the worst smile in the world. "Maybe I'll stop by the cafeteria today."

I didn't mean it. She knew that, yet she patted my hand and said, "I'll see you there," before taking Stephen's hand and heading to lunch.

Tossing my stuff into my backpack, I continued to fight the urge I'd fought for seven days—to run to Noah and beg him to take me back. I'd lost not only him, but the routine I'd come to depend on: studying, tutoring, plotting to get into our files, and Isaiah and Beth working on Aires' car. Losing Noah meant losing a life. It also meant losing my chance for answers.

Noah had been the mastermind behind all of our plans and I'd drawn upon his courage to succeed. Or had I? I dropped my last book in my pack and an eyebrow rose with the thought. My mind began to churn as I left the room. *I* convinced Mrs. Collins and my father to change the appointment time—not Noah. *I* found his brothers' foster parents' last name. Maybe, just maybe, I could find my answers on my own.

I turned the corner of the empty hallway and froze. With her back against my locker, Grace inspected her nails.

"What are you doing here?" I asked.

"Talking to you. If you'd stayed with Luke, we could have re-mained friends." She wiped at her thumbnail before glancing at me.

"Shouldn't you be at lunch proving to the world you're per-fect?" I asked. For the first time in my life, I didn't feel like bow-ing down to her.

"He'll take you back," she said. "Luke. When he heard you broke it off with Noah, he about flipped. He's ending it with Deanna. He wants you. Not her."

No, he didn't want me. It was a rumor even I had heard, but I knew what no one else did—Luke couldn't handle my scars. My head fell back before I refocused on the issue blocking me from my locker. "Why do you even care? Last I heard you were making everyone laugh in the gym at my expense."

Grace became insanely interested in her shoes. "So I'm not a saint, Echo. Shoot me. It's not like you make anything easy." She snapped her mouth shut and tilted her head, a sure sign she was trying to gain composure. "I still want to be your friend, and we can salvage everything—our friendship, what people think of you, everything. Now that you've dumped the loser, we'll just say Noah was a brain fart. That he used you. Manipulated you. And then you saw him for the moron he is. Everyone will be-lieve that."

Anger snapped inside of me. How could she not understand? "I'm in love with Noah."

She pushed off the lockers, her face twisted in rage. "And look where that got you. Boyfriendless. Friendless. Damn, Echo, you went through the social lynching of the year the moment you kissed that boy in public all in the name of love. All of that for nothing!

"*Nothing* about you has changed. You still hide your scars, you still hide from lunch and you still hide from the world. You were better off before you met Noah Hutchins. What I wouldn't give to have January back. At least then you came to lunch. At least then you tried."

Her words became knives slashing against my skin, pricking and prodding more than I thought they should. "I'm not the one that put conditions on our friendship. I'm not the one terrified of what people will think of me if I'm friends with someone you think of as beneath you."

Grace laughed and it wasn't the happy kind. It was the type that said she was ticked beyond belief. "Yes, you did, Echo. You put conditions on our friendship the moment you slid those gloves on your arms and you asked me to lie to everyone on your behalf. I had to tell the world that I didn't know what happened to one of my best friends. And as for pointing a finger at me and accusing me of being terrified of what people think, turn that finger back around, sister. If you're so high and mighty, why the hell are you still hiding those scars?"

I swallowed and all of the anger I'd felt seconds before drained from my body and into the air. She was right. Grace was utterly right.

I STARED INTO MY OPEN LOCKER and drummed my fingers against the door. I could do this. I could definitely do this…tomorrow, or next month, or never…. No, no. I could do this. I could live life to please myself or everyone else. Me. I wanted to please me.

As far back as I could remember I'd lived to please everyone else: my mother, my father, teachers, therapists. Terrified if I stepped out of line I would lose their respect. And in the case of my parents—their love. But no more. I wanted answers about my past and I was only going to discover them if I found some courage.

Yesterday, Grace completely called me out and today, I was calling her bluff.

For the first time in two years, I'd worn short sleeves to school, though I kept a sweater over my shirt. But I didn't want to wear a sweater. I was hot and uncomfortable and the sweater itched. Reaching behind my shoulders, I yanked it over my head and took a refreshing breath the moment the cooler air hit my arms. The sensation reminded me of those summer commercials where obviously hot people jumped into the cool, inviting water. This was what freedom felt like.

I left my books and sweater in my locker and headed down the empty hallway toward the cafeteria. Funny, I felt naked, like I was only sporting my bra and underwear, not my favorite blue short-sleeved shirt and a pair of faded jeans.

To keep myself from turning back, I hitched my thumbs in my pockets and counted the floor tiles. The tile stopped at the edge of the cafeteria's concrete floor. Laughter and loud conversation flowed from the room. I prayed for two things. One: I wouldn't pass out. Two: Lila would still love me.

My throat swelled and my chest constricted when I lifted my foot and crossed the barrier from the hallway to the lunchroom. The immediate gasps of "Oh, my God" to my left stopped my progression forward. Note to self—this was probably my worst idea yet.

I surveyed the room and watched as people leaned over from lunch table to lunch table, informing the masses that the freak had entered the room. *Go ahead, stare. Maybe next time I'll be smart enough to sell tickets.*

From across the room, a pair of warm brown eyes met mine.

Everything inside of me hurt—Noah. For a week, we'd each pretended the other one never existed. He strutted through school with his delicious dark looks and dangerous attitude like I'd never entered his life. Noah laughed and cut up at his lunch table and sat stoic in class.

But he wasn't stoic now. Sitting between Isaiah and Beth, he slowly rose from his table, never once taking his eyes off me. I bit my lip and willed myself not to cry and him not to approach me. I couldn't do both in one day. I couldn't be strong enough to expose myself to the world and stay away from him.

When he took a step in my direction, I shook my head and pleaded with my eyes for him to sit back down. Noah stood still and ran his hand over his face, a curse word I'd heard him say more than once forming on his lips. Was this breakup killing him as much as it was killing me?

He closed his eyes for a second and when he reopened them, he slammed his hand into the door as he left the lunchroom. Isaiah bolted after him.

Laughter broke out in the direction of my old lunch table and when I glanced over, they were staring at me. Grace included, though she was the only one at the table not laughing. She gave a brief nod and looked away.

"Fuck them."

I jumped when I noticed Beth standing so close that her arm touched mine. "Excuse me?"

She motioned to the rest of the cafeteria. "Fuck them. They aren't worth it."

"For once, I agree." Lila linked her fingers with mine. "You could have told me you were planning on doing this. I would have come in with you."

I turned my attention back to Beth, but she was already gone.

I caught her black hair trailing behind her as she left the cafeteria through the same door that Noah used.

"Are you hungry?" Lila asked.

More like I wanted to puke. "Not really."

Lila gave me her Glinda the Good Witch radiant smile. "Good. Then we won't feel guilty for eating only dessert." She tugged on my hand. "Come on, they have fudge brownies."

NOAH

My fist collided with my locker and the loud banging accompanied the curse flying from my mouth. Echo finally found the courage to expose her scars and she wouldn't let me stand by her side.

"Nice dent, man." Isaiah rested his hip against the corner of the hallway as he crossed his tattooed arms over his chest. "I appreciate you choosing my locker to beat the shit out of. I was looking for an excuse to never open it again."

My head jerked as I did a double take. Damn, I hit the wrong one. The shock of my mistake zapped the anger out of me, leaving behind a dull throb in my knuckles. "Sorry."

"Did it get out whatever it is you've had up your ass?"

I was wrong, some of the anger still simmered in my gut. "What is that supposed to mean?"

"It means the girl you love is in that cafeteria baring her soul and you're out here punching lockers. I call that something up your ass."

I ran a hand over my face. "She broke up with me. Not the other way around. Besides—" I pointed toward the cafeteria "—I wanted to be by her side. She waved me away."

"When did you become a fucking sheep? Way I see it, she may have said the words, but you must have wanted to break up, too."

My muscles flinched and my fist curled, causing Isaiah to push away from the wall. He stood with his feet apart, arms held stiff near his sides. Isaiah sensed a fight and he wasn't wrong. My voice dropped. "What did you just say?" Because he knew how much I loved Echo and those words he'd just said bordered on betrayal.

Yet my brother continued, "That you must have had some doubt about the two of you because you seemed to easily walk away."

The urge surged through me to hit something again, but the throb in my knuckles kept me grounded. "I love Echo. I love her so much I asked her to marry me. Does that sound like I wanted to walk away?"

His eyebrows rose toward his shaved hairline as his muscles relaxed. "Tell me you're kidding about the marriage part."

Collapsing against the locker, I let the back of my head hit the metal. I wished I was kidding. That one question became the domino that destroyed my relationship with her. "I'm not. I fucked it all up, bro, and I don't know how to fix it."

Isaiah's combat boots thumped against the floor as he came closer to me. "All I'm saying is that I don't see you fighting for your girl, man. If you want her, then stop punching lockers and start focusing on the prize."

Echo

The smell of acrylic paint tickled my nose the moment I walked into the gallery. Landscapes filled the canvases on the wall. A painting of long blade grass bending with the wind caught my eye. Earlier today, I'd exposed my arms. This afternoon, I was finding answers.

Nerves caused my blood to skip in my veins. The last time I visited this place, Aires was still alive and my mother was on her meds. Mom had chuckled when Aires told her he didn't understand one of her paintings and he'd pulled my hair when I called him an idiot. He'd laughed when I smacked him in return. A weight pressed down on my lungs. Aires laughed. I should have hugged him then. I should have hugged him and never let go.

"Can I help you?" asked a female voice.

I plastered a smile on my face and turned. "Hi, Bridget."

Bridget's blue eyes widened. Her sleek midnight-black hair hung to her shoulders and angled her face. At six feet tall, she towered over me. As I always remembered her, she wore a chic black business suit. "Echo. My God, you've grown."

"It happens." I shifted from one foot to the next. "Do you have a few minutes?"

"For you, always. Would you like some water?"

"Sure." She led the way to her office.

"What can I do for you?"

Now or never. "I'm hoping you can help me with two things."

She handed me a bottled water and twisted the top off of hers. "Tell me number one."

"You told me once that if I was ever interested in selling my paintings you wanted me to call you first. Does that offer still stand?"

Bridget licked her lips and sat. "Your mom showed me your sketches for years. I've been dying for this day. Did you bring anything for me to look at?"

I shook my head.

"Pick out your five favorite paintings and bring a full sketch pad for me to peruse tomorrow." She narrowed her eyes. "You're still in school, right?"

"I graduate next month."

"Brilliant." Her eyes glittered as if her mind had gone to a far-off place. She blinked back to life. "Two?"

"I want to find my mom."

She lost the glitter and her smile fell. "Cassie doesn't work here anymore. You know that."

"Yeah, I do, but you were her best friend. I'm hoping you could at least tell me where she ended up. Maybe if she found another job, who hired her, or at least who called for references."

Bridget took a long drink from her water. "Your mom was in

a bad place for a very long time, Echo. What happened to you is a tragedy and she feels nothing but remorse."

My heart beat faster. "You know what happened to me?"

"Yes." Her long fingernails ripped at the label on the bottle. "And she said that you don't."

Adrenaline poured into my body. My foot tapped against the floor. "You still talk with her?"

"Yes." The sound of the label tearing filled the silence.

I reached around and pulled an envelope from my back pocket. "Please just give this to her. She can decide how to proceed. Okay?"

She stared at my outstretched hand. "I know your dad liked to keep you in a glass ball so maybe you're not aware of the restraining order."

"I'm not interested in sending her to jail. I just want to see her." I shook the letter in my hand and tried Mrs. Collins's puppy dog eyes. "Please, Bridget."

Bridget accepted the envelope. "I'm not promising anything. Do you understand?"

I nodded, too worked up to speak. Either I'd solved all my problems or I'd created a whole new set of them. It didn't matter. I was done living like a coward. It was time to be strong.

NOAH

"How are you, Noah?" Mrs. Collins smiled when I waltzed into her office and sank into the chair.

"I've been better."

That got her attention. "At least you're being honest today. What brought that on?"

I shook my head, not able to answer. I'd heard a rumor that Luke had broken up with his girl of the week with the intention of asking Echo to prom. The bastard barely waited three weeks before going after my girl.

Shifting in my seat, I tried to erase the thought of Echo as my girl. We'd broken up and Isaiah was right, I'd done nothing to stop it. I wanted Echo to be happy and there was no way she could with a boyfriend who was busy raising two little boys. Isaiah said I should have made it her choice and to try talking with Echo again. I wanted Echo in my life, but in the end her life would be better without me.

Beth promised to ask around and find out whether Echo accepted Luke's offer. Part of me hoped she said yes. I'd fucked up her Valentine's Dance. She deserved a good prom.

"You'll be happy to know the drug test the judge ordered came back negative."

I shrugged. I hadn't touched weed in months. "You expected a different result?"

She laughed. "I've met Beth."

I laughed along with her. At least she called a spade a spade. For the past couple of weeks, Mrs. Collins had tried to dig at me, but I kept our topics of conversation stuck on my brothers. Sometimes we discussed the possibility of a future in college I'd never have.

"How are things going with Jacob?" After my visit to Legal Aid, Carrie and Joe found a cutthroat lawyer and rescinded my visitation privileges. Some bullshit about me using drugs and partying and being a bad influence on my brothers. Hence the drug test. Smart move on their part. Before Echo their claim wasn't bullshit, but since her, it was.

"You know I can't discuss private details, but I can tell you a story about this wonderful child named Jack who had night terrors for three years."

My lips twitched. Mrs. Collins wasn't so bad after all. "So how's Jack?"

"Jack slept through an entire night without a nightmare this past week."

The air caught in my chest, making it a little hard to breathe. "Thanks."

"Thank you. I don't believe Carrie and Joe would have figured out what tormented him if you hadn't told me."

We sat in silence for a few seconds. I stared down at my combat boots.

"I'd like to discuss what torments you."

"Echo has been absent a lot." She'd missed three days two weeks ago and two last week.

She raised her eyebrows. "Not exactly what I was going for, but I'll bite. Yes, she has."

The more I talked, the more I backed myself into a corner, but I didn't care. Maybe I wanted to be cornered. "Is she okay?"

"Why don't you ask her?"

"We don't talk." But I needed to. The part Isaiah had ordered for Aires' car had finally arrived.

Mrs. Collins leaned forward on her desk. "What happened between the two of you?"

"We broke up," I bit out. "I changed my mind. I don't want to talk about Echo." I looked away. Thinking about Echo hurt.

She stared at me with those puppy eyes and opened my file. "Then let's discuss the upcoming ACT testing date."

Mrs. Collins bribed me into registering for the ACT. If I took the test and applied to a couple of schools, then she'd help prep me for my meeting with the judge after graduation. She wasted her time. Any doubts I had about gaining custody of my brothers ended when Carrie and Joe stole my visitation.

Mrs. Collins's cell phone rang, something that hadn't happened since I'd known her. She answered it immediately and then turned to me. "I'll see you next week. Please tell Echo that I'll be with her in a few minutes."

Our appointment had run over. I slid a hand over my face when I opened the door. For the past three weeks I'd busted ass out of this office to avoid being alone with Echo, and now.... Fuck.

She sat alone in the row of seats, skimming her iPhone, rocking her foot in her own silent rhythm. I shut the door behind me and leaned my back against it. "Isaiah has the part you need to finish Aires' car."

She flashed a surprised smile and her green eyes glittered. "You're kidding? I assumed that after...you know...he wouldn't want to..."

"Isaiah's been a walking hard-on since he saw that car. Besides, I promised I'd help you fix it." Part of my heart soared from seeing her happy; the other part drowned in misery. "He said he'd come by this weekend and finish it."

"This weekend?" Echo hopped out of the seat. "Isaiah is going to fix my brother's car this weekend? Oh. My. God!" She placed a hand over her mouth. "That is amazing!"

She launched herself at me. I closed my eyes the moment her arms slipped around my neck. I slid my hands to familiar places and reveled in her delicious smell. For three weeks I'd felt like a puzzle with missing pieces. Her body fit perfectly into mine, making me feel whole again. "I've missed you."

I swore Echo clutched me tighter before stepping back. "I'm sorry. That was totally inappropriate."

Begrudgingly I let go, chuckling. "I'm all about inappropriate."

Her laughter healed and stung at the same time. "Yeah, you are." She bit her lip and my smile grew when her eyes wandered down then back up my body. Echo blinked. "How are things going with your brothers?"

I motioned with my chin toward the chairs and we sat next to each other. Her knee and shoulder barely brushed against me and I wished more than anything that I could run my fingers through her hair. "The judge set a date to hear me out after graduation. Mrs. Collins has been prepping me."

"That is awesome!"

"Yeah." I forced optimism into my voice.

Her cheeks fell, as did her joy. "What's wrong?"

"Carrie and Joe hired a lawyer and I lost visitation."

Echo placed her delicate hand over mine. "Oh, Noah. I am so sorry. Have you seen them at all?"

I'd spent countless hours on the couch in the basement, staring at the ceiling wondering what she was doing. Her laughter, her smile, the feel of her body next to mine, and the regret that I let her walk away too easily haunted me. Taking the risk, I entwined my fingers with hers. Odds were I'd never get the chance to be this close again. "No, Mrs. Collins convinced me the best thing to do is to keep my distance and follow the letter of the law."

"Wow, Mrs. Collins is a freaking miracle worker. Dangerous Noah Hutchins on the straight and narrow. If you don't watch out she'll ruin your rep with the girls." Echo waggled her eyebrows.

I lowered my voice. "Not that it matters. I only care what one girl thinks about me."

She relaxed her fingers into mine and stroked her thumb over my skin. "With Mrs. Collins on your side, you'll get them back."

Minutes into being alone together, we fell into each other again, like no time had passed. I could blame her for ending us, but in the end, I agreed with her decision. "How about you, Echo? Did you find your answers?"

Echo let her hair fall forward as her knee bounced. "No."

If I continued to disregard breakup rules, I might as well go all the way. I pushed her curls behind her shoulder and let my fingers linger longer than needed so I could enjoy the silky feel.

"Don't hide from me, baby. We've been through too much for that."

Echo leaned into me, placing her head on my shoulder and letting me wrap an arm around her. "I've missed you, too, Noah. I'm tired of ignoring you."

"Then don't." Ignoring her hurt like hell. Acknowledging her had to be better.

"We're not exactly the friends type." As if to prove her point, she tilted her head up. Echo's warm breath caressed my neck, causing my body to tingle with the thought of kissing her.

I swallowed, trying to shut out the bittersweet memories of our last night together. "Where've you been? It kills me when you're not at school."

"A little bit of everywhere. I went to an art gallery and the curator showed some interest in my work and sold my first piece two days later. Since then, I've been traveling around to different galleries, hawking my wares."

"That's awesome, Echo." I absently stroked her shoulder. Part of me was thrilled for her; another part was upset she'd made such big leaps without me. "Sounds like you're fitting into your future perfectly." No custody battles, flipping burgers or single parenthood in her future. "Where did you decide to go to school?"

"I don't know if I'm going to school."

Shock jolted my system and I inched away to make sure I understood. "What the fuck do you mean you don't know? You've got colleges falling all over you and you don't fucking know if you want to go to school?"

My damned little siren laughed at me. "I see your language has improved."

Poof—like magic, the anger disappeared. Anger Mrs. Collins

would love to analyze. Guess her scheme to get me thinking about my future worked. I pulled Echo back into me. "If you're not going to school, then what are your plans?"

"I've got paintings and drawings in a handful of different galleries in this and surrounding states. I'm not going to be rich, but I make a little bit with every painting I sell. I'm considering putting college off for a year or two and traveling cross-country, hopping from gallery to gallery."

Damn if her whole world wasn't changing. "And your dad's okay with this?"

"Not his call to make." Fury crept out behind her light tone. Maybe some things hadn't changed. "I don't want to live with him and Ashley anymore. Selling my paintings—it's my way out. I don't want to stare at the walls and think of my mother. I don't want to sit in my room and think of all the nights Aires used to stay up talking to me. I don't want every moment of my life filled with reminders of a life I will never get back."

Normal. We both craved it and neither one of us would ever experience it again. She had hoped learning the truth of what happened between her and her mother would solve her problems and I had promised to help. "I feel like a dick. We made a deal and I left you hanging. I'm not that guy who goes back on his word. What can I do to help you get to the truth?"

Echo's chest rose with her breath then deflated when she exhaled. Sensing our moment ending, I nuzzled her hair, savoring her scent. She patted my knee and broke away. "Nothing. There's nothing you can do."

She crossed the room and leaned against the counter. "I've tried hypnosis several times and I remember nothing more. I think it's time that I move on. Ashley's due in a couple of weeks. Dad's ready to complete his replacement family. As soon as I graduate, this part of my life will be over. I'm okay with not knowing what happened." Her words sounded pretty, but I knew her better. She'd blinked three times in a row.

Mrs. Collins opened her door. "So sorry, Echo, but I had an emergency...." Her eyes fell on me then flickered to Echo. I shook my head when her lips twitched up. "You can come in whenever you're ready." Without waiting for a reply, she shut the door.

"Guess I should go in." Echo walked back to the chair beside me and picked up her pack.

I stood as she straightened and snaked my arms around her, pulling her close to me, savoring the feel of every delicate curve. For three weeks, I spent my time convincing myself that our breakup was the right choice. But being this close to her, hearing her laugh, listening to her voice, I knew I had been telling myself lies.

Her eyes widened when I lowered my head to hers. "It doesn't have to be this way. We can find a way to make us work."

She tilted her head and licked her lips, whispering through shallow breaths, "You're not playing fair."

"No, I'm not." Echo thought too much. I threaded my fingers into her hair and kissed her, leaving her no opportunity to think about what we were doing. I wanted her to feel what I felt. To revel in the pull, the attraction. Dammit, I wanted her to undeniably love me.

Her pack hit the floor with a resounding thud and her magical fingers explored my back, neck and head. Echo's tongue danced manically with mine, hungry and excited.

Her muscles stiffened when her mind caught up. I held her tighter to me, refusing to let her leave so easily again. Echo pulled her lips away, but was unable to step back from my body. "We can't, Noah."

"Why not?" I shook her without meaning to, but if it snapped something into place, I'd shake her again.

"Because everything has changed. Because nothing has changed. You have a family to save. I…" She looked away, shaking her head. "I can't live here anymore. When I leave town, I can sleep. Do you understand what I'm saying?"

I did. I understood all too well, as much as I hated it. This was why we ignored each other. When she walked away the first time, my damn heart ruptured and I swore I'd never let it happen again. Like an idiot, here I was setting off explosives.

Both of my hands wove into her hair again and clutched at the soft curls. No matter how I tightened my grip, the strands kept falling from my fingers, a shower of water from the sky. I rested my forehead against hers. "I want you to be happy."

"You, too," she whispered. I let go of her and left the main office. When I first connected with Echo, I'd promised her I would help her find her answers. I was a man of my word and Echo would soon know that.

Echo

Nerves took dominion over my body and I concentrated on not peeing my pants. My bladder shrank to twelve sizes smaller than normal and sweat soaked the armpits of my cotton short-sleeved shirt. I was sure I looked excellent.

A slimy cold boa constrictor wrapped around my heart and squeezed—the scars. I wore short sleeves most of the time now and was getting better at not obsessing about my arms...until someone stared, anyway. Sure, she knew about them, but seeing them could be difficult. I sighed heavily as I parked under the large oak trees. Too late to head home and change clothes now.

She stood by Aires' grave. I kept my eyes to the ground and counted each step from the car. Somewhere between steps three and five, adrenaline began tickling my bloodstream, making me feel like a balloon floating away. The April Saturday was warm, but my skin felt clammy.

I'd asked to see her, proving I'd officially lost my freaking mind. Tucking my hair behind my ear, I stopped. Aires' grave lay between us. My mother on one side and me on the other.

"Echo," she whispered. Tears glistened in her green eyes and she took a step toward me.

My heart rammed through my rib cage and I took an immediate step back. For a second, I considered running and struggled hard to remain where I stood.

Mom retreated and put her palms in the air in a gesture of peace. "I just want to hug you."

I considered her request for a brief moment. Hugging my mom should be natural, an automatic reaction. I swallowed, shoving my hands in my back pockets. "I'm sorry. I can't."

She nodded weakly and glanced at Aires' tombstone. "I miss him."

"I do, too."

All of my memories of my mother didn't fit the woman before me. I remembered her as a youthful beauty. Now she rivaled my father. Crow's-feet were embedded around her eyes and lines framed the sides of her mouth. Instead of the naturally wild, curly red hair I remembered, she wore it flat-iron straight.

During her highs, my mother had appeared to walk on air. In her lows, she clung to the ground of the earth. Standing in front of me, she was neither high nor low. She just was.

She seemed almost normal. Like any other aging woman grieving at a cemetery. In this moment my mom wasn't some out-of-control superwoman or a dangerous foe. She was just a woman, human, almost relatable.

Relatable or not, every instinct inside of me screamed to run. My throat swelled and I fought the compulsion to dry heave. My options were faint or sit. "Do you mind sitting down? Because I need to."

My mother gave a brief smile and nodded while she sat. "Do you remember when I taught you and Aires to make bracelets and necklaces out of clover?" She picked a few of the small white flowers and knotted them together. "You used to love wearing them as tiaras in your hair."

"Yeah," was my only answer. Mom enjoyed the feel of the grass on her bare feet so she never forced Aires or me to wear shoes. The three of us loved being outside. She continued to weave the clover into a single strand as the awkwardness grew.

"Thanks for texting me back. Which letter did you get?" I'd purposely visited art galleries where my mother had once sold her paintings, leaving a letter for her at each one.

"All of them. It was Bridget, though, who convinced me to come."

A quick spark of pain pricked my stomach. My letter hadn't been enough to convince her?

"Do you come to visit Aires often?" I asked.

Her hands stilled. "No. I don't like the thought of my baby in the ground."

I hadn't meant to upset her, but Resthaven had seemed safe. If someone spotted us together then we could say we just happened to stop by at the same time. No one could accuse her of breaking the restraining order.

I should just ask her about that night and leave, but watching her, seeing her…I realized I had so many more questions. "Why didn't you call me back over Christmas?"

Last December, the grief of losing Aires became so unbearable that I called her. I'd left a message, giving her the number to my cell, to the landline. I'd told her what times to call. I never heard back. Then of course, in January, Dad changed the number to the landline, then my cell in February.

"I was having a rough time, Echo. I needed to focus on myself," she said simply and without apology.

"But I needed you. I told you that, right?" At least I thought I had left it in the message.

"You did." She continued to link one clover to another. "You've grown into a beautiful young woman."

"Except for the scars." I bit my tongue the moment the comment slid out. Mom stayed silent and my foot rocked back and forth. I yanked a large blade of grass from the ground and methodically peeled it apart. "I don't know much about the restraining order. Surely it's gotta end soon."

Maybe the hole in my heart wouldn't feel so huge if I could see Mom every now and then.

"Bridget showed me your artwork," Mom said, ignoring me again. "You're extremely talented. What art schools did you apply to?"

I paused, waiting for Mom to lift her head so I could look into her eyes. Was she evading me? A warm breeze blew through the cemetery. The length of Aires' coffin separated us, yet it felt like the Grand Canyon. "None. Dad didn't allow me to paint after what happened. Mom, did you read any of the letters I left for you?"

The ones that begged her to meet with me so I could finally understand what happened between us. The ones that said I missed having a mom. The ones that told her how broken I was because in a span of six months, I lost both her and Aires.

"Yes," she said, so softly I almost missed it. Then she sat up straighter and spoke in her professional gallery curator voice. "Stop trying to change the subject, Echo. We're talking about your future. Your father never understood us and our need to create art. I'm sure he jumped at the opportunity to cleanse you of anything that had to do with me.

"Good for you for sticking it to him and continuing to paint. Though I wish you would have stood up for yourself more and applied to a decent school. I guess you could try for spring admission. I have significant pull in the art community. I wouldn't mind writing you a recommendation."

Writing me a recommendation? My mind became a blank canvas as I tried to follow her train of thought. I'd asked about the restraining order out loud, right? "I don't want to go to art school."

My mother's face reddened and an undercurrent of irritation leaked into her movements and words. "Echo, you aren't business school material. You never have been. Don't let your father bully you into a life you don't want."

I'd forgotten how much I hated the constant tug-of-war. Ironically, I spent my entire life trying to make them both happy—my mother with art, my father with knowledge—yet in the end, they both threw me away. "I take business classes at school and I've aced every single course."

She shrugged. "I cook, but that doesn't make me a chef."

"What?"

Mom looked me square in the eye. "It means you're just like me."

No, I'm not, cried a small voice inside my head. "I paint," I said aloud as if to prove that was our only link.

"You're an artist. Just like me. Your father never understood me, so I can't imagine he understands you."

No, Dad didn't understand me.

"Let me guess," she continued. "He's on you all the time. Whatever you're doing, it's not good enough. Or not to his standards and he just keeps on you until you feel like you're going to explode."

"Yes," I whispered and felt my head sway to the right. I didn't remember this about her. Yeah, she'd taken the occasional verbal punch at my father and she'd always wanted me to choose the path she envisioned for my life over Dad's, but this felt different. This felt personal.

"I can't say I'm surprised. He was a failure as a husband, and he completed his failure by being a terrible father."

"Daddy's not that bad," I mumbled, feeling suddenly protective of him and wary of the woman sitting across from me. Never did I think this meeting would be easy, but neither did I imagine it would be so strange. "What happened between us that night?"

She dropped the clover strand and once again avoided my question. "I went away for a while. At first not voluntarily, but then once I understood what happened, what I did…I, um…I stayed. The doctors and staff were very nice, nonjudgmental. I've been faithfully on my medication ever since."

A low, dull throb pulsed near my temples. Goody for stinking her. She took her meds and all was right with the world. "I didn't ask that. Tell me what happened to me."

My mother rubbed a hand to her forehead. "Your father always checked on me before he let you visit. I depended upon that. Owen was supposed to take care of me, you and Aires and he messed it up for all of us."

What the hell? "How did he mess it up for Aires?"

Her eyes narrowed. "He allowed Aires to join the military."

"But that's what Aires wanted to do with his life. You know it was his dream."

"That wasn't your brother's dream. It was something that

witch your father married planted in his mind. She was the one that filled Aires' head with stories about her father and brothers and their careers. She didn't care if he died. She didn't care *what* happened to him.

"I told Aires not to go. I told him how much his decision would hurt me. I told him..." She paused. "I told him I'd never speak to him again if he went to Afghanistan." Her voice broke and all of a sudden I wanted to leave, yet I couldn't move.

A weird sort of edgy calmness took over my brain. "Those were your last words to Aires?"

"It's your father's fault," she said flatly. "He brought her into our lives and now my son is dead."

This time, *I* spoke as if she hadn't said anything. "Not 'I love you.' Not 'I'll see you when you get home.' You told him you'd never speak to him again?"

"That witch broke up my home. She stole your father."

"This isn't about Ashley or Dad or even Aires. This is about you and me. What the hell did you do to me?"

Wind chimes from a neighboring grave site tinkled in the breeze. My mother and I shared the same eye shape and color. Those dull and lifeless eyes stared at me. I hoped mine looked happier.

"Does he blame me for that night?" she asked. "Did your father even bother telling you how he just dropped you off? How he didn't answer the phone when you called for help?"

"Mom." I paused, trying to find the right words to explain. "I just want you to tell me what happened between us."

"He didn't tell you, did he? Of course he didn't. He's shoving the blame onto me. You don't understand. I lost Aires and I couldn't cope. I thought if I could paint, I would feel better." She tore handfuls of grass from the ground.

"Dad's not shoving anything onto you. He's accepted responsibility for his part, but I don't remember what happened with us. I fell into your stained glass and then you lay next to me while I bled." My voice rose higher as I continued to speak. "I don't understand. Did we fight? Did I fall? Did you push me and why didn't you call for help and why were you telling me bedtime stories when I was bleeding?"

She tore at the grass again. "This is not my fault. He should have known better. But that's your father for you. He never tried to understand. He wanted a cookie-cutter wife and divorced me the moment he found one."

"Mom, you came off your meds. Dad had nothing to do with that. Tell me what happened."

"No." She lifted her chin and jutted it out in the stubborn style I remembered so well.

I flinched. "No?"

"No. If you don't remember, I'm not telling you. I heard he's got some overpriced, fancy Harvard therapist helping you." A bitter smile curved her lips. "Did your father find something else he couldn't fix with money and control?"

For a fleeting moment, the cemetery resembled a chessboard and my mother moved her queen. If Aires and I were pawns in our parents' game, had she noticed that I quit playing?

"Heard?" I repeated as her answer struck me. "There's a restraining order. How did you hear anything?"

Mom blinked several times and the color seeped from her cheeks. "I wanted to know how you were doing, so I contacted your father."

A sickening feeling slid down my throat. "When?"

She lowered her head. "February."

"Mom...why didn't you call me? I gave you my numbers." I

paused, unable to keep up with the emotions and questions flying in my head. *February.* The word vibrated through me. That was the month my father took away my cell and my car without telling me why. He'd lied to me so he could conceal me from her. "I wanted to talk to you. I begged you back in December to call me. Why would you call Dad? I mean, you could have gone to jail. There is a restraining order!"

"No, there isn't," she said simply. "The order was rescinded thirty days after you turned eighteen."

Now I felt as if someone drop-kicked me in the stomach. "What?"

"It was the terms of the order when the judge signed it over two years ago. Your father tried to have it extended until you graduated, but enough time had passed that the judge no longer saw me as a threat."

I couldn't breathe and my head shook back and forth. "You mean you could have contacted me since February and you didn't?"

She hesitated. "Yes."

"Why?" Was I that unlovable? Weren't mothers supposed to want to see their daughters? Especially when their daughters asked them for help? Not knowing what to do with myself, I stood and wrapped my arms around my shaking body. "Why?" I screamed it this time.

"Because." Mom stood and raised her hands out to her sides. "Because I knew this is how you'd react. I knew you'd want to know what happened between us and I can't tell you."

"Why not?"

"Because you'll blame me and I can't take any more guilt. It wasn't my fault, Echo, and I'm not going to let you make me feel that way."

A Mack truck hit my body and my shoulders rolled with the impact. What an unbelievably selfish answer. "You don't know that's how I'll react. I'm not happy you went off your meds, but I get that you didn't understand what you were doing. I understand that you weren't in the right frame of mind that night."

She released a loud sigh and it echoed in the lonely cemetery. "I do know how you'll react, Echo. I told you before, you and I share the same skin. Once we're betrayed, we never forgive."

The dark sludge that had inhabited my veins since I found out my father's role in that day moved slowly in my gut, chilling me from the inside out. "I'm not like that."

"Aren't you? How's the bimbo your father married? You once loved her."

I wasn't her. I wasn't my mother. I blinked and stared at Aires' tombstone, half hoping he'd tell me she was wrong. What did this mean? What did this mean about me? And Ashley? And my father?

"Let's not discuss bad things," she said. "I've been on my medication for two years and I'm never coming off. Besides, I came here to catch up on the present, not rehash the past. I've got a fantastic job and a beautiful loft apartment. Echo? Echo, where are you going?"

From over my shoulder, I looked at the woman who gave birth to me. She'd never once said she was sorry. "I'm going home."

NOAH

Water trickled from my parents' fountain. Children laughed and yelled from the playground behind the neighborhood. Frank had told me to take the day off. I didn't need a day off. I needed to work. I needed the money. I didn't need so much damn time on my hands.

I brought Echo here once. Either to impress her or seduce her, or maybe I brought her here to prove to myself I was someone worth loving. Who the hell knew, for all the good it did.

My mind had wrestled with the same question since Tuesday. How could I help her? I drew nothing but blanks. So much for those damn problem-solving skills Mrs. Collins said I was so good at.

"Noah!"

I whipped my head at the sound of Jacob's voice and my heart squeezed in my chest. Wide-eyed, I stood just in time for the blond-haired midget to tackle me in a hug. "Noah! Noah! It's you! It's really you!"

Wrapping my arms around him, I quickly scanned the area. Joe slowly walked across the street, his hands shoved in his pockets, shoulders slumped forward. Carrie held the hand of a struggling Tyler. He extended his other hand toward me.

"Noah," said Joe.

"Joe."

Jacob faced Joe, but kept his arm around me. "You did this, didn't you?" He glanced excitedly at me. "He does things like this all the time. He tells us that he's taking us to the store and then does something great like get ice cream. Except this time he said we were going to the fountain and he gave us you."

The faith and love that radiated from Jacob tore at my heart.

"Didn't you, Dad?"

My muscles tensed and I held tighter to Jacob. *Dad.*

Joe's eyebrows furrowed together. "Jacob, I had no idea…"

"That I'd be early," I cut in. Joe eyed me warily, but didn't contradict me. Maybe if I played nice, he'd let me see them for a few seconds. "But I don't have much time, bro."

Jacob's smile fell. "Did you know that our mom and dad built these houses?"

I blinked. *Our mom and dad.* "Yeah. I was about your age then. I helped Dad put up every single porch swing."

Mom's smile returned on Jacob's face. "That must have been cool."

"Yeah, it was."

Joe gestured for Carrie to join us. A flash of worry covered her face before she slowly walked over. Like a fish, Tyler slipped out of her grasp and ran headfirst into my leg.

"Hey, bro."

Tyler responded with a dazzling smile. No bruises. No staples. Just happiness. I mussed the hair on his head.

"Hey, Mom," said Jacob, "did you know that Noah helped our mom and dad build these houses?"

The smile on her face seemed forced. "Did he?"

"Yep, because Noah is awesome."

Her lips turned down, but she shoved them back up.

"Wanna come play with us?" Jacob asked me.

Tyler attached himself to my leg and propped both of his feet on top of mine. I cleared my throat. "I've got to get to work later and I need to eat before that." Even though I didn't work today and even if I did, I cooked food for a living.

"Eat wis us," said Tyler.

He spoke to me. My youngest brother uttered his first words to me since the day of my parents' funeral. I stared helplessly at Carrie and Joe. I was trying to do the right thing here. The exact opposite of what I wanted and my brothers were tearing out my heart.

"Come home and have lunch with us," blurted out Carrie.

Joe touched her arm and spoke soothingly. "Are you sure?"

Carrie turned to him. "You were right, Joe."

"Noah, would you like to follow us home and have lunch with your brothers?" asked Joe.

"Yes!" Jacob pumped his fist. "Wait until you see my room and my bike."

Tyler still hung on my leg. "Yes, sir."

I forced down the ham-and-cheese sandwich, chips and iced tea, even though sitting here on the back patio at Carrie and Joe's made me nervous as hell. Part of me waited for the cops to show so Carrie could point at me and say I broke some sort of court order. To cover my ass, I called Mrs. Collins on the way here to tell her about lunch. She reminded me three times to watch my language.

"Come on, Noah, come see my room." Jacob tugged on my hand and I glanced at Carrie and Joe for permission. Joe nodded.

This was the grandest house I had ever seen. The house may have been Victorian-era style, but the entire inside rocked out in contemporary. Granite kitchen counters, stainless steel appliances, hardwood floors throughout the first floor and a foyer the size of Dale's basement.

Jacob rattled on about school and basketball while we walked up the massive staircase. "Tyler's room is across from mine and Mom and Dad's is right down the hall. We have two guest bedrooms. Two! Mom and Dad said that if I keep working with my counselor and go another month without nightmares then I can have friends over for a slumber party. I can't wait...."

He led me into a large room and I stopped in the doorway. It was like entering the grade-school version of *Pimp My Room*. A wooden bunk bed lined the wall. The bottom bunk was a full-size mattress and a slide attached to the top bunk. Jacob had his own television and toys. Toys were everywhere.

A picture frame on Jacob's dresser caught my eye and made it impossible to breathe. Jacob continued to talk, but I tuned him out as I picked up the frame. I rushed out the words, unsure I could say them without my voice breaking. "Do you know who this is?"

Jacob looked at the picture and then returned to the Bat Cave on the floor. "Yeah. That's our mom and dad." He said it so casually, like everyone had a picture of them.

I sat on the bed and ran a trembling hand over my face. My mom and dad. This was a fucking picture of my parents and they looked…happy. I sucked in a breath, but it sounded more like a sob.

"Jacob?" said Carrie. "Dessert is on the table."

Jacob jumped up and then hesitated. "You coming?"

I blinked rapidly. "Yeah, in a sec." I kept my eyes locked on the picture.

My brother hurried out the door and I tried hard to shove down the pressure building on my chest. Men don't cry. My parents. Men don't cry. Fuck. Men don't cry. I wiped at my eyes. I missed my parents.

"Are you okay?"

My head shot up; I'd been unaware that Carrie remained in the room. "Yeah. Sorry." I motioned with the frame before putting it back on the dresser. "Where did you get this?"

"Joe contacted Habitat for Humanity and asked if they had pictures of your parents. We felt it was important to keep them a part of the boys' lives."

I took a deep, shaky breath and faced her. "But not me."

Carrie immediately looked down. "Please don't take my boys away from me. They're my whole world and…and I can't live without them."

Joe walked into the room and placed his arm around her waist. "Carrie."

She shook like a damn leaf in a hurricane. "We'll give them everything. Everything. Whatever they want. I swear to you, they're happy here and I love them. I love them so much my heart hurts."

I tried to reach for the anger that had propelled me forward over the past couple of months, but I only found confusion. "They're my brothers and you've kept them from me. What did you expect me to do?"

Carrie began to sob. Joe pulled her into his chest and rubbed her back. "We were scared they'd choose you over us. That we'd lose them. Now, we stand to lose them regardless."

Joe whispered something into Carrie's ear. She nodded and left the room. He scratched the back of his head. "Thank you for what you did for Jacob. You transformed this entire family."

Family. Why didn't he use razor blades and rip me open that way? "You have a nice way of showing your appreciation."

"And we were wrong about that." Joe knelt by some Legos on the floor and absently dropped them, one at a time, back into the container. "All Carrie ever wanted was children. We tried for years, but Carrie has a medical condition. She had surgery to try to correct it, but it created scar tissue."

Unfortunately, I understood scar tissue.

"After she came to terms with the fact that we'd never hold our own natural-born child, we decided on adoption. We met Keesha through a friend and she convinced us to look into foster care. We attended classes, but never really planned on doing it until we met your brothers. Against everything we learned and were told, Carrie and I fell in love with them."

He continued to plunk one Lego piece on top of another. "After a few months, we decided to adopt. We had to prove to the court that no one else had claim to them, which we thought would be easy, but it turns out that your mother had living relatives."

My eyes narrowed. "Mom and Dad were only children. Mom's parents died her first year of college. Grandma and Papa died six months apart from each other when I was ten."

"Actually, your maternal grandmother is still alive, as well as your mother's brothers and sisters. She ran away from home to go to college. According to our findings, your mother had a... less than tolerable upbringing."

Besides to turn my world upside down and confuse me more… "Why are you telling me this?" And why hadn't my mom told me herself?

Joe shrugged. "In case you want to know that you still have living blood relatives. And to make you understand that we spent two years negotiating and fighting to keep your brothers from a place your mom ran away from. We won, only to be faced with our greatest challenge…you."

Just when I thought my life couldn't be more fucked up, Joe found a way to do it. He stood and assessed me—the way Isaiah did when he decided whether or not he was going to take a swing. "We've been wrong in how we've handled you and your relationship with your brothers. In our defense, you had just hit your foster father when we first took on your brothers. The system labeled you emotionally unstable and we were concerned about your influence on the boys, especially when we saw you bouncing around to several different foster homes. At first, we kept the boys away from you in order to protect them."

"And after the system began to figure out I wasn't the problem?"

"Then you scared us." He stared at me and after a second continued, "When you announced your plans to seek adoption, I had people dig deep to find information on you, to use against you in court."

Joe came closer to the bed and propped an arm on the wooden beam. "What you did to help those children in your previous foster homes was honorable, and what's happened to you is deplorable. Noah, my wife and I were wrong about you, but we weren't sure how to stop what we started without hurting our chances of keeping the boys."

My mind went blank. Joe and I had spent the past couple of

years at each other's throats and because of one chance meeting, he was waving the white flag? He scratched the back of his head, obviously feeling as unsure about this moment as I did.

Joe began again, "The way I see it, you've got three options. You can walk out of this house and continue to fight for your brothers and possibly win, yanking them away from their friends, their school, this house and us. You can fight and lose and only end up seeing your brothers on whatever visitation schedule the court allows, if any.

"Or you can withdraw your claim on the boys. Let us adopt them and raise them as we already see them, as our own. But with this option, you become a part of this family. You'll have unlimited access to them. Phone calls, visitation, school plays, basketball games. Hell, come have dinner with us once a week."

"Why?" I asked him.

He blinked, surprised by the question. "Why what?"

"Why are you offering the last option?" They'd gone this long hating me. Why be so generous now?

"Because they love you, Noah, and we love them. In ten years, I don't want to explain to my sons that I let fear and pride keep them away from their only blood relative who cared about them."

"I don't trust you," I said. Because adults lied.

Joe looked me straight in the eye. "I'll have my lawyer put it in writing."

I'd heard enough and I needed air. Joe had thrown out too much information, screwing with my brain. I pushed past him so I could find my brothers. Carrie lurked in the hallway, clutching a stuffed bear. For years I'd seen her as the hateful bitch who kept my brothers away from me. Thanks to Joe's little speech I couldn't see that anymore. Instead, I saw a broken woman who couldn't complete her own dreams because of me.

Yeah, I knew all about scar tissue. Problem was, helping her was only going to increase mine.

Echo

I slammed the door to my car and ran up the dark driveway. Thank God, Isaiah was under the hood of Aires' car.

"I am so sorry I'm late. I had this thing—" I met my mom, whom my dad would freak about if he found out I saw "—and it got screwed up—" she'd rather I spend years never sleeping again because she's scared of what I'd think of her and then pointed out I'm a heartless, unforgiving bitch "—and I lost track of time." I'd driven around trying to convince myself she was wrong.

Isaiah poked his head out from under the hood and gave me a crazy smile. "S'all good. Your dad told me I could go ahead and work on it."

Okay. Sort of not my father's style to let pierced, tattooed people hang out alone in our garage, but maybe he was too busy with Ashley to care. The door to the kitchen closed and Beth entered the garage with a can of Diet Coke. "All you've got is diet shit in your house. And fruit. Lots of fucking fruit. Don't you have any frozen pizzas?"

"Ashley doesn't like preservatives." What was I doing? "Why were you in my house?" I glanced around and my heart dropped. "Where's Noah?" My slow mind caught up with the fact that my father's car was gone. "Where's my father?"

Beth stared at me blankly, then snapped out of her trance. Lovely, she was high. "Oh, yeah, your stepmom went into labor and your dad said something about telling you." She scrunched her eyes together. "Was there more to the message, Isaiah?"

He mumbled from under the hood, "Fuck, I don't know. You were the one who was supposed to be listening."

Beth giggled. "Right. I was." Her giggling stopped. "Wow. When did it get to be night?"

My heart tripped in my chest. "Ashley's in labor? She can't be. She still has like…" I don't know—something weeks left. Crap, how come I never paid attention? Dad had to be freaking out. "Lots of time left. The baby isn't done yet."

Beth tilted her head. "Do babies have timers?" Her smile grew. "If not, they should."

Isaiah shut the hood with a feverish look in his eyes. "I need the keys."

I experienced mind whiplash. Oh. My. God. He'd never asked for the keys before. I pointed crazily in the air toward the hook on the workbench, unable to do more than stutter, "There… there…they're there."

He grabbed the keys and hopped into the front seat of the car. I swore time moved in slow motion as he placed his foot on the gas pedal and inserted the key into the ignition.

In my mind, I saw Aires. His brown hair, long legs and ever-present smile. "It's gonna run someday, Echo," he once said. "Can't you just hear the engine purring?"

Tears burned my eyes and I swallowed down the sob. *Yes, Aires. It is going to run. I did this for you.* How I wished he was here.

Isaiah turned the key and the sweetest rumbling sound filled the garage. He pressed his foot against the gas and hollered as the engine roared with life. "Oh, yeah, baby, that's what I'm fucking talking about!"

He stepped out of the car with his arms wide open. "I'm getting me something for this."

And I happily complied. I jumped into those arms and kissed his cheek. "Thank you. Thank you. Thank you."

I let go of Isaiah, sat in the warm leather seat and clutched the vibrating steering wheel. Isaiah closed the door and I shifted the car into Reverse.

And then everything inside of me froze. I pressed down on the brake to stop. The hole in my heart that was supposed to be filled with this moving car…grew. "Isaiah, where's Noah?"

NOAH

Carrie's arms strangled my neck and, for a moment, I hoped she'd kill me. Death had to be better than this. I swallowed, but the heavy lump in my throat remained. Every muscle in my face pulled down and I sucked in air in an attempt to wash away the despair.

"I want to talk to Mrs. Collins first," I choked out. "I haven't completely made up my mind." Goddammit. Why did everything have to hurt so bad? Every part of my body throbbed with pain to the point that I either had to die or explode.

"God bless you, Noah," Carrie whispered in my ear.

I wanted a family. I wanted a fucking family and Jacob and Tyler already had one.

She sniffed as she released me, but her smile lit up the room like a thousand stars put together. "I know you'll do the right thing by the boys. I know it."

They had normal.

And I wasn't it.

Carrie waited for a reply, but I couldn't form a response to save my life. Joe placed a hand on my shoulder, saving me from speaking. "Mrs. Collins will be here soon."

As if we were living out a bad sitcom, the doorbell chimed on cue and Carrie escorted Mrs. Collins into the kitchen. She wore paint-covered sweatpants and a Nirvana T-shirt. Joe mumbled something about giving us a few minutes.

The dishwasher beside me entered a rinse cycle. The rhythmic beating of the water against the dishes filled the room. Mrs. Collins tapped one finger against the black granite countertop. My gaze trailed to her face, expecting to see agitation for dragging her into this mess. Instead, the pain in her puppy dog eyes ripped open the dam of emotions I struggled to suppress.

Wetness invaded my eyes and I closed them, shaking my head repeatedly to stop any of it from falling. I did not want to hurt. I did not want to care, but dammit, this was killing me.

"Talk to me, Noah," she said in the most serious tone I'd ever heard from her.

I glanced around the kitchen and back to her. "I can't give them this."

"No," she replied softly. "You can't."

"And I can't afford basketball camps and the private school they love so much and the gifts for all the birthday parties they're invited to." My throat became thick.

"No," she repeated.

"And they have grandparents." I didn't recognize the hoarse sound of my voice. "Jacob couldn't stop talking about Joe's parents and Tyler goes fishing with Carrie's dad every Wednesday as long as it's above freezing. I can't offer them that."

"You're right."

"I love them," I said with determination.

"I know you do." And her voice quavered. "I have never doubted that."

"I love Echo, too." I stared straight into Mrs. Collins's eyes. "I
miss her."

She shrugged and gave me a sad smile. "It's okay to love someone besides your brothers, Noah. You aren't betraying them or
your parents because you're living your life."

And it happened. After years of holding it in, the grief within
me snapped. All of the anger and sadness and hurt I'd stored
away in my quest to never feel those emotions burst through to
the surface. "I want my mom and dad." I couldn't suck in air. "I
just want my family back."

Mrs. Collins wiped her eyes and crossed the room to me. "I
know," she said again and pulled me into a hug.

"THANKS AGAIN, NOAH." JOE SHOOK my hand for possibly the fifti-
eth time since I told him and Carrie I was no longer pursuing
custody after I graduated. "I promise you'll see them whenever
you want."

I nodded and glanced over my shoulder. Mrs. Collins and
Carrie stood near the stairs at the end of the second-floor hallway. Mrs. Collins sent me an encouraging smile and I took a
deep breath.

Joe opened the door to Jacob's room and the two of us entered. "Boys, Noah would like to talk to you."

"Noah!" In Batman pajamas, Jacob raced across the room and
rammed into me. "You're still here!"

"Yes," said Joe. "And he'll be here a lot more."

With eager eyes, Jacob marveled at Joe. "You mean it?"

"I swear to it." Joe patted my shoulder. "I'll give you guys some
time to talk."

And just like that he walked away, closing the door behind him. I hadn't been alone with my brothers in over two years. With my hand on Jacob, I stared at the picture of my parents. They weren't coming back and I could never re-create what we had, but I could move forward.

I sat on the floor and my heart floated when Tyler, in footed pajamas, inched closer to me and placed his small hand in mine. His thumb in his mouth. A blanket in his fist.

Jacob superglued himself to my side. "Dad never swears unless he means it, Noah. He says it's a sin to lie."

I nodded. "It is. Our mom used to say that, too." I cleared my throat and began the hardest conversation of my life. "A couple of years ago, I made a promise to you. At the time I meant it, but now I don't think it's the best thing for any of us."

I looked at Tyler. He was too young to remember the way Mom laughed when Dad tried to dance with her as she washed the dinner dishes. Too young to remember Dad showing him pictures of buildings and explaining how his sons would know how to hammer in a nail correctly before the age of ten.

And Jacob. Old enough to remember, but too young to fully understand everything he lost. He'd never know the pride of walking in with Mom on parent appreciation night. He'd never know the explosion of joy when Dad told him that he was a natural when he used his first power tool.

They'd never know that they lost the two most amazing people on the face of the planet. They'd never know how the loss had torn me up every single day of my life.

I took a deep breath and tried again. "How would you feel about the two of you living here forever and me just coming to visit?"

Mrs. Collins ran the stop sign at the end of Jacob and Tyler's street. I sat in my car, alone.

Echo.

I had let her walk away and it wasn't over custody of my brothers. Mrs. Collins was right. Deep down I'd thought loving her was a betrayal of my parents and my brothers.

But I loved Echo. I needed her. And I was going to win her back.

I turned on the car and the engine sputtered to life. Foster care was educational—in a "five to seven years with the possibility of parole" kind of way. The question was what to do with all of the information I'd gathered.

Echo

"He's where?" I screeched. I turned off Aires' car and flew out of the seat. The entire world had gone insane. First Ashley went into early labor. Now Noah insisted upon being crazy.

"Dammit, Beth. I told you not to smoke that shit. Noah is going to be pissed." Isaiah rubbed a hand over his buzzed head. For once, I was glad that Beth was stoned into near-incomprehension and rambling.

"What exactly does he think he's going to get?" I asked. "He already knows everything about his brothers and he told me that he's following the letter of the law. Breaking into Mrs. Collins's office is not following the letter of the law!"

Isaiah clapped his hands together. "Let's take it for a ride."

Had Isaiah also lost his mind? "Your best friend...your brother is going to break into school and then break into Mrs. Collins's office and you want to take the car for a ride?"

Isaiah rubbed his hands together in mock excitement, but frustration marred his eyes. "Yes."

"No." I waved my hand in the air. "No. We've got to stop him. He cannot be caught or he'll lose his brothers. Oh, my God, he can be such a stubborn idiot. What could breaking in possibly accomplish?"

"He wants you back," slurred Beth.

Lightning bolts could have flashed out of the cloudless night and set my tennis shoes on fire, and I would have been less surprised. "Excuse me?"

Beth sat on the concrete and rested her head against the workbench, eyelids fluttering in exhaustion. "He's in love with you and wants you to be his one and only. And some other bullshit about you not being in second place and proving you wrong."

Ding, ding. Noah wanted my file and he wanted me back. My heart squeezed in warmth and joy then dropped and became cold. No, he couldn't risk anything for me—not when it could cost him his brothers. I turned to Isaiah. "We have to stop him. When did he leave?"

"He wanted to wait until it got dark. Noah came home all messed up. I assumed he saw you and you guys had a fight. Babbled on about how he screwed things up with you and was determined to set it right. He asked me to come here, fix the car and then to keep you here until he showed."

"Why didn't you stop him?" I dug my keys out of my pocket.

"You don't stop Noah."

Guess again.

ISAIAH SLID HIS CAR INTO A spot at the supermarket across the street from the high school and cut the engine. I tried Noah's cell and for the millionth time it went to voice mail.

"Why don't you park at the school?" I asked.

Isaiah gave me an are-you-a-moron glance. "Police patrol the school grounds every two hours. They'll know something is up if there's a car in the school's lot."

Sure enough, Noah too had parked his car at the supermarket. "Done this before?"

"Just for kicks to play ball in the gym, but never to break into an office."

I squeezed the door handle and eyed Beth, who was passed out in the backseat. "She okay?"

"Yeah, just fucked up." He pulled at an earring. "I can't leave her in the car like this and if we wake her up, she'll make enough noise to raise eyebrows. Odds are Noah would have picked the side entrance nearest to the main office. He'll place something small in the doorway to keep the door from relocking him in. Make sure you keep that there. Grab him and tell him you two can argue later."

"Thanks."

I ran across the street and tried to keep my lungs from exploding. Good God, I was breaking and entering to keep my stupid, stubborn, sweet-as-can-be—boyfriend? Ex-boyfriend? Maybe boyfriend again?—out of jail.

Just like Isaiah said, Noah had left the side door next to the office propped open. I slipped in, making sure I kept the door exactly how I found it. Mrs. Collins would love finding the two of us locked in her office.

I had that eerie horror flick feel as the lights flashed on ahead of me with every step I took. My heart flew up to pound in my throat. I kept looking over my shoulder, waiting for someone to rush up from behind me and suck my blood or drag me off to prison.

At first I skulked against the lockers, then realized what a fool I was. The freaking lights were already on and would turn off once all movement stopped. No more skulking—I ran.

Thank God, the office lights were switch only. I'd had enough of motion sensors. Problem? Mrs. Collins's office door was closed and no light shined from underneath the door. Had Noah already left?

The hallway went dark, but seconds later the lights flickered back on. Talk about freaking completely out. I grabbed the handle to Mrs. Collins's door and almost yelped when it came open. As quietly as I could, I closed the door and backed away from it, hoping and praying that whoever entered the office was either Noah or wouldn't find me.

The urge to scream zapped from my toes to my mouth when something warm and strong came up behind me and jerked me into the coat cabinet. The door of the cabinet shut before my eyes.

Noah hissed in my ear, "What are you doing here?"

I harshly whispered back, "I could ask you the same thing! I'm here to save your butt from going to jail over something stupid and losing your brothers."

Footsteps echoed from the main office. I clutched Noah's hand, which was still wrapped around my waist, and he pulled me closer to him. He barely whispered, "Side door?"

I nodded. If the security guard found the side door propped open, they'd know someone entered the building. I reached into my pocket and withdrew my phone, texting Isaiah rapidly: **unprop side door asap!**

Seconds later Isaiah texted back: **on it.**

Noah lowered his head so his nose skimmed the tender area right behind my ear. His warm breath tickled my sensitive skin.

I'd missed him and his touch. Why did he have to go and do something so idiotic?

I wasn't worth losing his brothers. If Noah got caught he'd get arrested. My stomach dropped to my toes. What did I have to lose? I was a two-bit artist roaming the country with her canvases. So I'd have a record (every muscle cringed) and I'd have to stay at least one night in jail (vomit burned the back of my throat). Yeah, it would be great.

Noah's arms tightened and I could have sworn he kissed my hair. I could do it—for him. I could give myself up and tell Noah to stay hidden. I was reaching out to shove open the door when Noah's hand smacked it back down and held it to my stomach in a death grip. "What the fuck do you think you're doing?" he asked in a low voice.

"Taking a peek to see if we're in the clear?" Crap, I sucked at lying.

"Hell, no, and you're full of shit. You're staying here with me."

"Your brothers…"

"I gave them up."

I shifted so I could see his face and the pain in his eyes sliced through me. "Not for me."

His throat moved as he swallowed and he shook his head. "For them."

My cell vibrated. Isaiah texted back: Bad. Get out thru window now. Car ready.

"Fuck," whispered Noah. "I must have triggered an alarm. Come on."

He quietly opened the door to the coat cabinet. In a methodical yet somehow fluid motion, he opened one of the windows. Without headlights, Isaiah's car moved stealthily into the student parking lot.

Noah picked up one of my feet to help lift me out the window. "Keep running until you can get in Isaiah's car."

"What about you?" Pure panic shook my insides. I thought my eyes were going to wheel out of my head.

He gave me his relaxed, wicked grin. "I'll be right behind you, baby. Did I ever mention you're uptight?"

As he gave me a boost, I noticed that Mrs. Collins's desk sat file-free. Oh, well. I rapidly climbed through the window and sprinted across the parking lot toward Isaiah, peeking behind my shoulder to see Noah crouched near the wall. Blood pounded in my veins and the cool night air burned my lungs as I raced to freedom.

The back passenger door flew open and I dove inside, landing on Beth's feet. I slammed the door behind me. My gut twisted at the sight of Noah running full speed toward the car. Lights in the main office flashed on. Isaiah continued to drive closer to Noah. My eyes darted between Noah and Mrs. Collins's dark office. Isaiah threw the front passenger door open and took off the second Noah landed in the front seat.

"We've got to get out of here." Isaiah glanced in his rearview mirror.

"Take me to my car then go home." Noah was watching the dark, closed window of Mrs. Collins's office. He cackled and hooted when the light turned on the moment we crossed the invisible freedom line of the grocery store parking lot.

Isaiah pulled up next to Noah's car and the two of us got out. Beth still lay sound asleep in the back. Isaiah called out to us, "Fight someplace else. Don't stay here."

Noah offered Isaiah his hand. "Thanks, bro."

Accepting it, Isaiah answered, "Anytime, man."

Isaiah drove off as Noah started his car and followed after

him. Two blocks from the school, a police car with lights flashing and no siren drove past us going the opposite direction. That
had been freaking close.

Noah covered my hand with his. "You okay, baby?"

"Yeah." But I didn't feel okay. I felt anything but okay. I waited for my pulse to stop beating my veins like a gang initiation,
for the blood to leave my face and for my lungs to not burn as I
gasped. We were safe now. We were free, but my body still re-
acted like the devil was chasing me.

Another cop car drove past and the blue and red flashing
lights hurt my eyes. In my temples, a slow, steady throb mim-
icked the rhythm of the blue light—away and near, away and
near.

The left side of my face felt numb and my head grew light.
"Noah, I think I'm going to be sick."

"Hold on." Noah turned into an abandoned parking lot. He'd
barely parked the car when I threw the door open and stumbled
out, hacking up the remains of my long-ago lunch.

Noah held my hair away from my face. His body shook with
silent laughter. "Seriously, you are way too uptight."

Part of me wanted to laugh with him, but I couldn't. I sat back
on my knees and stared into the dark night. I couldn't get the
flashing lights out of my head. The red and the blue. Near and
away. Near and away.

And then…darkness. No lights. No sounds. Darkness…

Vibrant, colorful images flashed forward in my mind in rapid
succession, hitting me like bullets from a machine gun. My head
dropped forward and I covered it with my arms to drown it all
out. My mind pulled at the images, attempting to sort them, to
categorize them, but it couldn't—and the loss of control, the
bombardment, caused sharp, excruciating pain to tear through

my brain. Voices and sounds and high-pitched screams clawed at my mind.

I realized that I was screaming and heard Noah speaking rapidly to me. The sound of glass shattering and my own screams drowned him out.

"What happened?" A man with a small light in his hand hovered over me. Red lights flashed behind him and beyond that constellations glowed in the night sky. My mother's voice whispered in my ear, crooning to me to return to her story.

"No!" I fought to keep myself from falling back into the pit, back to her floor…to keep away from my own blood. "Noah!"

His voice had a husky edge as he called out to me, "I'm right here, baby."

The man withdrew the light. A stethoscope hung from his neck. "Have you taken any drugs tonight? Have you been drinking?"

The rage in Noah's voice tasted bitter in my own mouth. "Listen, you fucking asshole, for the fifth time, she's clean."

He ignored Noah as he rubbed his hands under my neck. "Pot? Meth? Pills of any kind?"

You're not allowed sleeping pills. My own voice echoed from the back of my mind. No. No. God, no. Gravitational forces pushed me into the ground and my mind got sucked into itself and yanked reality from my grasp.

"You suffer from depression." I shook the empty pill bottle and stumbled out of my mother's bathroom, stopping when my knee hit the stained glass window she had propped between two chairs to let dry.

My mother sat on the couch, a glass of iced tea in one hand and a picture of Aires in the other. She took a methodical sip.

Her eyes darted from my own empty glass of tea on the coffee table to me. Her wild red hair fell from its clip. "I know."

I swayed to the side as the entire world tilted. "What did you do?"

She took another sip of tea. Everything inside of me became heavy as steel. "What did you do to me?"

"Don't worry, Echo. We'll be with Aires soon. You said you missed him and would do anything to see him again. So would I."

The room flipped to the left. I struggled to stay upright and overcompensated to the right, but I fell regardless of my efforts. The world collapsed in on itself. The sound of glass shattering accompanied searing pain and screams. Screams from my mother. Screams from me. I opened my eyes and watched as a shower of red and blue followed me to the floor. A fleeting thought ripped through the pain…I'd loved that stained glass window.

Blood.

Blood poured from the exposed veins on my arms. It soaked my clothes and stained my skin. It pooled at the crook of my elbow and a small river streamed out and flowed toward my mother, who was now lying next to me.

"I'm bleeding!"

A strong hand gripped mine. Noah came into view. "No, you're not." Behind him, white lights glared and a beeping noise kept in sync with the pounding of my heart. He spoke with unwavering determination. "Focus, Echo! Look at your arms!"

He held my arms up. Clear tubing gently rubbed against my skin. I'd expected blood, but there was none. White scars. Raised scars. And no blood.

"Noah?" I gasped, trying to understand through the screams in my head.

"I've got you. I swear to God, I've got you," said Noah. "Stay with me, Echo."

I wanted to. I wanted to stay with him, but the shouting and screams and glass breaking in my mind grew louder. "Make it stop."

He tightened his grip on my arms. "Fight, Echo! You've got to fucking fight. Come on, baby. You're safe."

Noah wavered in front of me and swirled. Pain sliced through me and I screamed again. A nurse pulled glass out of my arm. My father wiped the tears from my eyes and kissed my forehead. Blood soaked his white button-down shirt and smeared his face. "Shh, sweetheart, don't cry, you're safe now. You're safe."

"You're safe, Echo." Noah rubbed the scars on my arm.

"She can't hurt you ever again." My father held my bandaged hand, tears pouring down his face.

"Go to sleep," my mother cooed, lying on the floor next to me, my blood creeping toward her on the floor.

My father scooped me up and cradled me in the hospital bed. "I'll scare the nightmares away. I promise. Please, just sleep."

And the constant screaming stopped and I gasped between shallow breaths and a cold, calm hospital room blinked into view. A woman in blue scrubs finished pushing something in an IV line and gave me a small smile before walking away.

My eyelids became heavy and I fought it.

"Go to sleep, baby." Noah's voice soothed like balm on a wound.

I swallowed and turned my heavy head to the sound of his voice. "She drugged me."

He gave me a sad smile and squeezed the hand he held. "Welcome back."

My voice was slurred. "She put all of the sleeping pills in the tea without me knowing and she gave me a glass."

His lips pressed against my hand. "You need to rest."

My eyes flickered. "I want to wake up."

"Sleep, Echo. I'm right here and I swear I'll never let anyone hurt you again."

NOAH

"Still here, Noah?" Mrs. Collins strode into Echo's hospital room. "Mr. Emerson said you brought her in."

I raked a hand through my hair in an attempt to wake my brain. Echo had slept through the entire night. I spent most of it staring at her, holding her hand, and sometimes drifting off in the chair. "Yeah."

Mrs. Collins's blond hair was pulled back in a ponytail. She wore blue jeans and a Grateful Dead T-shirt. Dragging a chair to the other side of the bed, she took Echo's hand. "Has her dad been down?"

"He stayed here for a couple of hours last night, but they'd already put her to sleep before he showed. He talked to the doctor before he went back to help Ashley feed the baby."

"What did the doctor say?"

"That he'll know if her mind cracked when she wakes up."

She let out a brief sarcastic chuckle. "Is that how he put it?"

"That's my own spin." My thumb caressed Echo's hand. She

slept on her own now. They hadn't given her anything else to keep her calm or help her sleep. Nothing to do now but wait. "Do you think she'll be okay?"

Mrs. Collins cocked an eyebrow. "I'm surprised you asked. You know better than I do that she's a fighter."

I relaxed back in the chair. It felt good to hear someone else say it. But still, after watching her fight for her sanity last night... How much could a mind take?

"Did you know she saw her mother yesterday?" asked Mrs. Collins.

Muscles tensed again. "What?"

"Yep. She sure surprised me. I didn't know Echo had it in her to defy her father. Guess you were a bigger influence than I gave you credit for. She used her trips to different art galleries to find her mom. Left letters for her everywhere until her mother finally agreed to meet."

"How do you know this?"

"I guess the meeting didn't go well and her mother called her father and told him to find Echo."

Damn. Just damn. And she'd tried to save me. Echo wanted to know what happened to her, but had been terrified to remember. I'd never really understood. Yesterday must have pushed her mind over the edge—seeing her mother, fixing Aires' car, almost becoming a felon. I knotted my fingers with her lifeless ones. *I promise, Echo, I'll take care of you now and forever.*

"You really didn't know, did you?"

"Had no clue." I thought about what she said. "Mr. Emerson didn't go after her, did he?"

Mrs. Collins tucked the blanket tighter around Echo. "Ashley went into labor after the phone call. The baby came early."

Once again, second place. The story of Echo's life. Echo had a habit of making me feel like a dick in comparison to her and today would be no exception. She left me so I could have a family, making her—alone. How could I ever have let her walk away?

"I'm proud of you, Noah."

The past twenty-four hours had been one long nightmare. I lost my brothers. Echo came close to losing her mind. "Why is it when people are proud of me that my life sucks?"

"Because growing up means making tough choices, and doing the right thing doesn't necessarily mean doing the thing that feels good."

We sat in silence and listened to the sound of Echo's light breathing and the steady beep of the heart monitor. My heart ached with the promises I silently made to her and longed to fulfill. She'd never be alone again.

"She had a moment before she fell asleep," I said. "She said her mother drugged her with sleeping pills. Echo cried a lot during the hallucination or whatever you want to call it. Sounded like her mom was in a depression, decided to kill herself, and then Echo showed. Psycho mom changed the plan to include her."

Mrs. Collins sighed and patted Echo's hand. "Then she remembers."

Echo

Mrs. Collins sent me an encouraging smile when the tiny pieces of tissue fell from my hands onto the blanket. "Sorry," I said. I shifted in the hospital bed and sighed when more tiny pieces fell to the floor.

The hospital psychiatrist, a balding man in his late forties, laughed. "Tissues were made to be torn. Don't worry."

I felt like I had done nothing but cry since I woke up this morning. I cried when I opened my eyes to find Noah at my side. I cried when the doctors immediately came in and asked Noah to leave so they could examine me. I cried when I told the psychiatrist and Mrs. Collins what I remembered. I cried when they talked me through the events.

And here I was, hours later, still crying—a pathetic, constant trickle of tears.

I plucked another tissue from the box and tried to discreetly blow my nose. I remembered. Everything. Showing up and finding Mom in a deep depression. Deciding to stay to see if I could convince her to see her therapist. Drinking the tea and then feeling ill.

Going to the bathroom, finding the empty bottle of sleeping pills on the sink and calling my father only to end up in his voice mail. The sinking realization that my mother planned to kill herself and then decided to include me without my consent. Becoming woozy and falling into the stained glass. The time spent on the floor, begging my mother to get me help, and then…closing my eyes.

No wonder I hated sleep.

I blew my nose again. "So, can I go home?"

The psychiatrist leaned forward and patted my knee. "Yes. I recommend that you continue private therapy to deal with any residual feelings now that you've remembered the incident. I hear Mrs. Collins has kept a few private clients on. Maybe she'd be willing to help."

Mrs. Collins all but wagged her tail and panted. "My door is always open."

"I think I'd like that." Who knew? The woman I'd assumed was dead-set on making my life a living hell had actually delivered me from it.

IN TYPICAL GLINDA THE Good Witch fashion, Lila brought me stuff from home. Once I had something to change into other than puke-covered clothes or a hospital gown, I enjoyed a long, hot shower. When I left the bathroom, I found Noah standing by the window.

"Hey," I said.

"Hey." Noah flashed his wicked grin. "I hear they're springing you."

"Yeah." I walked over to the small bag Lila had left and shoved my stuff back in, trying to think of anything else to do to keep myself busy.

He'd witnessed me lose it. But he also stayed with me the entire time. Maybe he felt bad for me. Yet he broke into Mrs. Collins's office to get my file because, according to Beth, he wanted me back.

"Noah." But he said my name at the exact same time. He hitched his thumbs in his pockets as I drummed my fingers against the nightstand.

"How are you?" he asked.

Was he asking because he was buying himself time before he dumped me? Who would want to stay with a crazy girl? I shrugged and watched my fingers continue to tap. "Fine."

In an uncharacteristic movement, Noah scratched the back of his head. He looked almost…unsure. Crap, I'd freaked him out so badly he was terrified to be in the same room as me.

"You scared the shit out of me last night, so forgive me if I don't want to hear fine as an answer."

I rubbed my eyes, hoping it would keep the burning tears away. The warm water of the shower had finally calmed the tears, but the thought of Noah walking away brought them back. "What do you want to hear? That I'm exhausted? Terrified? Confused? That all I want to do is rest my head on your chest and sleep for hours, but that's not going to happen because you're leaving me?"

"Yes," he said quickly, then just as quick said, "No. Everything but the last part." He paused. "Echo, how could you think I would leave you? How can you doubt how I feel?"

"Because," I said as I felt the familiar twisting in my stomach. "You saw me lose it. You saw me almost go insane."

The muscles in his shoulders visibly tensed. "I watched you

battle against the worst memory of your life and I watched you win. Make no mistake, Echo. I battled right beside you. You need to find some trust in me...in us."

Noah inhaled and slowly let the air out. His stance softened and so did his voice. "If you're scared, tell me. If you need to cry and scream, then do it. And you sure as hell don't walk away from us because you think it would be better for me. Here's the reality, Echo: I want to be by your side. If you want to go to the mall stark naked so you can show the world your scars, then let me hold your hand. If you want to see your mom, then tell me that, too. I may not always understand, but damn, baby, I'll try."

I stared at him and he stared at me. The air between us grew heavy with the weight of our next unsaid words.

"Okay," I said.

He closed his eyes for a second, the tension draining from his face. "Okay."

My heart pounded in my chest. Did this mean we were back together? I wanted it to mean that, but the ground beneath me felt unstable. Maybe we'd be okay if we could just be us again. "Stark naked?"

"We all have dreams, Echo." The right side of his mouth tipped up. "You know, there's a bed here and the door's already closed. It'd be a damn shame not to take advantage of the situation."

I laughed and the action took me off guard, but, oh, it felt good.

Noah didn't walk, he stalked and I loved the mischievous glint in his eye when he stalked me. He placed his hands on my hips and nuzzled my hair. "I love the way you smell."

"Thanks." Heat flushed my cheeks and I blew out a breath.

So much had changed in twenty-four hours. "Why did you give up your brothers?"

Noah stroked his fingers through my curls, gently pulling on them in tantalizing movements. "Because they love Carrie and Joe and living with them is what's best."

Unable to stop myself, I caressed the rough stubble on his cheeks. "But you love them."

His smile became forced and a muscle clenched in his jaw. "I'll still be a part of their lives. A big part. I'm not going to lie, it hurts like hell, but I'm honestly relieved. I can go to college. I can decide my own future."

I swallowed and tried to reign in the mutant pterodactyls having a roller derby in my stomach as I dared to think about a future for the two of us. The moment Aires' car rumbled beneath me, I'd known that I needed Noah in my life. Aires' death had left a gaping hole in my heart. I thought all I needed was that car to run. Wrong. A car would never fill the emptiness, but love could. "I hope your future includes me. I mean, someone has to continue to kick your butt in pool."

Noah laughed as he snagged his fingers around my belt loops and dragged me closer. "I was letting you win."

"Please." His eyes had about fallen out of his head when I'd sunk a couple of balls off the break. "You were losing. Badly." I wondered if he also reveled in the warmth of being this close again.

"Then I guess I'll have to keep you around. For good. You'll be useful during a hustle." He lowered his forehead to mine and his brown eyes, which had been laughing seconds ago, darkened as he got serious. "I have a lot I want to say to you. A lot I want to apologize for."

"Me, too." And I touched his cheek again, this time letting my fingers take their time. Noah wanted me, for good. "But can we hash it all out some other time? I'm sort of talked out and I've still gotta go see my dad. Do you think we can just take it on faith right now that I want you, you want me, and we'll figure out the happy ending part later?"

His lips curved into a sexy smile and I became lost in him. "I love you, Echo Emerson."

I whispered the words as he brought his lips to mine. "Forever."

Echo

Noah held my hand and my bag as he escorted me to the third floor—the Women's Pavilion. The elevator bell rang and the doors opened.

"Jesus, Echo, circulation in my hand would be a good thing," said Noah.

"Sorry." I tried to let go, but Noah kept his fingers linked with mine.

We walked down the hallway and passed women strolling slowly with their husbands, balloon- and flower-filled rooms, and the nurse's station. At the end of the hall, I paused right outside the room I'd been told was Ashley's.

"Do you want me to come in?" he asked.

I shook my head. "She might be breast-feeding." Plus I didn't need an audience for this.

Noah tensed. "Too much information. I'll be in the waiting room."

"All right."

He kissed my lips softly. "Text me and I'll be here in a heart-beat, breast-feeding or not."

"Thanks."

Noah waited until I stepped into the room before he retreat-ed. No ordinary room for Ashley. My father had upgraded to the private room with full spa bathroom, leather couches, wood floors and flat-screen television. He and Ashley were giggling over something when I stepped inside. "Hi."

Ashley stretched out on the inclined hospital bed with my father right beside her. His arm was draped over her shoulder. There was no sign of the constant worry lines on my father's face. His gray eyes shone as he looked down at the bundled baby she held in her arms.

They stopped laughing and Dad sat up on the bed. "Echo. Are you okay? Do you need me?"

My foot tapped against the floor. Nausea roiled deep inside. I'd had no idea how badly seeing the replacement child would hurt. "I'm fine. Am I interrupting something? Because if so I could go, because I know that you just had a baby and all…"

"No." Ashley's blue eyes softened. "You're not interrupting anything, Echo. Please come in. I'm sorry I couldn't be with you last night, but…well…I was sort of preoccupied."

"Yeah. It's fine. You had a baby. I think that sort of trumps—" Watching me have a breakdown.

I took the seat next to the bed and tried to peek at the baby without seeming like it. "Is he okay? I mean, he was born early and stuff."

Not that I should care or anything. This thing was my and Aires' replacement. But still, it was a small, defenseless baby and it should have been cooking in Ashley's belly, not out too soon in this horrible world.

My dad gave me an honest-to-God smile. "He's perfect."

"Good." I crossed my ankles and my foot rocked in rhythm to the finger tapping on my knee.

"Would you like to hold him?" Ashley asked.

Um...no. "Okay?"

My father retrieved the swaddled baby from Ashley's arms and handed him to me. Becoming the queen of awkward, I moved my hands three times before I finally accepted him.

"Support his head and hold him close," my father said. "That's right. See, you're a natural."

"Sure." People naturally wanted to run screaming when they held a baby. My heart rate rose when the little pink thing yawned and opened his eyes. He blinked three times and let them close again. When I blinked like that, a lie typically followed. I wondered how closely related we were.

"Would you like to know his name?" Ashley asked.

"Yeah. What's his name?" Because people named their children and I was supposed to want to know.

My father caressed Ashley's hand and answered, "Alexander Aires Emerson."

A shiver ran through me until the name settled in my heart. Alexander's little hand broke free from the blanket and grasped my finger. Aires. They named the baby after Aires.

Aires would have loved this baby, regardless of who his mother was, regardless of how our father treated him. Why? Because that's the way he'd loved me. Aires loved me unconditionally. He loved me when I was a scared child. He loved me when I was a bratty preteen. He loved me as a hormonal teenager. When nobody else in this world could love me for being an unsure, self-absorbed, timid scaredy-cat, he loved me.

More than once, Aires had sucked up his pride for me. He

took crap from my father, my mother and from Ashley to stick up for me. Aires did only one selfish thing in his life and that was to fulfill his dream of becoming a Marine, but even then, he fought for me. He wrote my father and Ashley letters, telling them to lay off. He called and wrote me all the time. He sacrificed his free time in order to be up-to-date on every detail of my life.

Aires would have moved heaven and earth for this baby, just like he had moved heaven and earth for me.

I'd thought repairing Aires' car was going to fix my life. I'd thought the same thing about recovering my memory. But neither of those things fulfilled the magical hope I'd clung to—that somehow my life would rewind to three years before.

Alexander shifted in my arms. God, he was so small, and from the giddy looks on my father's and Ashley's faces, they already worshipped him. We all started off this way—small little bundles of joy. Me, Aires, Noah, Lila, Isaiah and even Beth. At some point, someone held and loved us, but somewhere along the way, it all got screwed up.

Not for this baby though—not for Alexander. Over the past few weeks, I'd learned several harsh lessons about myself. The most devastating? That I was selfish like my mom. Like her, I saw the world in black and white instead of the vibrant colors and shades I knew existed. And not only that, I'd chosen to see the world through her eyes instead of my own.

But not anymore. I could do more than rebuild a car to honor Aires. I could become the sibling he would have wanted me to be. Alexander would never face this world alone. He'd have an advocate—he'd have me. "Alexander Aires. I like it."

Ashley let out a relieved breath and glanced at my father with a smile on her face. "I'm happy you're here, Echo."

Oddly enough… "Me, too."

A nurse walked in with a rolling bassinet. "Sorry to intrude, but I'm here to take little Alexander to be weighed." She expertly took Alexander from me and placed him in the bed. "And someone will be in to examine you, Mrs. Emerson."

"He'll want to eat soon, so don't keep him long." Ashley grasped my father's hand and her blue eyes became worried.

"We'll bring him right back," the nurse assured her.

We watched him roll away. My father slid to the edge of the bed. "How are you?"

"Good." For having a slight mental breakdown and remembering that my mom had tried that murder-suicide thing with me. "They released me."

"Already? The doctors and nurses have been keeping me updated, but they told me you wouldn't be released until two. I planned on being there to take you home." He checked his watch. Sure enough, it was only one-thirty. "I promise I sat with you."

"I know. Noah told me."

My father exchanged a perplexed glance with Ashley. "Are you and Noah back together?"

Heat burned my cheeks at the thought of the way he kissed me in the hospital room. "Yeah."

"He stayed with you, Echo. All night." He stared down at his shoes as he spoke and I heard the heavy hint of regret. Noah stayed with me—he didn't.

My mother's words chose that moment to echo in my head. "You and I share the same skin." *No, Mom, we don't. I share Aires' skin. I'm going to do better than you.*

Every few seconds Ashley's face flickered between worry and hope. I'd loved her once. My mother reminded me of that. There was a time as a child I possibly could have called her Mom with-out feeling a twinge of regret. Yes, things happened. A marriage failed and a family fell apart, but Ashley…Ashley wasn't evil. "I'm sorry, Ashley."

Her forehead furrowed. "For what?"

I forced myself to look at her. "For always blaming you." Ash-ley's eyes watered. I swallowed my pride and continued, "My mom isn't who I thought she was, so maybe you're not the per-son I've made you out to be either."

At first, I meant the apology as a truce in order to start fresh with Alexander, but as I said the words, my heart became lighter. I really was sorry and forgiveness felt…enlightening.

Ashley placed a hand over her heart while the tears streamed down. "I'm sorry, too. So sorry. I never meant to hurt you. Never. Sometimes I say things and the words just fall out, and I can see by the look on your face that I said it wrong. But you have to know—I have always loved you. I'll do better, Echo. I prom-ise."

I glanced at my bouncing foot. Guilt ate at me. She wanted a clean slate. If we were starting off on a new foot, we needed to begin with honesty. "And I'm going to really try with you. Not fake try. Really try."

Ashley smiled through her tears and nodded, accepting my treaty.

"Mrs. Emerson, I'm here to examine you," said a nurse in purple scrubs. "Would the two of you mind stepping out?"

My father stood. "No problem."

The appropriate thing to do would be to hug her. Yeah…I should. But I couldn't. I'd save that for when I really felt it. Re-pairing my relationship with Ashley was going to require baby steps. I held my hand out to her and she squeezed it.

"I'll see you at home," she said.

"Okay."

Almost shocking the red out of my hair, my father placed an arm around my shoulder and escorted me out of the room. "Have I told you lately how much I love you?"

A floor-to-ceiling window ended the hall next to Ashley's room. My father closed the door behind him and the two of us looked out on the busy parking lot. *Do you realize that you haven't touched me like this in years?* "No."

He pulled me closer to him and kept his eyes locked on the outside world. "I love you more than you could ever know."

"I love you, too," I whispered. "I wish…" That Aires had never died. That my mother wasn't so selfish. "I wish things didn't have to be so difficult between us."

"I didn't know how to talk to you, Echo. Not that I ever did before, but after what happened with your mother…I had a hard time facing you. Every time I looked at you, I saw how I failed—and how could I ask for your forgiveness if you didn't even remember what I did?"

"What happened?" I glanced up to him. "On your side?"

The gray that shadowed his face made him appear way older than a man in his forties. "Fifteen minutes. That's how long your message sat in voice mail. I called 911 as soon as I heard the panic in your voice. I begged them to check on you and your mother. Ashley and I left immediately, but I knew we wouldn't be fast enough.

"If only I'd answered my phone when you called, I would have told you to lock yourself in the bathroom. You never would have fallen through that glass. If I'd checked my voice mail earlier, you would have been conscious when EMS found you." He closed his eyes. Pure torture weighed his features. "You almost died."

I pressed my face into his chest and squeezed him tighter. "I'm alive, Daddy." *And say it, Echo.* "And it's okay. I don't blame you."

My father hugged me back as he whispered, over and over, "I'm so sorry."

I turned my head, listening to his heart as I looked out the window. Just like always, the world continued. People left and entered the hospital. Cars scurried to their destination points. And as glad as I was to have gotten through to my father, I knew my destination wasn't here.

"You know those times I left town to sell my paintings?" I pulled back, but my father kept his arm around me even as he turned his head and glanced away. The quiet, painful recognition that he'd lost control of me several weeks ago was still evident on his face.

"Yes."

How exactly should I explain this? "I slept through the night while I was gone."

"Echo, that's great!"

And he didn't understand. "It made me realize I need to find a space of my own. When I graduate from high school, I'm moving out."

It had to be said, but I regretted the heaviness that returned to my father. He rubbed my shoulder. "I know I've made mistakes. I can't tell you how many nights I've sat up and watched those brief precious hours that you actually slept and wondered how I could make all of your problems disappear. I know it wasn't good enough, but I did the best I could by you. No matter how hard I tried, I could never find a way to fix you."

The image in my head made sense. I was a broken vase and my father's tight reign was the glue. He thought if he pressed hard enough, I'd go back to normal.

"You really tried with Mom, didn't you?" My conversation with her had made me rethink everything she raised me to believe.

His tone grew hoarse. "I loved her, Echo. She was that someone that tilted my universe. But I loved you and Aires more. I tried everything possible to minimize the effects of her behavior on the two of you. I became what they call an enabler until I finally realized that the only person who could help your mother was herself."

My father wiped at his face and I pretended that maybe he had dust on it. "I came home one night and found you and Aires in your bedroom closet, hiding from her. It wasn't the first time, but I swore to myself it would be the last. I couldn't change your mom, but I could take care of the two of you. I hired Ashley full-time and told your mother that if she didn't get it together I'd file for divorce.

"You were too young to remember, but your mother did try and there were periods where she stayed on her medication and did fine. When she got really bad, I'd admit her to a psychiatric hospital. The cycle never ended. From good to okay, from okay to bad, from bad to the hospital and then back to good. One night I came home from visiting her at the hospital and I found Ashley reading to you in your room. You sat on her lap, played with her hair and looked at her like she hung the moon. She helped Aires with his science project and recorded his basketball game. She even cooked you guys dinner and warmed me up leftovers.

"Ashley brought a sense of normal into a house where normal was hard to come by. I swear, Echo, neither of us meant to fall in love. Sometimes life happens."

Maybe my father and I were more alike than I'd ever imagined. We both craved normal. Nerves swelled inside. "Am I like Mom?"

He looked at me from the corner of his eye. "Is this a trick question?"

My eyes pleaded, hoping he wouldn't make me spell it out. He rubbed my shoulder again. "You have her beauty, her artistic talent and her tenacity if that's what you mean."

Was he saying I was stubborn? Wait until he got to know Noah. "Anything else?"

"Your mother never would have uttered to anyone those words you just said to Ashley…or to me. You're your own person, Echo, and I'm proud to be your father."

The nerves went away and I rested my head on him. "Thanks, Daddy."

"Give me another chance. I promise to let you run your own life. Anyhow, I think Ashley is going to be overwhelmed with Alexander. She didn't start babysitting you until well after you were potty-trained."

What a crazy, crazy world I lived in. My teenage babysitter, turned nanny, turned stepmother, had given birth to my new brother. I wanted so badly to give my dad the answer he wanted and make him happy, but then I wouldn't be true to the person I was beginning to believe I was. "Honestly, Daddy, it has nothing to do with chances. That house is full of memories. Some of them are wonderful and some…aren't. I spent years hoping and praying and plotting for a life I never really had to begin with. I'm scared if I stay, I'll keep looking back and never look forward."

"Funny." But he didn't laugh. "Aires said the same thing when he enlisted. Promise me you'll come home and visit. You're my baby, too."

I wrapped both of my arms around him and he hugged me. "I promise."

NOAH

In a tent set up in Shirley and Dale's backyard, Echo lay on her stomach studying a huge map of the United States. Because of the warm April night, she'd pulled her shirt up a few inches to expose her skin. At least that was the reason she gave when her fingers inched the material of her blue tank away from the small of her back. Personally, I think she did it to drive me insane.

"Sorry," Echo said. "I'm not an ocean kind of girl. Birds and sand and seaweed." She shivered and stuck out her tongue. "Not my scene, but we can go there if you want."

A week ago, I'd held her hand in the hospital and wondered if she'd come back to me. Tonight, I watched her in complete awe. Echo was here and she was mine. Sitting beside her, I traced patterns on the exposed skin of her back. "I'll go wherever you want, baby."

The light from the old camping lantern the two of us bought flickered and she raised an I-told-you-so eyebrow. Echo was not a fan of the treasures that could be found at Goodwill, nor was she a fan of sleeping outdoors. But she'd promised to give camping a shot on our trip this summer.

"The tent's in good shape," I said to prove my point. "It would have cost us a hell of a lot more at a real store."

"If you say so." She moved her finger west of Kentucky. "I want to see snow-capped mountains."

I brushed her curls away, bent down and kissed the nape of her neck, loving how her muscles relaxed as she leaned into me. I whispered into her ear, "Then that's what we'll see."

"Noah," she moaned in equal parts pleasure and reprimand. "How am I supposed to schedule appointments with art galleries if I never plan where we're going?"

Her sweet smell drove my body higher as I nibbled on the edge of her earlobe. "I'm not stopping you. You plan. I'll kiss."

Echo turned her head to look at me over her shoulder. My siren became a temptress with that seductive smile on her lips. A mistake on her part. I caressed her cheek and kissed those soft lips.

I expected her to shy away. We'd been playing this game for over an hour: she plotted while I teased. Leaving for the summer was important to her and she was important to me. But instead of the quick peck I'd anticipated, she moved her lips against mine. A burning heat warmed my blood.

It was a slow kiss at first—all I meant it to be, but then Echo touched me. Her hands on my face, in my hair. And then she angled her body to mine. Warmth, enticing pressure on all the right parts, and Echo's lips on mine—fireworks.

She became my world. Filling my senses so that all I felt and saw and tasted was her. Kisses and touches and whispered words of love and when my hand skimmed down the curve of her waist and paused on the hem of her jeans my body screamed to continue, but my mind knew it was time to stop.

With a sigh, I moved my lips once more against hers before shifting and pulling her body to my side. "I'm in love with you."

Echo settled her head in the crook of my arm as her fingertips lazily touched my face. "I know. I love you, too."

"I'm sorry I didn't say it sooner." If I had, then maybe we never would have been apart.

"It's okay," she murmured. "We're together now and that's all that matters."

I kissed her forehead and she snuggled closer to me. The world felt strange. For the first time in my life, I wasn't fighting someone or something. My brothers were safe. Echo knew the truth. Soon, I'd be free from high school and foster care. Hopefully, I'd be admitted on late acceptance to college. Contentment and happiness were unfamiliar emotions, but ones I could learn to live with.

"Do you mind?" she asked in a small voice that indicated nerves. "That we're taking it slow?"

"No." And it was the truth. Happiness and contentment were going to be a little harder for her than for me. Echo, Ashley and her dad had reached a new understanding, but old habits were tough to break, especially when they all lived in the same house. A new baby didn't help the stress level. Echo's therapy sessions had increased instead of decreased. Regaining the memory and the confrontation with her mom had created a whole new set of issues, but ones Echo felt she could deal with as long as she had Mrs. Collins.

Everything in her life was in flux and she needed strong, steady and stable. Oddly, she found those three things in me.

Who would ever have guessed I'd be the reliable sort? "Besides, taking it slow creates buildup. I like anticipation."

Her body rocked with silent giggles and my lips turned up. I loved making her happy.

"And you're sure you want to leave your brothers and you swear you won't lose your job?"

She'd asked those two questions a million times this past week, but I understood her fear. She didn't want me to end up full of regret. "They're closing the Malt and Burger for a month in July for renovations and my boss thinks a vacation would be good for me. As for my brothers..." I paused. "I need the space. It's hard flipping off the switch. Maybe if I go away for a while I won't feel like they're my sole responsibility."

She propped herself up on her elbows and tilted her head. Those beautiful green eyes searched mine. "You're sure?"

"One thousand percent."

The smile I loved so much graced her face. "Then we're going west."

NOAH

"When are you coming back?" Jacob asked. We sat in the tree house in Carrie and Joe's backyard the day after graduation. Carrie and Joe had made a large dinner in celebration and told me to invite my friends. I'd brought Echo, Isaiah and a very sober Beth.

Echo was currently helping hide Tyler in a very bad game of hide-and-seek with Isaiah and Beth. "Latest? September. I start school after Labor Day."

His little legs dangled from the edge. "Our mom's school?"

"Our mom's school." With a major in architecture. The deal for foster kids covered my college costs and housing, but I planned on living off-campus with Isaiah and Beth once Echo and I returned. Beth and Isaiah would only be seniors next year, but Shirley and Dale didn't care where they lived. As for Echo, she had accepted her scholarship to "our mom's school" and planned on living in the dorms.

He extended his fingers and counted down. "But that's at least three months."

How could I explain to my little brothers why I needed to leave? How could I explain that for three years the only thing that kept my head above water was the thought of being a family with them again? I'd lost and I'd won. I'd lost the dreams I had, but won new dreams.

I needed time to rewire my brain, figure out how to be a responsible eighteen-year-old college student and carefree older brother. "I'll call every day and I'll send you presents and postcards from every place I visit."

Jacob brightened at the word *presents*. "Promise?"

"Promise."

Echo and Tyler laughed as Isaiah flipped Tyler over his shoulder, grabbed Echo's hand and ran across the yard to keep Beth from "finding" them. Beth slowly followed, pretending she had no idea where the three of them had gone. My throat swelled at the sight. I finally had a family.

"Tyler likes her," Jacob said as he watched Tyler reach for Echo.

I cleared my throat and swallowed down the emotions overwhelming me. "What do you think of her?"

When I first introduced them a month back, my brothers had been shy around her. Then Echo drew a picture of Jacob and Tyler and the wall between them shattered. They thought it was cool that a grown-up loved crayons as much as they did. It took them longer to warm up to Beth and Isaiah, but eventually they'd been won over by Isaiah's tattoos and by the gifts "Aunt Beth" bought them.

Jacob shrugged. "She's cool for a girl."

I laughed. "Yeah. She is."

"Where are you going when you leave?"

"Everywhere, but mainly Colorado. There are a couple of art galleries Echo wants to visit there."

He tackled me in a hug. "Colorado. They have mountains. Cool."

Cool. We played a few more rounds of hide-and-seek until Tyler couldn't keep his eyes open. Echo left with Isaiah and Beth to pick up the rest of the items she needed for our trip and to make her dad swear, yet again, that he'd take care of Aires' car until she came back to town. Though she wouldn't admit it, I think she also wanted another few minutes to rock Alexander.

Carrie let me read stories to my brothers, listen to their prayers and tuck them in for the night. Tonight, Tyler slept with Jacob in the bottom bunk.

"Love you, Noah." Tyler yawned and closed his eyes. I touched the side of his head. It wasn't the first time he'd said the words to me, but it was the first time since Carrie and Joe allowed me back in my brothers' lives.

"Me, too. I love you," Jacob added.

"I love you both. Take care of each other and listen to Carrie and Joe."

Jacob flashed me Mom's smile. "We will."

I kissed them both on the forehead and forced myself out of the room. The house had that peaceful quiet. The refrigerator hummed. The dishwasher quietly swished. The smell of rich coffee drifted from the kitchen.

I followed the scent and poked my head into the room. Carrie and Joe sat at the breakfast bar, sipping from mugs. "I'm not kidding. I plan on calling every day."

Joe gave me a genuine smile. "We wouldn't expect anything less."

"Noah." Carrie slipped off the stool. "I have something for you and I didn't want to give it to you in front of your friends."

She handed me a manila envelope. "Open it later, okay? I promise you'll love it."

"All right."

Joe extended his hand. "Have a safe trip and don't buy the boys anything too big."

I laughed. Like I could buy anything bigger than the stuff in that toy-store basement of theirs. "I will. Thanks again."

The moment I stepped out onto the front porch, I opened the envelope. Inside were lots of drawings from Jacob and Tyler, a picture of me and my brothers, and then a copy of the picture of my parents. I remembered this picture. I'd taken it after Mom and Dad handed over the key to the first resident of the Habitat neighborhood. The memory made me smile. Carrie and Joe weren't the devil. They were people who loved my brothers and had hearts big enough to possibly love me, too.

I pulled out my cell phone and texted Carrie: thanks.

Seconds later she texted back: welcome. b safe.

Across the street, Echo sat on the hood of her gray Honda Civic. Her red curls shone in the street light and her spaghetti-strapped tank top dipped just low enough that my mind already wondered how I could get her to deviate from the plan of driving at least six hours tonight before setting up the tent.

Her siren smile lit up my world. "Noah."

"Echo. You look…" I let my eyes wander up and down as I approached the car. "Appetizing."

Her laughter tickled my soul. "I think we've had this conversation before."

I settled between her legs and cradled her face with my hands. "And I think at the end of that night something like this also happened."

Her lips feathered against mine and she giggled. "You ready for a new normal?" she whispered.

I kissed her lips one more time and plucked the keys from her hand. "Yes, and I'm driving."

* * * * *

ACKNOWLEDGMENTS

To God—Luke 1:37

For Dave—it is because of you I know love.

Thank you to…

Kevan Lyon—I can think of no one else I'd rather have in my corner. You're the right mixture of energy, enthusiasm, and kindness.

Margo Lipschultz—You are brilliant plus you have a heart of gold. I am honored that you took a chance on me, Echo and Noah.

Everyone at Harlequin and Harlequin Teen who touched this story, especially Natashya Wilson—I am thankful to you all.

Angela Annaloro-Murphy, Veronica Blade, Shannon Michael and Kristen Simmons—my beta readers. You were brave enough to sludge through first drafts and tell me your very honest opinions.

Anne Cook and Rodolfo Lopez Jr.—Thank you for answering my questions, thus enriching the story.

Colette Ballard, Bethany Griffin, Kurt Hampe and Bill Wolfe—
You are more than a critique group. You are my lifeline.

Louisville Romance Writers—you are a terrific and talented group of ladies.

My parents, my sister, my Mt. Washington family, and my in-laws…I love you.

My friends and family—thank you for all your love and support. There are too many of you to mention, but know that I think of you always.

Don't miss Beth's story,
DARE YOU TO,
coming soon from Katie McGarry
and Harlequin TEEN!
Read on for a sneak preview....

Chapter 1

Ryan

Ty Cobb once said, "I never could stand losing. Second place didn't interest me."

Doesn't interest me either. Which sucks because my best friend is seconds from scoring a phone number from the chick working the Taco Bell counter, placing him in the lead.

What started as a simple dare had twisted into a night-long game. First, Chris dared me to ask the girl in line at the movies for her number. I then dared him to ask the girl at the batting cages for her number. The more we succeeded the more momentum the game gained. Too bad Chris owns a grin that melts the hearts of all girls, including the ones that have boyfriends.

I hate losing.

Taco Bell Chick blushes when Chris winks at her. Come on. I chose her because she called us redneck losers when we ordered. Chris rests his arms on the counter, inching closer to the girl, as I sit at the table and watch the tragedy unfold.

Every muscle in the back of my neck tenses as Taco Bell Chick giggles, writes something on a piece of paper and slides it over to him. Dammit. The rest of our group howls with laughter and someone pats me on the back.

Tonight isn't about phone numbers or girls. It's about enjoying our last Friday night before school begins. I've tasted everything—the freedom of hot summer air in the Jeep with the panels down, the peace of dark country roads leading to the interstate, the exciting glow of city lights as we made the thirty-minute drive into Louisville and, lastly, the mouthwatering taste of a greasy fast-food taco at midnight.

Chris holds the phone number like a referee holding up the glove of the prize champion. "It's on, Ryan."

"Bring it." There's no way I'm getting this far to have Chris outdo me.

He slouches in his seat, tosses the paper into the pile of numbers we've collected over the evening and tugs his Bullitt County High baseball cap over his brown hair. "Let's see. These things have to be thought through. The girl chosen carefully. Attractive enough so she won't fall for you. Not a dog because she'll be excited someone gave her a bone."

Mimicking him, I shift back in the seat and fold my hands over my stomach. "Take your time. I've got forever."

But we don't. After this weekend life changes. On Monday, Chris and I will be seniors starting our last fall baseball league. I only have a few more months to impress the professional baseball scouts or the dream I've been working toward my entire life will dissolve into ashes.

A shove at my foot brings me back to the here and now.

"Stop the serious shit," Logan whispers. He knows my facial expressions better than anyone. He should. We've been playing together since we were kids. Me pitching. Him catching.

For Logan's sake, I laugh at a joke Chris told even though I didn't hear the punch line.

"We close soon." Taco Bell Chick wipes a table near ours and gives Chris a wink.

"I may call that one," says Chris.

I raise a brow. He worships his girlfriend. "No, you won't."

"I would if it weren't for Lacy." But he has Lacy, and loves her, so neither one of us continues that conversation.

"I have one more try." I make a show of glancing around the purple tex-mex-decorated lobby. "What girl are you choosing for me?"

A honk from the drive-through announces the arrival of a car full of hot girls. Rap pounds from their car and I swear one girl flashes us. I love the city. "You should choose one of them."

"Sure," Chris says sarcastically. "In fact, why don't I hand you the title now?"

Two guys from our group hop out of their seats and go outside, leaving me, Logan and Chris alone.

"There she is." Chris's eyes brighten as he stares at the entrance. "That's the girl I'm calling as yours."

I suck in a deep breath. Chris sounds too happy for this girl to be good news. "Where?"

"Just came in, waiting at the counter."

Black hair. Torn clothes. Total Skater. Damn, those chicks are hard-core. I slap my hand against the table and our trays shift. Why? Why does Skater Girl have to wander into Taco Bell tonight?

Chris's rough chuckles do nothing to help my growing agitation. "Admit defeat and you won't have to suffer."

"No way." I stand, refusing to go down without a fight.

All girls are the same. It's what I tell myself as I stroll to the counter. She might look different from the girls at home, but all girls want the same thing—a guy who shows interest. A guy's problem is having the balls to do it. Good thing for me I've got balls. "Hi. I'm Ryan."

Her long black hair hides her face, but her slim body with its hint of curves catches my attention. Unlike the girls at home, she isn't wearing marked-down designer labels. Nope. She's got her own style. Her black tank top shows more skin than it covers and her skintight jeans hug all the right places.

Skater Girl turns her head toward me and the drive-through. "Is someone going to take my fucking order?"

Chris's laughter from our corner table jerks me back to reality. I pull off my baseball cap, mess my hand through my hair and shove the hat back in place. Why her? Why tonight? There's a dare and I'm going to win. "Counter's a little slow tonight."

She glares at me like *I'm* a little slow. "Are you speaking to me?"

Her hard stare dares me to glance away. *Keep staring, Skater Girl. You don't scare me.* I'm drawn to her eyes though. Her eyes are blue. Dark blue. I wouldn't have thought someone with black hair could have such brilliant eyes.

"I asked you a question." She rests a hip against the counter. "Or are you as stupid as you look?"

Yep, pure punk: attitude, nose ring and a sneer that can kill on sight. She's not my type, but she doesn't have to be. I just need her number. "You'd probably get better service if you watched your language."

A hint of amusement touches her lips and dances in her eyes. Not the kind of amusement you laugh with. It's the taunting kind. "Does my language bother you?"

Yes. "No." I don't care for the word, but I know when I'm being tested.

"So my language doesn't bother you, but you say—" she raises her voice and leans over the counter "—I could get some *fucking* service if I watched my language."

Time to switch tactics. "What do you want to eat?"

"Fish. What do you think I want? I'm at a taco joint."

Chris laughs again and this time Logan joins in. If I don't salvage this, I'll be listening to their ridicule the entire way home. I lean over the counter and wave at the girl working the drive-through. I give her a smile. She smiles back. Take lessons, Skater Girl. This is how it's supposed to work. "Can I have a minute?"

Drive-Through Chick's face brightens and she holds up a finger as she continues taking an order. "Be right there. Promise."

I turn back to Skater Girl and instead of the warm thank-you I should be receiving she shakes her head, clearly annoyed. "Jocks."

My smile falters. Hers grows.

"How do you know I'm a jock?"

Her eyes wander to my chest and I fight a grimace. Written in black letters across my gray shirt is Bullitt County High School, Baseball State Champions.

"So you are stupid," she says.

I'm done. I take one step in the direction of the table then stop. I don't lose. "What's your name?"

"What do I have to do to make you leave me alone?"

"Give me your phone number."

The right side of her mouth quirks up. "You're kidding."

"Give me your name and phone number and I'll walk away."

"You must be brain damaged."

"Welcome to Taco Bell, can I take your order?"

We both look at Drive-Through Chick.

I pull out my wallet and slam ten dollars on the counter. "Tacos."

"And a Coke," Skater Girl says. "Large. Since he's paying."

Drive-Through Chick enters the order and returns to the drive-through window.

We stare at each other. I swear this girl never blinks.

"I believe a thank-you is in order," I say.

"I never asked you to pay."

"Give me your name and phone number and we'll call it even."

She licks her lips. "There is absolutely nothing you can do to ever get me to give you my name or number."

Ring the bell. Playtime ended with those words. Purposely invading her space, I steal a step toward her and place a hand on the counter next to her body. It affects her. I can tell. Her eyes lose the amusement and her arms hug her body. She's small. Smaller than I expected. That attitude is so big I hadn't noticed her height or size. "I bet I can."

"Eight tacos and one large Coke," says the girl from behind the counter.

Skater Girl snatches the order and spins on her heel before I can process I'm on the verge of losing. "Wait!"

She stops at the door. "What?"

Her *what* doesn't carry much anger. Maybe I'm getting somewhere. "Give me your phone number. I want to call you."

No, I don't, but I do want to win. She's wavering. I can tell.

"I'll tell you what." She flashes a smile that drips with a mixture of allure and wickedness. "If you can walk me to my car and open the door for me, I'll give you my number."

Can.

She steps into the humid night and skips down the sidewalk to the back parking lot. I never would've bet this girl skipped. I follow, tasting the sweet victory.

Victory doesn't last long. Before she can even make it past the yellow lines confining an old rusty car, two menacing guys climb out.

"Something I can do for you, man?" Tattoos run the length of his arms.

"Nope." I shove my hands in my pockets and relax my stance. I have no intention of getting into a fight, especially when I'm outnumbered.

Tattoo Guy crosses the parking lot and he'd probably keep coming if it wasn't for the other guy with hair covering his eyes. He stops right in front of Tattoo Guy, halting his progress, but his posture suggests he'd also fight for kicks. "Is there a problem, Beth?"

Beth flashes an evil smirk. "Not anymore." She jumps into the front seat of the car.

Both guys walk to their car while keeping an eye on me, as if I'm stupid enough to jump them from behind. The engine roars to life and the car vibrates as if duct tape holds it together.

In no hurry to go inside and explain to my friends how I lost, I stay on the sidewalk. The car slowly drives by and Beth presses her palm against the passenger window. Written in black marker is the word signaling my defeat: *can't*.

PLAYLIST FOR
PUSHING THE LIMITS

Music is my muse of choice. These songs helped shape the overall theme of the story:

"Push" by Matchbox Twenty
"Bad Romance" by Lady Gaga
"Scar Tissue" by Red Hot Chili Peppers
"Use Somebody" by Kings of Leon

To help get into character for Noah, I listened to the following:

"Down" by Jay Sean
"Changes" by 2Pac & Talent
"Hey, Soul Sister" by Train

For Echo, I listened to:

"Paint" by Roxette

"Sometimes Love Just Ain't Enough" by Patty Smyth & Don Henley
"The End of the Innocence" by Don Henley & Bruce Hornsby

Songs used for specific scenes:

"Undone (The sweater song)" by Weezer—This song inspired the moment between Noah and Echo at the party
"Crash Into Me" by The Dave Matthews Band—I listened to this song whenever I needed to write a kiss between Echo and Noah
"Free" by Zac Brown Band—This song represents everything I wanted Echo and Noah to have gained by the end of the story. If you're curious as to what happened between them the summer after the story ends, just listen to this song.

A song special to me:

"Can You" by Angela McGarry—After reading a draft of *Pushing the Limits*, Angela was inspired to write "Can You." Check out the song performed by Mason Stonebridge on my website: www.katielmcgarry.com.

Q&A WITH KATIE MCGARRY

Q: What was your inspiration for writing *Pushing the Limits?*

A: I had two main inspirations:
One, I knew from the beginning that I wanted to write a story in which my characters felt strong enough to leave their pasts behind and create new futures for themselves. The first scene I ever saw in my mind was Echo and Noah leaving town after graduation.
Two, I wanted to write two characters who were facing overwhelming issues and who, through battling these issues, found hope at the end of their journey.

Q: How did you come up with Echo's name?

A: Echo went through several name changes as I wrote the manuscript. For a while, she had a very normal name, but it always felt off. It wasn't until I looked at Echo from her mother's point of view that I found her name. Echo's mother loved Greek mythology so it made perfect sense that she would name her children after the myths. I read several Greek myths and the moment I found Echo's, I fell in love. Echo, to me, was the girl who lost her voice. Thankfully, she finds it by the end.

Q: Which character is the most "like" you?

A: All of them. I gave each character a piece of me (though some have larger slices of me than others). Overall, I'd say I'm a strange combination of Echo, Lila and Beth. Echo has my need to please, Lila has my unfailing loyalty to my friends and Beth encompasses my insecurities.

Q: Did you experience friendships with Grace types when you were in high school?

A: Yes. And the more people have read this story, the more this question comes up. Grace has struck a stronger nerve in people than I ever would have imagined. It seems most of us have unfortunately experienced a relationship where a person wants to "like" you and wants "be your friend," but only if it serves their needs. In case anyone is wondering, that isn't friendship.

Q: Are there any parts of the story you feel particularly close to?

A: Yes. The relationship between Noah, Isaiah and Beth. Beyond my parents and sister, my nearest family members were over fourteen hours away. My friends became my family. The people

I grew up with were more than people I watched movies with or talked to occasionally on the phone. These were people with whom I shared life's most devastating moments, but also my hardest laughs. These were people who I would have willingly died for and I know they would have done the same for me. They shared my triumphs with smiles on their faces and congratulatory hugs. They held me when I cried and offered to beat up whoever hurt my feelings. These were also the same people who were more than happy to get in my face if they thought I was making a wrong decision.

Q: Did anything that happens to Echo happen to you?

A: Sort of. I was bitten by a dog when I was in second grade and repressed the memory. It felt very strange to have no memory of an incident that other people knew about. It was even stranger to have injuries and not have an inkling where they came from. In college, I finally remembered the incident when a dog lunged at me. I relived the horrible event and sort of "woke up" a few minutes later to find myself surrounded by people I loved. Even though I "remember" the incident, I still don't remember the whole thing. I only see still frames in my mind and there is no blood in any of the memories.